DC 5/14

Jm2
LB
PR 4/16
DC 7/16

WAITING FOR SPRING

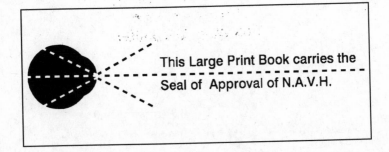

WAITING FOR SPRING

AMANDA CABOT

THORNDIKE PRESS
A part of Gale, Cengage Learning

GALE
CENGAGE Learning·

Detroit • New York • San Francisco • New Haven, Conn • Waterville, Maine • London

GALE
CENGAGE Learning·

© 2013 by Amanda Cabot.
Thorndike Press, a part of Gale, Cengage Learning.

Thorndike Press® Large Print Christian Romance.
The text of this Large Print edition is unabridged.
Other aspects of the book may vary from the original edition.
Set in 16 pt. Plantin.

LIBRARY OF CONGRESS CATALOGING-IN-PUBLICATION DATA

Cabot, Amanda, 1948–
    Waiting for spring / by Amanda Cabot.
        pages ; cm. — (Thorndike Press large print Christian romance)
    (Westward winds ; book 2)
    ISBN 978-1-4104-5665-6 (hardcover) — ISBN 1-4104-5665-X (hardcover)
    1. Wyoming—History—19th century—Fiction. 2. Large type books. I. Title.
PS3603.A35W35 2013b
813'.6—dc23   2012050189

Published in 2013 by arrangement with Revell Books, a division of Baker Publishing Group

Printed in Mexico
4 5 6 7 8 9 17 16 15 14 13

For Suzanne "Betty Boop" Dawson,
whose faith and friendship have
enriched so many lives, including mine.
Thanks, Suzanne. I'm so glad you
interrupted your birthday celebration to
attend one of my book signings.

Cheyenne, Wyoming Territory 1886

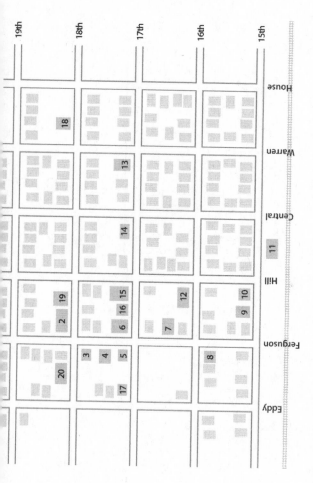

1 *Barrett's Home*
2 Charlotte's Church
3 Yates's Dry Goods
4 *Élan and Charlotte's Home*
5 James Sisters Millinery
6 Post Office
7 Myers Dry Goods
8 *Rue de Rivoli*
9 *Mrs. Kendall's Boardinghouse*
10 *Sylvia's Brothel*
11 The Depot
12 InterOcean Hotel
13 The Cheyenne Club
14 Ellis Bakery and Confectionary
15 Opera House
16 Arp and Hammond Hardware
17 *Mullen's Jewelry*
18 *Miriam's Home*
19 *Maple Terrace (Richard's Home)*
20 Central School
21 *Warren's Home*
22 City Park
23 The Capitol

Italics indicate fictional locations.

1

Cheyenne, Wyoming Territory, October 1886
It was only the wind.

Charlotte Harding wrapped her arms around her waist, trying to convince herself there was no reason to tremble like a cottonwood leaf in a storm. The creaks that had wakened her were simply the building shuddering from the force of the wind. That was all. No one had broken in. No one had found her. She and David were safe. But the brave thoughts had no effect. They never did.

With a sigh, she fumbled to light the lamp. As the soft yellow flame chased away the darkness, she slid her feet into slippers and padded across the room. Perhaps it was foolish. She could see that the intruder had been nothing more than a figment of her imagination, the product of her fears. Her bedchamber was empty, except for David. Sweet David. The love of her life.

Charlotte stood at the side of his crib, looking down at the red hair so like his father's. Other than his eyes, which were the same shade of brown as hers, her son was the image of his father. The trembling that she'd managed to quell returned as thoughts of David's father and the fears that always accompanied those thoughts assailed her once again. Taking a deep breath to soothe her ragged breathing, Charlotte shook her head. She had to stop this worrying. It had been almost a year since she'd moved to Cheyenne, and no one had come looking for her and David. She had done everything she could to ensure that no one would know she had once lived at Fort Laramie as the wife of First Lieutenant Jeffrey Crowley. What she feared most would not happen. The baron would not find them.

Though the lamp that she held over the crib did not disturb him, David stirred, perhaps alerted by the sound of her breathing or the scent of her toilet water. "Mama," he murmured as he held out his arms.

Charlotte smiled and set the lamp on the floor. She knew what her son wanted. Slowly, she stroked the length of each of his arms, then let him grasp her hands. "Yes, David, Mama's awake, but you need to go to sleep." Crooning softly, she moved his arms back to his side and pressed a kiss to his forehead. "Sleep now."

As his breathing became regular, Charlotte's smile faltered. Today was her son's first birthday. Though she intended to celebrate only that wonderful event, she could not forget that today was also the anniversary of Jeffrey's death and the day her life had changed forever. Pampered, coddled Charlotte Crowley was gone, replaced by Charlotte Harding, a woman who had learned that while life could be more difficult than she had thought possible, it had many rewards. Though this year had been far different from her dreams, Charlotte could not regret what it had brought. She had new friends and a new life in a new city. She had learned that she could be self-sufficient. Best of all, she had kept her son safe. It was worth the lies.

"Gentlemen, I call this meeting to order." Barrett Landry used his fist to rap on the table. His visitors looked up in surprise.

"A meeting?" Warren Duncan lit his cigar, taking a puff before he continued. "I thought it was simply an opportunity to sample some of Mrs. Melnor's fine food." The older of Barrett's two guests, Warren was a distinguished-looking man with steel-gray hair, light blue eyes, and a nose that would have made a hawk proud. Though he confided little about his background, other than his graduation from an unspecified law school, his cultured accent led Barrett to believe that he was originally from the East, perhaps even Boston. But Barrett did not pry. If there was one thing he had learned since arriving in Cheyenne, it was that a man's past was best left in the past. He certainly had no desire to advertise many aspects of his own.

Richard Eberhardt leaned forward, his keen brown eyes sparkling. "Does this mean you've come to your senses and decided to take our advice?"

"It does." Barrett smiled at the man who was almost a decade older than his own thirty. Rail thin and an inch or two under six feet, Richard was not a man anyone would call handsome, and yet his confident gait told onlookers that he was not to be overlooked. The combination of his shrewd mind and what some called his Midas touch had turned Richard into one of the city's wealthiest merchants.

"The trip to Rawlins was the final step," Barrett told his advisers. The convention had confirmed what Richard and Warren had claimed, that the political power brokers were looking for new blood and that Barrett had a good chance of winning their approval. If everything went the way he hoped, even the residents of Northwick, Pennsylvania, would have to admit that Barrett Landry was an important man.

"And so, gentlemen . . ." Barrett paused when a soft knock announced the butler's arrival. Only when Mr. Bradley had placed the tray of coffee and cinnamon rolls on the low table and closed the door behind him did Barrett complete his announcement. "You're looking at a man who hopes to have a future in governing this fine territory."

"Hallelujah!" Warren raised his cigar in a salute. "This calls for a round of brandy." Barrett's lawyer was nothing if not predictable. He let out a melodramatic sigh at the sight of coffee before taking another puff of his cigar. Less inclined to imbibe strong spirits, Richard poured himself a cup of coffee.

The three men were seated in what the architect had called the morning room of Barrett's home, perhaps because it was situated at the back of the house and faced east. This morning the sunshine that seemed to be a Cheyenne staple was strong enough that Barrett had drawn the heavy velvet draperies half closed, leaving the room bright but not blindingly so.

"Brandy?" Barrett stirred a spoonful of sugar into his coffee. "You know you won't find any strong drink in my house, and before you reach for the flask I know you carry with you, consider that we need our wits about us if we're going to plot strategy."

Richard settled back in the leather upholstered chair, balancing a plate on his knee. "What strategy? It seems to me you have everything Wyoming will need in a senator. You have plenty of money and a nice house for entertaining when you're not in Washington. You're not too hard on the eyes." Richard shrugged his shoulders. "The only thing you're lacking is a wife."

Warren nodded. "I agree."

Their reaction was not what Barrett had expected. His friends had been encouraging him — haranguing him was more like it — to enter politics, claiming that when Wyoming became a state, its citizens would need a man like him representing them in Washington. He had invited them here this morning, rather than meeting at the club, because he wanted their discussion to remain confidential. It seemed he shouldn't have worried. There would be no discussion, at least not of anything important.

"Doesn't either of you think that political

views and plans for the state — assuming we can convince our citizens and Congress that Wyoming should become a state — are important?" he demanded.

Warren raised an eyebrow, deepening the wrinkles that half a century of living had carved in his forehead. "Do you really believe that voters listen to that? Especially with women voting, what's important are appearances."

"And that means you need a wife," Richard interjected.

"Exactly," Warren agreed. "You've got the trappings. Now you need a good woman to stand at your side and convince voters that you're a family man."

This was definitely not going the way Barrett had planned. He'd imagined discussions of platforms, politics, and public appearances, not matrimony. His friends' advice was enough to make him reconsider the whole idea. "Why are you so focused on a wife? I don't see either one of you enjoying marital bliss."

"True." Richard drawled the word. "We're also not attempting to convince the citizens of Wyoming that we'd serve them better than F. E. Warren or Joseph Carey."

Warren and Carey were the primary reasons Barrett had convened the meeting here. Both were prominent members of the Cheyenne Club, and he hadn't wanted any mention of their names to be overheard.

"What chance do you think I have of defeating either one of them? Carey's been a popular mayor, and Warren — the other Warren," Barrett said with a nod toward his friend, "was territorial governor. I'm a virtual unknown compared to them."

"They both belong to the other party," Warren said after another puff of his cigar. "We need a change. That's where you come in. You're a fresh face. You've got good ideas. I heard you address the cattlemen's association, and you're as convincing as F.E. You're what we need."

Richard nodded. "I agree with Warren. You're what the territory needs. Your ideas are fine, but you need more than that." He took a sip of his coffee, keeping his eyes fixed on Barrett, as if waiting for his reaction. "Voters like family men. They believe they can trust them. That's why you really ought to be thinking about marrying. Besides, a pretty lady at your side will help draw in the crowds." Richard raised an eyebrow. "It's not just for the campaign. A wife would make your life better. Think about it. You don't see F.E. or Carey living alone."

Barrett didn't live alone. Not precisely. He had a cook and a butler, both of whom had quarters in the house, and assorted other servants who spent the day making certain that the house was in impeccable condition. But he had no wife. That was true.

"I've been thinking about it," he admitted. It wasn't only his friends' admonitions that had triggered the thought. It started with a letter from his brother Camden, saying that he and Susan Miller would be wed by the time Barrett received the news. Though two years Barrett's senior, Camden had claimed that he would be the last of the three Landry boys to marry. Now it appeared that he would be the first, for Harrison had shown no sign of romantic entanglements.

"What do you think of Miss Taggert?" Barrett asked. Of all the women he'd met in Cheyenne, she was the only one he could envision marrying. That was why he'd been spending more time with her lately, even though they were not officially courting.

"Miss Miriam Taggert?" Richard's voice sounded strained.

Barrett nodded. "I believe she is the only Miss Taggert in Cheyenne."

Warren snuffed his cigar as he nodded

17

vigorously. "It's a brilliant choice. She's blonde; you're dark. You'll make a striking couple. Plus, having her father's newspaper behind you will help sway undecided voters. I don't always agree with Cyrus Taggert's views, but there's no doubt his editorials are powerful." Warren rose and laid a hand on Barrett's shoulder. "I knew I was right to support you."

Leaning back in his chair, Barrett gave his attorney a wry smile. "And the fact that I pay you handsomely for legal work and that there will undoubtedly be more work if I run for office didn't influence you?"

Warren shook his head. "Not for a minute."

It was a lie. "Be careful, Warren. You know how I feel about liars."

His friend wrinkled his impressive nose. "How could I forget? You're this generation's Honest Abe."

The slightly mocking tone made Barrett want to wipe the smirk from Warren's face, but before he could speak, Richard crowed, "That's it. Warren, you're a genius. We've got our campaign slogan: Landry Never Lies."

"I'm so glad Barrett's coming." Miriam Taggert gasped as Charlotte tightened the

18

corset strings. Though Charlotte had advised her friend and best customer otherwise, Miriam had insisted that the gown she was about to don be made with a waist an inch smaller than any of her other dresses. "Men like small women," she had informed Charlotte, "and since no one could call me small . . ." With a laugh, Miriam gestured from the top of her carefully coiffed head to her elegant shoes, a length of five feet eight inches. "One part of me needs to be tiny."

Though some might quibble that Miriam was not beautiful in the classical sense, with a mouth a bit too wide and eyes a bit too small, she was a striking woman who'd used her slender form and her father's wealth to make herself one of Cheyenne's fashion leaders. And thanks to Miriam's patronage, Élan, Charlotte's dressmaking shop, had become the most popular in the city for wealthy ladies under the age of thirty. The older women either ordered their gowns directly from Paris as Miriam's mother did or joined the city's less affluent citizens in frequenting Miss Smith's establishment. That knowledge assuaged many of Charlotte's fears. With Élan catering to a wealthier clientele, it was less likely that one of the officers' wives from Fort Laramie would discover that Charlotte now resided in Cheyenne. She'd known she was taking a chance by not leaving Wyoming, but the feeling of peace she'd experienced when she'd stepped off the stagecoach in Cheyenne had told her this was where she was meant to live.

"Why is Mr. Landry coming?" she asked. Few men entered Élan, and those who did were normally husbands.

Miriam chuckled. "I told him I wanted him to see the color, but the truth is, I want you to meet him. We've been seeing each other a lot, and Mama thinks he's going to court me. She and Papa believe he'd be the perfect son-in-law, but . . ." Miriam winced as Charlotte gave the corset strings a final tug. "I'm not so sure. I want your opinion," she said when she could breathe again. "Sometimes I think you know me better than my parents do."

Though they saw each other only within the confines of Charlotte's shop, the two women had become friends as Miriam enlivened fitting sessions with tales of her mother's matchmaking attempts. "She's convinced I'm an old maid at twenty-four," Miriam said with a rueful smile. "How old were you when you married?"

"Twenty-four."

"And was your mother worried you'd die

an old maid?"

Charlotte shook her head as she removed Miriam's gown from its hanger. "She was so ill the last few years of her life that I think she was glad I wasn't married then. A husband might not have been happy that I spent all my time nursing her." Jeffrey wouldn't have been pleased. Charlotte tried to dismiss the thought. She didn't want to think about Jeffrey now. There would be time later to mark the anniversary of his death.

Turning back to her customer, Charlotte smiled. "Is this gown for a special occasion?" When she'd ordered the silk, Charlotte had had Miriam in mind, knowing that the deep forest green would highlight Miriam's blonde hair and draw attention to her striking green eyes.

Miriam nodded. "We're going to a concert." The smile that lit her face turned Miriam into a beautiful woman, if only for an instant. "The symphony's playing Beethoven's Ninth. That's one of my favorites."

"Mine too. My mother used to sing 'Ode to Joy' while she was working."

Miriam stretched her hands above her head as Charlotte prepared to slide the dress onto her. "Before she was so ill, was your mother a modiste like you?"

Though Miriam couldn't see her, Charlotte shook her head. "No. Just a wonderful mother." While she was confident that Miriam would never knowingly betray a secret, Charlotte was careful about the stories she told her. There was no reason to tell Miriam — or anyone — that her mother had been a minister's wife and that her work had involved visiting infirm parishioners and making some of the best jams and jellies in Vermont. To deflect attention from herself, Charlotte spoke while she arranged the demi-train behind Miriam. "I imagine your mother enjoys music as much as you do. The newspaper always lists her among the who's who at every event."

An unladylike snort greeted Charlotte's words. "Don't tell anyone I said this, but my mother is tone deaf. It's my opinion that she attends concerts only because it's expected . . . and because it gives Papa something to write about. He's always saying that the paper needs to include information that will appeal to ladies, even if it is boring."

And ladies, despite the fact that they'd been given the vote and had even served on juries in Wyoming Territory, weren't deemed intelligent enough to care about politics. It was, Charlotte knew from the conversations

22

she'd overheard, a common enough opinion.

"You needn't worry. Your secret's safe with me." Charlotte had become a master at keeping secrets, her own and others'. "What about Mr. Landry? Does he enjoy music?"

Miriam shrugged, then grimaced as a pin scraped her shoulder. "I don't know. He might be like my mother."

Charlotte suspected that was the case. Though she had never met Barrett Landry, enough of her customers had mentioned him that she had formed a picture of the cattle baron who'd moved to Cheyenne five years ago. Rich and ambitious, he owned one of Cheyenne's finest mansions. Though only three blocks farther north on Ferguson Street from the building that housed Charlotte's shop and her living quarters, the Landry residence was a far cry from the simple brick structure where she plied her trade. It might not possess a ballroom, as some of the neighboring houses did, but Barrett Landry's home was clearly designed to impress. Having seen it, Charlotte did not discount the rumor that he was planning to enter politics. The mansion would be an ideal place to entertain the territory's most influential men, including Miriam's father. Charlotte tried not to frown at the thought that Cyrus Taggert might be part of the reason Barrett intended to court Miriam, if indeed that was his intention. She hoped that was not the case, for Miriam deserved a man who loved her for herself, not for the votes her father could deliver.

The bell that Charlotte had positioned on the front door tinkled.

"That's probably Barrett." Color rose to Miriam's cheeks. "Go on out. Molly can help me finish dressing."

"Are you sure?" Charlotte asked as she moved toward the dressing room door. It was true her assistant could button the three dozen pearl buttons that decorated the back of the gown.

Miriam nodded. "I want your opinion. Your honest opinion."

"Of course."

When she entered the main part of her shop, Charlotte found Molly staring. It was no wonder. The man who stood inside Élan was more handsome than even the most breathless rumors had claimed. At least six feet tall, he boasted dark brown hair, blue eyes, and a face that was saved from perfection by the small bump in the middle of his nose. Though he was not as muscular as the farmers Charlotte had known at home in Vermont, his finely tailored coat left no doubt that this man possessed his share of brawn, and yet that brawn was so beautifully packaged that the overall impression was of a gentleman. An important gentleman. Barrett Landry was a man no one would ignore.

"Mr. Landry?"

He nodded. "You must be Madame Charlotte. I beg your pardon, but Miriam never told me your full name. She simply described you as Madame-Charlotte-who-makes-the-most-beautiful-gowns-in-Cheyenne-better-even-than-Mama's-Paris-originals."

Charlotte chuckled. "Miss Taggert exaggerates." Though Mr. Landry had given her the opening to reveal her surname, she did not. When she'd opened Élan, Charlotte had deliberately chosen a French name for the shop and had called herself Madame Charlotte, though she possessed not a drop of French blood. Not only did most of her clients prefer the illusion that they were buying gowns with a connection to France, but by using the title with her first name, Charlotte avoided hearing herself referred to as Mrs. Harding. It was true that she'd signed the bill of sale for Élan as Charlotte Harding, but she still cringed whenever someone called her Mrs. Harding. She'd been Miss Harding, then Mrs. Crowley, never Mrs. Harding. Perhaps she should have chosen another name altogether, but Papa's sermons about the dangers of lying had led Charlotte to use the name she'd had for most of her life.

"Please, have a seat. Miss Taggert will be ready shortly." Charlotte gestured toward one of the gilded chairs that flanked a small table. It was here that customers waited, occasionally perusing the fashion magazines she carefully arranged on the table. The room — indeed her whole shop — was designed for women. Perhaps that was why she felt so uncomfortable having Barrett Landry here. As for the mission Miriam had given her, to form an opinion about the man who might or might not plan to court her friend, Charlotte could hardly begin a conversation by asking him if his intentions were honorable.

"Would you like a cup of coffee?"

Mr. Landry shook his head before walking toward the shelves laden with bolts of fabric. To Charlotte's surprise, he fingered several pieces.

She bit back a smile as she thought of the report she would give Miriam: *Your gentleman caller was the only man to take an interest in a piece of silk.* At least in that regard,

Barrett Landry was not what Charlotte had expected.

The object of her thoughts turned back toward her. "You have very fine merchandise. If I'm not mistaken, that's China silk." He gestured toward the display of bolts that stood on end rather than being stacked as the less costly fabrics were.

"It is, but I'm surprised you recognized it." Many of the women who patronized Élan could not distinguish between silk and satin, and not one would recognize the difference between silk from India and China. Barrett Landry wasn't merely breathtakingly handsome; he possessed unexpected facets.

As if he sensed her thoughts, he grinned, the self-deprecating smile only making his face more appealing. "I haven't always been a cattleman. Before I moved here, I worked in my family's mercantile in western Pennsylvania. We didn't normally carry silk, but my father ordered it occasionally."

The mystery was solved. The cattle baron who might be entering politics had a logical reason for being knowledgeable about fabric.

"Nothing else drapes quite like silk," Charlotte said. "That's why I enjoy using it for evening gowns."

Mr. Landry turned back to the bolts and

touched one. "This green is particularly attractive. It would complement Miriam's eyes."

Keeping her expression impassive, Charlotte gestured toward two others. "Then you would prefer it to the sapphire or the apricot." When Miriam had commissioned the gown, Charlotte had suggested either the sapphire or the forest green, but Miriam had been drawn to the apricot, perhaps because it was similar to a shade Charlotte had been wearing that day.

"Yes." Mr. Landry's reply was unequivocal. "The orange — er, apricot — would suit you far more than Miriam." He was right. The apricot would complement Charlotte's dark brown hair and eyes far more than Miriam's coloring. It appeared the scope of Barrett Landry's knowledge was wider than simply recognizing fabric.

He turned at the sound of the dressing room door opening. "Ah, there you are," he said as Miriam emerged.

She revolved slowly, letting him see the gown from all directions. "What do you think?" The sparkle in her eyes when she glanced at Charlotte suggested that Miriam viewed this as some sort of test. Perhaps she was trying to learn what kind of husband he would be, whether he'd care about her clothing.

"It's a nice dress."

Though Charlotte suspected that Mr. Landry was teasing Miriam, her friend pursed her lips as if she were annoyed. "The color, Barrett. What do you think about the color?" She took a step closer to him. "Don't you think it makes me look like a Christmas tree?"

"No, it does not. It makes you look absolutely beautiful. I'll be the envy of every man in Cheyenne."

Charlotte tried not to stare. Though Mr. Landry did not resemble Jeffrey physically, the tone of his voice and the words he'd chosen sounded like Charlotte's former husband. The casual, friendly tone he'd used when discussing the silk had changed, and the sincerity she had thought she'd heard when he'd told her his color preference had disappeared. The changes were subtle, but to Charlotte's ears, the words he'd spoken to Miriam rang false.

Afraid that her friend was making a mistake, Charlotte waited until Miriam returned to the dressing room before she said, "I've heard rumors that you're considering entering politics."

Barrett Landry leaned against the counter, his blue eyes sparkling. "I am. Don't tell me you disapprove. I was counting on your vote."

His smile was engaging, and Charlotte did not doubt that he was accustomed to charming women with it. She would not succumb to that charm.

"It's too soon for me to know whether I approve or disapprove," she told him. "I am curious, though, about your reasons for running for office." In Charlotte's experience, too many men were like Jeffrey, seeking fame or fortune or both. For Miriam's sake, she hoped Barrett Landry was not one of them.

"What would you consider a valid reason?"

Charlotte noticed that he had not answered her question but had instead turned the tables. "I've always believed that each of us was put on Earth to make it a better place. We can't change the past, but if we make the present the best it can be, we can influence the future. Whatever we choose to do with our lives should be done with that in mind." Now she was sounding like Papa, preaching a sermon. That wasn't what she had intended. She was supposed to be learning more about Barrett Landry, not telling him her deepest beliefs.

He was silent for a moment, absentmindedly rubbing the bump on his nose while his eyes remained fixed on her face as if he were assessing her sincerity. "I have no doubt that the citizens of Wyoming would be better off if we were a state instead of a territory. We could elect our governor, not have some crony the president appointed running Wyoming. We know how to manage our resources, especially water, better than a man who's never set foot in the territory. The politicians back East don't understand how scarce water is or how lives depend on its being managed wisely."

He was not a dilettante or a man out for only personal gain. The passion in his voice convinced Charlotte of his sincerity about running for public office. "And you believe you're the man to change Washington?"

Barrett Landry shook his head. "Not alone. But with the right advisers, yes, I believe I could make a difference."

Charlotte heard the sound of muted laughter coming from the dressing room. Whatever Molly and Miriam were discussing, it was lighter than her conversation with Mr. Landry.

"What about you, Madame Charlotte?" he asked, his lips quirked into a semblance of a smile. "Do you believe that sewing fancy gowns for wealthy women is making the world a better place?"

Charlotte blanched as his words registered. She was doing what she could to provide for herself and David, but she wasn't improving the world by dressing women like Miriam. She should never have introduced the subject. "No, I don't," Charlotte admitted. "I guess that makes me a hypocrite. I apologize, Mr. Landry." She forced herself to keep her gaze steady, though she longed to duck her head.

To Charlotte's surprise, Barrett Landry shook his head. "I'm the one who should apologize." The sparkle faded from his eyes. "My mother would have washed my mouth out with soap if she'd heard me. If there was one lesson she drummed into us boys, it was that a gentleman is never rude to a lady. I was, and I'm sorry."

"You were only being honest with your question."

"Honest. Indeed." Though there was nothing remotely amusing about her words, once again Mr. Landry's eyes betrayed a hint of mirth. "May I ask your opinion about something? Your honest opinion." He stressed the adjective.

Charlotte nodded, trying not to reflect on the irony that this was the second time in less than half an hour that someone had asked for her honest opinion. What would Miriam and Mr. Landry think if they knew that she had begun the day reflecting on her own deception? She was still undecided what she should tell Miriam about this man, and now he was asking her opinion. She could only hope it did not concern Miriam.

"My advisers tell me I need a campaign slogan."

Not Miriam. Thank goodness. "They're probably correct."

"Since we're agreed on that, what do you think of 'Landry Never Lies'?"

Charlotte swallowed, trying to dissolve the lump that lodged in her throat at the memory of all the lies and half-truths she had uttered.

"It has a nice cadence to it," she said at last. "You could turn it into a jingle. You know, like 'Tippecanoe and Tyler, Too.' " Though it had been more than forty-five years since that campaign, Charlotte knew the words to the song that had helped William Henry Harrison and his running mate John Tyler gain the White House. All three Harding sisters had heard the story of their maternal grandparents' one serious disagreement and why their grandmother would croon the song only when Grandpa was not home.

Mr. Landry chuckled. "I'd forgotten about that and fervently hope that my advisers have too. If I have to sing a song, I'll lose every last voter. Bullfrogs are more melodic than I am." He wrinkled his nose before turning serious again. "Ignoring the musical possibilities, what do you think about it as a slogan? Do you think voters will like it?"

Not wanting to dwell on the idea of lies, Charlotte forced a smile. "I do, Mr. Landry. Indeed, I do."

2

"You brought the carriage." Miriam tightened her grip on Barrett's arm as her face lit with pleasure. It seemed he'd done something right today. There were times when Miriam's mood was difficult to read, when he felt as if he were playing a role, trying to coax her into a smile, but the sight of his cabriolet with the top folded down seemed to have chased away her pensive mood. She'd been unusually quiet when she'd emerged from the dressing room, and he'd had the impression that he was intruding, keeping her from a private conversation with Madame Charlotte. That was absurd. Miriam had asked him to meet her at the shop. She wanted him there. He'd done exactly what Miriam had asked, and she'd seemed miffed. But now, fortunately, she was smiling again.

"I thought we might go to the park," he said when he'd helped her into the carriage.

It was a perfect October day, the sky a deep blue that seemed unique to Wyoming, highlighted by a few fluffy cumulus clouds. The sun had warmed the air enough that strolling through the park would be pleasant, and though the trees the schoolchildren had planted were still saplings, providing little shade, that was not a problem, for Miriam had brought her parasol. "You can show off your new hat," Barrett told her as he tightened the reins.

Miriam wrinkled her nose, the look she gave him indicating he'd done something wrong. Again. "This is not a new hat. You've seen it before. Everyone has seen it."

"It still looks very nice. You look very nice." Barrett could have kicked himself. Compared to women, cattle — even the ornery ones that tried to hide during roundup — were the most agreeable creatures on the face of the earth. It appeared that he shouldn't have said anything about the hat, but Camden had claimed that ladies wanted to be complimented on their appearance. His brother had neglected to mention that a man had to be careful about referring to a specific piece of clothing. As he considered his words and Miriam's reaction, Barrett realized he should have simply said that he wanted the privilege of having her, the loveliest lady in the city, on his arm when he strolled through the park.

Were all women this prickly? Barrett doubted that Madame Charlotte was. She hadn't seemed that way. She wasn't the most beautiful woman Barrett had ever seen. Other women had dark brown hair and eyes the color of Mr. Ellis's best chocolate. Other women wore skirts that whispered when they moved, attracting a man's attention even though the fabric covered practically every inch of skin. Other women wore soft floral perfume that hinted at a summer garden. But no other woman Barrett had met had displayed the same intriguing combination of confidence and vulnerability.

When Madame Charlotte walked around her store and spoke of the silks, she was the consummate shopkeeper: knowledgeable, helpful, seemingly genuine in her interest in Barrett, even though he was not a customer. She'd even forgiven him for embarrassing her with his question. Question? It had been little more than a taunt. She had challenged him when she'd asked about his motives, and he'd felt the need to retaliate. Barrett wasn't proud of that, any more than he was proud of the fact that his initial motivation for seeking office had not been as pure as he'd claimed. When Richard and Warren had first suggested he run for public office, he'd seen it as a way to prove he could do something his brothers hadn't. It hadn't been easy, growing up in Harrison and Camden's shadow. They'd been big and strong, whereas he'd been small for his age, not reaching his full height until he was almost eighteen. When his brothers had called him the runt of the litter and refused to include him in their games, he'd retaliated by playing pranks and had soon earned a reputation as a mischief maker. Though he'd outgrown that and had mended his relationship with Harrison and Camden, he'd never felt completely at home in Northwick. That was one reason he'd left as soon as he could.

It had been a challenge, building a new life in Wyoming, but he'd succeeded. He now had wealth and a social position far beyond his brothers'. Running for office would be the final proof that he was no longer the runt of the litter.

The urge to prove that was powerful, but the more Barrett learned about his adopted home, the more he realized that he could make a difference in Wyoming — a positive difference. And so he'd told Madame Charlotte that, not his earlier selfish motive.

She had appeared to believe him. It was only when they'd discussed his slogan that she had seemed to retreat into herself. Her demeanor had changed, reminding Barrett of the porcupine he and Camden and Harrison had found when they'd been wandering through the woods back in Pennsylvania. The instant the animal had spotted them, it had curled into a ball, its fiercely sharp quills protecting its soft underbelly, and though they'd stood there for what felt like hours, waiting for the porcupine to straighten out, it had not.

Madame Charlotte was protecting something, perhaps a daughter. Though Miriam had said nothing more than that Madame Charlotte was a widow who lived above the shop, he had heard a young girl's voice coming from upstairs. A child lived there, in all likelihood Madame Charlotte's child. Barrett could understand that she might want to shelter her daughter, but that didn't explain why she'd seemed so disturbed by his slogan.

"Turn here." Miriam tapped Barrett's arm.

He blinked, surprised when he realized they'd reached the corner of 22nd Street. The park was only one block east. Somehow, he'd traveled four blocks without being aware of it.

"I'm sorry," he said honestly. "My mind wandered."

"You should be sorry." Miriam's normally sweet voice was laced with asperity. "You've practically ignored me since we left Madame Charlotte's."

Madame Charlotte. Did the woman have a surname? Of course she did, even if Barrett had never heard Miriam refer to her any other way. Though the question of the lovely dressmaker's name teased him almost as much as her protective air had, Barrett knew better than to ask his companion. Speaking of another woman, even if it was only the one who created her dresses, was no way to treat a lady, especially one he was considering courting.

"I'm sorry, Miriam. You didn't deserve that. I assure you that you have my full attention now."

The look she gave him told Barrett she was still skeptical. "What were you thinking about?"

It would be sheer folly to tell her the truth. Instead, Barrett changed the subject as they approached the four-block expanse of City Park. "Has your father said anything about beef prices dropping again? I've heard stories that some of the other cattlemen are selling more head than normal because they're fearful of a harsh winter."

Miriam shot him another look, as if to say she recognized his deliberate evasion. She wasn't simply an attractive woman, Barrett reminded himself. She was also intelligent. That was one of the reasons why she would be an ideal wife. Even if he never learned to love her, he could at least respect her.

Twirling her parasol in what might have been a flirtatious manner, Miriam nodded. "Papa mentioned something, but you know Mama doesn't like him to talk about business at dinner. She says it's not good for the digestion." Miriam waved at a friend on the other side of the street before she added, "He did say someone reported that beavers were making bigger dens than normal. It's a silly story, if you ask me. What do beavers know about weather?"

Her expression intent, Miriam laid her hand on Barrett's arm and waited until she was certain she had his full attention. "Tell me the truth, Barrett. Are you certain green is the right color for my gown?"

"It's beautiful." Tears sprang to Charlotte's eyes as she looked at the two-layer cake with its carefully swirled icing. Though the frosting was chocolate, Gwen had piped a white

41

border around the top and at the base. She had even placed multicolored candies on the sides and had used them to outline a *D* on the top. It was a work of art, a great deal of effort to expend for a boy who could not see it. "This must have taken you hours."

Charlotte gave her son another hug, then placed him back on the floor, handing him the gourd rattle that had been his favorite toy for the past week. He'd been waiting for her as he did each day, sitting on the floor of the room that served as kitchen, dining room, and parlor, his head turning in her direction when she opened the door, his face lighting with a smile that made the day's minor annoyances fade. This was her son, and today was his birthday. Though she doubted he would remember it when he was older, Charlotte had been determined that it would be a special one. Tonight she wouldn't worry about the baron. She wouldn't let her mind wander toward Barrett Landry. She wouldn't even wonder what the future held. Tonight was for David.

Charlotte smiled at the woman who shared the small apartment. "Thank you, Gwen. For the cake and everything."

The other woman shrugged, as if the effort of preparing a fancy cake while she cared for two rambunctious children had been insignificant. That was Gwen. Ever since she and her daughter had come to live with Charlotte, Gwen Amos had done more than expected, brushing off Charlotte's thanks as unnecessary. "I'm glad to help" was the normal refrain from the heavyset woman who watched over David while Charlotte was in the shop. Shorter than average, Gwen would never be considered beautiful, even though her light brown hair was smooth and glossy, the envy of many, and her blue eyes sparkled with enthusiasm. She was a jolly woman who appeared to enjoy life, and for that alone, Charlotte felt blessed. It had been Gwen's optimism that had helped Charlotte through the dark days when she'd learned that her son was blind.

"Rose and I told David what we were doing, didn't we?" Gwen smiled at her daughter.

The three-year-old nodded vigorously. "I and David taste the candies." She smacked her lips. "I and David like them."

"I'll bet you did." Charlotte smiled at Rose, then hugged Gwen. "Every day I thank God for bringing you into my life. I don't know what I'd do without you."

When Jeffrey had been killed, Charlotte had been forced to make an honest assess-

43

ment of her talents. There were only two —
a clear soprano voice and the ability to
design and sew fashionable clothing. Since
opportunities to earn money by singing
were limited, her best chance of making a
living for herself and David was to open a
dress shop. Though there was no question
of remaining at Fort Laramie, once she'd
arrived in Cheyenne, Charlotte had realized
that the growing capital city could support
another dressmaker.

Finding and stocking the store had been
relatively simple. Juggling work with caring
for David and their apartment was a far
greater challenge. Fortunately for Charlotte,
Gwen had been shopping at Yates's Dry
Goods the day Charlotte had introduced
herself to the man whose building adjoined
hers, and she had heard Charlotte tell Mr.
Yates that she needed a housekeeper who
could also care for her son. Half an hour
later, Charlotte had the best housekeeper
she could imagine.

"You were the one who helped us," Gwen
countered, "but let's not be maudlin. Especially not tonight. Supper's ready."

Charlotte moved to the dry sink. "Did you
hear that, David? It's time to wash our
hands. Come to Mama." She watched, a
proud smile on her face as he crawled

toward her. Other children his age were starting to walk, but for David, crawling had been a major accomplishment.

"You know what comes next." David giggled before raising his arms so she could lift him onto the counter. "Now, give me your hands." When she positioned them over the pail, he giggled again. Getting wet was one of David's favorite parts of the day. "Okay, rub," Charlotte said when she'd poured water over her son's hands. "Now we'll dry them." She gave him a towel. Though he hadn't quite mastered the art of drying his hands, he seemed to enjoy the texture of the cloth. "Off to your chair now."

It had seemed strange at first, narrating every step she was planning to take, but when Charlotte had blindfolded herself and tried to imagine what David's world was like, she had realized how important it was to compensate for his lack of sight by stimulating his other senses. David's hearing appeared to be acute, and he would often sniff, wordlessly telling Charlotte he had detected an odor she had not.

The meal went well. David enjoyed eating, once he knew where the foods were placed, and though he made a mess of the cake, smearing it all over his face, his grin left no doubt that he'd savored it.

When she had washed her son's face and hands and tossed his bib into the laundry basket, Charlotte settled him on her lap and reached for the first of the packages Gwen had laid on the now clean table. "David, your aunts sent presents for you." She handed him a box wrapped in heavy brown paper and tied with a coarse string. "This is from Aunt Abigail. Feel the tie." She moved his fingers over the twine, showing him how it circled the box. "We need to pull it loose." Handing him one end, Charlotte encouraged her son to tug on it. When it came undone, he crowed with delight. "Feel the box now. The string is gone." She guided David's fingers over the package. "Let's open the box." When she'd slid the paper off it, Charlotte removed the top. "Oh, it's a book." A book her son would never read. Elizabeth's gift was another book with beautiful pictures, the perfect gift for most one-year-old boys but not for David. Though he'd enjoy hearing her read the stories to him, only the richly textured blanket Gwen had made was something Charlotte's son would fully appreciate.

"You need to tell them," Gwen said when the children were in bed and she and Charlotte had returned to the sitting area of their main room. Furnished with a horsehair settee and two tapestry-covered chairs, it was large enough for the four of them and accommodated the few visitors the women had. Charlotte lit an oil lamp. Although the apartment had electricity, there were times when she preferred the softer light of the lamps.

Gwen's expression was solemn as she set her empty teacup on the small table positioned between the two chairs. "Your sisters deserve to know that David is . . ." She hesitated for a second before saying, "Special. You should have told them at the beginning."

It was a familiar argument. "I didn't realize he was blind when I left Fort Laramie." Though Gwen was reluctant to voice the word *blind*, Charlotte was not. "Even if I'd known, I'm not certain I'd have told Abigail." It was only after she'd moved to Cheyenne that Charlotte had noticed that David's eyes never followed her. "Probably not. I couldn't disrupt my sisters' lives. Elizabeth would have postponed her medical studies, and Abigail and Ethan would have interrupted their honeymoon to be with me. I couldn't let that happen."

At the time that Charlotte had learned about David's blindness, Abigail and Ethan had been back East, paying a brief visit to

47

Elizabeth while Ethan made the final decisions about his inheritance. Though both he and Abigail were confident that he'd been right in renouncing all claims to the fortune his grandfather had amassed, leaving it instead to a distant cousin who shared the grandfather's passion for railroads, if Ethan had known that David was handicapped, he might have made a different decision. Charlotte could picture Ethan sacrificing his own happiness in order to provide for her and David, and she could not allow that to happen. David was her son. She alone was responsible for him.

And now? It was difficult to explain when she didn't fully understand it herself. Charlotte had always been reluctant to let her sisters see her life as less than perfect. That was why she hadn't told either Abigail or Elizabeth the truth about her marriage. She hadn't even mentioned she was expecting a child, for fear they'd visit her and discover that the man she'd believed to be her knight in shining armor was troubled.

Gwen poured herself another cup of tea, shaking her head when Charlotte refused a second piece of cake. "You think because you're the oldest you should be the strong one. Abigail and Elizabeth are grown women now. They could have helped you.

You don't always have to be strong."

"I wasn't." Charlotte closed her eyes, remembering.

Her legs quivered as she tied her bonnet under her chin and smoothed on her gloves. Though she could blame her weakness on recent childbirth, it was fear that made her tremble like a sapling in the wind, fear that she would be unable to do what she must.

"I'll go with you, if you like." Abigail, who had spent the summer with her, put her arms around Charlotte's shoulders and squeezed gently. "You don't need to go alone."

But she did. "Only I can forgive her." And that was best done alone.

If the soldiers who'd drawn guard duty were surprised when Lieutenant Crowley's widow asked to visit the prisoner, they were too well trained to show it. They offered to accompany her to the cell but seemed unfazed when Charlotte refused. "If you need us, ma'am, we'll be right outside," they said as they resumed their pacing in front of the guard-house. It was a routine day for them, but an anything but normal one for Charlotte.

She could hear the hesitation in her foot-steps and forced herself to walk briskly.

The woman who'd been captured two nights before glared as Charlotte approached her cell. "Who are you?" she demanded in a drawl that suggested she had been raised in the South. Before Charlotte could answer, the prisoner narrowed her eyes. "You must be the wife, the nosy one's sister."

Ignoring the slur to Abigail, Charlotte said simply, "I'm Charlotte Crowley. I came to tell you that I forgive you for your part in Jeffrey's death."

For a second, the woman stared at Charlotte, as if in disbelief. "I didn't kill him."

"I know that, but if it hadn't been for you . . ."

The woman with the graying brown hair interrupted. "I don't need your forgiveness. It won't help me, anyhow. I know where I'm going when I leave this world, and there ain't nothing anybody can do to change that."

When Charlotte started to speak, to tell the prisoner that there was hope, the woman held up her hand. "Save your breath and listen to me. Listen good, because I'm only going to say it once. The baron knows that Jeffrey found Big Nose's stash."

Charlotte gasped. Even though he had met his fate at the end of a hangman's noose several years before she had come to Wyoming Territory, Charlotte had heard of George Parrott, better known as Big Nose. The notorious outlaw had been famous for his robberies, and with his death, speculation about the large shipment of gold that had never been recovered had only increased. Now it appeared that someone named "the baron" thought her husband had it.

"The baron is a mighty determined man," the woman continued. "He won't rest until he finds the gold, and you're the only link. Watch your back, missy. You don't wanna cross the baron. He kills folks the way you'd swat a fly."

The next morning, the fort was buzzing with the news that the prisoner was dead. Somehow, someone had snuck into the guardhouse and slit her throat. Though there were no clues, Charlotte was certain the baron was responsible . . .

"I know it's David's birthday." Gwen's voice brought Charlotte back to the present. "But I have a gift for you. For both of us, really." She handed Charlotte an envelope. "I know how much you love Beethoven's Ninth Symphony, and I thought maybe you and I could go together." Gwen's habitual smile faded slightly, as if she feared Charlotte's reaction. "Molly will watch the children. I already asked her."

Charlotte turned the envelope over in her hand, gazing at her name, inscribed by Gwen's untutored hand. "I don't know what to say. This is so generous of you." Though

51

she paid Gwen a salary in addition to providing food and lodging, theater tickets were a luxury Gwen could barely afford.

The heavyset woman shook her head. "This is a thank-you for giving Rose and me a home. I didn't want to tell you at the time, but I was desperate. I had only enough money for another week. Once it was gone, I didn't know what I'd do. I'd looked everywhere for work, but no one wanted a widow with a small child. I was afraid I'd wind up at Sylvia's," she said, referring to the brothel next door to the boardinghouse where Gwen and Rose had taken refuge after her husband's death. "It was a miracle that you and I were in Mr. Yates's store at the same time."

Charlotte shook her head. "Not a miracle, but the hand of God. He put us together for a reason."

"Then you'll accept the ticket?"

Perhaps it was the fact that the memory of the woman's warning was so fresh. Perhaps it was only because this would be the first time she'd appeared at a large public gathering. Charlotte didn't know the reason. All she knew was that fear assailed her. The baron could be anywhere, even at the Cheyenne Opera House. If he recognized her . . . Charlotte swallowed deeply, reminding herself of what had become her favorite Bible verse. She didn't have to live in fear. Joshua 1:9 promised that the Lord would be with her wherever she went, even to the opera house.

Slowly, she nodded.

His mother used to say that envy was a sin. Warren Duncan tugged off his boot, placing it carefully next to its mate. No matter how annoyed he might be — and he was mighty annoyed — there was no reason to damage good shoe leather by not caring for it properly. That would be foolish, and he was not a foolish man. Far from it. But he was an envious one.

Warren did not doubt that envy was a sin and that his mother would have been displeased if she'd lived long enough to know of it. He reached for the blacking and began to polish his boots. Ma would turn over in her grave if she knew that he'd been guilty of other, far more serious, sins. Those Ten Commandments she was so fond of spouting also said, "Thou shalt not steal" and "Thou shalt not kill." But words, whether written on the pages of Ma's Bible or carved on stone tablets, hadn't stopped him from relieving more than one person of his valuables. They hadn't stopped him from slitting his partner's throat, and they most definitely were not doing anything to lessen his envy.

He wanted what Barrett Landry had: more money than any one man needed, a position within Cheyenne society, a future in the nation's capital, and soon a wife. Barrett had it all. It seemed as if the man hardly lifted a finger and everything fell into place. That was what Warren envied most of all: the ease with which Barrett had transformed himself from a former shopkeeper into one of Wyoming's leading cattle barons.

It hadn't been that way for Warren. He'd had to struggle for everything after the doctor and the sheriff had shunted his ma off to the asylum. They'd claimed she was having delusions, just because she'd raced down Main Street in her nightgown, shouting that her husband had risen from his grave and was chasing her with a meat cleaver. It was that quack of a doctor who was crazy. Sure, Ma had spells. Everyone did, only some folks hid it better than others.

Warren frowned at the memory of the simpleton who called himself a doc saying Warren would grow up to be like his ma. It hadn't been easy, but he'd proven him wrong. He'd managed to finish law school,

albeit at the bottom of his class. The sheep-
skin they handed him was supposed to be
his golden ticket. Unfortunately, it hadn't
turned out that way. Oh, he'd found a position with a law firm, but the partners hadn't
seen his potential and had refused to pro-
mote him. Instead, he'd been stuck drafting
memoranda for the senior members of the
firm, never getting credit for his work. All
that on a salary that barely put a roof over
his head and food in his mouth. He deserved
more, much more. That's why he'd headed
West.

Warren studied the first boot, ensuring
that he had blackened each inch before
beginning to buff it. Though he hadn't been
in the military, his boots outshone those of
the officers who entrusted their legal affairs
to him. That was one good thing about
Cheyenne. There was no shortage of men
who needed him. He had a good-sized
clientele, and he no longer worried about
paying rent. Perhaps he ought to be satisfied, but Warren had never been one to be
easily satisfied. Ma had told him to dream
big, and he had. The problem was, those
dreams hadn't come true . . . yet.

He was fifty-one years old, and he still
didn't have what he deserved. He lived in
two rented rooms, not an opulent home on

Ferguson Street; he had no wife; and the only time he entered the hallowed halls of the Cheyenne Club was as someone's guest. His membership application had been rejected. The sour-faced man who'd delivered the verdict had told Warren he wasn't the caliber of man to be admitted to the club. Absurd! He was as good as Barrett and the other members.

Warren laid his carefully polished boots on the floor and strode to the window, considering the excuses the membership committee might have invented to deny his application. Eddy Street wasn't as prestigious as Ferguson, where Barrett had his mansion. It couldn't compare to the blocks of 17th Street where F. E. Warren lived and where other cattle barons were planning to build their homes, but it wasn't a seedy area either. Come spring, the lilacs that his neighbors had planted would be blooming. For a few weeks, they'd brighten the yards, and if he opened his windows, they would bring in a pleasing scent. It seemed that wasn't enough. All right. He'd build himself a house. A big house that would impress the committee. But what if even that didn't satisfy them? What else could he do?

He glanced down at the street, his eyes narrowing when he saw a young couple strolling along the opposite side. Maybe Richard was right. Maybe it wasn't only Barrett who needed a wife. If a wife could convince voters to support Barrett, surely one could convince the old men on the membership committee that Warren should be admitted to the club.

Warren grinned, imagining the day when he would enter the hallowed building on 17th Street as a full-fledged member. A house and a wife. He could do that. He would do that. Come spring, Warren Duncan would have a new house and would take a wife, and directly on the heels of those accomplishments, he would be admitted to the Cheyenne Club.

All it required was money. Lots of money. Fortunately, it was there, waiting for him. The money Big Nose had hidden, the money Jeffrey Crowley had found, would be his. Soon.

3

"Do you believe that sewing fancy gowns for wealthy women is making the world a better place?" It had been a week since Barrett Landry had spoken those words, and they still reverberated through Charlotte's brain.

She frowned as her feet pumped the treadle while her hands guided the fabric under the presser foot. Elias Howe's invention had dramatically reduced the time required to sew a gown, making short work of the seams and leaving Charlotte more time to add the fancy touches her customers craved, including the double box pleated hems that had become one of her trademarks. The sewing machine also gave her time to think. Some days that was good. Today it was not, for Mr. Landry's words haunted her.

He was right. Charlotte had known that at the time. Ever since David's birth, she had thought of little other than making a living for them and keeping him safe. That wasn't enough. For much of her life, she'd been coddled, protected by well-meaning parents and even her younger sister Abigail because of the lingering effects of her childhood bout of pneumonia. Though Charlotte hadn't told Jeffrey that the doctor had predicted her lungs would always be weak, he'd insisted on treating her like one of the fragile porcelain cups he'd given her. But Jeffrey and her parents were dead, and Abigail was more than a thousand miles away. For the past year, Charlotte had relied on herself, and in doing so, she'd discovered that she was stronger than she'd realized. Equally important, her lungs appeared to be fully healed, perhaps the result of Wyoming's dry air. The fact that her lungs seemed to be improving was one of the reasons she hadn't wanted to move back East after Jeffrey's death. That and the fact that she had fallen in love with the territory's rugged beauty.

She was a healthy, able-bodied woman, capable of doing more than dressing Cheyenne's most fortunate women. It was time to help others. The question was, what could she do? While it was true that she had once been a teacher and that teachers could indeed make a positive difference in others' lives, Charlotte knew she was not as gifted as Abigail. There had to be something else she could do.

She snipped the thread, then inspected the seam she had just sewn. Perfect. All that remained were the hem and the yards of lace that would turn a seemingly ordinary *matinée*, as the French were calling long fitted bodices this season, into one that would be the envy of Miriam's friends.

Miriam would be pleased, and so would Charlotte, for at least two or three of Miriam's acquaintances would ask Charlotte to sew similar garments for them. Those sales would help pay for groceries and Gwen's salary.

The gowns Charlotte made pleased Cheyenne's wealthy women. They enhanced their beauty and camouflaged less than perfect bodies, making each woman feel special. That was what Charlotte had intended when she'd called her shop Élan. She wanted her store to generate enthusiasm, and so she had chosen the French word for high spirits as its name.

She rose and hung the partially completed garment on a padded hanger. Gathering the remnants, Charlotte smiled when she realized there was enough left to make a dress for Rose. Gwen would be delighted, for she was determined that her daughter would never wear tattered clothing. Even though Gwen herself had been clothed in little more than rags, sporting a shabby, ill-fitting frock with patched elbows and a frayed hem the day Charlotte met her, Rose had worn a relatively new dress. Sensing that Gwen was not one to indulge herself, three days later Charlotte had presented her with a new dress. The change had been little less than a transformation. Clad in a garment that flattered her, Gwen had gained confidence, and her demeanor had altered. She stood a bit taller, and her smile, which had been tentative the day Charlotte had met her, was broader, more assured. She even laughed out loud, causing both Rose and David to chuckle.

Of course. That was the answer to Mr. Landry's question. Charlotte didn't have to confine herself to clothing Cheyenne's wealthiest women. She could make dresses for the women who still lived in Mrs. Kendall's boardinghouse. As happiness bubbled up inside her, Charlotte began to sing. Gwen had told her of the poverty that had driven her and a dozen other women to take refuge in the rickety building on 15th Street. "Everyone wants to escape," Gwen had said, explaining that Mrs. Kendall's kindness and her excellent cooking were often overshadowed by the fear that the men who frequented the brothel next door would accost them. "We all wanted to get away, but I'm the only one who has."

Charlotte couldn't hire them all. She couldn't give them enough money to live in a safer area. But she could — and she would — provide them with respectable clothing. She'd have to order new fabric, for Élan was currently filled with silks, satins, and velvets in anticipation of holiday parties, and those were not suitable for Mrs. Kendall's boarders — but within a few weeks, Charlotte would be able to begin.

She was still singing when she heard the front doorbell tinkle.

"Charlotte! Are you there?"

Surprised that Miriam had arrived a day early for her appointment, Charlotte hurried to the front of the store. "I don't have your gown ready for a fitting, but . . ." Charlotte stopped abruptly, shocked by the sight of Miriam carrying four dresses. There was no doubt about it. They were the first four frocks Charlotte had made for her less than a year ago.

"Is something wrong?"

Miriam wrinkled her nose. "No. Yes." She sighed as she laid the dresses on the counter.

"Mama wanted to burn these. She insisted that I can't wear them again because they're last season's style, and she won't let me give them to the servants. It wouldn't be seemly, she says."

Charlotte could imagine Amelia Taggert pronouncing those very words. Miriam's mother had spent a year in England and had come home convinced that if she followed every rule of etiquette, she would be regarded with the same esteem as the British aristocracy. Far less pretentious, Miriam chafed at her mother's restrictions at the same time that she tried to be a loving and obedient daughter.

"I don't want them destroyed." Miriam fingered the brown calico that had been her favorite everyday dress. "Can you do something with them?"

Charlotte grinned. "Indeed, I can." It would take only a few hours to convert Miriam's elegant frocks into dresses better suited for the women at Mrs. Kendall's boardinghouse. Even before the new shipment of fabric arrived, Charlotte could provide a few dresses. "Your timing is perfect."

"This is the most beautiful gown I've ever had." Gwen turned slowly in front of the long mirror, admiring her reflection. Though normally they would have dressed in their apartment, tonight Charlotte insisted that they use the shop's dressing room, largely because she wanted Gwen to have the experience of being a customer of Élan. The woman who did so much for her had admitted that she'd never been able to afford fancy evening clothes. Tonight was different. Even if they weren't seated in one of the elegant boxes, Gwen would be as well-dressed as any woman at the opera house.

Her blue eyes sparkling with pleasure and perhaps a bit of astonishment, Gwen ran her hands over her hips. "This style makes me look almost thin."

That had been the plan. Charlotte nodded as she fastened the last of the thirty-four buttons that closed the back of the dress. "Simple lines are slimming." When she had designed Gwen's gown, Charlotte had forgone the intricately draped overskirt and pronounced bustle that were popular, instead choosing vertical panels to give Gwen the illusion of more height and less width. Even the choice of midnight blue silk had been deliberate. Not only did the color flatter Gwen's blue eyes, but the dark color made her appear pounds lighter.

"You have beautiful shoulders," she told

Gwen. "The gown draws attention to them." And to the strand of pearls her husband had given her. When Gwen had told Charlotte how long Mike had saved to buy her only piece of jewelry besides her wedding ring, she had decided to give the gown a low scooped neckline that would highlight Gwen's creamy skin and her necklace.

Gwen's expression turned wistful as she fingered the pearls. "I wish Mike was here to see me. I miss him so much. I miss being married." She blinked back tears before forcing a smile. "You understand."

Charlotte nodded, because she knew it was what Gwen expected. The truth was, she didn't miss being married. Marriage hadn't turned out the way she had expected. As a child and then a young woman, Charlotte had dreamt of falling in love with Prince Charming. In her dreams, they married and lived happily ever after. Reality had been far different. She had been wed less than a year and a half, and Jeffrey had spent so little of that time with her that, were it not for David, she could almost believe her marriage had been a dream. But David existed. He and the fear that the baron would find them were the legacies of Charlotte's marriage.

"Let me arrange your train." Gwen's

habitual smile was back in place as she turned her attention to Charlotte's gown. Made of apricot silk, it was similar in design to Gwen's but had a higher neckline and an apron-style panel of darker silk that dipped gracefully below Charlotte's waist and draped around her hips, flowing into an elaborate bustle and short train. Had she been making the gown for a ball, Charlotte would have lengthened the train so that it trailed behind her, but since they would spend most of the evening seated, she had left it the same length as the gown itself, barely clearing the floor.

"It's not that I'm anxious to leave you and David," Gwen said as she straightened the fall of silk. "I hate the thought of leaving you alone if I remarry, but I want Rose to have a father." She looked over Charlotte's shoulder, meeting her gaze in the looking glass. "Wouldn't it be wonderful if both of us found husbands?"

"I'm not ready." *I'm not sure I ever will be,* she added silently. "It would take a special man to accept David." And even if he did, Charlotte wasn't certain she could trust her judgment. She had believed Jeffrey was the man God intended for her, and oh, how wrong she'd been. Jeffrey had showered her with material possessions, but he had not given her what she craved: true love.

Gwen shook her head. "That special man is out there. I know he is. And if he's in Cheyenne tonight, he won't be able to take his eyes off you. Apricot is the perfect color for you."

"I wanted us both to be walking advertisements for Élan. That's why I made our gowns out of colors that complement each other." Charlotte wouldn't tell Gwen there was another reason she'd chosen the apricot for herself. Though she knew he'd be at the opera house tonight, she doubted Barrett Landry would notice her. But if he did, she wanted him to see that he was right about the color flattering her. And if that wasn't a silly reason to use the most expensive piece of silk in the store for herself, she didn't know what was.

Half an hour later, Charlotte marveled as the carriage she'd hired approached the opera house. She'd seen the building at least a dozen times when she'd strolled through her adopted city, but that had been during daylight. Now that the sun had set, everything looked different. Lights blazed from the arched windows. Though the mansard roof was shadowed, the windows in the two dormers and the fancy round one that some called an *oeil-de-boeuf* or cow's eye window gleamed, leaving no doubt that this was one of Cheyenne's most impressive buildings.

"Oh, look," Gwen whispered as they joined the crowd that filed through the front door, then up the grand staircase to the second floor lobby. "The chandelier is even more beautiful than I'd heard. Do you suppose there really are fifty-two lights?"

Charlotte didn't need to count the bulbs. Whether it had fifty-two or some other number, the chandelier was magnificent, providing decoration as well as illumination. Miriam had told her that until the city was electrified, the chandelier was rarely lit because of the unpleasant smell from the oil, but now it was one of the most admired parts of Cheyenne. Like the building itself, the chandelier was designed to impress, and it succeeded. As discreetly as she could, Charlotte looked up, wanting to see the skylights that were almost as famous as the lighting fixture. During the day, light spilled through them, but now though the glass expanses were dark, a close to full moon cast its glow on the symphonygoers, and a few stars twinkled, giving the opera house an almost magical aura.

"I can't believe we're here." Gwen's voice cracked with emotion as they reached their seats. "Look at those boxes." She gestured toward one of the four private boxes whose red velvet swags announced that they would be occupied by the city's elite. "It's a different world."

Charlotte nodded, trying not to frown. Gwen's innocent words had resurrected a host of painful memories. This was the world Jeffrey had wanted to enter. Places like this were the reason he had taken the risks he had, and ultimately, they were the reason Charlotte was a widow. Forcing herself to smile, she murmured something innocuous, then smiled with genuine pleasure when the lights dimmed and the music began. Within seconds, the glorious strains of Beethoven's epic symphony transported Charlotte to another world, a world where memories of Jeffrey's foolishness and worries about a man called the baron did not exist.

When the music faded and the conductor announced that they would take a brief intermission, Gwen touched Charlotte's arm. "Would you mind if we walked around? I'd like to see who's here."

"Looking for a husband?" Charlotte couldn't resist teasing Gwen.

Gwen's eyes widened as if she hadn't considered that. "Maybe we should both be looking. You never can tell where you'll find the right man." When Charlotte started to frown, Gwen continued. "A husband would be nice, but what I really want is to see the other women's gowns. I doubt any of them can compare to mine." She smiled as she fingered the rich blue silk. "When Rose is old enough to remember, I want to be able to describe everything about tonight."

Joining the throng, Charlotte and Gwen descended the staircase. It was almost amusing, seeing the momentary confusion of young women wearing gowns she'd fashioned. They would look at Charlotte, perplexed, as if struggling to recognize her. It was as Mama had claimed: people rarely noticed servants, and though Charlotte was not technically a servant, she was also a woman few of Cheyenne's elite would expect to see at a social gathering. Rather than embarrass the women by speaking, Charlotte merely smiled and continued the slow progress toward the first floor. There, the doors had been propped open, the cool air of mid-October helping to dissipate the heat that had been generated by more than five hundred bodies.

"Mr. and Mrs. Carey are here," Gwen said, inclining her head toward the couple whose mansion was considered the most beautiful in the city. Gwen lowered her voice as she added, "Her gown isn't as nice as mine, and I bet she ordered it from Paris."

"You're simply prejudiced, but I'm glad you are." Charlotte squeezed her friend's arm when they reached the floor.

"Madame Charlotte."

The voice came from the left, startling Charlotte. How had she not seen him? She had known he would be here, accompanying Miriam in her emerald green gown. Though she hated to admit it, she'd been watching the crowd, looking for . . . Miriam. Of course she had been looking for Miriam, wanting to assure herself that the gown was perfectly draped. She hadn't been searching for a tall, dark-haired man who was even more distinguished in formal clothing than he was in his ordinary suits. For a second, she stood speechless, drinking in the sheer masculinity that was Barrett Landry. Then, reluctantly, her gaze shifted further to the left, where she saw Miriam deep in conversation with two gentlemen Charlotte didn't recognize.

"I hadn't realized you planned to be here too." Mr. Landry raised an eyebrow, as if asking for an explanation.

"The tickets were a gift from my friend." She turned toward Gwen, who was standing silently watching the exchange. "Gwen, let me introduce you to Mr. Landry. Mr. Landry, this is Mrs. Amos."

Turning slightly, Mr. Landry included Miriam and the other men in the conversation. "You know Miss Taggert," he said with a smile for the woman he'd escorted to the concert. Miriam nodded as she greeted Charlotte, her smile promising they'd discuss this evening the next time they were together. For the present, neither woman would admit they were anything more than modiste and customer, lest Miriam's mother disapprove.

Oblivious to the silent conversation, Mr. Landry continued. "These gentlemen are Richard Eberhardt and Warren Duncan." Though of the same height, a couple inches shorter than Mr. Landry, the two men had little else in common. Mr. Eberhardt was thin with brown hair and eyes and undistinguished features, while Mr. Duncan appeared to be at least ten years his senior, with steel gray hair. Although his eyes were an unusual shade of light blue, it was his prominent nose that caught Charlotte's attention. It might be uncharitable — after all, the man couldn't help being born with it — but the nose, combined with his intent expression, reminded Charlotte of an eagle searching for its prey.

Fortunately, that attention was not directed at her. Instead, Mr. Duncan took a step forward, stopping only inches from Gwen. "Tell me, Mrs. Amos," he said in a voice that betrayed an eastern education, "why I haven't seen you before. A beautiful woman like you would not normally escape my attention."

A becoming flush colored Gwen's cheeks. "I live a quiet life," she said. "With my new gown, I feel like Cinderella tonight."

"One of your creations, I assume." Mr. Landry pitched his voice so that Charlotte could hear it but not loud enough to disturb the conversation Gwen and Mr. Duncan were having. From the corner of her eye, she saw Miriam's lips curve in amusement. More than once, Miriam had admitted that she was surprised that the man who might become one of Wyoming's first senators was interested in women's fashion.

Charlotte nodded in response to Mr. Landry's question. "It was the least I could do after she bought the tickets." For a man with his wealth, the cost was insignificant, but Charlotte knew the gift must have substantially depleted Gwen's savings.

His eyes moved slowly from the top of Charlotte's carefully coiffed hair to the hem of her gown. When he finished his appraisal,

Mr. Landry smiled. "I was right. The orange . . ."

"Apricot," she corrected him.

"Ah yes, apricot. Whatever you call it, the color flatters you."

A rush of pleasure swept through Charlotte. She shouldn't care what this man thought. While it was true that she would undoubtedly see him around Cheyenne, especially if he entered politics, his life and hers would intersect only if Miriam continued to buy her gowns from Charlotte and if Mr. Landry accompanied her to Élan. Charlotte turned, planning to include Miriam in the discussion, but before she could speak, Mr. Eberhardt gave Miriam a dazzling smile.

"Clothes may make the man, but when a woman's as beautiful as you," he said, his voice low and intimate, "she could wear rags and still attract every man in the room. Come, my dear," he said, bending his arm so she could place her hand on it. "Let's leave these boring people to their boring conversation. I want to talk to you about the symphony."

As Miriam and Mr. Eberhardt made their way toward the door, Mr. Landry appeared unconcerned. "Are you enjoying the concert?" he asked Charlotte.

"Very much. This is my favorite Beethoven symphony. What about you?" Miriam had speculated that Barrett, as she called him, attended concerts only because it was the thing to do.

He wrinkled his nose, and once again Charlotte found herself wondering how he'd broken it. That wasn't a question one could ask a mere acquaintance, and so she would probably never know the answer.

"I hesitate to admit it, but I prefer lighter music," he said with a self-deprecating laugh.

"Such as?"

"Stephen Foster," Mr. Landry whispered, his fingers cupped around his mouth, as though he were confiding a dark secret.

Pressing her hand to her chest and widening her eyes in feigned horror, Charlotte tried not to laugh. "I probably shouldn't admit this, but I used to like 'Old Folks at Home.' The problem was, my dog hated it. Every time I started to sing 'Way down upon the Swanee River,' he'd howl."

Though Charlotte had expected Mr. Landry to chuckle, his expression was quizzical. "You have a dog?"

"Not anymore. I gave him to my sister." Though she still missed Puddles and his antics, she knew that had been the right decision. "He was more her dog than mine. Besides, I couldn't picture him being cooped up in a city house."

"I know what you mean. My family always had dogs, but there was plenty of room for them to run." Mr. Landry brushed a speck of dust from his shoulder before he said, "Tell me about your sister. Is she older?"

Charlotte heard Gwen laughing. Whatever she and Mr. Duncan were discussing, it appeared that Gwen was enjoying their conversation. Charlotte, however, had ceased to enjoy her conversation with Mr. Landry. Though she hadn't intended it, they had ventured into personal subjects. Still, what he had asked wasn't anything more than she had told Gwen. Taking a deep breath, she said, "Both my sisters are younger. Abigail — she's the one with the dog — married a soldier. They're in Washington Territory now. Elizabeth is the youngest. She's finishing her medical studies in New York." Before Mr. Landry could ask questions she wasn't prepared to answer, Charlotte posed one of her own. "What about you? Do you have sisters?"

He shook his head. "No sisters. I'm the youngest of three boys. Camden and Harrison run our parents' mercantile back home in Pennsylvania."

"And yet you became a cattle rancher."

Once again, his smile was self-deprecating. "My brothers claim that I'm the renegade. The truth is, I wanted to see if the stories I'd heard about the Wild West were true."

"Are they?"

As a couple anxious to reach the door jostled him, Mr. Landry shrugged. "Hard to say. I haven't seen any shoot-outs, and I've never experienced a stagecoach robbery."

Charlotte felt the blood drain from her face as his last two words registered. He was only making conversation, she told herself. There was no special reason why he'd mentioned stagecoach robberies. He had no way of knowing that the very thought made her shudder because it resurrected memories best left buried.

Swallowing deeply in an attempt to dislodge the lump that settled in her throat, Charlotte feigned nonchalance. "If you were hoping that I could give you a firsthand account, I'm afraid I'll have to disappoint you. I confess that I've had no experience with either of those supposedly quintessential Western events. My life is very quiet." Except for the worry that the man known as the baron might find her and David. She wouldn't tell Mr. Landry that. Not even

Gwen knew of Charlotte's fears. She managed a smile as she said, "Some might find my life boring, but it suits me. You didn't say, though. Are you disappointed that the West isn't as wild as you thought?"

"Hardly, but then I'd never describe my life as quiet or boring. If you've ever seen a herd stampede, you'd agree that raising cattle is anything but quiet, and rustlers keep life from being boring." His eyes darkened until they resembled Gwen's gown, a clear indication that he cared deeply. "As much as we try to stop it, rustling is still big business in Wyoming. It's bad enough when they steal mavericks, but when they take full-grown steers and alter the brands, well . . . it sets my blood to boil."

Charlotte knew she would be angry if someone had stolen bolts of fabric from the store. How much worse must it be when a living thing was taken? As Mr. Landry's lips tightened, Charlotte knew she needed to do something to take his mind off the rustling. "You mentioned mavericks. What are they?"

"Motherless calves." To Charlotte's relief, he seemed to relax as he explained, "During the spring roundup, we separate the cows by their brand. The calves haven't been weaned, so they stay close to their mamas. That's how we know whose cattle they are. Some of the youngsters aren't attached to a cow, most times because their mothers died. Those are the mavericks."

"So, who do they belong to?"

A smile lit his face. "All of us. They're sold, and the money goes to the stock growers' association."

Charlotte's smile mirrored his. "I probably shouldn't laugh, but I still find the term 'stock grower' unusual. I keep imagining something planted in the ground."

He shrugged. "I prefer stock grower to cattle baron. That sounds so pretentious." And Mr. Landry did not appear to be a pretentious man.

He pulled his watch from his pocket. "We should probably return to our seats, but before we go, I hope you'll satisfy my curiosity. You know why I came to Cheyenne, but I'd like to know what brought you to Wyoming."

"My husband." Though few of the guests had started to move toward the staircase, from the corner of her eye Charlotte saw Miriam approaching with Mr. Eberhardt. Relief flowed through her at the realization that she would not have to say anything more and she wouldn't have to lie.

"Is it time already?" Mr. Duncan frowned as he asked the question. When Mr. Landry nodded, the older man murmured something that made Gwen flush. Charlotte's friend was not given to blushes, but this was at least twice in less than fifteen minutes that her cheeks had been pink.

"May I escort you and Mrs. Amos to your seats?" Mr. Duncan's words were polite. His suggestion was chivalrous. There was no cause for alarm, and yet Charlotte felt ill at ease.

"Thank you, but your friends are waiting for you." She gestured toward the trio to her left. Miriam had returned and had placed her hand on Mr. Landry's arm, while Mr. Eberhardt stood only a few inches away, his expression as solemn as if he were attending a funeral. Charlotte gave them all a smile as she linked her arm with Gwen's. "Good evening, Miss Taggert, gentlemen." No matter how pleasant it had been talking to Barrett Landry, Charlotte's place was in the back row with Gwen.

"Oh, Charlotte, I never thought it would be so wonderful," Gwen said as they ascended the stairway. Mr. Landry and his party had remained on the ground floor, chatting with Miriam's parents while other theatergoers began to crowd the staircase, their exuberant conversation almost drowning out Gwen's words.

"Truly, I feel like Cinderella. I've met my Prince Charming."

Though Charlotte raised an eyebrow, she tried to keep her voice even, not wanting to spoil Gwen's evening. "Mr. Duncan?"

"Yes. And please don't tell me he's too old for me. You know I'm over thirty."

Warren Duncan's age was not what concerned Charlotte. "I wasn't going to say anything about his age. I just wondered what you knew about him."

Gwen's face was suffused with a fatuous smile. "Other than that he's the most wonderful man I've ever met? Did you know that he's an attorney? He's one of Mr. Landry's advisers. Can you imagine, Charlotte? He's an important man about town, and yet he noticed me — me, Gwen Amos. It's like a fairy tale come true."

Charlotte tried not to sigh. Gwen's enthusiasm reminded her of when she first met Jeffrey. The young soldier had literally swept her off her feet, and she'd been convinced that it was a case of love at first sight. Only later had Charlotte realized that infatuation and love were two very different things.

"All I can say, Cinderella, is that I hope our coach doesn't turn into a pumpkin. I wouldn't want us to have to walk home in these gowns."

They'd reached their seats, and as Gwen settled into hers, she sighed with pleasure. "Oh, Charlotte, I'm so glad we came."

"So am I. The music is glorious." But when the orchestra resumed its playing, Charlotte found that she could not concentrate on the symphony. Instead, as she closed her eyes, pictures of Barrett Landry flashed before her.

4

"I'm disappointed in you, Barrett." Richard's normally placid brown eyes flashed with anger. For a second, Barrett considered ignoring his friend's comment, but he knew Richard too well. The man would not leave the morning room, where they were currently enjoying a late evening repast, complete with some of Mrs. Melnor's berry pie, until he was satisfied.

"What did I do wrong now?" Barrett helped himself to a second piece of pie. "I attended the symphony, although you know I enjoy that about as much as being thrown from a horse. Before and after the performance, I spent at least an hour talking to every potential constituent you sent my way. I —"

Richard's hand made a slicing motion. "You were stupid, and you don't even know how stupid you were."

"I'm sure you intend to rectify that lapse."

Barrett infused his words with sarcasm, hoping to deflect Richard's annoyance.

It didn't work. His newly appointed business manager frowned. "You ignored Miriam during intermission. Instead of devoting yourself to the finest woman in Cheyenne, possibly in the entire territory, you wasted time talking to a seamstress. Honestly, Barrett, I don't know what you were thinking, if you were even thinking."

Barrett decided not to respond while Richard reached for his cup and took a long swallow of coffee. The man was on a tear, and the easiest way to end it was to let it run its course.

"I'll admit the seamstress is pretty enough, if you like dark hair and eyes," Richard conceded as he forked a piece of pie, "but no one can compare to Miriam. She's a golden goddess, and yet you didn't seem to know she was there."

"That's not true. She was my companion for the evening. I escorted her to and from the opera house. I never left her side. As I recall, it was you who took her away. What was I supposed to do? Drag her from you? I don't think that would have accomplished anything other than make us all look foolish."

Richard didn't bother to swallow his pie

before he retorted. "I only took her away because you were gawking at the seamstress."

"Her name is Madame Charlotte, and I wasn't gawking."

Throwing up his hands in exasperation, Richard glared at Barrett. "See what I mean? You're defending the woman who sews your future wife's clothing rather than caring about Miriam, the woman who's going to share your life and help you get elected. You don't deserve her. A woman like Miriam should be cherished, not ignored for a mere seamstress."

That made four times Richard had called Charlotte a seamstress. It wasn't a matter of class. Barrett knew that. Unlike Miriam's parents with their rigid ideas of social standing, Richard had never before denigrated a person simply because of the work he did. There had to be something else bothering his friend. Barrett took another bite of pie, chewing carefully as he thought about what Richard had said.

"It sounds to me as if you fancy Miriam yourself."

There was a second of silence before Richard said, "It's you and your career I'm worried about. That's all."

The words rang false.

If Warren had been thirty years younger, he might have jumped with joy, but legs that were more than half a century old did not take kindly to such exuberance. Instead, he poured himself a glass of whiskey and toasted his good fortune.

She was perfect. Not beautiful, but not ugly, either. Not so young that people would gossip, but young enough that she could give him a child of his own. Best of all, she was respectable. Highly respectable, unlike the women who saw to his other needs. No one would look askance if Warren married a hardworking widow with a small child. They'd applaud him for his kindness. They'd see that he was indeed an upright citizen, a man worthy of membership in the Cheyenne Club.

Gwen Amos was perfect.

"You shouldn't have disappeared with him."

Miriam took a deep breath, exhaling slowly. "I didn't disappear. Richard and I remained on the sidewalk in full view of anyone who came outside. And, Mama, I might add that there were many who did."

Her mother picked up the silver-backed

mirror from Miriam's dressing table and scrutinized her reflection. Apparently pleased that she had not discovered any new wrinkles, she nodded briskly. "What exactly did you talk about?"

"Music. Richard told me that although he enjoyed the Ninth, his favorite piece by Beethoven is the allegretto from the Seventh Symphony." As Miriam had expected, her mother rolled her eyes. She might as well be speaking Greek for all Mama understood. Perhaps that was why the memory of her conversation with Richard lingered in Miriam's mind. It was the first time she'd found someone who shared her love of music enough to spend a quarter of an hour discussing the finer points of two melodies.

Barrett would have listened politely if she had told him that the tempo was slightly too slow during the first movement of tonight's performance, but he wouldn't have understood. Richard did. Barrett would have agreed if she'd announced that the "Ode to Joy" was a magnificent piece of music, and then he would have changed the subject. Richard was different. He'd asked her why she cared for the Ode, what specific aspect of the music touched her heart.

Richard might not be as handsome as Barrett. He might not be quite as wealthy.

He might not be a man her parents would consider a suitable son-in-law because he had no aspirations outside of Wyoming, but he challenged her in ways no other man had. That was the reason — the only reason — she couldn't stop thinking of him.

"Music!" Mama sniffed. "I suppose that's perfectly respectable, but make sure it doesn't happen again. Even though the man is almost old enough to be your father and no one would think you were interested in him, you wouldn't want people to have the wrong impression, would you?"

"No, Mama."

Two days later, Charlotte pinned on a hat and slid her hands into gloves. Though she was only going next door and could forgo a cloak, no well-dressed lady would consider leaving her home without a hat and gloves.

"I should be gone only a few minutes," she told Molly, who was watching Élan in her absence. It was a quiet time in the shop, and Charlotte needed a few items for David. Gwen had chuckled over the fact that Charlotte, whose creations dressed many of Cheyenne's wealthiest women, bought clothing for her son. A proverbial shoemaker's child, she had declared. Be that as it may, David had worn holes in his socks, and while Charlotte might be an expert seamstress, darning was not one of her accomplishments. Fortunately for her, Yates's Dry Goods occupied the northern half of the building that housed Élan. With the James Sisters Millinery just down the block, Charlotte and Mr. Yates had chuckled over the fact that the city's women could clothe themselves from head to foot, all without crossing a street. Men who wanted custom-tailored suits had a slightly more difficult shopping experience, for the best tailors were more than a block away, but for those less particular customers, Mr. Yates offered ready-made trousers, shirts, and coats.

Charlotte was reaching for the doorknob, preparing to enter Mr. Yates's establishment, when the door swung open.

"Mr. Landry." Though it was foolish in the extreme, Charlotte's heart began to race. The man looked even more handsome dressed in his ordinary clothes than he had at the opera house. She had thought nothing could compare to the sartorial elegance of his evening coat, but the tweed sack coat he wore this morning was at least as attractive. Or perhaps it had nothing to do with the clothing and everything to do with the man inside.

"Madame Charlotte." He doffed his hat

in greeting, then wrinkled his nose as he closed the door behind him and moved to her side, positioning himself so that the slight breeze would not chill her. "I suspect it's very forward of me, but would you object if we dispensed with formality? My friends call me Barrett, and I'd like to count you among them."

It was a simple request, yet it warmed Charlotte's heart more than the October sun. "I'd be honored if you called me Charlotte." She paused before pronouncing the name that then lingered on her tongue. "Barrett." She had called him that in her mind, but this was the first time she had spoken the word. It felt good and at the same time oddly unsettling to be so familiar with him. Taking a deep breath to calm her nerves, Charlotte gestured toward the package Barrett held in his left hand. "I see your shopping excursion was successful."

One of the crooked smiles that she found so endearing lit his face. "Promise you won't tell Mr. Bradley I was here."

"That's an easy promise to make, since I have no idea who Mr. Bradley is."

"He's my butler. Richard and Warren convinced me that I needed one if I was going to live on Ferguson Street."

Charlotte raised an eyebrow. "I live on

Ferguson Street," she pointed out, "and I don't have a butler."

"Touché. I should have said that they convinced me that if I was going to live in an excessively ornate house with enough rooms for a family of ten, I needed a butler. Now I find myself in a predicament, because that very same butler believes that he should be responsible for all of what he calls procurement." Barrett gave the brown-paper-wrapped package a rueful look.

Charlotte couldn't help it. She chuckled as she stared at the man who stood so close that she could smell the bay rum on his cheeks. Listening to Miriam's description of him, Charlotte had believed Barrett to be like Jeffrey. He wasn't. Jeffrey would never have mocked his station in life, especially if it was such an exalted one. Jeffrey would have found a way to ensure that everyone knew that he lived in a mansion, and Charlotte doubted that he would have done his own procurement, as Barrett called it.

"I have to disagree with you. Your house is not excessively ornate," she said firmly. "I find it tasteful and remarkably restrained." Though the three-story brick building boasted four chimneys and an equal number of bay windows, not to mention a turret, nothing about it seemed ostentatious. Compared to some of the other cattle barons' houses, it could almost be described as modest. "I can't disagree with one part of your description, though. Your home is large, especially compared to my lodging." She accompanied the last sentence with a gesture toward the second floor of the building.

"That's right. I heard you lived above your shop."

"With Mrs. Amos and her daughter." Charlotte couldn't help smiling at the irony. "Four of us live in a fraction of the space you own."

The instant the words were out of her mouth, Charlotte winced. Perhaps she would be fortunate and Barrett wouldn't notice that she'd said "four."

"Four people?" It was not her lucky day. "Who's there besides you, Mrs. Amos, and her daughter?"

There was no way out of the predicament save the truth. "My son," she said. Oddly, she felt a sense of relief once she'd made the admission. Barrett Landry was not the baron. She had no reason to fear him.

Barrett frowned, but Charlotte couldn't tell whether it was because of her words or the cloud that chilled the air and made her shiver. "You're fortunate to have Mrs. Amos and the children. My house can be lonely, but I doubt you have that problem."

"Indeed, I don't. David sees to that."

"David's your son?"

"Yes. He's a very special boy."

Barrett appeared intrigued, and for a second Charlotte expected him to ask her why her son was special. Instead, he said only, "Perhaps I can meet him someday."

"Perhaps." It was the polite response, even if it would never happen. Though she had made a major step forward by admitting David's existence to this man, she was not ready to expose her son to potential scorn. Barrett appeared to be kind, but there was no way of knowing how he would react if he learned that David was blind. As a cool breeze swept down the street, Charlotte shivered again. "If you'll excuse me, I need to buy a few items before I turn into an icicle." *And I want to end this discussion of my son.*

Seconds later, she was inside the store. A quick glance told her there were no other customers, and so she walked briskly toward the back counter, where the proprietor greeted her with a broad smile.

"I saw you talking to Mr. Landry." No more than medium height, Mr. Yates looked smaller than that because of his thin frame and stooped shoulders. *Weary* was the adjective Charlotte normally applied to him, and yet this afternoon his gray eyes sparkled with what appeared to be amusement. "Landry's a good man. He bought shirts from me when he first came to Wyoming, and he still comes here, even though he could shop anywhere. A good man," Mr. Yates repeated, almost as if he realized that Charlotte needed the assurance. "Now, what can I get for you?"

"David needs new socks. I'm afraid I haven't had time to knit."

Shaking his head, the man who seemed older than the sixty-five years he acknowledged reached for a box of children's socks. "Prudence used to say that knitting relaxed her, but I don't imagine you have time to relax."

"Unfortunately, you're right." She'd been busy before, but now that she was remaking Miriam's old gowns for Mrs. Kendall's boarders, Charlotte had even less time. Perhaps it was foolish, not telling Gwen what she was doing, but Charlotte knew that Élan's cachet would be compromised if anyone learned she was providing gowns to the city's less fortunate. While Gwen would never intentionally tell anyone, she might let something slip. And so Charlotte sewed in her room late at night, knowing that the light would not disturb David.

"I'm not complaining," she told Mr. Yates. "Business is good, and needing socks gives me an excuse to visit you." Charlotte took her time, choosing two pair each of brown and black stockings, darting occasional glances at the proprietor. It was as she had feared. Though Mr. Yates had appeared chipper when she'd entered the store, his demeanor changed when he didn't realize she was watching him. "Is something wrong?" she asked. "You look a bit glum."

His eyes clouded as he nodded slowly. "Nothing's the same without Prudence." His wife of more than forty years had died six months before Charlotte arrived in Cheyenne, and Gwen, who had known the elderly man for the half dozen years she had been in Wyoming, claimed that the difference in the man's attitude had been dramatic. "It's like he lost his zest for living," Gwen had said. "Poor man." That was one of the reasons the two women insisted that Mr. Yates join them for Sunday dinner a couple times each month. Even though David's and Rose's antics tired him, Charlotte knew he enjoyed both Gwen's cooking and their company.

"Some days I don't even want to get out

of bed," Mr. Yates admitted. "My sister down in Arizona keeps telling me I should move there. She says the weather would be kinder to these old bones." He frowned as he calculated the cost of Charlotte's purchase. When she'd handed him the few coins, he said, "The trouble is the store. I don't want to sell it to just anyone, not when Prudence and I worked so hard to turn it into a success. I want someone who'll do right by the customers." Mr. Yates paused for a moment, his expression lightening. "I don't suppose you'd be interested in taking over, would you?"

"I wish I could." Charlotte's heart went out to Mr. Yates and his dilemma. He had once told her and Gwen that since he and Prudence had had no children, the store was their only legacy, and they had hoped it would continue, even when they were both gone. "I don't know anything about running a store like this," she said, wishing she had another answer for her neighbor. "It's much different from Élan." And then there was the money. She had none to spare.

The gleam in the shopkeeper's eyes faded. "I figured you'd say that." As his lips tightened, he nodded slowly. "It'll be all right. I'll figure something out."

Charlotte wished she were as confident.

5

Charlotte retrieved a hat pin. Though the plain black bonnet with the heavy veil that would hide her face fit well, she would take no chance of the wind dislodging it. Once her arms were filled with packages, she would be unable to clasp the hat if it started to shift. Fortunately, this early in the morning, the wind had diminished. Even more importantly, David and Gwen were still asleep, and there would be few people on the streets. Few if any would see her, and anyone who did would not realize that it was Madame Charlotte who was approaching the boardinghouse. That was why she had chosen 5:30 as the time to make her delivery. Gwen had mentioned that Mrs. Kendall started breakfast preparations at that time but that none of her boarders entered the kitchen until close to an hour later. If Charlotte hurried, she'd be gone less than half an hour, and neither David nor Gwen would know that she'd left. But, just in case David wakened, Charlotte had left a note in her room, telling Gwen she'd be back soon.

Tiptoeing, she made her way to the door, closing it as quietly as she could. Moments later, she'd descended the stairs and was headed south on Ferguson. Mrs. Kendall's boardinghouse was less than three blocks away, and yet as Charlotte turned onto 15th Street, she felt as if she'd entered a different city. There were no fancy houses or shops like Élan here. Instead, the ramshackle buildings were testaments to despair and deprivation. It was no wonder Gwen had been anxious to escape.

Charlotte scanned the street, looking for the drunkards Gwen had claimed were all too often present. The Lord must have been watching over her, for Charlotte saw no one. She increased her pace, walking as quickly as she could without breaking into a run. While the widow's weeds that she'd chosen as her disguise had a fuller skirt than was currently fashionable, they would not accommodate running.

There were no streetlamps here, perhaps because the city fathers had no desire to encourage the establishments that lined this block, but Charlotte saw the light of a kerosene lantern in the back room of the second house. It was just as Gwen had described it.

Though she shivered from a combination of cold and apprehension, Charlotte knocked firmly on the kitchen door. Seconds later, an almost skeletally thin woman opened the door a crack.

"Who are you? What do you want?" Even in this part of town, it was unusual for a woman to be out so early.

Mrs. Kendall looked to be a year or two shy of forty, an inch or two shorter than Charlotte's five and a half feet, her hair a shade or two lighter brown than Gwen's. Though the voluminous apron covered most of her dress, Charlotte's trained eye recognized the style as one that had been popular almost a decade ago, and the faded line along the hem left no doubt that it had been turned more than once. It wasn't only the boarders who needed clothing. None of the frocks she had brought with her would fit Mrs. Kendall, but Charlotte resolved that when she returned, she would have a new dress for the woman who had been so kind to Gwen.

As Mrs. Kendall's eyes narrowed, Charlotte held out the packages. "I brought some clothes for your boarders."

The woman blinked in surprise. "I wasn't expecting nobody and no clothes." She gave Charlotte an appraising glance before nodding. "You might as well come on in."

Charlotte found herself in a kitchen so cramped that she wondered how Mrs. Kendall managed to cook for more than a dozen women. The stove was smaller than average, with only three burners. No wonder she wakened early. Even a juggler would have trouble preparing eggs, sausage, potatoes, and coffee here.

Mindful of the ticking clock and the need to return before David stirred, Charlotte unwrapped the dresses, spreading them on the large table that occupied most of the room. "I didn't know what sizes you might need, but I hope these will fit some of your boarders." When she'd altered Miriam's gowns, Charlotte had shortened one and let out the seams in another, guessing that the boarders were not all as thin as Miriam.

Mrs. Kendall stared at the four frocks that covered her table. Gingerly, she fingered the fabric, her eyes brightening when she touched the smooth poplin.

"They're beautiful, ma'am, but I can't pay what they're worth. I ain't got much money, and neither do my gals."

Charlotte shook her head. "I don't want

any money. They're a gift."

Mrs. Kendall stroked the poplin almost reverently. "A gift? For us?"

Charlotte nodded.

Still dubious, Mrs. Kendall lifted her eyebrows. "No strings attached?"

"None. And if you tell me what other sizes you could use, I'll bring more."

The older woman swallowed deeply, as if she were trying to control her emotions. "I'm much obliged, ma'am. Some of my gals ain't got decent clothes. They'll be mighty pleased to get these." She looked at Charlotte, her curiosity apparent. "Who are you?"

"Just a widow who wants to help."

Barrett strode back and forth in front of the depot, listening for the humming of the rails that would announce the incoming train. When he'd lived in Pennsylvania, black smoke had been the first sign, but Wyoming's prevailing westerly winds meant that trains from the East had no visual harbingers. He pulled out his watch, checking it for what seemed like the hundredth time. As he did, Barrett let out a short laugh. If his watch was correct, the train wasn't due for another ten minutes. It was only his own eagerness to see Harrison that had brought him here so early. Harrison would laugh at the notion that his youngest brother, the same one who'd once described him as the scourge of the earth, all because he'd refused to share his slingshot, was excited about his visit.

Striding past the existing depot, Barrett inspected the one that was taking shape. Workers scurried around the site of the new train station, but progress seemed slow compared to the speed with which his house had been built. Still, when the new depot was complete, it would be a much-needed improvement over the simple frame structure that served the city now. Barrett had seen the design, and he liked it. No doubt about it, the large red sandstone edifice with the arched windows and the tall clock tower would be impressive.

Warren had speculated that one reason the legislature was in such a hurry to construct a capitol building was that they didn't want to be outdone by the Union Pacific. Whatever the motive, ground had been broken on the territory's new capitol only last month.

The two buildings that were being constructed at the opposite ends of Hill Street had few things in common. The capitol was square and symmetrical and would boast a gilded dome, whereas the depot was Romanesque in design. And though both were being built of sandstone, the capitol's was gray, not red. Different styles, different purposes, and yet both would enhance Cheyenne's position as an important stop on the Union Pacific Railroad and the capital of Wyoming Territory.

The city's future was bright, and if Richard and Warren were correct, so was his own. What concerned Barrett today was his immediate future. His oldest brother, the one whose shoes Barrett had been told he would never be able to fill, was about to arrive. He pulled out his watch again and grinned. One minute left. If the UP's reputation for punctuality held, his brother would be here within sixty seconds.

Precisely on schedule, the train pulled into the station, and passengers began to disembark. Three women, their shoulders slumped with fatigue, were the first to step onto the platform. Then came a burly man whom Barrett would have recognized anywhere. He was heavier than the last time Barrett had seen him, his jowls more prominent, and yet the face still bore a distinct resemblance to the one Barrett saw in the mirror each morning. Folks had always said you could recognize a Landry at fifty paces. He wondered if that was true of Charlotte's family. Surely her sisters could not be as lovely as she.

Barrett shook himself mentally. This was not the time to be thinking about Charlotte, no matter how beautiful she was, no matter how often he replayed their conversations. His brother was descending the iron steps.

"I never thought I'd see this," Barrett said as he clapped Harrison's shoulder, "but it's true. You're here. You've come all the way to the wild Wyoming Territory."

Only an inch shorter than Barrett, Harrison had the same dark brown hair and deep blue eyes. Right now those eyes were sparkling, and his lips twisted in a wry smile. "You didn't leave me much choice, little brother. Camden and I figured you'd be back within a year, once you realized you weren't cut out for this life. Looks like we were wrong. It's been five years, and you haven't shown any signs of coming to your senses. I reckoned that if I wanted to see you, I'd have to come here. So, here I am." This was vintage Harrison. Whereas other men spoke in terse sentences, Harrison rambled on for paragraphs.

Harrison looked around, his expression giving no clue to his reaction to Barrett's new hometown. If he judged Cheyenne by

104

the seedy hotels and saloons west of the depot on 15th, he would be making a mistake. Every city had its less than desirable section, and this was Cheyenne's. Rather than say anything, Barrett decided to let Harrison form his opinions once he'd seen the whole town. Instead, he addressed his brother's last comment.

"I meant to go back. For a visit," Barrett clarified. "The time never seemed right." It was an excuse. He could have found time for a trip to Northwick, if he'd wanted to. The truth was, he hadn't wanted to return until he had everything: wealth, a wife, a glittering future. He doubted his brothers would understand. They'd seemed puzzled when he'd tried to explain his need to leave home, and though their letters had said little, he had sensed their bewilderment over his decision to raise cattle and remain in the West. Barrett had wanted everything to be settled before he faced Harrison and Camden again. Especially Harrison. The man had always been outspoken, believing that, as the oldest son, he knew what was best for everyone. Barrett doubted that had changed in the past five years. Fortunately, his plans were in place, even if he hadn't executed them all. No matter what Harrison said, Barrett would not change his mind.

"Speaking of the right time," Barrett said as the porter wheeled Harrison's trunk toward the wagon, "it's good that you arrived today. The old-timers are claiming we're in for some snow tomorrow." If it did snow, Harrison would have a surprise. He'd soon learn that winters in Wyoming were unlike those back East.

When the trunk was loaded into the back of the wagon, Barrett headed west one block to Ferguson. Though his brother spoke of inconsequential things, by the time they'd reached 19th Street, his tone had changed.

"Cheyenne's not what I expected," Harrison said as they passed the ornate home that many called Castle Dare. With its towers and crenellated roof, it was reported to be a replica of a European castle.

Barrett tried not to smile. "Were you envisioning tumbledown wooden shanties?"

"Maybe." A shrug accompanied Harrison's response. "I know you told us it was a wealthy city, but I thought you were exaggerating. These are mansions." He gestured toward the houses on both sides of the street. "Who lives here?"

Keeping his expression impassive, Barrett slowed the wagon. "Merchants, newspaper owners, bankers, your brother." He stopped in front of his home and nodded at it.

"This is yours?" Astonishment colored Harrison's voice, and for the first time Barrett could recall, he seemed at a loss for words.

Barrett climbed out of the wagon. Mr. Bradley would have seen him arrive and would send one of the boys to put the horse and wagon in the stable and bring Harrison's trunk inside. "I told you I built a house."

"You said a house, not a mansion." Harrison stared at the red brick building. Though less elaborate than some of its neighbors, the three-story house was far larger and more elaborate than any in Northwick. Harrison shook his head as if trying to clear his brain, then shrugged. "All I can say, little brother, is that you've done well for yourself." There was both approval and amazement in Harrison's voice, and it filled an empty space inside Barrett. This was what he'd wanted, his brother's approval, and at last he had it.

When they entered the front door and Mr. Bradley appeared to take their coats, Harrison pursed his lips. It was only when they were alone again, inside Barrett's office, that he spoke. "Camden won't believe this. When you said you owned cattle and were building a house, we figured it would be a farmhouse. Instead, you've got a mansion with a butler and who knows how many other servants."

"Six."

Harrison's eyes widened. "You have six servants?"

"Seven, counting Mr. Bradley."

Harrison shook his head. "I still can't believe it. And that's another thing. Why do you call him Mr. Bradley? I thought servants were addressed by only one name."

"That's what he told me, but I thought it made me seem too highfalutin, so I made it what my attorney calls a condition of employment. If the staff insist on calling me Mr. Landry — and they do — I'll address them similarly."

Harrison shook his head again. "My brother, the cattle baron. I still can't believe it."

"There are times when I can't either." It had taken a lot of work, a lot of hard work, but the profits from his first year of raising cattle had exceeded his dreams. Barrett had had more money than he'd imagined possible, and — even better — he'd gained respect. No longer the runt of the litter, he'd been invited to join the Cheyenne Club. Soon after, he'd started building this house.

"This sure isn't a farmhouse." Harrison

gestured toward the velvet draperies, the flocked wallpaper, and the Persian carpet. "Even the mayor of Northwick doesn't have anything like this."

Harrison would probably feel more comfortable when he saw the ranch house where Barrett stayed while checking on the cattle. It had begun as a dugout and had few amenities other than the one window in the room Barrett had grafted onto the front when he'd realized he could not live without sunshine.

"I have a ranch house," he admitted, "but I don't spend much time there."

Harrison crossed his legs and leaned back in the chair. "I don't suppose I would, either, if I had a house like this. The truth is, from the beginning, I couldn't picture you being happy raising cows. I thought you liked people too much." He slid his hands over the leather chair arms. "Of the three of us, you were the best with the customers. You could sell them anything."

"If they'd listen to me." That had been part of the problem. If Harrison or Camden was in the store, customers would ignore Barrett.

"Why do you think I left you alone so often?" The skin crinkled around Harrison's eyes as he grinned. "I'm not as dumb as you think. I may not have realized it while we were growing up, but once we all started working in the store, I saw what was going on. I also saw that customers bought more from you than they ever did from Camden or me."

Barrett stared at his brother. "Why didn't you tell me?"

"And let you get a swelled head? Besides, you needed to figure out what you wanted to do."

He had. "I knew there was no future for me in Northwick. Even if I enjoyed working in the store — and I'm not sure I did, the mercantile didn't need three people.'

Furrows reappeared between Harrison's brows, and he stared at the floor as if fascinated by the carpet pattern. "Right now it doesn't need two. Business hasn't been good recently." The furrows deepened. "Camden claims it's because I won't try new ideas. He calls me hidebound. Don't laugh, Barrett. You've probably said the same thing yourself."

"I prefer stick-in-the-mud."

As his lips twisted in a smile, Harrison nodded. "Sounds like you. But back to Camden. I got tired of arguing with him, so I decided I'd give him some time to run things the way he wants. Besides, with him being newly wed, I figured he and Susan deserved some time without an interfering older brother around."

"Mighty considerate of you. I probably shouldn't say this, lest you get a swelled head." Barrett tossed Harrison's words back at him. "But I'll take my chances and admit that I'm glad you're here, even though I imagine it's my life you're going to try to interfere in now. It's clear you disapprove of it."

"Aw, Barrett, you always were too sensitive. I don't disapprove. I'm just surprised." Harrison leaned forward, his expression earnest. "Tell me about those cows."

"Cattle," Barrett corrected, although he suspected his brother knew the correct term and was calling the animals cows simply to annoy him. "I'd rather tell you about something else." He might as well get everything out in the open right away. Besides, Harrison might have some good advice. "I have to warn you, though, old stick-in-the-mud, that it's a new idea."

"Not you too."

"Afraid so. It must be contagious." He took a deep breath, wondering how Harrison would react. "I'm considering marriage."

"It's about time." A grin split Harrison's

face, setting his jowls to quivering. "You're not getting any younger, you know." As Barrett opened his mouth to retort, Harrison's grin widened. "No need to point out that I'm even older and still haven't married. Some men are meant to be bachelors, but you're not one of them."

"So, you approve?" Harrison's letters hadn't sounded as if he was happy about Camden's marriage.

"Sure do. I hope you're planning to introduce me to your bride-to-be." Harrison's smile faded. "Or is this just theoretical?"

"Nope." Barrett shook his head. "I have a lady in mind, and if you promise to be on your best behavior, I just might let you meet her."

"Afraid I might steal her away?"

"Hardly." Harrison was too honorable to court Miriam when he knew that Barrett was considering marrying her. "There's more, though."

"Another new idea?" Harrison feigned shock. "I'm not sure I can handle two in one day."

"Brace yourself." As his brother gripped the chair arms, Barrett chuckled. This was the Harrison he remembered, always ready to play. "I may run for political office."

There was a second of silence as Harrison

digested the words, then he leaned forward and pounded his fists on Barrett's desk. "That's the best idea I've heard in months. You'll charm the voters the way you did customers." He rose and clapped Barrett on the shoulder. "Good move, little brother. Good move."

"The snow is getting heavier," Gwen said as she shook her cloak and hung it on one of the pegs near the door. "You might want to skip services today." She knelt on the floor and held out her arms, grinning when Rose raced into them. "Did you miss your mama?"

Rose nodded. "I play with David, but he cry."

Gwen looked up in alarm. "Did Rose hurt him?"

"It was a game." Gwen's daughter had been trying to teach David to stand, and when she'd let go of his hands, the inevitable had occurred: David had fallen and hit his head. A few minutes later, his tears gone, he'd attempted to rise without assistance and had fallen again, but this time Charlotte had seen a new determination on her son's face. Though he'd resisted her efforts to help him stand, somehow, Rose's encouragement had given him the impetus he

113

needed to try. "Don't be surprised if he falls again," she told Gwen. "You know it's part of the process. I moved everything I could out of the way."

She reached for her cape. Cut with what the fashion books called dolman sleeves, it was far more practical for Cheyenne's wind than an ordinary cape, because she could draw it close to her body.

"It wouldn't hurt you to miss church today," Gwen repeated. "Look at the snow."

Charlotte shook her head. "It's less than a block away." That was an advantage of living where she did, close to what residents called Church Corner. Charlotte's church was located on one corner, Gwen's on another, a third across the street. It was a short walk, and, fortunately for the two women, each church's services were held at different times, allowing them both to worship without worrying about their children.

"I want to go," Charlotte said as she picked up the Bible that had been one of her first purchases when she'd reached Cheyenne. "I need to go." Until she had married and moved to Fort Laramie, the only times she had missed Sunday worship were when she had been ill. Services at the fort had been irregular, and as often as not, Charlotte had worshiped at home, but since she had become part of a community with established churches, she hadn't missed a Sunday. A snowfall, even if it was unusually heavy for October, was no reason to break her pattern.

"You're stubborn." Gwen's smile took the sting from her accusation.

"Guilty as charged." Charlotte gave David one last hug, then slid the Bible into the pocket she had sewn into the cape. The leather binding was still stiff, and the book did not fit into her hand as comfortably as the Bible she had had since childhood, but Charlotte could not risk using that one in public. With its record of not only her birth but also her marriage to Jeffrey, it contained too much information that she was trying to keep secret, and so she hid it beneath a spare petticoat in one of her bureau drawers.

Charlotte bent her head as she crossed the street, trying to keep the snow from pelting her face. Unlike the snow of her childhood, where fat, lazy flakes drifted to the ground, snow rarely fell in Cheyenne. Instead, the wind blew it with such force that it seemed as if shards of glass were being catapulted through the sky. The tiny flakes that were more like pellets could hurt delicate skin, especially when they were driven sideways by a fierce wind.

As she entered the church and brushed away the snow that had coated her eyelashes, Charlotte heard a familiar voice. She looked up. It hadn't been her imagination. Though she had never before seen him in the church, Barrett Landry was indeed here. Even more surprisingly, he was accompanied by a man whose resemblance said he was a relative.

"Good morning, Charlotte." Barrett smiled as he covered the distance between them in two long steps. "I'd like to introduce you to my brother Harrison. He came to Wyoming to see how cow farmers live." The mischievous tone to his voice told Charlotte that Harrison must have referred to cattle ranchers as cow farmers, a term no one in the territory would use.

"It's nice to meet you, Mr. Landry." Though normally the narthex was crowded, it appeared that the snow had discouraged many parishioners, for today there was no one other than Charlotte and the Landry brothers.

"Harrison, please." The man was an older, less refined version of Barrett. Though his suit was well-cut, as befitted someone who ran a store that sold men's clothing, his shoulders were not as broad, his muscles

116

less defined, his face softer around the edges.

"It's nice to meet you, Harrison. Are you enjoying our snow?"

It was Barrett who answered, his lips twisting with irony. "Does anyone enjoy snow? I don't, especially when I consider what it means to the cattle. They're not used to having so much of the frozen white stuff so early in the season."

Charlotte looked at the sanctuary with its sparsely filled pews. "Judging from the few people here, I'd say many of the parishioners aren't happy about it, either."

Barrett nodded. "I usually attend an earlier service, but Harrison slept too late."

Seemingly unchastened by his brother's comment, Harrison grinned. "The train was tiring. Barrett wouldn't know about that, since it's been so long since he traveled on one."

Though Charlotte was curious about the currents that seemed to flow between them, this was not the time to ask. "We'd better take our seats."

As she led the way into the sanctuary, Barrett asked if they could join her.

With the church only a quarter filled, there was no reason for them to share a pew with her, and yet there was also no reason for her to refuse. "Certainly."

As the congregation rose for the first hymn, Charlotte discovered two things about Barrett. He sang badly off-key, and it didn't seem to bother him. Barrett sang like a man who knew that God heard the words of praise and knew they were sincere. The fact that his voice was less melodic than many didn't matter. How different from Jeffrey. Charlotte's husband had attended church services only when she insisted, and though he sang the hymns and recited the prayers with the rest of the congregation, she knew he had been there in body but not in spirit. Barrett was not like that.

Her heart filled with warmth, Charlotte settled back in the pew and waited for the minister to begin his sermon.

"Today we will be considering Proverbs 12:19."

In an instant, the warmth fled, replaced by a cold that penetrated more deeply than the frigid outside air. This had been one of Papa's favorite verses, and he had used it as the basis for at least one sermon at each of the churches he'd served.

" 'The lip of truth shall be established for ever: but a lying tongue is but for a moment.' " Though the minister was intoning the words, Charlotte heard her father's

118

voice. "Do you believe, as some do, that this verse condones lying, by saying it lasts only a moment?" Papa had demanded one Sunday. "That is false reasoning. Our God loves truth. He abhors lies. As God's children, we must live our lives based on truth. Only truth."

Charlotte closed her eyes and tried not to shudder. Both Papa and Mama had taught her the importance of truth. What would they think if they knew what she had done? More importantly, what did God think? She knew the answer.

"Men!" Miriam pretended to pout as she pronounced the word. "They don't understand anything. They think just because they decide to do something, we'll be thrilled. They don't know what's involved in getting ready." She accepted the cup of coffee Charlotte offered after settling in one of the gilded chairs that Barrett had refused when he'd visited Élan. Miriam's voice was little less than a wail as she continued. "I know there isn't enough time for you to make me a new gown, but Mama's adamant that I can't wear the green silk again. What am I going to do? I can't refuse Barrett's invitation."

Charlotte had anticipated this conversation ever since she'd left church on Sunday. When the service had ended, Barrett and Harrison had insisted on accompanying her back to her house, and as they'd crossed Ferguson Street, Barrett had announced that he wanted to have a dinner to introduce Harrison to his friends. "I hope you and Mrs. Amos will be my guests." Charlotte, still reeling from the sermon and the knowledge that her deception had to stop, had nodded. It was only afterward that she had realized Miriam would also be invited, and she would want a new gown.

"I would tell you that Barrett won't remember what you wore to the symphony," Charlotte said as she poured herself a cup of coffee and took the other chair, "but that would be a lie. Most men don't notice much about women's clothing. Barrett's different."

As Miriam nodded, Charlotte said, "There's only one answer. We have to make your green gown look like a new one. Here's what I thought I'd do." She handed Miriam the sketch she'd made the previous night. "It's the same dress with a few changes. I'll use the fabric in the overskirt to make long sleeves and a fichu, and I'll add a new overskirt of lemon yellow. It won't be as elaborate as the original, which means it'll be more suited for dinner." Charlotte looked at her friend. "What do you think?"

A smile as broad as the prairie was her answer. "Oh, Charlotte, it'll be beautiful. You're a genius."

Charlotte shook her head. "Hardly a genius. While I was growing up, my family didn't have much money, so I learned how to make simple changes that would make an old dress look almost new."

"I still say you're a genius." Miriam flung her arms around Charlotte and hugged her. "I'm so glad you're my friend."

"I never thought I'd have another chance to wear this gown." Gwen settled back in the carriage, her smile radiant. Unlike Miriam, she felt no need for a new dress and was delighted to have another occasion to wear her blue silk. "I still can't believe we were invited."

"I don't think Barrett knows too many unmarried women," Charlotte had told Gwen when the official invitation arrived. "He probably wanted to balance the numbers." She was certain Messieurs Duncan and Eberhardt would be there, along with Harrison. That meant Barrett had needed to find at least three single women in addition to Miriam.

According to Miriam, there would be fifteen guests, including four married couples, one of which was her parents. "I won't tell Mama that you've been invited, but I'll make certain she has her smelling salts." Though both Charlotte and Miriam knew that Mrs. Taggert was unlikely to be pleased by the presence of someone she considered little more than a servant, Charlotte did not regret having accepted the invitation, for it brought Gwen great pleasure.

"I don't care what the reason was," Gwen said, her face rosy with happiness. "I'm just glad we're going. And in this beautiful carriage too." Ever the gentleman, Barrett had insisted on sending his carriage for Charlotte and Gwen. Though it was only six days since the October 24 snowstorm and most of the snow had melted, Barrett had declared that the women must not walk the two and a half blocks from their home to his. "Mr. Bradley would be horrified," he had told Charlotte. And though Charlotte suspected the butler's disapproval was a figment of Barrett's imagination, she had agreed. Even though she'd taken long walks both at home in Vermont and at Fort Laramie, it was one thing to stroll during the daylight, quite another to walk at night in an evening gown. That was why she had hired a carriage the night she and Gwen had gone to the opera house.

"Oh, my." Though she'd been silent as they covered the short distance from the carriage to the double front doors, Gwen let out a deep sigh as they entered Barrett's house. Charlotte understood the feeling. The imposing foyer with its parquet floor was as large as the room she and David shared, and yet it served as nothing more than an entry hall. To the right, she saw a spacious parlor, to the left an elegant dining room. Finely woven carpets, intricately carved mahogany furniture, and crystal chandeliers left no doubt that this was the residence of a wealthy man. Charlotte had known that from the exterior, and yet seeing the inside of Barrett's home made her realize the width of the gulf that separated them.

"This way, madam." The heavyset man who had taken their cloaks directed Charlotte and Gwen toward the parlor. They stood in the doorway for a moment before anyone noticed their presence. Charlotte wasn't surprised, for although there were little more than a dozen people, all of them seemed engrossed in their conversations.

Mr. Duncan spotted them first and, disengaging himself from Miriam's parents, hurried toward the doorway. "I'm glad you could come." The direction of his smile left no doubt that he was speaking to Gwen. "I asked Barrett to seat you next to me at dinner. I want to continue the conversation we began at the opera house."

For all the attention he paid to her, Charlotte might have been invisible. It wasn't the first time she had been ignored, but though it was undeniably rude, that wasn't what bothered her. She could slough off uncouth behavior. What bothered her was that she couldn't pinpoint the cause of her uneasiness. All she knew was that she felt uncomfortable around Warren Duncan. Perhaps it was foolish, for he seemed the personification of courtesy when he was with Gwen, but Charlotte could not dismiss her concerns.

She left Gwen and Mr. Duncan conversing in the doorway and moved toward a cluster of chairs, intending to sit there until dinner was served. But before she was halfway across the room, Barrett appeared at her side.

"I'm sorry I wasn't able to greet you when you arrived." As he had been the night at the opera, he was dressed in formal clothing. It was not difficult to imagine this man walking the halls of Congress and helping to lead the nation.

Barrett wrinkled his nose and spoke softly. "This is my first dinner party, and I'm still learning." When Charlotte raised a questioning eyebrow, he explained. "Richard and Warren have told me it's time I started entertaining, and Harrison's visit seemed like a good excuse." Barrett nodded almost imperceptibly toward the man who had taken Charlotte's cape. "Mr. Bradley is in his element. You wouldn't know he started life as a gold miner, would you?"

Charlotte studied Barrett's butler. "I can picture him as a miner." He had the well-developed arms and shoulders of a man who had wielded a pick and ax for many years, though the somewhat haughty expression he had adopted would not have fared well in a mine shaft.

Barrett appeared startled. "What gave him away?"

"His shoulders. They're even more muscular than yours." Charlotte felt a flush rise to her cheeks. Mama would have been appalled if she'd heard Charlotte's remark. It was positively unseemly to have noticed Barrett's musculature, far worse to have admitted it.

Barrett must not have noticed her discomfort, for his voice was even as he said, "I hope you won't tell anyone about Mr. Bradley's past. I doubt he'd want that to become common knowledge."

Relieved that her faux pas had gone

undetected, Charlotte nodded. "I'm good at keeping secrets, but I am curious. How did he learn to be a butler?"

"He claims he read a book." Barrett looked around the room, as if assuring himself that his other guests were occupied. Miriam and a young woman Charlotte did not recognize were deep in conversation with Harrison Landry and Richard Eberhardt, while the elder Taggerts appeared to be entertaining one of the city's prominent bankers and his wife. Smiling, Barrett added, "It's amazing what you can find in books, isn't it?"

Though she read few books now other than those devoted to fashion, Charlotte nodded. "When I was a child, I was ill for a long time and had to spend my days in bed. Books were my best friends then. They helped me pass the time while Abigail and Elizabeth were at school. Unfortunately, since David was born, I haven't had much time to read."

"But surely you read to him. Or is he old enough to read to himself?"

Charlotte tried not to frown at the thoughts that Barrett's innocent question had provoked. "He's only one," she said, forcing herself to smile as Miriam and Richard Eberhardt approached. She would not tell Barrett that David would be unable to read, even if he were ten. She wouldn't burden him with her worries, for David was her responsibility, no one else's.

As Richard asked Charlotte her opinion of Barrett's political aspirations, Charlotte heard Barrett address Miriam. "Have I told you how attractive you are in that new gown?" From the corner of her eye, Charlotte saw Miriam smile. She smiled in return.

Charlotte was still smiling as dinner began. The food was delicious, and the guests congenial. Warren Duncan had indeed prevailed on Barrett for the seating arrangement, for Gwen was on his right, seemingly so entranced by whatever he was saying that she paid virtually no attention to the man on her right.

For her part, seated between Harrison and Miriam's father, Charlotte enjoyed the contrast between the two men's conversation. Harrison was outspoken, while Mr. Taggert couched his words carefully. They differed on many subjects, yet both were united in their belief that Barrett should become one of Wyoming's first senators.

"Of course," Harrison said with a twist to his lips, "you need to achieve statehood first."

"And Barrett needs to take a wife." Mr. Taggert nodded toward the head of the table where his daughter was seated on Barrett's right. "I think he might have someone in mind."

As if she sensed her father's regard, Miriam tipped her head to one side and gave Barrett a smile that could only be described as radiant. They made a striking couple, Barrett so dark, Miriam so blonde. Charlotte could picture them standing together, waving at voters, then nodding graciously when Barrett was sworn in as senator. She could hear the crowds crying out in adulation, "Mr. and Mrs. Landry." Everyone would smile. Why, then, couldn't Charlotte muster one? Marriage was what Miriam wanted and what Barrett needed. It was foolish, absolutely, positively foolish, that the thought made Charlotte feel empty inside.

The party had gone well. At least Barrett thought it had. His guests had lingered longer than he'd expected, and when they had departed, it had been with what appeared to be genuine reluctance. Now they were gone, and he was ready to sleep. But Harrison, who appeared as wide awake as he had at nine that morning, had insisted on a final cup of coffee. That was why Barrett was sitting in his office, staring at the clock on the wall and wishing he were upstairs in bed, while his brother poured himself a second cup of Mrs. Melnor's dark brew. He'd talked about the party, complimenting Barrett on the food, mentioning each of the guests by name. And all the while, Barrett had been waiting for the shoe to fall. When Harrison was like this, it was because he had something unpleasant to say and he was trying to soften the blow.

The sobering of Harrison's expression told Barrett the time had arrived. "You probably don't want to hear this, but I'm going to give you some brotherly advice anyway."

"Can't this wait until morning?" Though he knew the answer, it was worth a try. Barrett would have preferred to bask in the memory of a successful evening. Mrs. Melnor had outdone herself with the food, and Mr. Bradley had been the perfect butler, but the memory that shone the brightest was Charlotte's reference to Barrett's muscles. He wasn't certain what had touched him most, the fact that she had noticed his shoulders or her obvious embarrassment that she had. When he'd realized she would be even more chagrined if he acknowledged the comment, he pretended he hadn't noticed. Sweet Charlotte!

"Nope." Harrison's voice brought Barrett back to the present and the prospect of an unpleasant conversation. "You said we were going to the range tomorrow to check on your cows. Cattle," Harrison corrected himself. "When that happens, you won't be thinking about anything else. That's why it's gotta be tonight."

Trying not to sigh, Barrett nodded. There was no point in postponing the inevitable. "Go ahead. I'm listening."

Harrison placed the cup back on its saucer and faced Barrett, his eyes more serious than normal. "You're making a mistake if you marry Miriam Taggert."

It wasn't what Barrett had expected. He'd thought Harrison might try to dissuade him from running for office. He'd even considered that his brother might suggest selling the cattle. But he hadn't expected Harrison to care about his choice of a wife, much less disagree with it.

"Why on earth would you say that?" he demanded, his voice harsher than it might have been if he weren't so tired. "Richard and Warren think she's perfect. Miriam is an attractive woman who's been groomed for a role in society. As a bonus, her father

131

publishes an influential newspaper. What could possibly be wrong with her?"

"You don't love her."

"Don't I?" It was easier to counter with a question than to admit that Harrison might be right.

"I don't think you do."

Big brother saw more than he was supposed to. That was one of the problems with big brothers. Still, Barrett wasn't going to confirm Harrison's supposition. Instead, he equivocated. "I'm not sure I believe in love."

The way Harrison's eyes narrowed told Barrett he'd seen through the ruse. "Our parents loved each other."

"That's true. They did, but Pa said it didn't start out that way. The way he tells it, they grew to love each other. I figure that'll happen with Miriam and me."

Harrison leaned forward, pointing his index finger at Barrett. "Are you willing to risk your future happiness on that possibility? Seems to me it's a mighty big risk. Why would you do that when you've got a much better alternative?"

It was late. That was the only reason Barrett could find for his brother's nonsensical words. "What are you talking about?"

Harrison shook his head. "It's a who, not a what."

"All right. *Who* are you talking about?"

As he had when they'd been children, Harrison closed his mouth, looking around the room slowly, as if he wasn't about to deliver a salvo. The technique had never failed to irritate Barrett then, and it didn't fail now. But Barrett was older and, he liked to think, wiser. He rose and headed for the door. "Time for bed."

Harrison chuckled. "So, you've learned something. Well, you're not going to escape so easily, little brother. The woman you ought to be considering is Charlotte. She'd be a much better wife for you than Miriam."

Barrett stopped in midstride and stared at his brother. Surely he was joking. But Harrison's solemn expression said this was no joke. "Nonsense! A widow with a young child is all wrong for me." Barrett knew that. It was only a passing problem that he couldn't seem to get Charlotte out of his mind, no matter what he did. "You're wrong, Harrison. Dead wrong."

7

It was too nice a day to remain inside. Though it had snowed on Monday and Tuesday, most of the snow had melted, the sun had emerged, and the wind no longer howled. It was a beautiful Saturday afternoon, perhaps the last fine day of the year, and Charlotte had no intention of wasting it. She hung the closed sign in the shop window and settled David in the wagon. Though she doubted Rose would be able to walk the entire distance, the little girl refused to ride. "I big," she had announced when Charlotte offered to pull her. "I walk."

Rose had pouted when her mother left with Mr. Duncan — Warren, Charlotte corrected herself. He had insisted both Gwen and Charlotte call him Warren, although he continued to address her as Madame Charlotte. The little girl was decidedly miffed that Gwen had gone for a drive in the park without her, and rather than let Molly deal with the inevitable tantrum, Charlotte had offered to care for the children. It wouldn't hurt to close Élan early, especially since no one was scheduled for a fitting today.

"You've been very good," Charlotte told Rose and David, "so we're going for a treat. We'll see what Mr. Ellis has in store for good children today." They probably would not recognize the shopkeeper's name, but that didn't matter. Charlotte had learned that the word *treat* was enough to ensure good behavior.

Today's excursion was an experiment, the first time Charlotte had taken David for a long ride. In the past, she had told herself that he didn't need the exposure to possible scorn, that he could learn about the outside world in their backyard, where no one would stare at him. She had even convinced herself that if by some chance the baron were passing through Cheyenne, she was keeping David safe from his prying eyes by not taking him with her when she explored the city. But the minister's words about the dangers of lies had echoed through Charlotte's brain long after the sermon had ended. The truth was, she had been lying to herself. She hadn't wanted anyone to know about David's blindness because she feared the scorn — not for David, but for herself.

That was why she kept him sequestered. She had seen Molly's reaction when she realized David was blind, and although the girl had grown to accept him, the initial shock had wounded Charlotte. Her son deserved better. He deserved to be treated like any other child. David couldn't see the pity on others' faces, but Charlotte could. That pity hurt, and so she had protected herself.

No longer. She couldn't unravel all the lies until she was certain that the baron had given up his search for her and the money he believed she had, but she could stop acting as if she were ashamed of her son. She wasn't.

"We've just turned south, David," she said as they left the store. "Can you feel the sun on your face?" David nodded and giggled, his giggling intensifying when she told him they were crossing the street and he had to hold on tighter. A pang of regret stabbed Charlotte as she realized that her fears had resulted in her cheating her son out of such simple pleasures.

Determined that today would be different, she put a smile into her voice. "The post office is right here on the corner," Charlotte said, giving both children a verbal tour of the city.

David sniffed and wrinkled his nose as a horse made a deposit in the street. He tipped his head to one side, listening intently as a buggy with a squeaky wheel approached. And all the while, he grinned. There was no doubt that David was having fun.

So was Rose. She clapped her hands when they passed the hardware store. "Hammer," she said, pointing to the display in the plate-glass window.

"That's right. It is a hammer. And that's a shovel." Charlotte stopped to let the little girl enjoy the sight of tools. Though shoppers filled the street, no one seemed to mind that Charlotte and her wagon were blocking the view of Arp and Hammond's main window. The women smiled, and the men tipped their hats in greeting. No one paid them any undue attention. No one stared at David's sightless eyes. No one appeared to notice his resemblance to Jeffrey. Charlotte's fears had been unfounded.

"We're here." She lifted David out of the wagon when they reached their destination. Opening the door, she admonished Rose to stay by her side, then carried her son into Mr. Ellis's bakery and confectionary.

"Foo." David grinned as he turned his head in both directions, trying to absorb all the aromas. The smells of freshly baked rye and pumpernickel mingled with the aromas of chocolate and citrus, and it was clear that David was enjoying all of them.

"Yes, David, it's food." Though Rose had started to scamper toward the glass-fronted cabinets filled with pastries, Charlotte snagged her arm and placed her firmly on a chair. In the past, when Charlotte had shopped here, she had carried the baked goods home, but today she and the children would enjoy their treats seated at one of the small round tables that lined the left side of the store.

When she had ordered macaroons and hot cocoa, Charlotte seated David on a chair. "You need to be careful," she admonished him. "There are no arms on this chair, but you're a big boy. You can sit here."

His expression once more solemn, he felt the chair back, then as he let his hands grip the edge of the table, he smiled again. A round table was a novelty for David, and he appeared to be enjoying the sensation of curved wood under his palms. Charlotte was enjoying watching him. The store, with its pressed tin ceiling and elaborate chandeliers, had helped inspire the interior of Élan, and the pastries never failed to satisfy her craving for sweets, but nothing compared to the sheer pleasure of seeing her son's delight in the new surroundings.

"They're called macaroons," she told both David and Rose as the cookies were delivered to their table. "Here you go, David." Charlotte guided his hand to one of the coconut confections that she'd chosen because they would be simple for him to eat. Rose slurped her cocoa, giving herself a chocolate mustache, while David stuffed the macaroon into his mouth.

"I didn't expect to see you here."

Charlotte looked up, startled. Though she had glanced around when they'd entered the store to see if she recognized anyone, once the food arrived, she had been so engrossed in watching her son that she hadn't noticed Barrett's approach. Surely it was her imagination that he appeared more handsome than ever today, his blue eyes sparkling, his lips curved in a smile. He was the same Barrett Landry. It was only she who, like a schoolgirl, found something new to admire each time she saw him.

"Harrison's a bit under the weather." Barrett frowned as he added, "I don't think he's adjusted to the altitude yet, so I thought I'd risk Mrs. Melnor's wrath by buying him some of Mr. Ellis's pastries." Barrett glanced at the empty chair. "May I join you?"

When Charlotte nodded, he settled himself across from her, then gave her an expectant look. It was time for introductions. "I'd like you to meet my son David and Gwen's daughter Rose. Children, please say hello to Mr. Landry."

Predictably, David mangled the name, but he grinned in Barrett's direction before reaching for another macaroon, his hands moving slowly across the table until he encountered the plate.

"Yes, David, you may have another." Though she addressed her words to her son, Charlotte kept her eyes focused on Barrett, and as she did, the pleasure she had taken in the day evaporated. There was no disguising the pity and revulsion that flitted across his face. He did his best to hide it, trying to force his lips into a smile, but Charlotte knew she had not mistaken his initial reaction. This was worse — far worse — than Molly's response had been, because the pity came from Barrett.

"Your son is blind," he said slowly. There was something faintly accusatory in his voice, almost as if he were angry that she hadn't told him about David's blindness. Charlotte dismissed the notion, for anger or even disappointment would not explain the expression she had seen.

140

She took a deep breath, exhaling slowly as she tried to control her pain. "Whether or not he can see, David is my son, and I love him deeply."

Barrett waited until he'd given the waitress his order before replying. "As you should." His expression changed subtly, making Charlotte believe he pitied her as well as David. "I'm simply surprised you haven't placed him in a school or asylum where he can be cared for."

Charlotte took another deep breath. No good would be accomplished by responding in anger, although that was what she longed to do. Instead, she spoke softly, her voice little more than a whisper. "My son is not a package to be boxed up and sent away." The words were firm, but though she tried to remain calm, Charlotte knew that her flushed cheeks betrayed her distress. Rather than respond, Barrett rubbed the bump on his nose in what Charlotte had come to realize was an involuntary gesture when he was troubled.

It was what she had thought. He didn't understand. She had been foolish to believe that he could, when he had no children of his own. He didn't know what it was like to love and want to protect an innocent, helpless being. "David is my son, and his place is with me," Charlotte said firmly.

Unaware of the currents that swirled around them, David and Rose were chattering happily about the macaroons and cocoa, David making cooing noises while Rose expressed her approval with frequent repetitions of the word *dee-lish.* Though Gwen had reminded her that the word had three syllables, Rose preferred to abbreviate it. On another day, Charlotte would have been amused. Today she barely noticed, for her attention was focused on Barrett.

He kept his eyes firmly fixed on her as he sipped his coffee. Surely he must realize how hurt and angry she was. When he spoke, Barrett's voice was as low as Charlotte's. "Have you considered that you might be being selfish? Those places you don't want to talk about have teachers who are trained to deal with —"

She cut him off before he could finish his sentence. "That's a word I hate: *deal.* You deal a deck of cards, not a person. You love a person. You care for them. You keep them safe. That's what David needs, and no one can give him that better than me. As for teaching, I'm not as unskilled as you might think. I taught school when I lived in Vermont." Charlotte rose and reached for her son. "And now, if you will please excuse

142

us, it's time to take David home. At least there he will not be subjected to scorn."

She bundled both Rose and David into their coats, refusing Barrett's offer of a ride in his carriage. The sooner she was away from him, the better. She wouldn't listen to Barrett. She wouldn't send David to an asylum, not so long as she drew breath, and she was not — she absolutely was not — being selfish to want to keep him near her.

"Him not nice," Rose said as they left the store.

Charlotte sighed. It appeared that Rose had not been as oblivious to the conversation as she had hoped. Still, she could not prejudice the child. "Normally Mr. Landry is a very nice man."

Rose wrinkled her nose and shook her head. "Him not talk to me. Mr. Warren tol' me I'm pretty."

"You are pretty." Charlotte bent down and hugged David. "And you're the finest boy ever born." She turned back to Rose. "I'm sure Mr. Landry thought you were pretty. It's just that he was worried about grown-up things."

Nodding sagely, Rose said, "Grown-ups don't have fun."

That had been the case today, at least for Charlotte, and she had no one to blame but herself. She should not have let her anger rule her. She knew better, for whenever she failed to control her anger, she blurted out things that should not have been said. Like today. No one, not even Gwen, knew that she used to be a teacher and that she had once lived in Vermont. She had guarded that information, afraid that it might somehow lead the baron to her. No one was supposed to know anything of her past except that she was a widow. Now Barrett was privy to important details of her life.

Charlotte sighed. She had thought she was ready to unravel the cloak of deception she had woven with her lies, but it appeared she was not. She might tell Gwen — she probably should — but she would not reveal the truth to a man who regarded David as if he were an object.

Just a few hours ago, Charlotte had believed that Barrett was her friend. She had thought she could trust him, but as it had with Jeffrey, her judgment had proven faulty.

Barrett leaned back in the chair, trying to escape the smoke. "You may be one of the best attorneys in Wyoming Territory," he told Warren, "but those cigars are foul. Why on earth do you smoke them?"

Barrett's friend and lawyer shrugged.

"They're an acquired taste. I started with cheroots, but these taste better."

"And cost more too."

Warren exhaled carefully, creating a series of smoke rings. "That's true, but thanks to clients like you, I can afford them." He looked around as if checking for other clients. At this time of the morning, the smoking room of the Cheyenne Club was almost empty. Once the noontime meal had been served, it would fill with men who wanted to discuss the day's happenings or simply pass time until the evening meal was ready. The relative emptiness was one of the reasons Barrett had suggested they meet this morning.

Warren blew another smoke ring. "Is Richard coming?"

"Not today. Harrison'll join us for dinner, though." Whatever had ailed his brother on Saturday had passed quickly, and Harrison had declared himself well enough to attend church yesterday. Fortunately, he'd been ready for the early service, which meant they had not seen Charlotte. Barrett had no regrets about that, for he was still stinging from the rebuke she'd dealt him.

He glanced at his watch. An hour before Harrison would arrive. Thrusting thoughts of Charlotte aside, Barrett focused his attention on Warren. "I thought you and I could review the plans first." Richard had helped draft them, but Barrett wanted Warren's opinion before he put them into action. That was the reason he'd invited his adviser to join him at the club that Warren aspired to join.

"Doesn't your brother want to weigh in on them?"

"He already has."

Though Barrett believed he had hidden his reaction to Harrison's comments, he must not have succeeded, for Warren raised an eyebrow. "And you don't like what he said." It was a statement, not a question.

"Not all of it." Harrison's assertion that Barrett should marry Charlotte was absurd. Positively absurd, but he hadn't relented. Harrison had mentioned the ridiculous idea at least daily. His brother's persistence as they'd traveled to the ranch had almost made Barrett forget how bad the grasslands looked and what their condition might mean for the coming winter. He would be thankful when spring arrived for more than one reason. Not only would the winter have ended, but Harrison's harangues would have too.

"Let me see what you have." When Barrett handed Warren the two sheets of paper he and Richard had created, he watched while the attorney reviewed them. A few minutes later, Warren laid them on the table and took another puff of his cigar. "Not bad. Not bad at all. You might want to start earlier, though. I don't like waiting until the new year before you host a rally. You need to keep your name before the public, and if you wait that long, they might have forgotten you." Warren tipped his head back and blew another series of smoke rings. "A Christmas betrothal to Miriam would help."

Barrett was of the same opinion. "That's possible."

A cynical expression crossed Warren's face. "You ought to turn that into probable. Even a man with only one eye can see that she's bonnet over boots for you."

Barrett shuddered at the image Warren's words had evoked. Memories of a young boy with carrot-colored hair taunted Barrett. Charlotte's son had both eyes, but he could not see. Perhaps he would be like the blind calf that had been part of Barrett's herd. The poor critter didn't survive long enough for the spring roundup. The mother had tried to keep it by her side — Barrett had seen her nudge it back into the herd when it tried to stray — but somehow it must have wandered off. He had found it in a ravine with a broken leg, leaving him no choice but to put it out of its misery. Barrett didn't know if the cow grieved the loss of her calf, but he knew that Charlotte would be devastated if anything happened to her son. She was like the bear sows he'd been warned to avoid, protective of their cubs, ready to do anything — even kill — to keep them safe.

"Why are you frowning?" Warren leaned forward, shaking his finger at Barrett the way Mrs. Cranston, the schoolmarm the children in Northwick had feared, had done.

Schoolmarm. That was another surprise. He hadn't realized Charlotte had been a teacher. He'd known she was intelligent, but it appeared that she had more education than he'd realized. Had she . . . ? Barrett dismissed his thoughts of Charlotte, forcing himself to concentrate on what Warren was saying.

"Most every man in Cheyenne would like to be in your place. Miriam Taggert is a good catch."

"That she is." Even though Harrison disagreed. Of course, Harrison didn't know about David. He'd change his tune if he did. Even Harrison wouldn't argue that a woman as encumbered as Charlotte would be a good senator's wife.

Seemingly mollified by Barrett's acquiescence, Warren settled back in his chair. "I know I can trust you not to say anything, but you're not the only one contemplating matrimony."

His words took Barrett by surprise. "Who?" When there was no answer other than a smirk, Barrett raised his eyebrows. "You?"

"What's the matter? Do you think I'm too old?" Without waiting for a reply, Warren said, "A man's never too old if he finds the right woman."

"And you have?"

A satisfied grin crossed Warren's face. "I believe I have." He started to hum Mendelssohn's Wedding March.

Warren was right. He shouldn't waste any more time. If Barrett was going to marry Miriam — and he was — he needed to court her. That's why she was seated next to him in his carriage, headed for the Inter-Ocean Hotel. That hadn't been his plan. When he'd invited her to join him for dinner, Barrett had planned to take her to the Cheyenne Club. To his way of thinking, the club offered the best food in the city, and it had the added advantage that the other diners would be people he knew, members of the club and their guests. But Miriam had other ideas. When he'd mentioned dinner, she had commented that her parents had enjoyed the roast grouse at the InterOcean. Barrett knew a hint when he heard it, and so he had made the reservation.

He'd hesitated over inviting Miriam anywhere, because it meant leaving Harrison on his own. Though he didn't always like what Harrison said, he was enjoying his brother's company and hated to desert him. However, Harrison announced that he'd be happy to spend the evening with Richard. "If I were a betting man, I'd wager that I'll have a better time than you," he had said, his lips curving into a smile that bordered on mockery. "I know you don't want to hear it, but you're planning to court the wrong woman."

He wasn't. Harrison simply didn't understand. Miriam was the woman Barrett needed by his side if he was going to become one of Wyoming's first senators.

"Thank you for bringing me here," Miriam said softly as she handed her cloak to the attendant at the hotel. "I know it wasn't your first choice." She waited until they were seated and the waiter had handed them menus before she said, "Papa thought it would be good for us to be seen here."

Barrett glanced around the dining room. With dark wood paneling extending halfway up the walls and a matching coffered ceiling, the room was gloomier than he liked, but there was no denying the excellence of the food or the quality of the service. No one questioned the InterOcean's reputation as Cheyenne's premier hotel, and Cyrus Taggert was correct in believing this was a place for Barrett to be noticed. Being noticed was important, particularly when he had Miriam at his side. While it was true that Barrett preferred the intimacy of the Cheyenne Club, there were more potential voters here.

"Your father's a very astute man." Barrett took a sip of water as he prepared for the obligatory compliment. "I'm the envy of every man in this room, because I'm here with you." When Miriam said nothing, he continued. "If you don't believe me, look around. Not a one can keep his eyes off that red dress." It was eye-catching, and unless Barrett was mistaken, it was another of Charlotte's creations.

Miriam raised her eyebrows slightly, causing Barrett to expand his compliment. "A dress needs the right woman to display it to perfection. Otherwise, it's nothing more than a collection of cloth and lace. Your

151

gown is attractive, but you make it beautiful." Barrett had said the same thing to customers when they'd debated which of the Landry Mercantile's calicos to purchase and whether that extra yard of lace was an extravagance.

Miriam's smile seemed almost amused, as if she had realized he felt compelled to pay her a compliment. Surely he hadn't been that obvious. "Thank you, Barrett. Papa was right. You have a gift for words."

Charlotte would not agree, and Barrett couldn't blame her. When he'd seen David, he hadn't chosen his words carefully enough. Foolishly, Barrett had spoken from his heart, and he'd hurt Charlotte. He would not let that happen to Miriam. There would be no impulsive speech where this woman was concerned, for there was too much at risk.

The waiter appeared at the table, his hands folded behind his back, his manner more formal than Mr. Bradley's. "Have you decided what you'd like for dinner?"

"My mother suggested I try the roast grouse." And Miriam was nothing if not an obedient daughter. Though Barrett suspected she had opinions of her own, she appeared to defer to others. Warren would say that was good; Harrison would disagree.

And Richard? Barrett wasn't certain.

As if she'd read his thoughts, Miriam leaned forward ever so slightly. "Where did you and Richard first meet?"

Two hours later, as he escorted Miriam to her front door, Barrett realized that their dinner conversation had centered on Richard. How odd.

8

Thou shalt not hate. Warren held the cigar in front of his nose and sniffed. He'd never seen much point in smelling a cigar, but he'd heard that was what gentlemen did, and so he made it into a ritual, even when he was alone. That way he wouldn't forget in public and give the club's membership committee another excuse to deny his admission. He would play by their rules so that they'd agree that Warren Duncan was a man of sterling character, eminently suited to join the Cheyenne Club. He wasn't going to give them any reason to be like that doc back home who claimed Ma had delusions. She'd been perfectly fine. Warren knew that, but she hadn't played by the rules those silly townspeople set, and she'd wound up in a room with a locked door and bars on the windows. That would never happen to him. He'd learned from Ma's mistakes.

Thou shalt not hate. The words reverberated through Warren's brain. As far as he knew, it wasn't one of the commandments. That must mean it wasn't as serious as killing or coveting. Not that it mattered. He'd broken enough commandments to ensure that the pearly gates were not part of his future. But maybe he would not be consigned to fire and brimstone for hatred. After all, he wasn't certain he hated the man. All Warren knew was that it had taken more restraint than he'd known he possessed to keep from smashing his fist into Barrett's face. How dare the man look so surprised — so shocked — that Warren was planning to marry? Did he think he was the only one who deserved a wife and child? He'd learn. Oh yes, he would.

Warren lit his cigar, taking a puff before he strode to the window. No doubt about it. A good cigar could soothe a man's mood. That and the prospect of the night ahead. He grinned. Soon. Soon he'd have a far more pleasurable way to release his anger than smashing Barrett Landry's nose.

Though darkness came early at this time of the year, there were still too many people on the street. He'd wait another hour or two before he visited Sylvia, and even when he did, he'd take his normal precautions. No one must ever be able to connect Warren

Duncan, successful attorney and prospective member of the Cheyenne Club, with the masked man who frequented the crudest of Cheyenne's brothels.

"Oh, Charlotte, it's been three days, and it's still all I can think about." Gwen looked up from the gown she was hemming. Though normally Charlotte did not ask Gwen to help with sewing, the upcoming Christmas season had brought in more business than ever, and Gwen had volunteered her services. The help was a godsend, for it gave Charlotte a few extra hours to work on clothing for Mrs. Kendall and her boarders. Three of the four dresses she planned to take there were finished. Unless David had another restless night, she should have the final gown completed within a week.

Gwen was a great help, but tonight, while they sat with yards of fabric draped over their laps, she appeared to have trouble concentrating on her sewing.

"I loved Mike," Gwen said, furrows forming between her eyes, "but it wasn't like this. Saturday was the best afternoon I can imagine. We rode in the park and everyone waved at us and it was wonderful and afterwards he took me to Rue de Rivoli for tea and that was even better." She paused for a quick breath. "Oh, Charlotte, Warren's amazing. He knows everyone and everything. If it hadn't been for him, I wouldn't have known that Rue de Rivoli isn't really French. He said it was built by a Scottish businessman from Colorado who put his offices on the second floor and wanted good food, so he opened the restaurant downstairs. I didn't care about any of that. I only cared that everyone treated me like a real lady because I was with Warren. He's the most wonderful man I've ever met."

"I'm happy for you." It wasn't Gwen's fault that Charlotte's Saturday had been so different from her friend's. While Gwen had spent the past three days mooning over Warren Duncan, Charlotte had passed the time trying desperately to forget what had happened at Mr. Ellis's shop. Her efforts had failed. Every time she closed her eyes, the image of Barrett's expression when he realized that David was blind floated before her. When she smelled fresh bread, she was transported back to the bakery, and though she tried to block the memories, she was forced to relive the sight of Barrett's pity while David searched for another macaroon. Even the simple sound of cups rattling on saucers reminded Charlotte of the afternoon that had turned out so differently from her plan.

She could tell herself that Barrett had spoiled the day, but that wasn't true. She should have anticipated his reaction. It wasn't as if this was the first time someone had pitied David, and it wouldn't be the last. She needed to develop what Mama called a thick hide. Mama had claimed that that and the knowledge that God would never abandon her were what had sustained her through the times they'd been asked to leave a church when Papa's outspoken beliefs had angered the congregation. Those moves with three small children must have been far more difficult than dealing with one man's pity. Mama had survived, and so would Charlotte. She slid a length of thread into the needle, preparing to gather lace for the sleeve flounces.

"Warren said he likes children." Gwen continued the litany of praises. "He even said he wants to take Rose with us the next time we go riding." She held up the gown she'd been hemming for Charlotte's inspection. "I think he may love me. Oh, Charlotte, wouldn't that be wonderful? Warren would be the perfect father for Rose."

And Barrett would be the worst possible father for David. Not that Charlotte was searching for a father for David. She wasn't. Not that Barrett would consider her a potential wife. He wouldn't, for he was planning to marry Miriam . . . but having him as a friend would have been nice.

"Just be certain he's the right man for you," Charlotte cautioned. "It's dangerous to marry a stranger." Her marriage was proof of that. Perhaps if she and Jeffrey had known each other better before they married, they might have recognized their differences, but they'd been too caught up in the magic of what felt like first love to realize that marriage needed to be based on more than infatuation.

Gwen nodded. "I know that. We're not rushing into anything." She gave Charlotte a self-deprecating smile. "Warren hasn't mentioned marriage. Perhaps I'm being foolish and imagining something that isn't there, but it seems that he cares."

"He would be a fool if he didn't. You're a wonderful woman and a great mother, Gwen. Any man who doesn't see that doesn't deserve you." Gwen's flush made Charlotte realize the woman was unaccustomed to receiving praise. She would have to change that. Gwen deserved to be recognized for her gifts.

"I hope he does love me. I've been praying so hard for a father for Rose, and I'd like to think that Warren is the answer to those prayers." Gwen's smile faded. "The only thing that worries me is leaving you and David. What would you do if I married?"

Charlotte pinned the lace to the sleeve, then held it up to admire the effect. "I couldn't ever replace you," she admitted. "I doubt there's anyone in Wyoming Territory who could do all that you do as well as you do it, but I'd need to find someone to care for David during the day. Molly would rather work in the shop, but there must be someone else."

Charlotte was thinking out loud. Though she had known from the beginning that Gwen wanted to remarry and that she might have to find another person to help with David's care, until Warren Duncan had entered their lives, Charlotte hadn't given it serious consideration. As her needle darted in and out, attaching the lace to the velvet, Charlotte's thoughts whirled, recalling her initial mistrust of Warren. It had seemed irrational at the time, but now she wondered if there hadn't been a good reason for her reaction. Perhaps the fact that Warren might disrupt her life was the reason Charlotte felt so uncomfortable around him.

"Now that David's older, the woman wouldn't have to live here," Charlotte continued. "She could come during the day, or I could take him to her house."

"Or you could send David to a school for children like him."

Charlotte jabbed the needle into the velvet, trying to vent her anger on the fabric rather than her friend. "An asylum?" she asked, trying to keep her voice even.

Gwen shook her head, for she knew how much Charlotte hated the very word. "A school. A boarding school."

The words might be different, but the effect was the same. "Not you too."

Gwen seemed startled by Charlotte's reaction. "What do you mean?"

"Someone else suggested that." She wouldn't admit that it was Barrett, for that would mean telling Gwen about their painful encounter at the confectionary. "I thought you'd understand because you're a mother. Surely you can see that the best thing for David is to be with me."

For a long moment, Gwen said nothing. Then she raised one brow. "Is it?"

He couldn't stop thinking of her. Barrett took another spoonful of the pea soup Mrs. Melnor had made for lunch, knowing that it would seem as tasteless as everything had since he'd left Mr. Ellis's store. This was ridiculous. Three days had passed, and the memory hadn't faded. If anything, it had intensified. Meals were the worst. Though he managed to keep himself busy the rest of the day, whenever he sat down at a table, his memory was drawn back to the small round table at the confectionary. He'd been an idiot, a stupid, insensitive idiot. Charlotte didn't deserve the treatment he'd given her, nor did David.

"Are you going to tell me what's wrong?" Harrison laid his soup spoon on the liner plate and leaned forward. "Don't bother claiming it's nothing. I've known you too long to believe that."

Harrison was right. There was no point in pretending. "I've been a fool."

"And that's news?" Though Harrison's question was light, Barrett did not smile. "What did you do this time?" his brother continued. "Forget to tell the lovely Miriam just how lovely she is?" The sarcasm that laced his words left no doubt that Harrison expected Barrett to laugh. He did not.

"It's worse than that. I hurt Charlotte."

Harrison's grin faded. "That is serious. You'd better fix it."

Though he'd eaten only half his meal,

Barrett rose. "I'm not sure I can fix it," he admitted as he tossed his napkin onto the table, "but I'm going to try. Don't be surprised if I come back battered and bloody."

Harrison reached for a piece of corn bread, his lips curving into a smile. "She wouldn't do that."

"You don't know Charlotte." Barrett hoped he did.

"What's wrong, David?" Charlotte watched as her son cocked his head before starting to crawl toward the door. Gwen and Rose were out taking a walk, leaving Charlotte and David in the kitchen with Charlotte rolling out dough for gingerbread cookies while David played on the floor. Judging from his reaction, her son had heard something she hadn't. It wouldn't be the first time. Although he could not see, his other senses — particularly his hearing — were more acute than Charlotte's.

A moment later, someone knocked on the door. Charlotte brushed the flour from her hands before scooping David into her arms. Though he still wasn't comfortable standing, he had learned to crawl at a speed that continued to amaze her. She wouldn't take the chance that he'd scoot outside.

Holding her now squirming son, Charlotte opened the door. At the sight of her visitor, she started to slam it. He had no right to be here. It didn't matter that he was breathtakingly handsome and that his eyes were as brilliant as the Wyoming sky. Those were superficial trappings. What mattered was what was inside a man, and what was inside Barrett Landry was ugly.

He wedged his foot inside the door. "I know I don't deserve it, but I hope you'll give me another chance."

An apology. She hadn't expected that. That and his smile, which seemed to include David, were difficult to resist. The least she could do was listen. The common courtesy Mama had instilled in her daughters demanded that. "All right. Come in."

As she led the way toward the sitting area, Charlotte spoke to her son. "Mr. Landry has come to visit." Though she doubted he would recall the name, David probably recognized the voice and scent, a combination of bay rum, cold air, and something unique to Barrett. When she'd placed David on the floor and handed him the stuffed sock that was this week's favorite toy, Charlotte settled herself in one of the chairs and nodded toward the other. "Please have a seat."

"Thank you." Barrett removed his coat, folding it over the chair back, and laid a small sack at his feet. She hadn't noticed that he'd been carrying anything, but she'd been so surprised by his arrival that she might not have noticed if he'd had a bolt of fabric tucked under his arm.

Placing his hands on his knees, Barrett leaned forward, as if he sought to close the distance between the two chairs. "I want to apologize for my behavior on Saturday."

There was no stammering, none of the hesitation Jeffrey had shown the few times he'd apologized. Barrett's eyes radiated sincerity, and the look he gave David was that of any man looking at any child. The revulsion and pity Charlotte had seen on his face three days ago were gone, replaced by what appeared to be genuine remorse. "My mother taught me that when a man does something truly stupid, his apology should be accompanied by a gift. What I did was stupid, and so I hope you'll accept this." He reached into the sack and pulled out an easily recognizable box. When Barrett made amends, he did it with style.

Charlotte smiled. "Your apology is accepted. And so is your gift." She looked at the pale blue box that signified a special treat. "Thank you, Barrett. I've heard that

Mr. Ellis's chocolates are delicious." Henry Ellis wasn't simply an excellent baker. He was also an accomplished chocolatier. As Charlotte opened the lid, David sat up, his nose quivering. "Yes, David, it's chocolate. We'll have some later."

Barrett's eyes widened slightly. "Your words sounded as if you've never eaten Ellis chocolates."

"I haven't." There was no need to state the obvious, that indulgences like expensive chocolates were rare in this household. The mismatched chairs and the slightly frayed rug told their tale. A shiver made its way down Charlotte's back as she thought of the luxuries she had had at Fort Laramie. Those days were over. She had left the Steinway piano, the Wedgwood china, and the fancy furniture, bringing only what she could carry in a single trunk. The rest would have been reminders of a life that had brought more heartbreak than happiness. Charlotte shivered again. If the baron could see the way she lived, he'd realize that she did not have the fortune Jeffrey was supposed to have found.

Seemingly oblivious to her inner turmoil, Barrett reached for the sack and handed it to Charlotte. "I know David doesn't understand apologies, but my guess is that gifts are always welcome. This is for him." Barrett glanced at David before returning his attention to Charlotte. "If he already has one, I can choose something else."

Charlotte reached into the bag, smiling as she withdrew a medium-sized wooden ball. "It's perfect, and, no, David does not have one." She rotated the ball, checking for splinters. Of course there were none. A man with Barrett Landry's wealth would buy only the best.

His eyes sparkled as he watched her. "I'll take it as a good sign that you didn't throw that at me, even if I do deserve it. I warned Harrison that I might come home battered and bruised."

"Did you really think I'd do that?"

Barrett shook his head. "I didn't think you were violent, but I've learned that mother cows can be unpredictable when their young are threatened."

Charlotte couldn't help it. She laughed. "Just a hint, Mr. Landry." She feigned indignation. "If you want to win a woman's good graces, it would be prudent not to compare her to a bovine."

"If I had any doubts that you were once a schoolteacher, your etiquette lesson, not to mention your use of the word *bovine,* would have squashed them. Your point is well taken." Barrett's face sobered as he said, "I probably shouldn't judge human behavior by what I see on the range, but since I arrived in the territory, I've spent more time with cattle than people. I want you to know how sorry I am about how I behaved on Saturday. I was surprised — shocked is probably the better word — but that's no excuse for treating you and David the way I did."

Once again, his voice rang with sincerity, and Charlotte felt her last resistance melt. It took a strong man to humble himself with an apology. She nodded slowly, encouraging him to continue.

"The only thing I can say in my defense is that I was worried about what the future would hold for him . . . and for you."

"I can tell you right now that David's future will not hold an asylum."

"That's your decision. You're David's mother, and you know better than anyone what he needs. My only experience with blindness has been with cattle."

As he recounted the story of the blind calf, Charlotte gripped the chair arms. She'd been mistaken in judging Barrett. He had been worried, not disgusted. He'd spoken from sympathy, not prejudice.

"I'm sorry my thoughtless words hurt

you," he concluded. "I hope you'll forgive me."

"I do. I already told you that I accepted your apology. Now that I know the whole story, I realize that I was wrong." Charlotte laid her hand on David's head, tousling the red hair so like his father's. "I was hurt, probably more than I should have been. Any slight to David hurts me, but it was worse coming from a friend."

"Are we friends again?" Barrett's voice held a note Charlotte didn't recognize.

"I hope so."

"Then let's see how your son likes his ball."

To Barrett's surprise, Charlotte handed him the ball. "You should give it to him. Tell him what it is and that you're going to put it in his hand."

Though he had little experience with children, other than the ones who had come into the family's store in Northwick, Barrett had never seen parents go to such lengths to give a child a toy. There had to be a reason. He thought for a second before nodding. "That's so he's not surprised."

"Exactly." The smile Charlotte gave him made Barrett feel as if he'd accomplished something important, not simply understanding how to approach her son.

"I spent days with my eyes closed, trying to imagine David's world." What an amazing woman! Perhaps it was the fact that she'd once taught school that helped her think like a child, but Barrett suspected it was more than that. He was seeing a mother's love at work.

He rose, then squatted next to the boy. "David, it's Mr. Landry. I've brought you a ball. Hold out your hands, and I'll give it to you." When the child extended his hands at shoulder width, Barrett laid the ball on the floor and moved David's hands closer. "Ball," he said as he placed the child's hands around his gift. "Can you say that?"

For a second, David did not speak. As he rolled the ball between his hands, Barrett could see that he was teaching himself the shape and texture of his new toy. "Baw," he said at last.

"That's close. Ball."

David hugged the ball to his chest. Had he misunderstood the word *close*? "Balls are meant to be rolled on the floor," Barrett explained. "Can you do that?"

David shook his head and clutched the ball closer.

"He's never had a moving toy," Charlotte said. "Toys are something he holds or places on the floor. They're always stationary."

"I see." Barrett winced at the phrase. How often did he use it, not realizing that it might be painful to the mother of a child who could not see? "Come, David. Let's put the ball on the floor."

As the boy complied, the ball rolled away. Startled by the sound, David reached for his toy, encountering only bare floor. He patted the floor in all directions before beginning to wail.

"It's all right. You'll get it back." Barrett retrieved the ball, then sat on the floor a few feet in front of David. "I'm going to roll the ball to you, David. Put your hands on the floor. You'll feel it coming. Here it comes."

As the ball touched David's hands, he grabbed it and pulled it to his chest. "Baw."

"That's right. Now it's your turn. Roll it to me." But no matter how often Barrett tried, no matter how he phrased the commands, David would not relinquish his toy.

"He's the answer to prayer."

Charlotte reached for the plate Gwen was holding and began to dry it. Both children were in bed, and the women were washing dishes. "Who are you talking about?"

"Barrett." Gwen swished the cloth around

another plate. "While I was walking with Rose, I kept praying that God would send someone who could take my place here. He sent Barrett."

The thought was ludicrous. "He came to bring David a toy, not to change my life." Although, to a small degree, he had done that. Barrett's visit had restored Charlotte's sense of peace. Her anger had faded along with the sense of being on edge. The past few days had reminded her of a childhood summer when she had tried to walk on the railroad tracks. Though Abigail and Elizabeth had mastered the skill easily, it had been proven to be far more difficult than Charlotte had imagined to keep her balance. She'd tottered from one side to another, coming so close to falling that Abigail had grabbed her arm. Only when she'd been able to place both feet back on the ground had Charlotte felt as if the world had stopped spinning the wrong direction. For the past three days, she'd had that same sense of vertigo, but now, thanks to Barrett's visit, she had regained her equilibrium.

"He'd be perfect for you." Gwen was nothing if not tenacious. "Barrett Landry is one of Cheyenne's most eligible bachelors."

"I know." This was an absurd conversation. Just because Gwen fancied herself in love didn't mean she needed to play match-maker for Charlotte. "If I were considering marrying again — which I am not," Charlotte was quick to add, "Barrett would not be the man for me."

"Why not?"

"Any number of reasons." Some of which Charlotte would not reveal. "Let's start with the most important one. He's going to marry Miriam."

"But he doesn't love her."

Charlotte dried another plate. "Why do you say that?"

"Because he doesn't look at her the way Warren does when he's looking at me."

Though Charlotte had thought Warren's expression reflected avarice more than love, she had no intention of saying that.

"Be that as it may, they're practically engaged."

"But if they weren't, wouldn't you want to marry Barrett?"

Charlotte sighed as she looked at the stack of pots and pans still to be washed. This ridiculous conversation was going to be a long one.

"No," she said firmly. "He deserves better." Though his apology had been sincere and she believed he was beginning to recognize David as the boy he was, Barrett's future constituents might not be so accepting of a child they considered less than perfect. And then there was the baron. If he was still in Wyoming and if she were being courted by Barrett, he would have a good chance of seeing her and David while Barrett was campaigning. Charlotte couldn't let that happen. She couldn't risk the baron finding her. She seized on a subject that Gwen ought to understand. "I'm not meant to be a senator's wife."

"Nonsense." Waving her soapy hand in the air, Gwen dismissed Charlotte's concerns. "You'd be wonderful. I can picture you at Barrett's side while he's campaigning."

Perhaps. The image wasn't as foreign as Charlotte might have thought. She pictured Mama serving alongside Papa. Theirs had been a partnership as well as a marriage. Perhaps that was what Barrett sought from his marriage. And that brought Charlotte back to her first reason: Miriam, her friend Miriam. She was the future Mrs. Landry.

"He's going to marry Miriam."

Gwen waved her hand again, this time sending soap bubbles floating through the air. "Can you honestly say you're happy about that?"

"Of course I am." Even to Charlotte's ears, the words rang false.

Gwen let out a triumphant crow. "You care for him. I thought you did."

Charlotte shook her head slowly. "He's a friend. Just a friend."

"And cows fly."

9

"How do you know if you're in love?"

As Charlotte's hand moved involuntarily, she almost stabbed Miriam with a pin. A minute ago, Miriam had been speaking of the fire that had consumed the Depot Hotel and her father's disapproval of President Cleveland's newly appointed territorial governor, who was alleged to have engaged in illegal fencing of range lands. Now she wanted to talk about love. That meant Barrett, the man Miriam had described as honorable, contrasting him to Governor Baxter.

Charlotte had agreed. Barrett was honorable. He was also surprisingly humble for a man of his wealth and social standing. Only a humble man would have apologized the way he had, and only a caring man would have taken the time to try to teach David to roll his ball. Charlotte's heart warmed whenever she remembered the tall, handsome cattle rancher who might become a senator sitting on the floor, playing with her son. He'd been more than considerate. She could almost believe he'd been loving. Of course, there were many kinds of love. The one Miriam wanted to discuss was different.

"I'm hardly an expert."

Miriam smiled as she admired her reflection. "You are an expert, and not only at making the most beautiful gowns in Cheyenne. Just now, your eyes softened and your cheeks turned pink, so I know you were remembering a special moment you shared with your husband."

It was cowardly, but Charlotte lowered her head, pretending that Miriam's train needed adjusting. She couldn't let her too perceptive friend guess that the man who had brought about that blush was the same man Miriam planned to marry. "You really should discuss this with your mother."

"There are no discussions with Mama." Miriam let out a sound that in anyone less well bred would have been called a snort. "She gives lectures. In this case, I have no need to ask her, because I know what she'll say." Miriam pursed her lips as she imitated her mother. "Love is for books. What's important is a man's social standing."

Sadly, Charlotte could imagine Mrs. Taggert saying exactly that. "I don't want to contradict your mother, so I'll answer your question with one of my own. How do you feel when you're with him?"

While she waited for Miriam's response, Charlotte draped a length of lace around the neckline of the gown, then shook her head. As she had thought, the dress was more striking without it.

"Alive." Miriam's lips curved into a sweet smile. "That sounds odd, doesn't it? But when I'm with him, I see things I've never seen before. I think I hear birds singing, though I know they've all flown south. Even ordinary food tastes better when he's at the table. If I told Mama that, she'd either laugh or call Dr. Worland, but it's not just my imagination. That's how I feel. Alive."

Charlotte nodded slowly. "You've answered your own question. You're in love."

Heedless of the pins that held her gown together, Miriam twirled around. "Isn't it wonderful?"

It was. For Miriam.

"We'll be back by Thanksgiving Day." Barrett watched as Harrison shivered. With clouds obscuring the sun, the wind penetrated even the heaviest of woven fabrics, finding its way between the fibers, eventually turning the underlying skin red and then dangerously white. That was, Barrett suspected, the reason the Indians wore leather garments. Certainly, it was the reason he had brought two buffalo robes with him. Animal skins were virtually impervious to the weather, making them an essential part of winter in Wyoming.

If he hadn't needed to transport another load of hay, Barrett would not have subjected his brother to a ride in the wagon. Even being on horseback was warmer than sitting virtually motionless in a buggy or carriage. An open wagon was worse, but since the hay was the primary reason for this trip, it was necessary.

"I wouldn't want you to miss Mrs. Melnor's meal," Barrett continued. Perhaps thoughts of hot food would trick them into feeling warmer. "She's planning a feast." There would be four at the table that day. When he'd remembered that neither Richard nor Warren had family in Cheyenne, Barrett had invited them to join him and Harrison. Perhaps he should have included Miriam and her family, but Harrison had mentioned that he planned to return to Pennsylvania before Christmas. Since this might be his only holiday with his brother for some time, Barrett wanted it to be a quiet, relaxing day. He did not want to discuss politics, nor did he want to hear Mrs. Taggert boast that her gowns came from Paris. It spoke volumes about Miriam's determination that she had been able to overrule her mother on at least one subject and continued to frequent Charlotte's shop.

While his thoughts strayed to Cheyenne's most beautiful dressmaker and the child who bore only a slight resemblance to her, Barrett's eyes scanned the horizon, looking for signs of lost or dying cattle. Though it was still early in the season, there was always the danger of losing animals to predators or the weather. The spring calves weren't yet old enough to be left on their own, but sometimes inexperienced cows didn't know that and wandered away. Barrett's lips curved in a smile. Thinking of mothers and babies, even of the bovine variety, led his mind back to Charlotte and her son. Admittedly, it didn't take much to make him think of her. Those thoughts intruded all too often. But, he reflected, intruded was the wrong word. An intrusion was unwelcome. Thoughts of Charlotte were not. Barrett settled back on the wagon seat as he wondered how she planned to celebrate the holiday.

"Too bad you invited Richard and Warren to dinner. I wouldn't mind spending Thanksgiving on the range." Harrison stretched his legs in front of him, flexing his feet within his boots. "That dugout you call a ranch house isn't much, and Dustin could use a lesson or two on cooking, but there's something intriguing about the idea of my little brother with cows. Sorry," he said with an unrepentant grin, "cattle." Harrison rubbed his hands together. "Do you want me to drive the wagon?"

"Sure. You always were good with horses." And though it didn't involve much exertion, the effort of driving might help warm his brother. Days like this, with no sun to warm the thin air, were brutal. Barrett handed the reins to Harrison before sliding to the other side of the wagon.

As he threaded the reins through his fingers, Harrison grinned. "When I was a boy, I thought I'd become a horse breeder."

Barrett stared at the brother he'd thought he'd known. Not once in his thirty years had he heard Harrison mention anything about raising horses. "Why didn't you?"

Keeping his eyes fixed on the road, Harrison shrugged. "It should be obvious. Pa expected me to take over the store. I couldn't disappoint him."

Just as, no matter how restless he'd been, Barrett had not felt free to leave his hometown while his father was alive. All three Landry boys had done their best to meet their parents' expectations. "That's why I stayed in Northwick as long as I did," Barrett admitted. He had remained for the year of mourning, in part because he'd wanted to be certain his brothers didn't need him, but once he was convinced that he wasn't essential to the Landry Mercantile, he'd headed West. "The Bible tells us to honor our parents. I tried."

Unbidden, Barrett found himself thinking about Charlotte, wondering what her parents had been like. They must have been unusually strong people, for they had raised at least two independent women. Most widows would have moved into a sibling's house, but Charlotte had not. Instead, she'd established a successful business in a new town. He didn't know too much about her middle sister, but the youngest one was studying to be a doctor, even though she had to know that being a lady doctor would not be easy. They were definitely not an ordinary family.

"You succeeded." For a second, Barrett wondered what Harrison meant. Then he realized that his brother was responding to

Barrett's statement about honoring their parents. "Ma and Pa were proud of all of us. Even though it's not what Pa planned for you, I think he'd approve of what you're doing here." Harrison grinned as he gestured toward the gently rolling hills. "The snow sure is pretty."

"The cattle don't think so. Snow stands between them and food." Barrett wondered how much his brother wanted to hear. It wasn't as if he had any aspirations of becoming a stock grower, and yet perhaps he'd be interested in understanding another part of Barrett's life. "The dry climate is one of the reasons why cattle ranching is so profitable here. The grass may look like it's dead." He pointed toward a patch of golden brown turf that the herd had uncovered. "It's not. It's cured by the dry air." When Harrison looked skeptical, Barrett continued. "Like meat in a smokehouse. Cured prairie grass doesn't lose nutrients the way grass does back East. That's why it can sustain a herd all winter. The problem is, this past summer was unusually dry, so the grass didn't grow as much as normal."

"Maybe it won't be as much of a problem as you think."

Barrett smiled at Harrison's optimism, but he was not smiling when they reached the ranch house. He'd known something was wrong when Dustin, his foreman, was mending a wagon wheel when they arrived instead of being out on the range. The broken spoke was only the first piece of bad news. Dustin had run a hand through his curly blond hair, leaving a streak of grease on his forehead as he explained that while he'd been riding the range, he'd found ten head of cattle lying on the ground, either dead or so close to it that there had been nothing to do but put them out of their misery.

"The critters were starving." Dustin shoveled beans and corn bread into his mouth as if he feared he would be the next.

For his part, Barrett had lost his appetite. "It's too early," he said, as much to himself as to Harrison and Dustin. "We always have some losses over the winter, but we don't usually see them until late January or into February. Finding them now when it's not even the end of November . . ." He bit off his words.

"What will you do if the deaths continue?" Harrison asked when they'd finished dinner and were sitting by the stove, their boots off and drying, their sock-clad feet as close to the heat as they could manage without burning them.

"You mean if I lose the whole herd?" The thought had been whirling through Barrett's brain faster than snow in a January blizzard. Though it would be an exaggeration to say that all his plans depended on a successful cattle season, the loss of too many cows would mean a poor calf crop. And a poor calf crop . . . That was another sentence Barrett did not want to complete.

Harrison looked as if the possibility surprised him. "I wasn't thinking that many. Could that happen?"

Barrett turned to Dustin, who simply shrugged. Both men knew it was impossible to predict the weather, particularly here.

"It could happen, I suppose." Though Barrett wouldn't lie, he didn't want to alarm Harrison needlessly. "We haven't had a really bad winter since I've been in Wyoming, but the old-timers talk about some rough ones. That's why we brought the hay. I want my cattle going into this winter as healthy as possible."

His brother's expression sobered. "What if it's not enough?" Harrison always had been a worrier.

"Are you asking if I'd be destitute and desperate enough to go back to Northwick?" Though Harrison made no response, something in his expression made Barrett

185

realize he'd considered that possibility. "I doubt that. I haven't sunk everything into the herd," he told Harrison. "I took Pa's advice and built an emergency fund. That would tide me over for a while." Barrett did a quick mental calculation. "It would be enough to restock, but it wouldn't leave much for a political campaign."

"Then I guess we'd better pray this isn't a bad winter."

"Amen to that."

The warmth of Mrs. Kendall's kitchen was a welcome respite after Charlotte's walk in the wind. Even the heavy black hooded cape had not kept the cold from penetrating.

"Won't you have a cup of coffee, ma'am?"

Charlotte shook her head. She'd left the house later than normal this morning because it had taken her all night to complete the last dress. A wise woman would have slept, but Charlotte had been determined that Mrs. Kendall and several of her boarders would have at least one reason to give thanks tomorrow.

"I can't stay," she said as she unwrapped the first parcel, holding up the rust-colored calico dress she'd made for the boarding-house proprietor. Though the other frocks were more of Miriam's hand-me-downs that

Charlotte had reworked, this dress was brand-new. She had chosen the calico specifically for Mrs. Kendall, knowing that the color, although practical enough not to show stains, would flatter her.

"It's beautiful." The older woman smiled. "It'll be perfect for Madeline, once the baby's born."

"It's not for Madeline." Charlotte infused her voice with determination. "This one's for you."

A flush of pleasure rose to Mrs. Kendall's cheeks. "Me?" She touched the rows of pin-tucks that marched up and down the bodice. Though they'd taken hours to complete, even with the sewing machine, Charlotte had not considered eliminating them, for they would add a pleasing fullness to Mrs. Kendall's overly thin body.

"Yes, you. You deserve a new dress too." Sensing that the older woman was on the verge of tears, Charlotte opened the other packages, spreading the dresses on the table as she had the last time. "These are the sizes you asked for."

Her eyes still brimming with tears, Mrs. Kendall nodded. "I don't know how to thank you. The gals who live here ain't never had pretty things like this, and the ones who come for meals . . ." Her voice trailed off, as if in embarrassment. "I'm sorry, ma'am. It ain't proper, talkin' to a lady like you about them."

Charlotte couldn't let the conversation end, not when her curiosity had been aroused. Gwen had said nothing about women who took meals at the boardinghouse but did not live there.

"Where do these other women live?"

Her face now almost as red as the velvet gown Charlotte had made for Miriam, Mrs. Kendall bit her lips. "Next door. At Sylvia's."

The whorehouse. Charlotte flinched, remembering her own disdain for the women who'd sold their bodies to Fort Laramie's soldiers. If it hadn't been for Abigail, she might not have realized how wrong she'd been, condemning women when she had no understanding of what had driven them to such a deplorable profession. She wouldn't repeat that mistake.

"Can they use new dresses?"

Rose was cranky. The normally even-tempered three-year-old had started fussing early in the morning, and by the time Thanksgiving dinner was over, it appeared that a full-fledged tantrum was brewing. Charlotte was certain that was the reason

Mr. Yates, who'd been invited to spend the entire day with them, had pleaded fatigue and returned to his apartment once dessert was served. Even David seemed affected by Rose's pouts and wails.

"She needs a nap." Gwen mouthed the words, rather than upset her daughter further. Naps were not Rose's favorite thing. Soon after David's birthday, she had announced that she was a big girl, and big girls did not take naps. Only babies did.

Charlotte nodded. If the child was catching a cold or the grippe, sleeping would help. But that would happen only if the house was silent. "David and I will go for a walk," she offered. "The fresh air will be good for both of us." It might even help clear her mind. Though she had many reasons to be thankful, concerns still weighed heavily on her. Some days, she felt as if she had an entire shipment of woolens strapped to her back, and nothing she did seemed to lighten the load. Even Mrs. Kendall's delight in her new dress and Mr. Yates's obvious enjoyment of dinner had provided only brief respites from her worries. Though she couldn't explain why, it was easier to solve others' problems than her own.

"Come, David. We need to get you dressed

189

to go outside." Despite a mighty protest when she took the wooden ball from him, his spirits seemed to soar when he felt the scratchy plaid wool of his coat, and he grinned at her. If only everything were so simple. But few things were simple where David was concerned, which was why Charlotte's worries persisted. He wasn't making the progress he should be, and nothing she did was changing that.

David had stood by himself two weeks ago, his legs shaky, his expression betraying fear as well as excitement. He had even taken a single step toward Charlotte before falling on his face, banging his nose against the floor. Charlotte didn't know whether it was the pain of the fall or the fact that his nose had bled. All she knew was that, despite all her encouragement, he refused to try to stand again.

Perhaps Barrett and Gwen were right. Perhaps David did need a special teacher. Charlotte let out a bitter laugh. She was like her son, avoiding pain. David wouldn't try to walk, and she refused to think about letting him go.

David looked up, startled by her laugh. "I'm sorry, David. I didn't mean to frighten you. Come on. We're going for a ride." She scooped him into her arms and carried him down the stairs to the backyard. "Into the wagon now." Once he was seated, she placed his arms on the side rails. "Hold tight."

When she reached the front of the building, Charlotte hesitated. Normally she turned right and headed south, but today something drew her in the opposite direction. The streets were almost deserted, perhaps because it was a holiday, perhaps because the afternoon was colder than normal, even for late November. As David exhaled, Charlotte saw puffs of white emerge from his mouth. An ordinary sight, and yet one he would never experience. She closed her eyes, trying to calm her erratic pulse, wondering if it would always be like this, feeling that her heart was being cut into tiny pieces. She couldn't send David away. She couldn't. That couldn't be the right decision for him.

"We're going by the school now," Charlotte told him as they turned left onto 18th Street. Perhaps it was silly. He would never attend classes here; she was only torturing herself by imagining him entering the doorway, books clasped under his arm, and yet she could not stop praying for a miracle. That's what it would take for David to join the throng of children who climbed those stairs each day. A miracle. Though Papa had told her that miracles happened every day, there had been none of them so far.

As she pulled him past the school, David smiled, then twisted his head to let the sun warm his face when they reached the corner of Ferguson again.

How foolish she had been! Charlotte swallowed deeply. "You're right, David. The sun is shining." Papa had been right too. There were miracles every day, if you took the time to look for them. They might appear insignificant to others. They might not seem like the answer to prayer. But they were real. It was late November. The sun was weak, and yet Charlotte's miracle was sitting in a small wooden wagon, smiling at the warmth of a celestial body he would never see.

Oh, Papa. I wish you were here to see your grandson. You'd love him as I do. But Papa would never hold David, and when Abigail and Elizabeth learned the truth, they might be so angry at all that Charlotte had hidden from them that they might refuse to see her again. That prospect haunted her almost as much as the thought of taking David to a special school and leaving there without him.

"Charlotte."

She turned, startled by the familiar voice calling her name. If there was anyone who could dispel her somber mood, it was Barrett.

"I thought I was the only person outside this afternoon," he said as he reached her side.

Charlotte almost giggled with happiness. This was what she needed, an ordinary conversation with this man. Her friend. "David and I wanted some fresh air. We walked around the block and were trying to decide where to go next. Weren't we, David?" Her son nodded, as if he understood all that she'd said.

"May I join you?"

Charlotte couldn't think of anything she would enjoy more. "Certainly."

Though she kept a grip on the wagon handle, preparing to cross the street, Barrett shook his head. Crouching next to David, he said, "Remember me? I'm Mr. Landry."

A grin split David's face. "Baw."

Barrett's face sported a matching grin as he stood. "That's right. Ball."

Though the sun snuck behind a cloud, Charlotte didn't mind. The day seemed warmer simply because Barrett was here. "That's become David's favorite toy," she explained. "He insists on taking it everywhere, even to bed." She gave her son a fond smile, recalling his earlier protests. "We had a small disagreement when I wouldn't let him bring it outside." Charlotte nodded toward the wagon, hoping Barrett would understand that David needed to grip the sides while she pulled it. "Gwen tells me that tantrums don't start until children are two, but I thought I was going to experience one today."

"You were a good boy, weren't you, David?" Barrett laid his hand on David's shoulder and gave him a light squeeze. To Charlotte's relief, her son giggled. She hadn't been certain how he would react to being touched by someone who was almost a stranger.

"Do you suppose he'd like some c-o-c-o-a?" Barrett's blue eyes sparkled more than the piles of snow that still lined the street.

She nodded, recalling how David had savored the beverage at Mr. Ellis's shop. "David never turns down chocolate in any form. We both enjoyed the candies you gave me, but c-o-c-o-a is a special treat."

"Then I hope I can persuade you to come home with me."

Charlotte raised an eyebrow. As a widow, she had more freedom than many women, but Barrett could not afford to be touched by scandal.

As if he'd read her thoughts, Barrett gave

her a quick smile. "We'll be properly chap-
eroned. All my servants are there, and so is
Harrison."

Charlotte nodded. This was Wyoming.
Life was less formal here. Still, she'd be
causing extra work for Barrett's servants.
Surely they deserved a respite, especially on
a holiday.

She started to refuse when Barrett said,
"You wouldn't want to disappoint my cook,
would you? Just the other day she complained that the house needs children to
bring it to life. Having David there will
make her happy, and her hot chocolate will
make him forget all about tantrums."

Barrett's argument quenched her last
concern. "Mrs. Melnor is very different
from my first cook. She threatened to leave
because she didn't like my puppy." The
instant the words were spoken, Charlotte
realized her mistake. She'd given Barrett
another glimpse into the life she had tried
to keep a secret.

But Barrett did not appear to be troubled
or even curious that Charlotte had once had
a cook. "I don't know how she'd react to a
dog, but Mrs. Melnor likes children. Please
say you'll come."

She couldn't refuse. Visiting Barrett would
mean that she and David would be away

from their house longer, giving Gwen a chance to get Rose to sleep. They would be out of the cold, and David would have a treat. And yet . . .

"Will Mrs. Melnor . . . ?" Charlotte broke off, unwilling to put her thoughts into words. She knew she ought to be used to it by now. She ought to have perfectly phrased questions, but she did not.

Furrows appeared between Barrett's eyes. "If you're asking how my cook will handle David's blindness, I don't know. There's only one way to find out."

"I suppose you're right. I can't hide him forever." Furthermore, she had resolved that she was going to begin to unravel the lies and deception. "I never thought I was a coward, but this last year has proven me wrong."

"You a coward?" Barrett's eyes widened. "Nonsense." He reached for the wagon handle and began to pull it, walking slowly so that David did not bounce on the uneven roadway.

"You wouldn't think it was nonsense if you knew that I haven't told my sisters about David."

Barrett's head swiveled, his expression leaving no doubt that he was surprised. Perhaps shocked. "They don't know you

196

have a son?"

Inside her gloves, Charlotte felt her hands grow moist. Gwen had been adamant in her belief that Charlotte should have told Abigail and Elizabeth the whole story. Barrett, with his belief in total honesty, might condemn her for not having done so.

"They know that much," she said slowly. "What they don't know is that he's blind. I didn't want my sisters rearranging their lives for me, so I didn't tell them." Charlotte sighed. "That decision has come to haunt me, because they're thinking about moving to Cheyenne." Her worries had grown taller than the Rockies when she'd received letters from both sisters two days ago. Abigail had announced that her husband was considering resigning his commission and possibly taking up sheep ranching just outside Cheyenne, while Elizabeth had told Charlotte that she wanted to establish her medical practice in Wyoming and was planning to come to Cheyenne as soon as she finished her studies.

"What are you going to do?"

That question had plagued her ever since she'd opened the envelopes. "I'm not sure. Do you have any advice?"

They had reached the front of Barrett's house. He stopped and fixed his gaze on

Charlotte, nodding as he said, "Honesty. You can't hide David's condition forever. I think you ought to tell your sisters now. That'll give them a chance to get used to the idea before they see him."

"What if they hate me for not telling them earlier?"

Barrett looked down at David, his expression solemn, making Charlotte wonder if he was trying to picture Abigail and Elizabeth's reaction. When he spoke, his voice was firm. "They're your sisters. They won't hate you."

"I wish I were that sure."

10

Mama would be most displeased if she knew where Miriam was headed. That was the reason she had neglected to mention that she was making two stops this morning. As far as her mother knew, Miriam was going to Élan. She was. She planned to select a new dress for Christmas morning as well as give Charlotte half a dozen dresses Mama had declared deplorably out of fashion, but first Miriam intended to visit the library.

Mama would not approve. It was true that Papa's study had one wall lined with books carefully chosen because their bindings matched the room's décor, but to Miriam's knowledge, neither of her parents had ever read for pure pleasure. She, on the other hand, could not imagine a world without books.

Miriam smiled as she climbed the two flights of stairs to the new Laramie County

Library. The location was unpretentious, the third floor of an ordinary building on Ferguson, but the contents were magnificent — all those wonderful books just waiting to be read.

Her smile broadened as she pushed the door open. With a full half hour before Charlotte expected her, she would have plenty of time to choose this week's reading.

"Miriam! I didn't know you came here."

Her heart began to pound. Surely it was only because she was startled by the sight of Richard in the library. Surely it had nothing to do with the fact that those brown eyes seemed to penetrate the shell she'd built and saw inside her to the real Miriam, the one who loved books and music and who had no political aspirations. Surely it was not because she'd started to dream impossible dreams, dreams of a life as Richard's wife.

Miriam placed her index finger over her lips. "You mustn't tell anyone," she said with feigned melodrama. "It's a deep, dark secret." That was only a slight exaggeration.

"What will you give me to keep your secret?" Richard accompanied his question with an exaggerated leer, causing Miriam to giggle. His playful side was one of the things she admired about him. While it was true that he worked as hard as Barrett, he seemed to have more fun, and he certainly wasn't afraid to laugh. Miriam wasn't convinced Barrett knew how.

When the librarian frowned, Richard gestured toward the door. Seconds later, they stood on the landing, trying to control their mirth.

"I love the library," Miriam confessed, "but everyone's so solemn here."

"And reading is fun, or it ought to be."

Miriam nodded. "I didn't realize you were a reader."

Though she expected a joking response, Richard's eyes grew serious, and his voice was intense as he said, "There are many things you don't know about me."

"Tell me one. Then we'll be partners in crime, knowing each other's secrets. And," she added in a conspiratorial tone, "I won't have to pay you to keep mine." Somehow she had to lighten Richard's mood. Perhaps this was the way to do it.

The ploy must have worked, for he waggled an eyebrow at her. "You won't get away that easily. I still demand a reward." His eyes moved slowly from the top of her hat to the tips of her boots, as if he were searching for an appropriate forfeit. When his gaze returned to her lips, lingering there, Miriam felt herself flush. Surely he wouldn't demand a kiss. No gentleman would, and yet her heart beat faster at the very idea. A second later, Richard grinned. "A hat pin. Is your secret worth a hat pin?"

Relieved and yet oddly disappointed, Miriam nodded. Plucking one from the back of her hat, she handed it to him. "Paid in full."

"Indeed." Richard tucked it inside his waistcoat.

Miriam felt her cheeks redden again. She had been reading too many romance novels. That was the only reason to think he had chosen that spot because it was close to his heart. To cover her confusion, she asked, "Who's your favorite author?"

"This week?"

Surely he was joking. No one was that fickle. Though the seasons changed, her fondness for Mr. Dickens's works did not.

Richard nodded. "For me, it varies each week. Last week was Dickens. This week Shelley."

"Shelley? Percy Bysshe Shelley?"

Richard nodded again. "You're surprised, aren't you? I told you there were many things you didn't know about me, including the fact that I admire the Romantic poets."

Miriam searched her memory, trying to

recall a line from one of Shelley's poems. "Ozymandias" was too obvious a choice. Almost everyone knew that one. " 'Power, like a desolating pestilence,/Pollutes whate'er it touches,' " she recited.

Without missing a beat, Richard grinned. " 'And obedience,/Bane of all genius, virtue, freedom, truth,/Makes slaves of men, and of the human frame,/A mechanized automaton.' "

Laughing, Miriam shook her head. "I can't trip you up, can I? I didn't realize anyone memorized 'Queen Mab.' "

"It appears there are at least two people in Cheyenne who have. So tell me, Miss Miriam Who Quotes Shelley, what other poets do you admire?"

And before she knew it, Miriam was late for her appointment.

Barrett was whistling as he flicked the reins. He had another fifteen minutes before he was supposed to be at Miriam's house, and so he was driving slowly, grinning as he thought about Thanksgiving afternoon. Charlotte's worries had been for naught. Mrs. Melnor hadn't batted an eyelash when she saw David but had insisted on serving sugar cookies along with a pot of her famous hot chocolate. "Children like my cookies," she had announced. Though it was always difficult to know what the man who had perfected the art of the expressionless face was thinking, Mr. Bradley had solemnly placed a sheet under David's chair. "Just in case something should spill," he had explained. Drawn from the library by the sound of unfamiliar footsteps, Harrison had joined them in the dining room, claiming that the table was unbalanced with only three people seated at it. And, though he declined the plate of cookies, his brother spent half an hour alternating his attentions between Charlotte and David, demanding to know how a brunette without a spot on her face had produced a redheaded child who would probably wind up with more freckles than Barrett had cows. "Cattle," Harrison corrected himself.

When it became clear that no one would say a word about David's blindness, Charlotte began to glow. It was the only word possible, for her smile and the way it changed her face reminded Barrett of the fires he and his brothers had made before the family replaced their fireplaces with stoves. At first a few flames would flicker around the edges; then as the wood caught, the flames became a blaze. So, too, had Charlotte's happiness grown, suffusing her face with color. When she'd entered the house, her cheeks and the tip of her nose had borne the telltale redness of too much time in a biting wind, but as the chill faded and her worries disappeared, her smile had blossomed, leaving her face with a radiance that owed nothing to the weather.

Barrett smiled as he crossed Central Avenue. It had been a good afternoon for everyone, including David. He had thought it might have been difficult for the child, being assaulted by a barrage of new sounds and smells, but David had adjusted quickly. Apparently the aroma of chocolate convinced him that he'd entered a good place, and he'd crowed "co-co" when Charlotte had directed his hand to the pewter mug. After that, his only sounds had been loud slurps.

"Whoa." Barrett slowed the horses as he approached the Taggert mansion. Thanksgiving afternoon had been one of the most pleasant he could recall. He could only hope that today would be equally enjoyable.

"Miss Taggert awaits you in the drawing room," the formally clad butler announced when he took Barrett's hat and coat. Though the man said nothing more, Barrett was certain that Mrs. Taggert was also waiting for him. It would be unseemly for him and

Miriam to be unchaperoned.

He tried not to frown, thinking of Charlotte's concerns. Though he'd dismissed them at the time, afterward he worried that he'd been wrong, that someone had seen her and David entering his home and that there had been unpleasant speculation. Fortunately, when he'd spoken with Richard this morning, his friend had said nothing. That must mean there had been no repercussions. Barrett hoped that was true, for the last thing he wanted was to cause Charlotte any distress. Her life was difficult enough without him complicating it.

"Good afternoon, Miriam." Knowing that she liked formality, Barrett gave her a small bow, keeping his left hand behind him. "You're looking particularly beautiful today." The pale blue dress highlighted her golden hair, giving her the appearance of the ice princess in the book of fairy tales that had been one of Landry Mercantile's bestselling items each Christmas. Miriam would probably be flattered if he told her that. She would not, however, be pleased to know that her cool smile made him think of Charlotte, and that in contrast to the warmth of Charlotte's smile, Miriam's appeared stingy. This was absurd. Barrett was visiting the woman he planned to marry.

He should not be entertaining thoughts of Charlotte.

"It's always a pleasure to see you, Mrs. Taggert." Hoping his smile appeared genuine, Barrett took a step forward into the room crowded with furniture that Miriam's mother had imported from France.

His expression must have seemed sincere, for she tapped her cheek and gave him a playful smile in return. "You're a flatterer, Barrett, but I like that. A golden tongue will serve you well in politics." She gathered her embroidery and rose from the settee. "I know you and Miriam have matters to discuss. You needn't worry. I won't eavesdrop." Settling herself in a chair in the far corner, Mrs. Taggert bent her head over her sewing. She would be the perfect chaperone, present but not intruding.

When Miriam motioned to the chair directly opposite hers, Barrett brought his left hand forward and handed her the box of candy that he'd kept concealed behind his back. "It's only a trifle, but I thought you might enjoy it."

Surely that was not disappointment he saw in her eyes. A man who was courting had few choices in gifts. Flowers, books, and candy were acceptable, with other items being much riskier. It wasn't the season for flowers in Cheyenne, and to the best of his knowledge, Miriam did not enjoy reading. That left candy.

He must have been mistaken, for Miriam smiled as she untied the box and removed the cover. "Thank you, Barrett." She waited until he was seated, then leaned forward slightly. "You needn't bring gifts, though. I know you're courting me."

Barrett blinked, unsure how to respond. While it was true that he was courting her, it seemed awkward for her to announce it like that. He decided to skirt the issue. "I hope you enjoy Mr. Ellis's confections," Barrett said, pleased when Miriam popped one into her mouth and appeared to be savoring it. "He's making some new flavors for Christmas. He won't tell me what they are, but he promised to save me an assortment." Barrett had actually reserved two boxes, but there was no reason to tell Miriam that he planned to give one to Charlotte and David.

"That's nice." Miriam eyed the chocolates as if considering eating a second piece, then resolutely put the lid back on the box. "The invitations are going out tomorrow, but my parents and I hope you're already planning to attend our Christmas Eve party."

Invitations to the Taggerts' Christmas Eve

gathering were as prized as membership in the Cheyenne Club. Held from eight until eleven, the party was designed to fill the hours before guests left for church. Barrett had known he'd be invited. He also knew that Miriam's parents expected them to announce their engagement no later than Christmas Day. The party would be the perfect time.

"Yes, of course, I'm planning to be there."

From the corner of his eye, Barrett saw Mrs. Taggert nod. She'd been listening more closely than he'd realized. Perhaps that was the reason Miriam lowered her voice as she asked, "Have you read any of Shelley's works?"

What an odd question. They'd been speaking of Christmas. Surely Miriam wasn't hinting that she wanted a book instead of a betrothal ring.

"I can't say as I have," he admitted. "One of our customers ordered a copy of *Frankenstein* but said she didn't care for it. We never got another one."

This time there was no doubt about it. Miriam's eyes reflected disappointment. "Not that Shelley. The other one. Percy. The poet."

Barrett shook his head. "I never had time for reading." Miriam didn't seem to understand how different his life had been from hers. While she had been the pampered daughter of a prosperous newspaperman, he'd been working in a store that barely managed to support his family. And when the mercantile closed for the day, there'd always been chores — chopping wood, pumping water, milking the cow — not to mention repairing the house and outbuildings. Barrett's life had been far from leisurely.

"It's all right. I understand." Miriam darted a glance at her mother. "Mama hopes you'll go to church with us as well."

"It would be my pleasure." If the evening went the way Barrett planned, that would be only the first of many times he attended services with Miriam and her parents, for although it was Miriam he was marrying, there was no doubt that he was allying himself with the entire Taggert family.

Miriam glanced at her mother again. "Mama says we're the perfect couple."

Barrett refused to cringe at the realization that, at least in Miriam's mind, if Mrs. Taggert declared something, it had to be true.

"The red velvet is perfect on you." It wasn't flattery. The sumptuous fabric highlighted Miriam's willowy figure, and the ruby hue brought color to her face.

"I love the style." Miriam stroked the soft fabric. "Once again, you were right." Unlike most evening gowns Charlotte designed, this one had long sleeves and a modest neckline, because Miriam had announced that she intended to wear it to church as well as her parents' annual Christmas Eve party. "I feel like a queen in this dress."

"And you should." Though Miriam had said nothing, several other customers had repeated the speculation that Miriam and Barrett's betrothal would be announced at the Taggerts' party. There was no reason — absolutely no reason — why the thought should cause a lump to settle in the pit of Charlotte's stomach. Miriam deserved a wonderful husband, and Charlotte had no doubt that Barrett would be that kind of husband. When they stood together, they appeared to be the perfect couple. If Charlotte couldn't picture them as man and wife, well . . . that was her problem.

She managed a small smile. "He won't be able to keep his eyes off you when you're wearing this gown."

Miriam's smile broadened. "I hope so. Sometimes I don't think he notices what I'm wearing, but I don't mind — not really. It's so exhilarating being with him and talking about all the things we have in common. He's the only man I know who's comfortable talking about poetry."

That didn't sound like Barrett. Charlotte would have thought he'd be more likely to discuss current events or next spring's calf crop. Those and his hopes for Wyoming's future had been the subjects he'd mentioned while they'd sipped cocoa on Thanksgiving afternoon. It appeared that Barrett was a different man when he was with Miriam. Charlotte's smile faded as she reminded herself that that was natural. A man treated his future wife differently from a mere friend.

"He can even quote Shelley's 'Queen Mab,' " Miriam continued. "Are you familiar with it?"

Charlotte nodded. "It's not my favorite, but I had to memorize it at school."

Her green eyes sparkling with enthusiasm, Miriam asked, "Do you agree with Shelley that obedience makes slaves of men?"

As the lines from the poem reverberated through her brain, Charlotte arranged the small train that fell from Miriam's bustle. "I guess it would depend on the context."

"The Bible tells us to honor our parents, so I try to obey mine. And I know I'm supposed to obey my husband, but . . ." Miriam turned slowly in front of the twin mirrors that Charlotte had placed outside the dressing room, studying her gown from all directions. "I'm confused. I don't want to think that marriage will be like slavery."

"It isn't." Though life with Jeffrey had been far from perfect, Charlotte had never felt enslaved or even trapped. She simply hadn't felt as if Jeffrey loved her the way her father loved her mother. "When you love each other, it's not a matter of obedience or slavery. You respect each other, and so neither of you would do anything to hurt the other."

Mama and Papa had listened to each other; they'd made decisions together. Not once had Charlotte heard Papa claim that Mama should do something simply because it was his wish.

"That's what I was hoping you'd say. Thank you, Charlotte." Miriam's smile was once more radiant. "I don't know what I'd do without you."

"Are you certain you won't stay?" Barrett stamped his feet, trying to warm them while he and Harrison stood at the depot, waiting for the train to arrive. "I had hoped you'd be here for Christmas."

Harrison shook his head. "My feet are

starting to itch."

"Funny, mine are turning to ice."

"That's another reason for me to leave. It's too cold here." When Barrett feigned umbrage, Harrison grinned. "I don't want Camden to get too used to running the store by himself. He and Susan might decide they don't need me."

"If that happens, you can always come back. Maybe raise those horses you were talking about. You wouldn't have to worry about a place to live. You know I've got plenty of room for you."

The distant whistle heralded the approach of the eastbound train. "Maybe now," Harrison said with a rueful expression, "but once you're married, things will change. Your wife may not want a houseguest."

Barrett couldn't believe Harrison was spouting such nonsense. "That's absurd. You'll always be welcome in my house."

"Ah, little brother, you don't understand." Harrison reached for the small suitcase he planned to carry onto the train. "Once you're married, it's her house."

Warren grinned as he slid his arms into his shirtsleeves. Two months ago he would not have thought it possible, but his dreams were coming true. For the first time he had a reason to celebrate. This Thanksgiving had been the first one that he was truly thankful. That was unexpected. But so was Gwen. She would be the perfect wife. She wasn't beautiful, but he was old enough to know that beauty was overrated. What Gwen possessed was far more valuable than physical beauty. She had what his mother would have called class. She was well-mannered, soft-spoken, and never felt the need to draw attention to herself.

Warren fastened the last button before reaching for his collar. When they were married, he hoped Gwen would want to tie his cravat and nudge his collar points until they were perfectly aligned. He'd seen his mother perform those tasks for his father until the day Pa died. Warren didn't know whether that was part of every marriage. All he knew was that the thought of Gwen standing so close to him, her fingers perhaps grazing his cheeks as she arranged the cravat, was surprisingly appealing.

She wasn't like Sylvia's girls. Gwen was an extraordinary woman. More than that, she was a lady. The men who made the decisions about membership in the club would see that. They'd be impressed, just as Gwen was obviously impressed with him. Love — if that was what he felt — was meant to be

215

reciprocated. She did. Equally important, Gwen didn't feel the need to ask too many questions. She seemed content with the information he gave her and didn't probe too deeply. Unlike his former partner, Gwen was not nosy. The other woman . . .

Warren scowled as he remembered the last time he'd seen the woman who'd been his partner for half a dozen years. Though he had told her very little, somehow she had learned — or deduced — too much about him, leaving him no choice but to kill her. He'd seen her shock during her last moment, when she'd realized what was about to happen, and he knew she was remembering his vow never to kill a woman. He hadn't. Until that night. But there had been no alternative. He couldn't risk anyone connecting Warren Duncan with the man who'd masterminded a string of successful stagecoach robberies. That was why the woman who had been the sole occupant of Fort Laramie's guardhouse that night had had to die.

Gwen wouldn't ask questions. She wouldn't poke and pry. She'd believe him if he told her he had to meet with a client one or two evenings a month. She'd never realize that there was no client and that he was going to Sylvia's.

Gwen would be perfect. All he needed was Big Nose's money so that he could build a house. A big house. One to rival Joseph Carey's. Once construction was started, the Cheyenne Club would realize that Warren Duncan was a man they wanted as a member. But that took more money than he had. The question was, where was it? Only one person knew, and she had disappeared.

Warren walked to the window and stared at the street. Where was the Widow Crowley? Folks at the fort had claimed she'd taken her child back to Vermont. Though the story sounded plausible, it was a lie. Warren had sent a messenger east to find her, but no one in Wesley, Vermont, had seen Charlotte Crowley since her marriage. The town was still buzzing with the news that her sister had married a soldier. As if Warren cared. He didn't. Not a whit. All he cared about was finding Jeffrey Crowley's widow and all that money.

Where was she? As he watched two men striding down Eddy Street, their brisk pace telling him they were late for something, Warren scowled again. There was no point in staring out the window. Widow Crowley wasn't in Cheyenne or anywhere in Wyoming Territory, for that matter. Everyone knew that the gold Big Nose had taken from that stagecoach amounted to a fortune. With that much money, she could be living anywhere — Paris, London, New York. It was no wonder she hadn't returned to a backwater town in Vermont. Widow Crowley was living the life of luxury somewhere. He would find out where.

That money was supposed to be his.

11

It was surprising how empty the house seemed. Barrett walked briskly down Ferguson Street, thankful to be out of the place that now seemed as quiet as the empty prairie. Harrison had been in Cheyenne less than two months, but that had been long enough for Barrett to become accustomed to his brother's company. Now that he was gone, Barrett's days seemed longer than normal, his meals endless. Hoping to banish the unexpected loneliness, he had ridden to the ranch. At least there the news had been good. Not only had Dustin not found any more dead steers, but the snow had melted, and, thanks in part to the hay he and Harrison had brought to the ranch, the cattle once again had easy grazing. It was surely Barrett's imagination that they appeared a bit thinner than last year, for Dustin claimed they were as heavy as ever.

He ought to be happy, Barrett told himself

as he approached his destination. Christmas, always one of his favorite times of the year, was less than a month away. That was the reason he was visiting Mullen's jewelry store.

"Good afternoon, Mr. Landry," the proprietor said as Barrett entered the shop. Of medium height and weight, with medium brown hair and eyes, the man could have blended into any crowd without notice were it not for his moustache. Thicker than normal, it was waxed into elaborate curls that extended several inches past his cheeks. "Can I show you something today?"

Barrett approached the main counter and pointed to a display of rings. "I'd like a ring for a lady."

Mr. Mullen nodded as he fingered one end of his moustache. "Did you have a specific type of ring in mind?"

"Betrothal." Was it his imagination again, or did his voice sound strained? Even though Harrison claimed it was normal and that even normally unflappable Camden had been nervous when he'd asked Susan to marry him, Barrett disliked the feeling that he was entering an unknown world.

"Very good. We have some fine ones." Mr. Mullen opened a drawer, then looked up at Barrett. "Were you looking for a diamond or colored stones?"

This was definitely a new world. Barrett couldn't recall whether his mother's rings had any stones at all, and he hadn't thought to ask Harrison what type Camden had given Susan. He shrugged. "I'm not certain. Why don't you show me what you have?"

The jeweler nodded and placed a tray of rings in front of Barrett. "Any one of these would please a lady."

The assortment was more extensive than Barrett had expected, with stones in every color of the rainbow. Though he admired the rubies, sapphires, and emeralds, his eye was drawn to one that reminded him of a flower. Six petals of an unusual milky color surrounded a central diamond.

"Those stones are opals," Mr. Mullen said when he saw the direction of Barrett's gaze. "Came all the way from Australia." He withdrew the ring from the case and handed it to Barrett. "Hold it to the light."

When Barrett did, he discovered that the opals were not the simple color he had thought. Instead, they shimmered with sparks of red and gold and green. As he turned the ring, each new angle revealed a different combination of colors. He took a deep breath as he stared at the most beautiful piece of jewelry he'd ever seen. This ring had depths he'd never imagined possible.

"You've chosen well, Mr. Landry. This is my finest ring. Any lady would be proud to have it on her finger."

Not just any lady. Unbidden, the image of Charlotte's face floated before him. This was the perfect ring for her, a woman with depths as great as the opals, a woman who sparkled like the diamond, a woman whose beauty would complement the ring's magnificence. This was Charlotte's ring, but he wasn't buying a ring for her.

Reluctantly, Barrett handed the opal back to the jeweler. "I think a diamond would be better. A large one."

Trying to mask his disappointment, Mr. Mullen placed the opal ring back on the colored stone tray and pulled out one that contained only diamonds. "These are all fine rings too," he said.

And they were. Though none could compare to the beauty of the opal, these were rings Barrett could imagine Miriam wearing. He chose one with a large oval stone in a simple setting. Miriam would like the fact that the stone was a little different from her mother's round one, and she would probably be pleased that it was larger. Yes, this was the ring for Miriam.

As the jeweler searched for a box, Barrett

wandered around the shop, looking at the displays in the other cases. Though he had no intention of buying a second piece of jewelry, when he saw a gold filigree bracelet, he stopped and gave it another look. "I'll take this too," he told Mr. Mullen.

The man twirled the end of his moustache. "Your lady will be very happy."

"I hope so."

He ought to be happy, Barrett told himself as he headed home. He'd found a ring for Miriam. Her father had already blessed their courtship. All Barrett had to do was ask her to marry him. He'd do that. Soon. And then they'd begin planning their life together. The prospect ought to fill him with happiness or at least anticipation. But it did not. He felt as empty as he had when he'd left home.

Though his house was on the east side of the street, Barrett crossed to the west when he reached 17th Street. It was a ritual he'd begun the day he met Charlotte. Whenever he traveled that block of Ferguson, he walked next to her store, looking at the display in the plate-glass window. Sometimes he would see her, and he'd wave. Those were the good days. Other times, though the store was open, there was no sign of Charlotte, and he guessed she was in her workroom, putting her Singer sewing machine through its paces the way he did his horses. Those days, he was aware of a sense of disappointment.

Barrett looked ahead, trying to see whether the store was open, and as he did, he saw Charlotte locking the door. By the time he reached her, she had begun to climb the stairs to her apartment.

"Charlotte!" he called in greeting. "I'm surprised you're not still in the store."

She turned, nodding slightly at the yards of fabric in her arms. "I need to finish three gowns tonight, so I closed the store to work."

Barrett recalled her saying that, even though she had a workroom in the store itself, she found that she completed handwork more quickly when she was in her apartment. It made no sense to him, for he knew that David would interrupt, but Barrett suspected Charlotte preferred the interruptions to worries about what her son was doing.

From the first time he'd seen her with David, Barrett had wondered about her decision to open a dressmaking shop. While there was no doubt that she was talented, he didn't understand why Charlotte hadn't taken the path most widows would have: a second marriage. If she'd remarried, she would not have had to open the store, and she would have been able to spend all her time with David. A woman as beautiful as Charlotte should have had her choice of husbands, particularly here in Wyoming Territory, where men far outnumbered women and widows often remarried well before their year of mourning was completed, sometimes mere days after their first husband's death. The only reason Barrett could imagine that Charlotte was still unmarried was that the men were unwilling to consider a widow with a blind child. Stupid men!

When he realized that he'd clenched his fists in anger, Barrett straightened them. Inclining his head toward her sewing, he said, "I understand. You don't need any additional interruptions. It's just . . . I thought I'd stop by to see how David is doing." *And his mother.* Though thoughts of Charlotte were never distant, Barrett had been able to think of little else since he'd left Mr. Mullen's shop. He didn't need to close his eyes to picture himself sliding the opal ring onto her slender finger, nor was it difficult to imagine her smile of pleasure.

As he watched, Charlotte smiled, and for a second Barrett wondered if she'd read his thoughts. She must not have, for her words

225

were matter-of-fact. "You're welcome to come in. I can't promise I'll be much company, but David will enjoy your visit."

When they reached the landing, Barrett opened the door. Flashing him a smile of thanks, Charlotte hurried into the apartment, her eagerness to see her son almost palpable. "David, I'm home," Charlotte called as she laid the fabric on the table. A cry of delight was accompanied by the sound of knees slapping the floor as David scurried toward her, crawling faster than Barrett knew a child could. On the opposite side of the room, Gwen smiled a greeting while Charlotte scooped her son into her arms and hugged him.

"You're a lucky boy, David. Mr. Landry has come to visit you," Charlotte said as she tousled his hair.

Though David had raised his face to Charlotte's for a kiss, he began to struggle, clearly signaling that he no longer wanted to be held. "Baw!" he cried.

Charlotte gave Barrett a rueful smile. "I told you it was his favorite toy," she said as she placed her son back on the floor. "That appears to mean that you're now his favorite person. He used to let me hold him for a lot longer than this."

"Perhaps he knows you need to work."

"Perhaps." Charlotte's grin said otherwise. "But I won't complain, because I do need to sew." She gathered the crimson gown and a pile of lace from the table and settled onto the settee in the parlor area. "Where's Rose?" she asked Gwen.

"Napping. I didn't think it was possible, but playing with David wore her out today."

Even if getting worn-out would be Barrett's fate as well, it was a small price to pay for spending time with Charlotte.

Gwen rose and moved toward the door to what Barrett surmised was the front bedroom. "I'll keep Rose occupied if she wakens. That way she won't bother you."

"Rose is no bother."

Gwen's lips twisted into a smile at Charlotte's words. "Barrett's not used to one child, much less two. We don't want to scare him away." Softly, she closed the door behind her, leaving Barrett alone with Charlotte and her son.

David sat at his feet, the ball clutched to his chest. "I see you have your ball, David. Are you going to roll it to me?"

When David tightened his grip on the toy, Charlotte shook her head. "He still won't do that. I think he's afraid of losing it."

Closing his eyes for a second, Barrett tried to imagine what it must feel like for David, releasing his toy, not knowing where it was going. It could be scary, and yet he was missing so much by not playing with it. There had to be a way to show him that rolling the ball was fun.

Apparently convinced that no one would take his toy, David shifted the ball from one hand to the other, seemingly content to play by himself. Barrett turned his attention back to Charlotte, who was attaching lace to some part of the crimson dress. "Business must be good."

She nodded without looking up from the tiny stitches she was taking. "I have twice as many orders as last month. If this continues, I may have to hire another assistant, especially if I start making bridal gowns." She knotted the thread, then clipped it close to the lace. "Bridal gowns require considerably more time than ordinary dresses."

"The customers are probably fussier too." Though Barrett doubted that Miriam would be demanding, he was certain that her mother would insist on being involved. Barrett could imagine Mrs. Taggert changing her mind about the position of a piece of lace a dozen times before she was satisfied that it was absolutely perfect.

Her face reflecting mock horror, Charlotte looked at Barrett. "I hadn't considered that.

I should probably charge twice as much as normal."

"Somehow I can't picture you doing that."

"Probably not. It would seem like stealing."

"Baw!" Apparently bored by the adult conversation, David banged his toy on the floor.

"I think your son is reminding me that I'm supposed to be playing with him." Barrett grinned as he settled on the floor, stretching his legs out to the side. "All right, David. I'm here." He touched the boy's thigh so he could realize how close Barrett was. "Roll the ball to me."

"No!"

Charlotte chuckled. "You've discovered his favorite new word."

Undaunted, Barrett leaned closer to David. "Yes, David. Yes." He emphasized the word. "Balls are meant to be rolled. Please give it to me." His reluctance evident, David handed the ball to Barrett. "Now I'm going to roll it to you." Barrett scooted back a few feet so the ball had a chance to gain momentum. "Hold out your hands. No, put them on the floor." When David was properly positioned, Barrett sent the ball toward him. The boy caught it and giggled. "Good job, David. Now it's your turn. Roll it back to me." But the child would not. Once again he clutched it to his chest.

"I'm afraid my son is a little stubborn," Charlotte said, her voice tinged with amusement.

"He must have inherited that from his father." As he pronounced the word, Barrett realized that Charlotte had never spoken of her husband. Surely most widows referred to them occasionally. Gwen did. Barrett had overheard her telling Warren the story of their first meeting and how her husband had been stationed at Fort D.A. Russell until he died of influenza. But, though he'd spent considerably more time with Charlotte than with Gwen, Barrett knew nothing about the man she had married, not even his name.

Before he could ask, Charlotte shook her head. "I wouldn't be so quick to blame David's father. My sisters claim I'm stubborn."

Her sisters. That reminded Barrett of another conversation. "Have you told them about David yet?"

Charlotte's fingers flew as they wielded the needle. "I thought I'd wait until after the holidays. I know it's cowardly of me, but I don't want any unpleasantness now. I just want everyone to be happy."

"I understand." That was Charlotte, always thinking of others. Undoubtedly her life would have been easier if she had told her sisters that David was blind when she'd first learned of his condition, and yet she had not, because she hadn't wanted to distress them. "Don't wait too long, though. My experience is that delays only make it worse."

What a hypocrite he was! If he had taken his own advice, he would not be waiting until Christmas to give Miriam a ring. Everyone expected the betrothal. Now that he'd chosen the ring, he should have gone directly to Miriam's house and asked her to become his wife. Instead, he was sitting on the floor in a small apartment, trying to teach a blind child to roll a ball.

Charlotte chuckled, and as she did Barrett's heart began to pound. It was probably an ordinary chuckle, but somehow it seemed so intimate that he wanted nothing more than to hear it again.

"You sound like my father." A smile colored Charlotte's words. "He was a firm believer in not procrastinating."

Barrett raised an eyebrow, encouraging her to continue. He'd wanted to learn about her husband, but he'd take any glimpses he could get into what had made her the extraordinary woman she was. "Was he a teacher too?"

"No, a minister." Charlotte blinked, as if surprised that she'd said that. It was an unexpected reaction, and yet there was little about Charlotte that was predictable. Though she was forthcoming, even outspoken, on many subjects, she was uncommonly reticent about herself.

"Was the church in Vermont?"

Charlotte nodded. "Churches." She emphasized the plural. "We moved frequently."

"No wonder you weren't afraid to come to Wyoming Territory. You must have inherited your father's love for travel."

Biting her lip, Charlotte shook her head. "It wasn't that he loved moving," she admitted. "His ideas were sometimes too modern for the parishioners, and the church elders would ask him to leave. I hated being uprooted."

Which might explain why she had remained in Wyoming after her husband's death.

"What brought you and your husband out here?" he asked. "Was he stationed at D.A. Russell with Rose's husband?"

Keeping her eyes on her sewing, Charlotte shook her head again. "His family were farmers."

Though many had come to Wyoming Territory as part of the military or to build the railroad, others had been lured west by the Homestead Act. It was a difficult life, battling the harsh weather, and while Barrett couldn't picture Charlotte — perfectly coiffed Charlotte with her elegant gowns — as a farmer's wife, there was no reason to think she was lying.

"I don't know how I'm going to finish all this in time," she said as she resumed her sewing. The hint couldn't have been clearer: subject closed.

"I'll try to be quiet," Barrett said and turned his attention back to her son. Though Charlotte had not said a great deal, she'd given him new insights. An image of the opal ring flashed into his brain, reminding Barrett of the way light revealed its inner fire. He'd been right when he'd thought it the perfect ring for Charlotte. If he could give it to her. But he could not. That would be not only unseemly but downright scandalous. He could give Charlotte nothing more than trinkets and small gifts for her son.

"All right, David. What would you like to do?"

A grin on his face, David began to crawl toward the other side of the room.

"He wants you to chase him." Charlotte interpreted her son's activity. "I think he enjoys the sound of our footsteps."

Barrett rose and began to stalk across the floor, making his footsteps heavier than necessary, and as he did, David peered over his shoulder, grinning with obvious delight. "That's it!"

"That's what?" The lines that formed between Charlotte's brows told Barrett she was perplexed.

"You'll see." If he was right — and he thought he was — her simple words had unlocked the key to teaching David to roll a ball. "Does he have any wooden blocks?"

Though her expression still registered confusion, Charlotte nodded and gestured toward a small crate. "They're in the box."

Excellent. Barrett retrieved a dozen blocks, arranging them in a row three feet from where David had been sitting. "I'll chase you once," he told the boy, "but if I catch you, we're going to play my game. Okay?"

David scuttled into the kitchen. Barrett let him almost reach the stove before he strode across the floor and swept him into his arms. "My turn." While David squealed with pleasure, Barrett carried him back to the parlor and placed him on the floor in front of the settee. Though the child couldn't see them, the blocks were arranged directly in front of him. After retrieving the ball that David had abandoned when he began to play chase, Barrett handed it to him. "Now, you give it back to me. Just for a minute."

"No!"

"Please, David. This will be fun."

His reluctance evident, the boy handed his toy to Barrett. "Baw."

"The game we're going to learn is called bowling. We're going to bowl. Can you say that, David?"

"Bowl." To Barrett's surprise, the youngster's pronunciation was perfect. When Barrett looked at Charlotte, she mimicked eating. No wonder David knew the word. It was one his mother would have used every day as she taught him to eat.

"That's right. Now, listen." Barrett laid the ball on the floor in front of David, guiding the boy's hands to it, placing his own over David's. "We're going to roll it." Barrett aimed the ball and gave it a firm push before pulling David's hands away. "Listen," he said. As the ball gained momentum, the sound of it rolling across the floor changed, and then it happened. The ball hit the middle blocks, toppling them over in a loud crash.

For a second, David's face mirrored

puzzlement. Then he laughed. "Bowl!" He tipped his head to one side, considering the direction of the sound he'd heard. An instant later, he was crawling toward the blocks. Reaching out, he touched them, and as he did, Barrett could see comprehension dawning. David laughed again. "Bowl," he announced.

And they did. Again and again. Though David was too young to learn to arrange the blocks, he soon released the ball without Barrett's hands guiding him. And through it all, he laughed.

"I think you've created a monster." Charlotte had laid her sewing aside and watched the process of her son learning to bowl. "Now he'll want to play that all day."

If she expected Barrett to be repentant, she was mistaken. "Look at how much fun he's having."

Her face softened. "I know, and it's wonderful. Thank you, Barrett. *You're* wonderful."

Barrett felt his heart swell until it threatened to break through his chest. Perhaps this was the way those medieval knights felt when they scaled walls or slayed dragons or whatever it was they were supposed to do. Charlotte was no damsel in distress, waiting for him to rescue her, but her smile made him feel as if he were some kind of hero. That felt good. Very, very good.

"Where were you?"

Charlotte gasped as Gwen's hiss filled the kitchen. Perhaps it had been too much to expect that Gwen would not discover her early morning forays to 15th Street, but Charlotte had clung to the hope that she wouldn't have to explain why she disguised herself in widow's weeds and snuck out of the apartment. With a small smile, she switched on the light and waited for the reaction.

It wasn't long in coming. "You're wearing mourning clothes." Gwen frowned at the heavy black veil that covered Charlotte's face. "Charlotte Harding, what on earth have you been doing?"

"Let me make some coffee, and then I'll explain."

Gwen pushed back her chair. "I'll make the coffee. You'd better change out of those clothes. I know you won't wear them to the shop."

Minutes later, Charlotte returned to the kitchen, clad in a simple navy dress. "Why were you waiting in the dark?" she asked as she wrapped her hands around the cup of coffee, letting the warmth penetrate her still chilled fingers.

Gwen shrugged as if the answer should be evident. "I didn't want Rose to know anyone was awake. She had a nightmare last night, and I'd just gotten her back to sleep when I heard the outside door close. I thought we had an intruder, but it turned out to be you leaving. So, where did you go?"

"Mrs. Kendall's."

Gwen's eyes widened. "You went to 15th Street in the middle of the night?"

Nothing would be gained by pointing out that it was actually early morning. "When you talked about living there, you made it seem that that was the safest time, and it has been. I haven't seen anyone unsavory."

Though Charlotte hadn't thought it possible, Gwen's eyes widened further. "You've been there before." She no longer phrased her words as questions.

"This was my third trip. I've been making clothes for Mrs. Kendall and her boarders."

"Oh, Charlotte, that's wonderful." Gwen's disapproval evaporated as quickly as snow on a spring morning. "But why didn't you ask me to deliver them during the day? I'm not afraid of that area."

Charlotte shook her head. "I know you would have helped, but it was something I had to do myself." There was no reason to tell Gwen how good it made her feel to know that she'd accomplished that on her own, that no one had protected her as she'd walked to the seediest part of the city. Instead, she simply said, "My parents taught us that it was important to see where our gifts were going. It wasn't enough to send money. They wanted us to be involved in the actual giving. Whenever she heard of a family that needed food, Mama would leave a basket on their front porch so it would be waiting when they awoke."

"And no one knew who left the baskets?" When Charlotte shook her head, Gwen nodded slowly. "That's why you wore the veil."

"That and the fact that I didn't want anyone to know it was Madame Charlotte who had made those dresses. If my customers learned that I was providing clothes for Mrs. Kendall's boarders, they would be upset. They like to think they're buying exclusive creations and that only the wealthiest of women can afford something I've sewn." Charlotte took another sip of coffee. "I couldn't simply leave the dresses on the doorstep, because I had to know what other sizes Mrs. Kendall needed, but I wanted to be as anonymous as I could. And," Charlotte continued, "it seemed safer to be dressed as a widow. It's not just that the veil covers my face, but I also thought that if there were people out, they'd be unlikely to accost a widow."

Gwen refilled Charlotte's cup. "When I realized you were gone, all kinds of crazy thoughts went through my mind, but I never imagined something like this. What you're doing is wonderful. What I don't understand is why you didn't tell me."

"I should have." Just as she should have told Barrett the truth about Jeffrey.

" 'And it came to pass in those days, that there went out a decree from Caesar Augustus, that all the world should be taxed.' "

While the wind howled outside, blowing the light snow that had fallen earlier, Barrett settled back in the pew. Surely he could relax as the minister read the familiar passage from St. Luke. Though Barrett had heard the story so often that he had memorized it, it never failed to move him, and yet tonight he found himself preoccupied with thoughts of what would happen when the service ended. Another gift. A diamond ring could in no way compare to the gift of the Son of God, and yet the moment it was on Miriam's finger, Barrett's life would be changed forever.

The changes had already begun. For the first time, he had come to church with the Taggert family. For the first time, he was seated with them in the second pew. For the first time, he was sharing a hymnal with Miriam. Though their betrothal was not yet official, his presence in this particular pew was tantamount to an announcement. It should have come earlier today. Barrett had seen Mrs. Taggert's disapproval when he'd escorted Miriam to dinner and there had been no ring on her finger. She had obviously hoped that her daughter's engagement would be the highlight of the evening. It should have been. Barrett had the ring. He'd rehearsed the words he'd use to ask Miriam to join her life with his. But when the moment he had chosen came, he found he could not pronounce the words. Tonight was Christmas Eve. This was a time that should be spent in contemplation of the greatest gift the world had ever received, not in celebration of an earthly event. And so Mr. Mullen's box would remain in Barrett's pocket. When the service was over, he and Miriam would ride back to her parents' home for a midnight supper, and before they reached the Taggert mansion, Barrett would give Miriam her Christmas gift.

" 'And she brought forth her firstborn son, and wrapped him in swaddling clothes, and laid him in a manger; because there was no room for them in the inn.' " The minister continued reading.

Barrett closed his eyes for a second, trying to imagine the scene in that stable so many years ago. A newborn child, clasped in his mother's arms. Though St. Luke said no more, Barrett imagined Mary had been filled with wonder. Was that how every new mother felt? Was that what Charlotte had felt the first time she cradled David in her arms?

Compelled by an instinct he could not ignore, Barrett opened his eyes and glanced behind him. The church was filled, every seat occupied, and yet he saw her. She sat in the last pew, her son in her arms, an expression of pure joy on her face. And in that instant, Barrett knew what he must do.

12

"Merry Christmas, Mr. Duncan, ma'am. Your table is ready."

Warren looked down at the woman whose grip on his arm tightened as they followed the formally dressed man into the dining room of the InterOcean Hotel. She had done something different to her hair — it seemed fancier than normal — and she was wearing a blue dress that rustled softly as she walked. To the maître d'hôtel, she probably looked like every other woman who dined here, well-groomed and confident, but Gwen wasn't like those other women. She was different. The way she clutched his arm proved that. Though Gwen had no way of knowing it, that involuntary gesture touched a chord deep inside Warren, for it told him that no matter how calm she tried to appear, she was nervous. And that aroused his protective instincts.

He hadn't expected that. Truth be told, he

hadn't wanted it. The last woman he'd tried to protect was Ma, but that meddling doc claimed Warren didn't know what she needed, that she'd become dangerous to herself as well as to others. Warren took a deep breath, pushing aside the memories of the last time he'd seen his mother. Ma was gone; Gwen was here. Pretty, nervous Gwen. He'd chosen her because she was perfect for his plans, but she had soon become more than a means to an end. Now she was his Gwen, and he'd do whatever was necessary to make her happy. He hoped that once she overcame her nervousness, being here today would accomplish that.

Seen from Gwen's view, the dining room must appear impressive, with its dark paneling, snowy white tablecloths, and the clink of silver on fine china. Warren had always enjoyed eating here. The food was predictably excellent. Some folks claimed it was the best in Cheyenne, which was the reason he'd brought Gwen here. She deserved the best. The only thing wrong with the Inter-Ocean was that anyone could eat here. Anyone with enough money, that is. As a public hotel, it wasn't exclusive the way the Cheyenne Club was. But if Warren played his cards right, next Christmas he and Gwen would be dining there.

When the maître d'hôtel had seated them and handed them their menus, Warren leaned across the table to place his hand on Gwen's. It might be too familiar a gesture for a public place, but he could see that she was still trembling, and he needed to reassure her. "Having you with me is making this the best Christmas I can recall."

That sweet smile that tantalized his senses softened her face. "It's very special for me too. I always wondered what this room looked like."

"You've never been here before?" Though he'd suspected that she hadn't eaten here, Warren knew that many people would wander into the hotel, merely to say that they'd been inside.

She shook her head. "My husband was a corporal. Even before Rose arrived, his pay barely covered our food and housing. Afterwards . . ." She let her voice trail off. "There was nothing left for luxuries."

And if anyone deserved luxuries, it was Gwen. As the waiter approached to take their orders, Warren withdrew his hand, clenching it as he laid it in his lap. The money had been important before. Now it was vital. He had to find it, for it was the only way he could shower Gwen with the expensive clothing, furs, and jewels that should have been her birthright.

When they'd placed their orders, he leaned forward, keeping his voice pitched low enough that no one would overhear. "You may not have had a lot of money, but I envy you."

Warren saw the shock in her eyes as his words registered. "Why would a successful man like you envy me? You have everything."

That was what most people thought. Indeed, it was what he wanted them to think. The truth was different.

"You have a family," he said simply. "I'm fifty-one years old, and right now my life feels empty. I want a home that's more than a few rented rooms. I want a wife and at least one child." He paused, smiling as he said, "A daughter would be nice. I want . . ." *You.* But he couldn't say that. Not yet. It was too early. And so he turned the tables. "What are your dreams, Gwen?"

She was silent for a moment. "Probably simpler than yours. I don't mind rented rooms for myself, but I want more for Rose. I wish I could give her a house outside the city with lots of space so she could have at least one pony."

Warren tried not to frown. He'd planned to build his mansion on 17th Street, a block or two east of the club. That was the perfect location for him, but it appeared that it would not be perfect for Gwen. He thought quickly, then smiled. There was no reason why he couldn't have two homes. They'd live in the city during the week and spend Saturday and Sunday on the ranch.

Warren nodded briskly as he reached for his water goblet. "Rose should have all that." He took a long swallow, keeping his eyes focused on Gwen. Her hands no longer trembled, and she'd lost that scared rabbit look. It appeared that she was finally relaxing.

"Do you have any other dreams?"

For a second, he thought she would shake her head. Instead, she started to nod. "I would like . . ." She hesitated, color staining her cheeks. Warren hadn't known that women her age still blushed, but once again the simple reaction aroused his protective instincts.

"A father for Rose?" he suggested.

She nodded.

"It's a good dream. Rose deserves a father, and you deserve a husband who'll cherish you." As he spoke, Gwen's blush deepened, leaving her face almost cherry red. His own pulse began to race as he considered the reason for her blushes. This woman cared for him.

Warren stretched his hand out, covering hers with his. "In only a week, the new year will begin. I've never put much stock in fortune-tellers, but if I were one, I'd predict that 1887 will be the year our dreams come true."

Gwen smiled and turned her hand over so that he could clasp it. "I hope you're right."

He would be.

Charlotte sipped a cup of tea while she watched David and Rose playing. Though Rose was entranced with the wooden top Mr. Yates had given her for Christmas, David's favorite toy remained his ball. He was rarely more than a few feet from it and continued to insist on carrying it to bed.

"Look, David." Rose put his hand on the top so he could feel it moving. "Spin."

Rose was so excited by their neighbor's gift that she hadn't protested when Gwen left to dine with Warren at the InterOcean, wearing the midnight blue gown that Charlotte had altered by adding a lace fichu to make it more suitable for dinner at the hotel. Gwen's invitation was the reason she and Charlotte had held their Christmas dinner yesterday. Though he'd protested that he didn't mind being alone, Charlotte had been adamant that Mr. Yates join them for both dinner yesterday and breakfast and an exchange of gifts this morning. Now he and Gwen were gone, leaving Charlotte to entertain the children.

She took another sip of tea as Rose spun the top again. Though she'd probably lose interest soon, for the time being, Rose was having fun. Charlotte hoped Gwen was too. She'd been flushed with pleasure this morning as she'd donned the gown and the matching gloves that had been one of Charlotte's Christmas gifts to her and had declared that she would be the best-dressed woman in Cheyenne. Charlotte sighed. It took so little to please Gwen, and yet she couldn't help worrying about her friend, for she feared that in some ways Gwen was still innocent. She saw the best in everyone, whereas Charlotte was more realistic.

"Baw." Apparently tired of playing with Rose's top, David scrambled across the floor, searching for his toy.

"No, David! Play with me!" Rose shrieked her protest.

Five minutes later, after she'd convinced Rose that her doll would like to watch her spin the top, Charlotte drank the last of her now-cold tea.

She hoped — oh, how she hoped — that Warren wasn't trifling with Gwen's affections. There was no doubt that Gwen was infatuated, perhaps even in love, with the older attorney. Gwen believed he was the man she'd been searching for ever since Mike died, the one who would be a good father to Rose. Though Charlotte wished that were true, she couldn't dismiss her concerns. She was unable to pinpoint the reason, but the fear that Warren was more like Jeffrey than Gwen realized niggled at her.

Perhaps that was why, though the sun was shining, making yesterday's snow glisten like diamonds, Charlotte was unable to chase away her doldrums. It was surely that and not the fact that Barrett and Miriam's betrothal was official. Charlotte had seen them sitting together at church last night. That might mean that the announcement had been made at the Taggerts' party beforehand, but even if Miriam hadn't received her ring until Christmas Day, by now her parents would have begun to tell friends, and soon, perhaps even Monday, Miriam would ask Charlotte to design her wedding gown.

She would do it, of course, and not simply because an order for a new, elaborate gown and a full trousseau would be good for her business. She would do it because Miriam was more than a customer; she was a friend. And that friend was in love.

Charlotte knew she ought to be happy about Miriam's engagement, and yet she wasn't. Just as she worried about Gwen, she worried about her other friends, Miriam and Barrett. They were both wonderful people, but try though she might, Charlotte could not picture them together. That was absurd! They were adults. They knew what they wanted, and they wanted each other. It was only Charlotte's imagination that they would be happier with someone else.

She frowned, realizing that she needed a change of pace, a change of scenery, anything to take her mind off Barrett and Miriam.

"I think we should take a walk," Charlotte announced to the children as she rose. "What do you two think?"

"Yes!" Rose, her disposition once again as sunny as her mother's, clapped her hands. "I pull wagon. David ride."

He wrinkled his little nose. "Walk."

If only he could. But he still refused to try. Though he'd shrugged off other minor injuries, David seemed to remember the day he'd bloodied his nose attempting to walk. "We'll take the wagon," Charlotte said firmly. "Now, let's get you dressed."

When they were bundled into their winter clothes and David was seated in the wagon, Charlotte decided to head east on 18th Street. She would not — she absolutely would not — pass by Barrett's house, for there could be festivities in progress there. Seeing the Taggerts' carriage hitched in front would only cause her to worry about the wisdom of Miriam and Barrett's engagement. Monday would be soon enough for that.

"Cold." Rose jumped up and down as they crossed Ferguson.

Yes, it was, but the day was also beautiful. A few white clouds drifted across a sky that was as deep a blue as Barrett's eyes. Charlotte inhaled deeply as she tried to corral her thoughts. She didn't want to think about Barrett, his beautiful blue eyes, or his upcoming marriage. Nothing was gained by that. Instead, she focused her attention on the children. This was Christmas Day, a day that ought to be special for them. They'd had a fancier than normal breakfast and gifts, and now . . . Charlotte wished she had a horse and carriage. If she did, she could take David and Rose to City Park. The park was lovely at any time, but frosted with snow, it would be spectacular. Unfortunately, it was too far for Rose to walk and farther than Charlotte could pull the wagon with both children in it. They'd have to stay closer to home.

Charlotte smiled as they passed her church. Though David would not recall it, last night's service was etched in her memory. The church had been filled with people, but — more than that — it had been filled with the wonder of a love that exceeded human understanding. What a joyous night it had been.

A sudden tug on her skirt brought Charlotte back to the present. "Horse!" Though the street was unusually quiet, Rose jumped up and down as she pointed toward a horse and carriage stopped midblock at the exclusive townhomes called Maple Terrace. "Horse!" Rose had become fascinated with all things equine, and had Charlotte not snagged her coat, she would have run toward it, heedless of the danger of passing too close to those huge hoofs.

As the driver dismounted, looping the reins over the hitching post, Charlotte recognized him. Barrett! Blood drained from her face, and her hands grew clammy inside their gloves. She didn't understand why he was here. Surely he and Miriam should be celebrating their betrothal with friends.

"Charlotte." It wasn't her imagination. Barrett was smiling as if he were delighted to see her. Though she found herself unable to move, he lengthened his stride until he reached her. "I didn't expect to see you out today." Still smiling, he greeted Rose and David. "Where's Gwen? I hope she's not ill."

"Not at all. She's at the InterOcean, having dinner with Warren."

Though Barrett nodded, he appeared surprised by the news, and the speculative expression she saw in his eyes made Charlotte wonder whether Barrett had the same reservations about Warren's apparent courtship of Gwen that she did.

"I see." The corners of his lips twisted upward, making Charlotte wonder if he'd somehow read her thoughts. Of course not. "I was on my way to visit Richard. He lives here," Barrett said with a glance at Maple Terrace. "But he can wait. Would you and the children like to take a ride?"

Though he'd spoken softly, Rose's sharp ears heard the critical word. "Ride!" she cried. "I ride horse!" She began to scamper toward the buggy. This time it was Barrett who restrained her. Though the gelding appeared docile, Charlotte was grateful that Barrett was taking no chances.

"I'm afraid not," he said. "My horse, Midnight, has to pull the carriage. He couldn't carry a big girl like you too."

Apparently mollified by being called a big girl, Rose tugged on David's wagon. "You ride," she told him.

Barrett chuckled as David began to clap his hands. "It seems that the children haven't given you much choice. I probably should have spelled the word."

He was standing close enough that Charlotte could smell the scent of bay rum that clung to him. Other men wore bay rum. Even Mr. Yates did. But it never tantalized her senses the way Barrett's did. Charlotte cleared her throat, wishing she could settle her thoughts as easily.

"A ride sounds wonderful, but what will I do with David's wagon?"

"That's no problem. I can fit it in the back. Come on, big boy." Barrett lifted David out of the wagon and placed him in Charlotte's arms.

David squirmed and turned his head toward Barrett. "Bowl," he shouted. "Bowl."

Barrett, who was securing the wagon in the back of the buggy, turned, a smile lighting his face. "Is he still playing that?"

Charlotte shook her head as she tried to restrain her son. "It's the strangest thing.

255

Gwen and I arrange the blocks the way you did. Even Rose helps. But no matter what we do, David won't bowl. I don't understand."

"You're right. That is strange."

David twisted, stretching his arms toward Barrett. "Bowl," he announced. "Bowl."

"It looks as if he's ready now."

Barrett helped Charlotte climb into the carriage. Once there, she settled David on one side of her, Rose on the other while she waited for Barrett. "Perhaps David thinks it's your game. That would explain why he won't play with anyone else."

"Should I be flattered?" Barrett's expression said he thought otherwise.

"I don't understand it. Gwen, Mr. Yates, and I have all given him toys, but he's not attached to them the way he is to your ball." Perhaps that was something her son had inherited from her, a foolish and inexplicable attachment to Barrett Landry.

As if in response to her thoughts, David nestled closer to Barrett. "Bowl," he said, his little hands moving as if to roll a ball across the floor.

"Maybe later." Barrett raised an eyebrow as he looked at Charlotte. "What do you think about a drive in City Park?"

Perhaps she should refuse. The park was

such a public place that they were sure to be seen, and if they were, people would wonder why Barrett was with her and not Miriam. She ought to refuse, and yet she did not, for Rose and David would enjoy the ride. And, if she were being totally honest, so would she.

"Are you sure you're not a mind reader?" Charlotte didn't try to hide her pleasure. "Just before I saw you, I was thinking about how wonderful it would be if I had a carriage and could take the children to the park."

Doffing his hat, Barrett grinned. "Your wish is my command, fair lady."

"You need hat. It's cold," Rose chided.

"You're right, little one."

"I not little."

As Barrett chuckled, his gaze met Charlotte's, and for a second she could hardly breathe. He looked at her as if she were more than a friend. But she wasn't. She couldn't be, for Barrett was going to marry Miriam and possibly become a senator, while she was going to live a quiet life, trying to teach David everything he needed to learn. Charlotte swallowed deeply. She and Barrett were friends. Just friends. And there was nothing unseemly about friends riding together, especially when accompanied by two children. Wrapping an arm around each child, she settled back on the seat, determined to enjoy the simple pleasure of a drive through the park.

It was even better than Charlotte had imagined. When Rose oohed and aahed over the snow that still blanketed the shrubs, Barrett stopped the carriage. As Rose and Charlotte strolled along one of the paths, he lifted David into his arms and carried him to a bush. "Snow," Barrett said as he removed one of the boy's mittens. "Snow on bushes." Carefully, he guided David's hand to the shrub, letting him feel the texture and size. And then he raised him up so that he could touch the top and experience the softness of the snow. "Snow," Barrett repeated. David said nothing, but the grin on his face as Barrett chafed his hand and replaced the mitten told Charlotte he had enjoyed his time in the park.

When they were back in the carriage, Barrett turned to Charlotte. "Might I suggest another pot of c-o-c-o-a? Mrs. Melnor and Mr. Bradley would be pleased to have guests again."

"After cooking and serving Christmas dinner?"

Barrett nodded. "You've met them. You

know they enjoy having children in the house."

"But isn't there somewhere else you need to be?" Something must have taken him to Richard's house, and even if that wasn't pressing, surely he should be spending the day with his new fiancée. When Charlotte had accepted Jeffrey's proposal, he had taken her around West Point, introducing her to everyone he knew. It had been an almost magical day, sharing the news of their love with others. But Barrett had not so much as mentioned Miriam. Why not?

"I have nothing planned this afternoon," he said as he turned the carriage onto Ferguson. "Miriam and her parents left an hour ago, and my meeting with Richard can wait until tomorrow. Besides, if you come to my house, you'll save me a trip."

"I don't understand."

"You will."

When they entered the house, as Barrett had predicted, Mr. Bradley came as close to smiling as Charlotte imagined he ever did, and Mrs. Melnor insisted that Charlotte sample her plum pudding. "The children won't like the pudding," she said, "but I can bake some cookies for them." And though Charlotte protested, Mrs. Melnor would not be dissuaded.

While they waited for the cookies and hot chocolate to be prepared, Barrett led them into the parlor. A small but exquisitely decorated tree stood in one corner, several open boxes and a bag filled with oddly shaped items beneath it. Barrett reached for the bag. "This is the trip you're saving me. I had planned to deliver it later today, but now is better."

The children thought so. Rose was enchanted with her new doll, and David seemed intrigued by the wooden animals Barrett gave him. He sat contentedly on the floor, turning each one over in his hand, as if trying to learn the shapes.

Barrett pulled out a box whose distinctive color left no doubt that it had come from Mr. Ellis's shop. "The candy is for Gwen, although I imagine she'll share it with all of you." Barrett explained that this was Mr. Ellis's special holiday assortment. "I was going to buy a box for you, but I found something I thought you'd like better." He handed Charlotte a package that could only contain a book.

"Thank you, Barrett, but I'm feeling overwhelmed." She had accepted the first box of candy and David's ball as part of Barrett's apology, but she had not expected anything else, and she most assuredly had not expected him to buy Christmas presents for four people who were neither family nor close friends.

Barrett shrugged as if the gifts were insignificant. "One thing led to another. I'd already ordered the candy and your gift. Then last month I was in the Union Mercantile with Harrison. When I spotted the animals, I thought of David, and once I bought those, I knew I couldn't neglect Rose." He wrinkled his nose. "She was the biggest challenge. You'd think that after working in my family's mercantile, I'd be better at this, but I don't know much about little girls. It was Harrison who suggested the doll."

The happiness that had filled Charlotte's heart when she'd seen David's delight over his toy animals overflowed, suffusing her with its warmth. It might be insignificant to others, but the fact that the presents were not last-minute purchases, that Barrett had thought of her son so much in advance, was an even greater gift than the animals themselves. Barrett's thoughtfulness reminded Charlotte of her childhood. Though money was invariably scarce, the family planned their Christmas celebration months in advance. Gifts were often simple and hand-made, but they always reflected both the giver and the recipient, and so they were cherished long after Christmas Day.

Blinking away the tears that threatened to fall, Charlotte smiled at Barrett. "I don't know how to thank you for making this such a special day."

Though a muscle in his cheek twitched, his expression was inscrutable. "You might want to open your gift," he suggested.

"I love books," Charlotte said as she untied the ribbon. "You probably expected that, since you know I was once a teacher, but it started way before then."

"That night at the opera house, you told me books were your best friends as a child."

Charlotte's eyes widened at the realization that Barrett had recalled the details of their conversation. It was true that she remembered almost everything they'd discussed that evening, but she hadn't expected him to.

"You also mentioned being ill," he continued. "That must have been difficult. Children — at least my brothers and I — like to be active." He rubbed the bump on his nose.

She laid her gift on her lap, more interested in learning about Barrett's childhood than in unwrapping the book. "Is that how you broke your nose?"

Barrett shook his head. "I was small for

my age, the perfect target for bullies. A couple of them caught me after school one day and decided to punch my face. The next thing I knew, I had a broken nose. The worst part is that my brothers had to come to my rescue. They never let me forget that I was the little one."

"I was the biggest one, but it wasn't always easy," Charlotte said softly.

"Because you were ill and confined to bed." He made it a statement rather than a question.

She shook her head. "That was hard enough, but what I hated most was the aftermath. I was used to being in charge of my sisters, but after I was ill, everyone thought I needed to be protected, so they coddled me. I wasn't allowed to do a lot of things that normal children did, because the doctor had warned that I'd always be weak."

"You don't appear weak now." Barrett's gaze was approving, and it warmed Charlotte's heart.

"I'm as healthy as can be." She looked down at her son. "Now it's David who needs protecting. I worry about his future."

His smile extending all the way to his eyes, Barrett gestured toward the package in

Charlotte's lap. "You might want to open it."

With the paper loosened, Charlotte carefully withdrew the book, gasping as she read the title. This was no novel or poetry collection. Instead, it was something of far more value. Barrett had given her a book for teachers of the blind. "I had no idea this existed."

As Charlotte leafed through the book, glancing at the chapter headings, she felt hope welling inside her. Perhaps with the author's advice, she could teach David everything he needed to know. Keeping a firm grip on the book, she looked up at Barrett. "I don't know how to thank you." He'd given her something more precious than diamonds and gold; he'd given her the chance to help her son.

Barrett shook his head. "No thanks are necessary. As you once told me, David is a special boy."

The tears that leaked from Charlotte's eyes were tears of happiness. Barrett's kindness had chased away her doldrums, replacing them with memories that would linger for the rest of her life. It might not have been a perfect day, but it was very, very close.

The weak December sun had barely risen when Barrett reached for his coat. As unpleasant as the next hour would be, he knew he should not postpone it any longer. As one of his advisers, Richard needed to know what had happened. Or, more precisely, what had not happened. That was why Barrett had gone to Maple Terrace yesterday, to tell Richard that his engagement was not yet official. His Christmas gift to Miriam had been a gold filigree bracelet, not a diamond solitaire. When he'd left his house after the sumptuous feast Mrs. Melnor had prepared for him and the three Taggerts, Barrett had planned to visit first Richard, then Warren. Instead, he'd seen Charlotte and the children, and suddenly nothing seemed as important as spending the afternoon with them.

It had been the right decision, for being with them turned it into the happiest Christmas Barrett could recall. The children's pleasure alone would have made it special, but seeing Charlotte's wonder at the book filled an empty space deep inside him. The gifts had been far less costly than the items he'd given Miriam's parents, and yet Charlotte had acted as if Barrett's generosity had known no bounds.

"You're a fool!" The front door banged open, and Richard strode into the foyer. "I thought you had more sense, but obviously I was mistaken."

Barrett sighed. The news had spread more quickly than he'd expected. "I was on my way to see you," he said, gesturing toward his coat. "But since you're here, we might as well sit down like civilized men."

Shrugging off his coat, Richard sneered. "There are many adjectives I'd use to describe you, but this morning, *civilized* is not one of them. I thought you were serious about running for office."

Barrett led the way into the morning room and gestured toward a chair. "I am serious."

"Then why did you risk alienating a powerful newspaper publisher?" Richard's normally pale face was suffused with color. "I thought we all agreed that you and Miriam would be engaged by Christmas. I expected it, and I know Cyrus and Amelia Taggert did." Richard clenched his fist. "I've never seen Amelia so distressed."

Richard had seen them. That explained how he'd heard that Miriam's left hand did not yet bear a diamond ring. "When did you see them?"

"Yesterday afternoon. I was outside when their carriage passed Maple Terrace. Though they didn't say, they must have been returning home from here. Miriam asked if I'd like to join them for a ride in the park."

"City Park?" Thank goodness the Taggerts hadn't been there when he'd taken Charlotte and the children. That could have been awkward.

Richard shook his head. "Minnehaha. It's Miriam's favorite park. She likes the lagoons."

Odd. Barrett hadn't known that. "Was Miriam distressed?" Though dinner had been a bit strained, in large part because of Mrs. Taggert's uncharacteristic silence, Miriam had done her best to keep the conversation moving, and she'd smiled each time she fingered the bracelet he'd given her. He might have been mistaken, but Barrett did not believe he was. When he'd wished Miriam a merry Christmas and handed her a narrow rectangular box, he'd seen relief in her eyes. Miriam, it seemed, was as unsure of their future as he was. And so long as either one of them had reservations, it would be wrong to become engaged, no matter how much the elder Taggerts favored the match, no matter how the union might help Barrett's career.

"Was Miriam distressed?" Barrett repeated the question.

Richard shook his head. "Not that I could see, but her parents are. Getting them riled was downright stupid of you."

"Perhaps it was." But it was his life that was at stake. Christmas afternoon had been so different from the previous evening at the Taggerts' mansion. A simple drive in the park compared to a party with Cheyenne's most influential citizens. Hot chocolate instead of champagne and oysters. The laughter of children instead of music provided by a string quartet. If only a stupid man would find the time with Charlotte preferable to the Taggerts' glittering party, then Barrett was a stupid man.

Richard's glare intensified. "Without Taggert's support, your chances of getting elected are lower."

"You're probably right, but he hasn't withdrawn it yet, has he?"

"No, but he will if you don't marry Miriam. Amelia Taggert has her heart set on her daughter becoming the wife of a senator. You cross her at your peril."

"I know."

"If I were you, I'd have a heart-to-heart with Mrs. Taggert. Tell her your plans. Let her know when you intend to ask for Miriam's hand." Richard's eyes clouded with what appeared to be pain. "Tell her you're a romantic, and you want to propose on Valentine's Day. Tell her whatever it takes to convince her you're sincere. You can do that, can't you?"

Barrett looked at the man who'd given him so much good advice. What Richard asked sounded reasonable, and yet . . . *Landry never lies.*

13

"Your work is exquisite, Madame Charlotte." Mrs. Slater, a tall woman with a waist so slender she hardly needed a corset, smiled as she admired the dark brown poplin dress that Charlotte planned to finish by the end of the week. It was the first Tuesday of the new year, and though Charlotte did not have many customers at this time of the year, Mrs. Slater was one of her best, ordering at least one new dress each month. Like Barrett, Mr. Slater had made his fortune in cattle, and he gave his wife a lavish clothing budget.

"Even Mr. Slater complimented me on my new Christmas gown," the cattle baroness said, "and he never notices what I wear. Men." She wrinkled her long nose. "Who can figure out what they're thinking?"

"I'm glad you both liked the gown. Lemon yellow is particularly attractive on you." Mrs. Slater had been surprised when Charlotte had pulled out the bolt of heavy satin, saying she'd ordered it specifically for her. "I don't know anyone else in Cheyenne who could wear this shade," she had explained, holding the fabric in front of the older woman so she could see how the light shade highlighted her dark hair.

"It wasn't just Mr. Slater. I had a dozen women telling me they'd never seen such a pretty gown. You're a genius, Madame Charlotte."

"Hardly that." If it was true as Mama had claimed that she had an eye for color, it was a gift.

"You should accept praise, my dear, when it's deserved. And in this case, it is." Mrs. Slater pursed her lips as she studied her reflection before smiling. "You were right again. The draped panel looks good over the pleated skirt. I'll be the first lady in the city with a dress like this." Her eyes narrowed ever so slightly, and Charlotte suspected she was choosing her words carefully. "You're wise, not like some people I could name. You know I don't like to gossip, but . . ."

Charlotte tried not to sigh. If there was anything Mrs. Slater enjoyed more than being a trendsetter, it was gossip. Though Charlotte had tried to dissuade her from relating tales in the past, she had failed, and so today she didn't even try. Instead, she busied herself pinning the hem so that she did not have to see the expression of contentment on her customer's face as she recounted some juicy bit of news.

"I was shocked when I heard it," Mrs. Slater said, "but it appears to be true. Mr. Landry seems to have lost whatever common sense he possessed."

A shiver ran down Charlotte's spine as she realized that Barrett might be paying a high price for having befriended her and the children on Christmas afternoon.

"The stories are very confusing." Mrs. Slater needed no encouragement to continue. "All I know is that no engagement has been announced, and Miriam Taggert and her parents were seen driving with Mr. Eberhardt on Christmas Day when they should have been with Mr. Landry."

Charlotte forbore pointing out that the Taggerts had been Barrett's guests for Christmas dinner. If Mrs. Slater didn't know that, Charlotte would not be the one to add that to her gossip bag.

"I tell you, Madame Charlotte, I never thought Mr. Landry was foolish," Mrs. Slater continued. "I thought he'd be a good senator. Why, he's so handsome, and his voice is so nice that I could listen to him talk for hours. But any man who lets a prize like Miriam slip away is foolish. Mark my words. He'll see his political career slip away too, if he doesn't marry her soon."

"Do you really think so?"

"I know so. The man needs a wife, and he won't find a more suitable one than Miriam."

Charlotte wasn't certain of that. What she was certain of was that Wyoming needed a man like Barrett. She shook her head as she put the final pin in Mrs. Slater's hem. Though others seemed willing to tackle tough issues and to fight for Wyoming's rights, Barrett was the best advocate for sensible water laws Charlotte had seen. His explanations of the problems were easy to understand, even for men who lived in parts of the country that had never suffered from drought and where adequate supplies of water were taken for granted. More important, he did more than explain the problems. He provided concrete suggestions for how to solve them. That combination of oratorical eloquence and practical policy was unique to Barrett. If he withdrew from the race or if he lost, the real losers would be the citizens of Wyoming.

By the time she closed Élan, Charlotte was

exhausted. Mrs. Slater had been followed by four other women. Though each of them had ordered a new dress, they had spent the majority of their time in the shop discussing Barrett and Miriam and the engagement that had not been announced. Charlotte's head ached, her feet ached, even her fingernails ached. The year that she had believed to be so full of promise had not begun well. It was a day when she could hardly wait for spring to arrive. Surely by then Barrett and Miriam would have announced their betrothal and his political future would be assured.

Gwen was not suffering from the doldrums. Her face wreathed with a smile, she dished a fragrant beef stew into four bowls before she settled onto her chair. "It's only January fourth, but I'm convinced this is going to be the best year ever," she said as she buttered a piece of freshly baked bread. Charlotte had known that Gwen was happy, simply by the aromas that had greeted her when she entered the kitchen. A contented Gwen added more spices than normal to whatever she was cooking, making the whole apartment smell wonderful.

"Warren told me this would be the year my dreams would come true," she continued, "and I believe him."

Charlotte managed a smile. "I hope he's right. You deserve everything good." So did Barrett and Miriam. Most of all, so did David. While some might believe that the problems he faced were not as important as those looming over the territory, to Charlotte there was nothing more critical than assuring that her son had the prospect of a happy, productive future.

Once supper was over, David returned to what had become his favorite pastime, playing with the wooden animals Barrett had given him. Each time he would pick one up, he would run his fingers over the edges, as if learning the shapes, while Rose would recite the names. The pleasure that both children derived from the simple gift told Charlotte that Barrett understood children better than he admitted.

Unbidden, the memory of how he'd shown David the snow on top of the bush brought a genuine smile to Charlotte's face. She was David's mother. She spent her days trying to devise ways to teach him, but though she had introduced him to snow, she had not thought to demonstrate that snow fell on everything, not merely the ground. Barrett, a man with no children, not even any nieces or nephews, had done that. Ever since that day, when they'd gone outside, David had raised his arms and spread his hands as if he were searching for evidence of snow.

Barrett had recognized a need. Perhaps he had also recognized how little Charlotte knew about teaching the blind, and that was why he had given her the book.

"Oh, Gwen, I don't know whether I can do this," Charlotte said when the children had been put to bed.

"Do what?" Gwen looked up from the table runner she was embroidering while Charlotte studied the book.

"Teach David. There's so much I don't know." Charlotte hated the whining tone of her voice. If only her head didn't ache so much, the book might not seem so overwhelming. "I want David to be able to read, but if I'm going to teach him, I need to learn Braille." She lifted her right hand and felt the pads of her fingers. "My fingertips have calluses from sewing. I wonder if I'll be able to distinguish those dots. They're so small."

Gwen flashed her a smile. "You've got years to learn. I know that David's unusually clever, but even he won't be ready to read for four or five more years. By then you'll be an expert. I know you will."

Charlotte did not share her confidence. She was still troubled when she went to bed, her mind jumbled with thoughts of Barrett's future and worries about her ability to help David. Somehow she had to find a way to give him everything he needed, and — God willing — that way would not involve sending him away.

Her gaze settled on her son, watching him as he slept, his arms tucked close to his chest, his legs splayed in a wide V. With his lips curving at the corners, David appeared at peace. If only Charlotte could share that tranquility. As she turned away, she recalled her father reciting one of his favorite Bible verses, and the words of Proverbs 16:9 echoed through her mind: "A man's heart deviseth his way: but the Lord directeth his steps." That was the answer. Papa was right. Charlotte had been so concerned about establishing her independence, about proving that she did not need to be coddled or protected, that she had forgotten the fundamental truth. She could deny it all she wanted, but she did need help. God's help.

Help me, Lord, she prayed. *I can't do it all alone. I need you to guide my steps.* She reached for the Bible on her nightstand, then shook her head. What she needed was her childhood Bible, the one she'd kept hidden since she'd reached Cheyenne. The words were the same, but the soft, slightly worn leather felt different in her hands, providing a tactile comfort that the newer one did not. The older one had been a gift from her parents on her eighth birthday, and if she opened it, she would see her name and birth date carefully inscribed inside it, followed by the other milestones of her life: her marriage, Jeffrey's death, David's birth. Perhaps it was because she had been thinking of Papa and remembering his wise counsel that the only book she wanted to hold was the one he and Mama had given her.

Removing it from its hiding place, Charlotte opened it randomly, searching for the Lord's words. Her eyes landed on the forty-first chapter of Isaiah, the thirteenth verse. "For I the Lord thy God will hold thy right hand, saying unto thee, Fear not; I will help thee."

She smiled as she looked down at her hands, her eyes focusing on the right one. Less than an hour ago, she had worried that that hand would be unable to read Braille. It was no coincidence that this was the first verse she had read. God had heard her worries, and he'd answered them. He would hold her hand. He would help her. That was all Charlotte needed.

Reluctantly, she placed the Bible back in the bottom drawer, covering it with clothing. As much as she wanted to use it daily, she could not risk Rose finding it and showing it to Gwen. She would wait until David's second birthday. Surely by then the baron would have forgotten her. Then she and David would be safe.

"Oh, Charlotte, it's lovely." Miriam admired her reflection in the long mirror. "I never thought brown would look good on me."

Charlotte smiled. "It's russet, not brown."

Fingering the lightweight wool, Miriam smiled again. "Only you would know the difference and which one I ought to wear. Mama would have insisted on blue again, but I wanted something less . . ." She hesitated, as if searching for a word. "Flamboyant," she said at last. "I want to look nice when I'm at his side, but I want the attention to be on Barrett."

Nodding, Charlotte handed Miriam the pair of gloves she had made to match the new dress. It appeared that Mrs. Slater and the other women were mistaken, for if there were any estrangement between Miriam and Barrett, Miriam would not be planning to be with him at the polls next week.

"Did you have a happy Christmas?" Miriam asked as she slid her hand into the gloves, smoothing each finger.

"Indeed, I did. This was the first year David understood opening gifts." Charlotte smiled, remembering how excited her son had been by the wooden animals Barrett had given him.

"I heard that Mrs. Amos dined with Mr. Duncan at the InterOcean."

Charlotte turned abruptly, startled by the odd note in Miriam's voice. Surely she did not disapprove of Gwen having a special meal. "Yes, she did."

"Mama was horrified, but you know Mama. She has a set of rules, and woe to anyone who dares to flout them."

Charlotte knew she shouldn't have been surprised that the story of Gwen's dinner had spread or that Mrs. Taggert found something disagreeable about it, but she could not imagine what social convention Gwen had broken. "What bothered your mother?"

"His age." Miriam pursed her lips as if she'd bitten into a sour lemon. "A woman should not marry a man old enough to be her father, especially here in Wyoming where there are a dozen men to every woman," she announced, mimicking her mother.

"I don't believe marriage has been mentioned, but even if they were considering it, I think a man's character is far more important than his age." And it was Warren's character that worried Charlotte, not the fact that he was twenty years Gwen's senior.

"That's what I told Mama." Color flooded Miriam's cheeks. "She wouldn't listen. She claims anyone who's foolish enough to consider an older man is doomed to be a young widow."

Though that was possible, it was by no means assured. Besides . . . "Gwen is already a widow, and her husband was only two years older."

Miriam looked confused. A second later, she nodded. "You're right. We were talking about Gwen."

"I'm surprised you're here." Herb Webster clapped his hand on Barrett's shoulder and motioned toward a less crowded corner of the courthouse. Though the older man held no official position within Barrett's party, he was well known as one of the organization's men behind the scenes. If he wanted to speak with someone, a man refused at his own peril.

"Why wouldn't I be here?" Barrett asked as they made their way through the lines of people waiting to vote. It was January 11, Election Day in the city of Cheyenne. "I agreed to help, because we all know some voters need encouragement as they enter the polls."

Herb's lips formed a crooked smile. "Most of the men who are providing what you refer to as encouragement are also trying to advance their own prospects."

"I won't deny that that's part of the reason I volunteered to be here."

Nodding slightly, Herb lowered his voice. "And that's why I'm surprised to see you here. I thought you'd abandoned your hopes of running."

"That's a false rumor."

"I'm glad to hear that. The party needs you, and so does the territory. We've got to get past this stage of having the president decide who'll govern us."

"You don't like Moonlight?" It had been less than a week since President Cleveland had appointed Thomas Moonlight as territorial governor.

Herb shrugged. "I don't know enough about him to say. He may be a fine man, but he's from Kansas. The citizens of Wyoming deserve a governor who lives here."

"You'll get no argument from me on that." While he'd been greeting voters, discussing issues with them and promoting his party's candidates, Barrett had also been stressing the importance of Wyoming's becoming a state. Like Herb and many of the politicians, he believed that self-government was essential.

"Where's Miriam?" Warren clapped Barrett on the shoulder and led him away from Herb. "I thought she was supposed to be with you today."

"She'll come." In the two and a half weeks since Christmas, Barrett had seen Miriam three times. They'd attended a New Year's party at a friend's house, they'd gone for a ride in Minnehaha Park so that Miriam could admire the frozen lagoons, and they'd attended a play last night. Each time, Miriam had mentioned that she would be at Barrett's side on Election Day. She'd even said that she was having a new dress made for the occasion. She would be here.

"There she is." Barrett gestured toward Miriam, who stood in the doorway, her smile radiant, her hand on Richard's arm. As her gaze met Barrett's, she nodded and headed toward him, never letting go of Richard.

"You look lovely today," Barrett said when

she reached him. It was no lie. The reddish brown dress made her hair seem as bright as sunshine, and the smile she'd been wearing when she entered the room set her face aglow. Barrett had never seen her looking more beautiful. While Warren engaged Richard in a discussion of the various candidates' chances, Barrett kept his attention focused on Miriam. "You and Richard appeared deep in conversation when you arrived." Though she'd been smiling, her animated expression had left no doubt that she had been engaged in something that touched her emotions.

Miriam's smile widened. "We were talking about 'The Raven.' Richard doesn't agree with me that there are several layers of meaning to it."

"I'd have to agree with him. How much meaning can a bird have?"

"Oh, Barrett." He could see that Miriam was trying not to laugh. "You may be the territory's best hope for sensible government, but your knowledge of literature is sadly lacking. 'The Raven' is a poem by Edgar Allan Poe."

A poem. No wonder he was confused. The only book Barrett had thought about in the past month was the one he'd given Charlotte, and that one had assumed almost monumental importance. He'd spent far too much time worrying whether it would help her learn the specialized techniques that were needed to teach David. He'd worried about why the child wouldn't roll his ball unless Barrett was there and what that might mean for his future. Most of all, he'd worried about David growing up without a father. That was far more important than poetry.

"I'm going next door," Charlotte told Molly as she snipped the last thread and pulled the fabric from the sewing machine. "I shouldn't be long, but if someone comes, you can offer them coffee or tea and a few cookies while they look at the new pattern books." Though she never ate or drank while sewing, Charlotte kept pots of tea and coffee for customers. Some days, like today, when she also had freshly baked cookies, the shop was redolent with delicious aromas.

A perplexed expression crossed Molly's face. "Now? You're going now?"

Charlotte nodded. It was no wonder that her assistant was confused. Charlotte had a firm schedule, and it was rare for her to deviate from it. She wouldn't be leaving now, for there was still work to be done on

Mrs. Slater's new dress, but Charlotte couldn't ignore the feeling that she ought to check on Mr. Yates immediately. Normally, she stopped in at the end of the day, making excuses because she knew the elderly man would protest if she admitted that the reason she visited his shop was to provide him with a bit of companionship. He'd seemed sadder than normal since Christmas, though he'd denied that anything was wrong other than missing Prudence and wanting to move to Arizona.

Charlotte could find no reason for her feeling of urgency, but her instincts told her this was the time to visit Mr. Yates, and so she hung the partially finished dress on a hook, tossed her cloak over her shoulders, and headed for the door. Though she would occasionally dash next door without a coat, yesterday's snow and the continuing bitter cold made that impractical today.

"Good morning, Mr. Yates," Charlotte called as she entered the mercantile, a covered plate in her hand.

"Ah, Madame Charlotte. It's good to see you." To Charlotte's relief, her neighbor seemed more cheerful than he'd been yesterday. Perhaps that was because she'd come during the morning today. Perhaps Mr. Yates was a person who dreaded sunset. She had heard that some people, particularly the elderly, were afflicted with that malady.

"What can I do for you?" he asked, leaning forward on the counter. "More socks for David?"

Charlotte laughed. "You know he doesn't need any." Mr. Yates had given him half a dozen pairs for Christmas. "I thought you might enjoy some of Gwen's cookies." She removed the covering before handing him the plate.

As the scent of gingerbread filled the room, a broad smile crossed the shopkeeper's face. "My favorite. Thank you, but do you mind if I share them with someone?"

"Of course not. They're yours."

Charlotte took another step toward the counter, intending to cover the plate again, but to her surprise, Mr. Yates called out, "Mrs. Cox, would you and Nancy like a cookie?"

Charlotte spun around, startled by the realization that there were other customers in the store. She had neither seen nor heard anyone. The reason for the first was evident as a woman emerged from behind the counter stacked with table linens. Less than five feet tall, the tiny blonde who was carrying a child had been hidden by the display.

"Thank you, Mr. Yates. We'd enjoy that."

Her voice was soft, almost tentative, as if she were afraid of drawing attention to herself. Perhaps that was why Charlotte had heard no sounds. Mrs. Cox settled the little girl on the counter and turned toward Charlotte, a question in her eyes.

Before Charlotte could speak, Mr. Yates performed the introductions. "Mrs. Cox, I'd like you to meet Madame Charlotte. Her shop is next door. Madame Charlotte, this is Mrs. Cox, one of my best customers, and her daughter Nancy."

Charlotte tried not to stare at the little girl with the clouded, unfocused eyes. Instead, she smiled at the mother, a woman Charlotte guessed to be in her midthirties.

"I'm pleased to meet you," Mrs. Cox said in response to Charlotte's smile. "I've heard so much about you, and I've seen the wonderful work you do." Her smile faded slightly. "I'd like to own one of your dresses, but it's difficult to find time for fittings. Nancy occupies almost every hour of my days, and I know you're not open past her bedtime." She kept her hand on Nancy's shoulder, perhaps to reassure her, perhaps to keep her from falling.

"You could bring Nancy with you."

The woman shook her head. "Oh, I couldn't do that. I always hold her when we're in a store, but I couldn't do that if you were fitting a dress. You see . . ."

"Yes, I see." Charlotte couldn't ignore the irony in the words. She and Mrs. Cox might see, but Nancy could not. Like David, she was blind.

"Cookie," the little girl said.

Charlotte watched as Mrs. Cox handed her daughter a gingerbread man. Though David was adept at breaking them into smaller pieces and eating the morsels one at a time, Nancy tried to stuff the entire cookie into her mouth at once, with the inevitable result that pieces fell out and onto the floor.

"I'm afraid she's not a very neat eater."

"That's not a problem." Mr. Yates's voice was calm and reassuring. "I'll get a broom." He headed toward the back room, leaving Charlotte alone with his customer.

She looked at the little girl who was obviously enjoying her treat, even though half of it was on the floor. Small and thin like her mother, the child appeared to be older than David, though her eating skills were less developed.

"How old is she?"

Mrs. Cox's expression said she understood Charlotte's unspoken concerns. "Nancy will be two next week. That's why I was shopping today. I wanted to buy a new dress for her birthday. I had hoped she'd be walking by now, but . . ." Her voice trailed off.

"Have you tried having her hold on to a doll carriage?" Barrett's book had suggested that technique for encouraging children to walk. Though he still wasn't walking independently, David seemed to be gaining confidence from holding on to Rose's little carriage.

"I haven't." Mrs. Cox's light blue eyes clouded with confusion. "How . . . ? Why . . . ?" She seemed unable to complete her questions.

"How do I know about using a perambulator?" When Mrs. Cox nodded, Charlotte said simply, "My son is blind."

To Charlotte's surprise, Mrs. Cox smiled. "You don't know how happy that makes me." As soon as the words were spoken, the woman flushed, and her smile disappeared. "I'm so sorry. Please don't misunderstand me, Madame Charlotte. I'm not happy that your son cannot see, but I am happy that I'm not alone. It's been so difficult." She picked up another cookie, this time breaking off a bite-sized piece to hand to Nancy. "I love my daughter dearly, but sometimes it's hard to know what to do, and there's been no one to ask. I've met several mothers whose children are hard of hearing, but none who are blind."

Mrs. Cox stretched out her hand and touched Charlotte's arm. "Oh, Madame Charlotte, I'm so glad you were here today."

14

Charlotte drew her cloak closer, trying not to shiver as the wind buffeted her. It had howled all night, its mournful cry keeping her from sleeping and making David restless. When it seemed to lose some of its ferocity in the predawn hours, she'd donned her widow's weeds and set out for the boardinghouse. Mrs. Kendall had admitted that the women needed warm clothing, so today's delivery consisted of half a dozen heavy flannel petticoats. Though they lacked the fancy stitching and crocheted edging Charlotte's customers expected, she had added pintucks to each garment, wanting Mrs. Kendall's boarders to have at least a small touch of luxury. They had so little.

But it wasn't the women from 15th Street who had occupied Charlotte's thoughts for the past four days. It was Nancy Cox. Like Nancy's mother, Charlotte had believed she was the only person in Cheyenne raising a blind child. Now she knew that she was not alone and that at least one other person believed as she did, that children benefited from being with their parents.

"We'll do anything we can to help Nancy, but we can't send our only child away." Mrs. Cox confided that Nancy's had been a difficult birth and that the midwife had warned she would be risking her life if she had another baby. "Mr. Cox and I won't do that, especially since Nancy is . . ." She hesitated before saying, "Special. We want to be close to her as she grows up."

Just as Charlotte wanted to be close to David. The problem was that the book Barrett had given her stressed the importance of having trained teachers, particularly after the first three years. Charlotte would not delude herself. While she had indeed been a teacher, she was not trained to work with blind children. But there had to be a solution.

Scraping her boots on the step to dislodge the packed snow, Charlotte knocked on the boardinghouse door. There would be time to worry about David's and Nancy's education on her walk back home. For the present, she would devote her attention to Mrs. Kendall.

"I have hot coffee if you'd like some," the

older woman said when she'd ushered Charlotte into the kitchen.

Charlotte shook her head. Though she would welcome the warmth, she did not want to raise her veil. While she doubted Mrs. Kendall would reveal her identity if she knew it, there was always the possibility that one of the boarders would enter the kitchen and recognize Charlotte. It was better to remain anonymous.

"I will warm my hands at the stove, though," Charlotte said as she removed her gloves. She nodded toward the package she'd placed on the table. "I brought petticoats today."

Eagerly Mrs. Kendall unwrapped the garments, her face glowing with pleasure when she felt the heavy fabric. "My gals are convinced you're an angel."

"Hardly. I'm just a widow who wants to help."

"That's why Sylvia's gals have took to calling you the angel widow." Mrs. Kendall hung one of the petticoats over a chair and stepped back to admire it. "They don't mean nothin' bad by it, ma'am. They give all their regular customers nicknames. You're different, though. When they say your name, it's respectful-like, not like when they talk about the baron."

Charlotte felt the blood drain from her face, and she grabbed a chairback when light-headedness threatened to overcome her. "The baron?" she asked, hoping her voice did not betray her distress. "Who's he?" It was probably coincidence, nothing to worry about, but she had to be certain.

Pursing her lips, Mrs. Kendall let out a small huff. "He's a bad man, is what he is. Sylvia's gals don't say much except that no one wants him as a customer. He's real mean."

That sounded like the same man. Tamping down her fear and revulsion, Charlotte managed to squeak out a question. "What does he look like?"

Though Mrs. Kendall's eyes narrowed as if she were puzzled by Charlotte's curiosity, she merely shrugged. "Nobody knows. The girls say he wears a mask — more like a hood with holes cut out for his eyes and mouth. We reckon he's somebody important-like and he don't want nobody to recognize him."

As her legs turned to jelly, Charlotte sank onto the chair. There was little doubt about it. The baron was in Cheyenne.

"It feels like spring, doesn't it?" Warren flashed Barrett a grin as he climbed the steps to the Cheyenne Club.

The rocking chairs that provided a comfortable place to meet friends and be seen by passersby during the summer months were still in storage, but the unseasonable warmth had brought Barrett and a few other men out onto the porch. Though it was only January 20th, the Chinook wind was a welcome change from the bitter cold that had plagued the city for what felt like an eternity.

"I sure hope it lasts." Barrett opened the door to usher Warren into the club. "I don't mind telling you that I've been worried about my cattle. This is the worst winter I've seen."

"But it's over now." Though Warren grinned again, Barrett wasn't certain whether it was because of the change of weather or the fact that he was inside the club. He seemed to derive an inordinate amount of pleasure from the time that he spent here. Barrett hoped Warren's membership would be approved this time. Maybe then he'd realize that, while the club was a pleasant place to while away a few hours, there was nothing magic about it.

"Amazing, isn't it?" Warren continued. "A week ago the men started harvesting ice, and now we've left off our overcoats."

"That's not amazing. That's Wyoming. You know the weather's fickle." And that was what Barrett feared: a resumption of winter's frigid temperatures and this year's unusually heavy snowfall. "I'm heading up to the ranch tomorrow. Want to come along?"

Warren lit a cigar, shaking his head as he blew out the match. "Absolutely not. Why would I want to spend time with you and some bellowing, odoriferous cattle when I could be with a charming, soft-spoken, sweet-smelling woman?"

"The one you want to marry?"

"Exactly." Warren nodded at Derek Slater as he entered the room. Rumor had it that Warren was hoping to land him as a client. "I just need to get a few things in line. Then I'll ask her to be mine."

Leaning back in the comfortable wing chair, Barrett studied his friend. The man had seemed calmer, more relaxed, happier for the past few months. Could the difference be attributed to his plans to marry?

"Who is this mysterious woman? Do I know her?" Though Barrett suspected it was Gwen, Warren had never admitted it. He'd seemed taken with her when they were introduced at the opera house, and he'd asked Barrett to seat them together at his dinner, but Warren had not spoken of Gwen other than those two occasions. He hadn't even mentioned sharing Christmas dinner with her at the InterOcean, though he had to have known that the rumor mill would have taken note of that. Barrett hoped Gwen was the woman Warren was planning to marry and that he wasn't toying with her affections.

As a puff of smoke circled his head, Warren nodded. "You do know her. Mrs. Amos. Gwen."

The relief that coursed through Barrett's veins was almost palpable. "She's a fine woman." And, according to Charlotte, she was eager to remarry and give her daughter a father. It would be an ideal situation, for if Warren married Gwen, they would both be happy. What concerned Barrett was Charlotte. He knew that she had limited experience living alone and that Gwen was her friend as well as the woman who shared her apartment, and so he wondered how Charlotte would fare when Gwen left.

"Gwen will make a fine wife." Warren's eyes narrowed. "You know, Barrett, you shouldn't be waiting so long to take a bride. You need to show the voters you're a stable man."

"You sound like Richard and my brother.

They're both convinced I won't be elected unless I'm married. The only difference is, Richard thinks Miriam is perfect, while Harrison spent most of his visit trying to convince me that I shouldn't marry her."

Warren rubbed his prominent nose, his eyes narrowing still further as he gazed at Barrett. "Is that why you haven't asked Miriam to marry you?"

The conversation had entered dangerous territory. "What's between Miriam and me is private." Barrett had no intention of telling Warren or anyone else that increasingly, every time he thought of marriage, the woman he pictured sitting on the opposite side of his breakfast table was a beautiful brunette, not a lovely blonde. This was one time he couldn't depend on others. Harrison would be pleased if Barrett chose Charlotte, while Richard was certain Miriam would be the ideal wife. Warren didn't seem to care whom Barrett married so long as he did it quickly. Though he'd never thought of himself as ambivalent, Barrett was confused. Until he resolved his feelings, there would be no proposals of marriage.

Warren was silent for a moment, puffing his cigar as he considered Barrett's declaration. "I'm beginning to think I was wrong," he said at last. "You're too soft to be a politician. You need more starch."

"Starch is for shirts."

"And politicians. Now, if you're really serious about running, here's what you need to do . . ."

Almost twenty-four hours later, Barrett was still considering Warren's advice as he rode north toward the ranch.

"You need to be more visible," Warren had announced. "Find excuses to make speeches. Get your views and your face — especially your face — in front of voters. You need to be better known." Though Warren had spoken for the better part of an hour, his advice boiled down to two things: visibility and marriage. They were both essential, at least in Warren's opinion.

But Warren's opinions were relegated to the back of Barrett's mind once he reached the open rangeland. The effects of the Chinook were different here than in Cheyenne. While the city's residents had welcomed the warmth and the partial melting of the huge piles of snow, out here there were no artificially created piles of snow, just rolling grassland covered with more than a foot of the white stuff. And now, thanks to the rapid melting, the low-lying areas had become ponds because of the several inches of water that had accumulated on top of the snow.

"I don't know, Boss," Dustin said when Barrett entered the ranch house. "I ain't never seen a winter like this. It's mighty peculiar weather."

It was, indeed, and Barrett feared that the worst might be ahead. "I'm afraid that the snow under all that water is icy. Cattle might slip and break a leg."

Dustin nodded, his lips twisted into a scowl. "I reckon that could happen. We gotta hope it don't turn cold again."

But it did. By the time Barrett returned to Cheyenne on the 24th, another blast of bitter cold had pummeled Wyoming, changing open water to a thick layer of ice. The ponds and streams froze, leaving the cattle with nothing to drink. That would have been dangerous enough, but the cold dealt a double blow, for the ice that now covered the snow was so thick that cattle could not break through it to reach the grass that was their only source of nourishment. With no food or water, Barrett's cattle and that of all the other stock growers were endangered. They needed an early spring. Desperately.

Barrett was back. Charlotte felt her lips stretch as she smiled. She couldn't help it. Her spirits had lifted when she'd seen him

301

ride past, and now she wanted to dance. It was silly, of course, just as it had been silly to be so disappointed when she hadn't seen him in church on Sunday. She had known there was nothing Barrett could do about the baron, but somehow knowing that he was gone had brought back the trembling that had plagued her at the boardinghouse. Each time her limbs had quaked, she had forced herself to take a deep breath and recite Joshua 1:9, and as she did, she felt the fear subside. God was with her. He had promised that.

And now Barrett was back. He might not visit the shop this afternoon, but Charlotte was certain he would come within the next few days, for he had made a point of stopping in at least twice a week to ask about David.

She was about to close Élan for the day when Barrett opened the door, his cheeks reddened by the wind. Though he'd been on his horse when she'd seen him earlier, he must have walked the few blocks from his home to hers, for there was no sign of a horse outside.

"You look cold," she said as he doffed his hat. "Would you like some coffee? I always have some ready for customers."

His lips curved in a smile that made Charlotte's heart beat a bit faster. It was foolish, acting like a lovesick young girl, and yet Charlotte could not seem to control her emotions. Barrett was a friend, she reminded herself. Only a friend.

"I'm not a customer," he said as he folded his overcoat and laid it on one of the counters.

"True, but you can have coffee anyway." When Barrett nodded, Charlotte brought out a tray with a pot of still fresh coffee and a pair of cups and placed it on a small table. Taking one of the two chairs, she gestured toward the other. "How was your trip?"

If Barrett was surprised that she knew he'd been gone, he gave no sign. Furrows appeared between his eyes as he said, "Worrisome. This weather is not good for cattle. The Chinook was probably the worst thing that could happen, because now we've got ice instead of only deep snow. The cattle can paw their way through snow, but I don't know how they'll fare with ice." He frowned. "Dustin and I tried to break through it, but there's no water underneath. It's all solid ice."

And that could be disastrous. "Is there anything else you can do?"

Barrett shook his head. "They've eaten all the hay I took out last fall, and there's no more to be had. All I can do now is pray that most of them survive."

"I wish I could help you." Barrett had done so many things for her that Charlotte felt almost guilty that she had nothing to offer him.

After he swallowed his coffee, Barrett leaned forward and smiled. "Actually, you can. I'd like your advice about something."

How ironic. She had planned to ask for his counsel. "Certainly. What is it?"

"Richard and Warren tell me it's important that I remain in the public eye. They want me to address the legislature. I had planned to talk about water rights, but after this winter, I wondered if that's our most pressing problem."

"What else would it be?"

"Regulating us cattle ranchers. I doubt anyone will admit it, but even in a good year, the range can't sustain the number of head we've got. The grass is overgrazed, and that's part of the problem."

"So what's the solution?"

"Limits."

Charlotte took a sip of coffee as she thought. "I see two problems with that. First, I suspect it would be difficult to enforce, and secondly, it would be unpopular with the men whose support you need if you're going to be elected."

Nodding slowly, Barrett settled back in his chair. "Are you recommending I do whatever increases my chances of election?"

Though he said nothing more, Charlotte sensed he was asking about more than a speech, and so she chose her words carefully. "Shakespeare had good advice when he said, 'To thine own self be true.' I don't think you should do anything that compromises your principles, but I wonder whether cattle growing is the right issue for you to tackle."

"Why do you say that?"

"I'm not sure it's broad enough. Sheep ranchers and farmers and city dwellers won't care about cattle the way you do. Even worse, they might think you were being self-serving." When Barrett nodded, Charlotte continued. "Water rights affect everyone."

Draining his cup, Barrett inclined his head when Charlotte offered to refill it. "You've made good points, Charlotte. I still need to think this through, but I'll probably stay with water. Now, tell me about David."

She paused to take another sip of coffee, enjoying the liquid's warmth as much as its flavor. "I hope you don't mind, but I need some advice too."

"About David?"

"Yes, or more precisely, about his schooling." There was no one whose opinion she valued so highly. Gwen would have been honest, if Charlotte had asked her, but she didn't have the same perspective. As a businessman and an entrepreneur, Barrett would understand the challenges Charlotte would face.

"The book didn't help?" Disappointment flickered across Barrett's face.

"To the contrary, it did. It showed me how to encourage David to walk." Charlotte smiled as she thought of what had happened after breakfast the day before. "He took his first step alone yesterday."

Raising his cup in a celebratory gesture, Barrett said, "We should celebrate. Why don't I take you and David back to Mr. Ellis's for a treat?"

That was Barrett, kind and generous. "It's too close to dinner. Besides, I'm not finished. The book also showed me how little I know. It made me realize that I'm not qualified to teach David everything he needs to learn. I had almost decided that I should move back East where there are special schools, but then I met Nancy Cox." Briefly, Charlotte described her meeting with the blind girl and her mother. "That's when I realized there was another answer."

"And that is . . ." Though he let his voice trail off, Barrett's expression was enthusiastic. This was why she had wanted his advice. Even though David's education didn't touch him directly, he was still interested.

"A school right here."

It must have been her imagination that Barrett's enthusiasm seemed to evaporate. "A school for the blind in Cheyenne?"

"Not just for the blind. It would include deaf children too. I believe the two groups could help each other." Charlotte winced as she looked at Barrett. Though he was trying to hide it, she could see his skepticism. "You think it's a foolish idea, don't you?"

"Not foolish. Difficult, perhaps." He turned to gaze out the window, to where the sun was even now beginning to set. "Cheyenne is still such a young city. Twenty years ago, it didn't even exist."

"That's true, but it's also a wealthy city. I've heard that we have more millionaires here than any other city in the country. Our citizens can afford a school."

Barrett nodded slowly. "That's true, but just because they can afford one doesn't mean they would approve. I'm sure many would consider a school for half a dozen pupils to be a luxury, not a necessity. They'd rather spend taxes on trolleys that everyone can use than on another school, especially one that would serve so few."

Charlotte had feared Barrett would react this way. She had told him she wanted his advice, and she did, but she had hoped that he would agree with her. "There are probably other blind and deaf children in the state," she said, trying to influence his opinion. "Their parents could send them here. It would be better than having a child at a school back East. At least they could visit more often."

For a long moment, Barrett said nothing. His expression remained inscrutable, but the flexing and releasing of his fingers told Charlotte he was pondering the concept. "You're right," he said at last. "It's a good idea."

"You really think so?" Charlotte hoped he wasn't simply trying to placate her.

Barrett's lips curved into a smile as he nodded. "Remember, Landry never lies."

"I'm so relieved." Charlotte felt her shoulders slump as the weight of worry was lifted. "Ever since I saw Nancy, I kept thinking about a school. You'll probably think I'm silly, but I even dreamt about it."

He shook his head. "I'd never call you silly. You're honest and courageous, and your idea is a good one."

Honest and courageous. If only he knew how wrong he was. Charlotte still felt like a coward, sneaking away from Fort Laramie, pretending she was returning to Vermont, then using her maiden name rather than admitting she was Jeffrey Crowley's widow. She ought to tell Barrett the whole truth, and she would . . . someday.

"I'm not sure what I can do," he said slowly. "It's not something one man can do alone. I'll need to talk to some people, get their support. I don't know how long that will take or whether they'll even agree, but I can promise you one thing: I'll do what I can to make your dream come true."

The wistful tone of his voice made her ask, "What about your dreams? Are they coming true?"

His eyes darkened, and furrows re-appeared between them. "I can't say. The problem is, my dreams are no longer as clear as they used to be. Sometimes I feel as if I'm in the middle of a cattle stampede. I'm being swept along, powerless to change direction, and I don't know how to escape."

Charlotte shuddered at the image his words conjured. "That sounds uncomfortable."

"It is."

15

"I don't know what to do." The way Miriam clasped her hands around the coffee cup rather than sip her favorite beverage communicated her distress as effectively as her words. Though normally calm, this morning she appeared upset.

"What's wrong?" Charlotte hoped she would be able to comfort Miriam, but the truth was, she was feeling inadequate. She didn't know what to do to help Barrett realize his dreams. Gwen was out of sorts because she hadn't seen Warren for a week, and nothing Charlotte said appeared to lessen her concern. And then there was the school. Though she'd thought and prayed about it, Charlotte had no new ideas of how to turn that dream into reality if Barrett's colleagues did not agree that it was important for the city and the territory.

As Miriam's eyes filled with tears, she blinked furiously to keep them from falling.

"It's all so complicated. I love him, and I believe he loves me, but he hasn't said anything. Oh, Charlotte, I want nothing more than to be his wife." Miriam sighed. "I know my parents think it would be wonderful if I lived in Washington, but I don't care about that. All I care about is marrying the man I love. He must know that, so why doesn't he propose?"

Raising her cup to her lips to buy herself some time, Charlotte tried to corral her thoughts. She shouldn't have been surprised by Miriam's declaration, for she knew that her friend had deep feelings for Barrett, but she was surprised by his delay in asking for Miriam's hand. Charlotte had heard that some men were reluctant to commit themselves. Though she would not have thought that was true of Barrett, it might explain his statement that his dreams were no longer as clear as they'd once been, and he felt as if he were being carried in an unplanned direction.

"I don't know why some men are slow to declare their intentions." It wasn't what Miriam wanted to hear, but it was the truth. "One of my sisters asked me the same thing when we lived at . . ." Charlotte stopped, horrified that she had almost said Fort Laramie. "Home," she amended. "In her

311

case, the man was worried about a number of things. He needed to resolve them before he could think about marriage." Charlotte laid her hand on Miriam's arm. "If it's any consolation, they're happily married now."

Miriam managed a faint smile. "So you're advising patience?"

Charlotte nodded. That was what she needed too.

It was perfect. Warren laughed out loud as he headed his horse back to Cheyenne. He'd been pleased when Derek Slater had asked him to handle his legal affairs, but this was an unexpected bonus. While he'd been discussing the mundane details of his feed contract, Derek had mentioned that a man he knew, a farmer, had fallen on hard times and wanted to sell his land.

"It's too small to be worth my while," Derek had said. Warren had translated that to mean that Derek had little free cash. All the better for him. When Warren paid a call on Anthony Franklin, he'd been hard-pressed to contain his excitement. What Derek Slater found too small was perfect for Warren. The farmhouse was large enough for him and Gwen and Rose, and there were several outbuildings, including a good-sized barn that could house the pony he planned to give Rose. An hour later, he and Anthony Franklin had shaken hands. All that was left was for Warren to draft a bill of sale and give Franklin the money. Within a week, the home Gwen dreamt of would be his. Yes, indeed, 1887 was the year for dreams to come true.

"You have a letter from your sister."

Charlotte gave the treadle one last pump, then let the sewing machine slow to a stop. Though she was rushing to finish Mrs. Slater's dress, a letter was a treat and a good reason to take a brief break. Gwen knew that, which was why she had interrupted Charlotte's sewing.

"Which sister?" Charlotte asked as she rose and stretched her back. As much as she enjoyed sewing, there was no doubt that it took its toll on her, cramping the muscles in her back and legs.

"Abigail." Gwen held out the envelope. "I can always tell by the penmanship. Hers is perfect and precise. Elizabeth's is a bit messier."

Gwen was right. "I could defend Elizabeth by saying that she's so busy, but the truth is, my sisters' handwriting reflects their personalities. Abigail can be impulsive, but normally she thinks things through, while Elizabeth lets her feelings drive her. She's so tenderhearted that she couldn't bear to see anyone ill. She always wanted to heal people, and now she's only a few months from being a doctor." The thought continued to amaze Charlotte. Little Elizabeth, the baby of the family, would soon be Dr. Harding. "She'll be a wonderful physician."

When Gwen returned to the apartment, Charlotte stared at the envelope, savoring the prospect of reading Abigail's news, hoping it included good tidings. Perhaps the letter would include the long-awaited announcement that Abigail was expecting a child. She and Ethan had been married for over a year now, but there was no sign of a baby, and Charlotte knew that distressed her sister. Abigail had even mentioned consulting Elizabeth, for their youngest sister had a special interest in women's health.

Charlotte slit the envelope carefully. Even if Elizabeth could help Abigail, there was nothing she could do for David. No one could cure his blindness, nor Nancy Cox's. What they needed was a teacher, not a doctor. Though she knew there had to be a way to give David and Nancy and the other children the schooling that would enable them to live almost normal lives, for a few moments at least, Charlotte would not think about that. She would concentrate on Abigail's letter.

She smiled as she read the first page, which described the antics of Abigail's dog. Puddles, it seemed, had not outgrown his curiosity about unusual smells and had had an encounter with a skunk. Predictably, the skunk had emerged victorious. *Puddles was not happy about being banished to the stable until the smell subsided,* Abigail wrote. *I only hope he learned his lesson.*

Charlotte turned the page, her smile fading as Abigail's letter took a more serious tone. *I know that if I were sitting there with you and asked this question, you'd freeze me with one of your famous cold looks, but I'm taking the chance that, once you reflect on it, you'll answer my oh so personal question.*

What could Abigail want to know? As children they'd shared everything. It was only after her marriage that Charlotte had not felt comfortable confiding in her sister.

Do I detect a romance developing between you and Mr. Landry? Charlotte stared at the sheet of ivory paper, wanting to toss it across the room. *Before you crumple the paper or deny that there's any truth to my question, let me tell you that I've noticed that his name appears more often in each of your letters.* Charlotte hadn't been aware that she'd written much about Barrett, but most evenings she'd been so tired that she hadn't reread her epistles before sealing the envelopes. Trust Abigail to notice something she hadn't.

The summer I tried to deny my feelings for Ethan, her sister continued, *my letters were filled with him. That's why I burned so many. I couldn't send them when they revealed so much of my heart.*

Charlotte leaned back in the chair, closing her eyes as she considered Abigail's words. She hadn't meant to reveal her heart. She took a deep breath, then opened her eyes and returned to the letter.

It may simply be my imagination, but I hope it's not. From what you've written, Mr. Landry appears to be a kind, honorable man. He was all that and much more. *I know you're reluctant to marry again. I understand your reasons.* Charlotte shook her head. Abigail knew only part of the reason she was wary of marriage. *You'll probably want to toss this away, but I'm going to give you some sisterly advice. Man was not meant to live alone, and neither was woman. Put aside your fears, Charlotte, and let yourself live. The right man will bring you and David untold happiness.*

Laying the letter on the sewing table, Charlotte stared at the wall, scarcely noticing the pattern sketches she had tacked in front of her work area. The right man. Abigail's words reverberated through her mind. Barrett wasn't the right man for her.

Charlotte wouldn't deny that she cared for him. It would be foolish to even try, when she thought of him so often, when the mere prospect of seeing him brightened her day. He wasn't like Jeffrey. She knew that now. But even if he weren't on the verge of asking for Miriam's hand, someone as much in the public eye as Barrett was not the right man for Charlotte, nor was she the right woman for him.

Each of them had the potential to hurt the other. Voters expecting perfection from their candidates might look askance at David, and that could lessen Barrett's chance of being elected. Equally concerning was the attention Charlotte would attract if she were at Barrett's side while he campaigned. Now that she knew the baron was in Cheyenne, she had no choice but to be extra vigilant. Under ordinary circumstances, it was unlikely she would encounter the baron, but she could not afford to take David to any public gatherings. If the baron saw David, he would likely realize he was Jeffrey's son, for the resemblance grew each day.

No matter what Abigail thought, Barrett was not the right man for Charlotte.

Barrett stared at the sheet of paper, reading the words that had taken him hours to compose. The whole speech would last no more than ten minutes. Others might speak far longer, trying to impress the legislature with their oratorical skills. Barrett knew only too well how boring those long lectures could be. He didn't want to bore the legislators. To the contrary, he wanted to excite them, to make them understand how critical water rights were, how vital it was that Wyoming had a policy that would protect its most important resource.

He had agonized over each word, wanting the cadence to be perfect. Knowing he had only a short time to convince the lawmakers, he was determined that each word would be so powerful that by the time he finished, no one would doubt the importance of his beliefs.

He rose and, holding the paper in front of him, recited his speech. It was good. It was more than good. It was excellent. It would accomplish what he sought.

Slowly, deliberately, he tore it into tiny pieces.

Her neighbor was ill. Charlotte blanched as she entered the store and heard Mr. Yates coughing. This was no ordinary cough but a prolonged racking that made Charlotte fear he would injure himself. Elizabeth had once told her that people, particularly elderly people, could crack a rib simply by coughing. Concerned, Charlotte rushed toward the counter. "Are you all right?"

The shopkeeper thumped his chest with his fist, then took a sip of water as the cough subsided. "I've been better." He took another sip, his color starting to return to normal. "This winter has been worse than any I can remember, or maybe it's just that these old bones don't tolerate cold anymore." A rueful expression crossed his face. "I can't wait until spring arrives."

Charlotte nodded, thinking of the small garden in Mr. Yates's backyard. "Your lilacs are always beautiful."

"I won't see them where I'm gonna be."

Though she didn't want to believe the situation was so dire, there was only one way to know. "What do you mean?" she asked.

He looked at her for a second, seemingly

startled by the intensity in her voice. "I'm not gonna die, if that's what you thought. I've made up my mind, though. I'm gonna go to Arizona. I'm tired of working, and my cough will be better there." He took another sip of water, frowning as he said, "First I need to find a buyer for the store. I can't move into my sister's house empty-handed."

Charlotte let out a sigh of relief. Though she would miss her neighbor when he moved, she was thankful that he was not seriously ill.

He looked at her, his expression hopeful. "I don't suppose you've changed your mind about buying it, have you?"

There was no reason to dissemble. "I'm afraid not."

Charlotte was humming as she frosted the cake. Though she wasn't as good a cook as Gwen, she didn't want the other woman to do all the work, especially when the cake was designed for Charlotte's visitor. Barrett was coming to spend the afternoon with her and David, and she wanted to be able to offer him refreshments.

"David, Mr. Landry is here," she called half an hour later as she opened the door to admit Barrett. Gwen had taken Rose into their room so that the little girl would not interfere with David's playtime, but she had agreed that they would come out for cake.

"Bowl!" David, who'd been sitting in the doorway to the room he shared with Charlotte, leaned forward, his arms reaching out to the sides as he searched for his ball.

While Barrett hung his coat on the hook near the door, Charlotte spoke softly. "I'm afraid he expects you to play with him. Ever since I told him you were coming, bowling is all he can talk about."

"I don't mind. As I recall, when I invited myself, bowling was part of the plan."

The ball firmly in his grip, David struggled to his feet, then toppled over, losing the ball in the process. "Ow!" It was a scene that was repeated a dozen times each day. Each time David would yowl, more from the loss of his precious toy than any injury.

"Let me help." Barrett crossed the room and knelt next to David. "You need to stand up first," he explained. "Then I'll give you the ball."

Though David appeared dubious, he nodded. "Bowl."

"Yes, David, we'll do that. But not here. We need to go into the other room."

Charlotte watched as David gripped the door frame for balance, then rose to his feet. A grin on his face, he extended his arms, chortling when Barrett placed the ball in his hands.

"Now, follow me," Barrett said as he began to walk slowly toward the part of the room that served as a parlor. "You're a good walker, David."

Charlotte smiled and pointed toward the book that she consulted each evening. "Thanks to that, he does better every day." She was still uncertain of her ability to teach David all he needed to know, but at least they had made progress with walking.

"Bowl." Her son was nothing if not persistent.

Nodding, Charlotte gathered a handful of blocks and set up the row. "All right, David, bowl."

He shook his head. "No."

Barrett, who was standing next to him, put his hand on David's shoulder. "Bowl." To Charlotte's surprise, her son looked up at Barrett, his confusion apparent.

David wasn't the only one to be confused. "I don't understand. He did it the last time you were here." She looked at Barrett, then focused her attention on her son. "Bowl, David." Again, he refused.

Wrinkling his nose, as if he were pondering a serious topic, Barrett said, "The only difference is, I was by the blocks last time."

With a shrug, he walked the five feet to stand at Charlotte's side. "Bowl, David," he said.

And this time David did. "Bowl!" he cried triumphantly when several of the blocks toppled. "Bowl!" David scampered back to his starting position, clearly ready for another chance to play.

Charlotte shrugged as she looked at Barrett. "That's strange. It seems that he listens to your voice and rolls the ball toward it. I don't understand why he won't do that for me."

Barrett's eyes twinkled as he set up the blocks and cued David. "You never know how children's minds work, do you? I don't suppose it matters. I'm just glad he's happy."

"He's an amazingly happy child," Charlotte said as she moved to the settee and waited for David to tire of the game. When he did and seemed content to play by himself in the corner, she gestured toward the chair opposite her.

"You like making people happy, don't you?" Barrett asked as he settled into the chair.

It was an unexpected question. "Doesn't everyone?"

Barrett shook his head. "Not to the same

extent." When he frowned, she wondered if he was thinking of a specific person. "Some people are more concerned with themselves. They seek power or wealth or influence — things that benefit them, not others."

"Power has never held much appeal to me, but wealth . . ." Charlotte chuckled as she said, "I could certainly use some of that."

"And what would you do with it?"

"Build a school and . . ."

His eyes twinkling with amusement, Barrett nodded. "If I were Warren, I'd say something like 'I rest my case.' Listen to yourself, Charlotte. You weren't planning to use the money for yourself."

He made her sound as if she were some kind of saint. She wasn't. Far from it. "It was for myself, in a way. My sisters used to laugh at me, but I always wanted everyone to be happy. I think it might have been because I was sick so much of the time when I was a child. I could see how worried everyone was, and I knew it was my fault, so I made it my mission to make the others happy."

"Who are you trying to help today?"

Charlotte blinked. "I didn't know it was that obvious."

"Only to someone who knows you well. So, who is it?"

"Mr. Yates. I don't like the idea of losing him as a neighbor, but he wants to move to Arizona."

Barrett let out a soft tsking sound. "He didn't tell me that."

"I don't think he wants his customers to know until it's all settled. He still hasn't found a buyer for the store."

"Unless it's someone new to Cheyenne, I imagine that will be difficult."

"Cake!" Suddenly tired of playing with his wooden animals, David shouted the word.

"Yes, David," Charlotte agreed, "we'll have cake. But you need to wait a few minutes." She wanted to understand why Barrett believed Mr. Yates would have trouble selling his shop. "The store seems to be doing well. I don't see why it would be hard to find a buyer."

His expression solemn, Barrett shook his head. "People come out of loyalty to Mr. Yates. That's why I buy my shirts there. It wouldn't be the same with a new owner. I'd probably go to Myers Dry Goods. He has a better selection."

And selection was critical for readymade items. Charlotte's customers knew they would have to wait when they ordered a dress from her, but people who went into a

325

dry goods store or a mercantile hoped to walk out with their purchases. "I knew Mr. Myers's store was bigger, but I haven't spent enough time there to compare the selection."

"Size is part of the reason why selection is a problem. Mr. Yates's shop is too small for the city we've become. If the new owner wanted to be successful, he'd have to expand it to have room to stock everything his customers expected." When David started to fuss, Barrett bent down and ruffled his hair. "Just a little longer. I know it's boring for you, David, but the grown-ups need to talk a bit more. You can wait, can't you?"

David nodded.

"There are only two ways to expand the store," Barrett continued. "The first is to turn the second floor into a shop. The problem is, there's no interior staircase, and adding one would be costly. Plus, the new owner would need to hire someone to work up there, and he'd have to find another place to live."

As she listened, Charlotte's frown matched Barrett's. "That doesn't sound very feasible. You said there were two ways. What's the second?"

"Take over Élan. That would double the space. A dry goods store could definitely be profitable that way."

"But I don't want to sell my store." Charlotte's gesture encompassed the large room that served as kitchen, dining room, and parlor. "Even if I could still live here, that would leave me without a source of income." And that was unthinkable. "Mr. Yates keeps hoping I'll buy his store, but I can't. I don't need more space for Élan, and I don't want to run a dry goods store."

Barrett nodded. "I agree with you on the last part. When I left Pennsylvania, I swore I'd never work in another mercantile. It's not an easy life, catering to customers. I hate to say this, Charlotte, but you can't make everyone happy."

"I don't want to believe that." There had to be a way to help Mr. Yates.

16

Barrett took a deep breath as he looked at the men who'd nodded politely when he'd been introduced. He knew most of them by sight but only a quarter or so well enough to call them acquaintances. According to Richard, that was a problem. A successful politician, Richard had declared, forged strong ties to other lawmakers. It wasn't enough to be elected; a man had to accomplish great things during his term, and the only way that happened was by enlisting others' support. That was why Barrett was here today, to convince these men, the duly elected representatives of the citizens of Wyoming, that his proposal was vital to their interests.

"Gentlemen, I thank you for allowing me to be here this morning. I know many of you expected me to speak of water rights. The truth is, that had been my plan. I even wrote the speech."

As he looked around, Barrett saw a flicker of interest light several faces. Perhaps those men would at least listen to him. He'd noticed that a number of the others appeared to be close to sleep, possibly because they'd enjoyed the capital city's nocturnal pleasures. He had heard that the saloons' business increased dramatically when the legislature was in session.

Barrett took another breath, keeping his expression neutral as he said, "Water rights are important to every one of us in Wyoming, but there is another subject that I believe is more urgent."

Being in the middle of a cattle stampede would have been more pleasant than what he had endured this morning. Barrett frowned as he climbed into the carriage. It had been awful, worse than anything he'd imagined, and the worst was yet to come. He flicked the reins and headed south on Ferguson. He had to tell Charlotte. As painful as it would be, he couldn't risk letting her hear rumors of what had happened. Reality was bad enough; he could only imagine how the rumor mill would exaggerate and distort it, turning a bad situation into a disaster.

Forcing a smile onto his face, Barrett

hitched the horse and opened Élan's front door. "Can you close shop early?" he asked when Charlotte approached him, a genuine smile on her face. "I thought we might go to Rue de Rivoli for tea."

Her smile faded faster than the snow had melted under the force of the Chinook. "What's wrong?"

"That's the first time anyone's responded to an invitation to tea that way." Barrett forced a light tone to his voice. "I thought you might enjoy it."

She nodded slowly. "I would if I weren't worried about you. Your expression tells me something's very wrong."

There was no reason to deny the truth. He'd only be postponing the inevitable. "You'd better sit down," he cautioned. When she was seated and he'd taken the chair next to her, he blurted out, "I addressed the legislature this morning."

Tipping her head to one side, as if she were trying to determine why that had caused him distress, Charlotte said, "I wish I'd known. I would have tried to be there. I never tire of hearing you speak about water rights."

"I didn't talk about water rights. I kept thinking about what you said, about being true to myself, and I knew that I had to address the issue of cattle grazing. You were right, though. No one supported me. Support?" Barrett let out a brittle laugh. "They told me I was a traitor to the cause and that any hopes I had of being the party's candidate for senator were gone."

"Oh, Barrett, I'm so sorry. But maybe it's not as bad as you think. People do forget."

He shook his head. "They won't. My political aspirations are ended." He swallowed deeply, not wanting to admit the rest but knowing that he had to. "I scuttled both my career and your dream of a school."

For a second, her eyes registered confusion. "What do you mean?"

"I tried talking to a few of the men afterwards. You know what they did?"

Though he didn't want to tell her all that had transpired, he knew she would hear some version of this morning's events. It was best that she heard the story from him, undistorted by scandalmongers. "They laughed, Charlotte." And that had hurt. Not himself. He could withstand ridicule. What had hurt was the casual disregard for Charlotte's dream. "They said it was a frivolous idea and that anyone with a grain of common sense would realize that the territory has far more important problems." The knives the party's influential men had thrown at him had lodged deeper at the realization that they believed giving a child like David an education was a frivolous idea. "It isn't frivolous," Barrett said firmly, "but that's what they thought."

He extended his hand and covered hers, trying to give her some measure of comfort. "I'm sorry, Charlotte. I thought I could help, but all I did was destroy your chances of getting support."

As tears filled her eyes, she brushed them away, then straightened her shoulders.

"Don't blame yourself, Barrett. I know you did everything you could, and that's the best gift you could have given me. It's not over, though. I won't give up hope. There has to be a way to get the school established. I just have to look harder."

His heart lighter than it had been all day, Barrett returned her smile.

He was angry. She could see it in his gait, the way he swung his arms, the rigid line of his neck. Perhaps she should ignore it. Mama claimed that the best thing a woman could do with an angry man was to ignore him until the mood had passed, but Miriam could not.

"Richard!" She reined in the horse and halted the carriage next to him. "Come for a ride with me."

He shook his head. "I'm not fit company."

"All the more reason why you need a ride. It will take your mind off whatever is bothering you."

"Nothing can stop me from thinking about the idiocy," Richard said as he climbed into the carriage.

For the first time in her memory, he looked haggard, and that worried Miriam. Normally Richard was even-tempered, able to slough off disappointment. Something was obviously different today. "What happened?" she asked. Though she had been on her way to Élan, she did not turn on Ferguson, sensing that whatever had bothered Richard would be more easily revealed if there were fewer people around.

Richard waited until they'd headed north on Eddy before he spoke. "It's Barrett. He's committed suicide." When Miriam gasped, Richard laid his hand on her arm and gave it a small squeeze. "I'm sorry. I didn't mean to alarm you. That was a poor choice of words. Barrett didn't kill himself, but he did kill his best chance at being elected."

Miriam slowed the horse so that she could focus her attention on Richard. "How did he do that?"

"He addressed the legislature."

333

"About water rights." Though she would not have admitted it to him, Miriam had found Barrett's almost incessant discussion of water boring. Perhaps the lawmakers did too.

"No." Richard's lips curled in disgust. "He talked about limiting the stock growers, about putting quotas on how many cattle they could have."

"What's so wrong about that?"

"Besides the fact that no one wants to have government tell them how to run their business?" Richard's voice dripped with scorn. "He made it sound as if anyone who disagreed was selfish, that they were putting their own interests over the well-being of the land. I can tell you, that didn't go over well. I've never seen the legislators so angry. If they'd had tar and feathers, Barrett would be wearing a new coat."

"How awful for Barrett! He must have been mortified." Miriam knew he'd been anxious about his speech at the same time that he was eager to become better known. What she didn't know was why he'd decided not to talk about water rights.

Richard tightened his grip on her arm. "I don't care about Barrett. I care about the fact that in being so stupid, he jeopardized your future. Unless rivers start flowing upstream, your chances of being a senator's wife are gone."

"I don't care about that."

It seemed as if Richard did not hear her, for he continued. "I would not have done that to the woman I love. I love you too deeply to do anything that would hurt you."

Miriam stared at Richard, wondering if she'd heard correctly. It sounded as if he'd said he loved her, but never — not even in her most far-fetched fantasies — had she imagined a declaration of love like this. As the blood drained from his face, then rushed back, turning his cheeks cherry red, Miriam knew she was not mistaken.

"Do you love me, Richard?"

He clenched his jaw, and for a moment Miriam feared he would deny it. "Yes, but . . ."

She loved him. There was no denying it. She loved everything about him, from the bump on his nose that kept his face from being perfectly handsome to the way his fingers wrapped around David's ball, almost caressing the smooth wood before he rolled it across the floor. She loved his honesty, his sense of humor, his integrity. She loved the way his eyes sparkled when he was happy and how he tried to mask his disappointment. She loved his kindness and his generosity. The simple fact was, Charlotte loved Barrett. She would never so much as hint that she cared so deeply for him, but she could not help wishing for one day — one perfect day — of loving and being loved by him.

Charlotte let out a sigh. There was no point in wishing for the impossible. Look what those foolish thoughts had wrought. She'd sewn a crooked seam. With another deep sigh, she began to pick out the stitches. Next time she'd be more careful.

She had the seam half undone when the doorbell tinkled. Rising to greet her customer, Charlotte heard the distinctive sound of Miriam's laughter.

"Oh, Charlotte!" Miriam flung her arms out and twirled in a circle. "I'm the happiest woman alive. He told me he loves me."

"What were you thinking?" Warren demanded the instant the study door closed behind him.

Barrett sighed. It had been a week since the debacle at the state legislature. Although the rumor mill had been kinder than he'd had any reason to hope, he knew that Warren would not be pleased. He'd expected a reaction almost immediately and suspected the only reason he'd been spared for so long was that his friend had been out of town on some mysterious business.

"You told me to be more visible, to let people know my views," Barrett said as he poured Warren a cup of coffee. "That's what I did."

"Regulating your peers?" Warren's voice was harsh with sarcasm. "I thought we agreed that water policy would be the problem you'd tackle."

"This was more urgent."

"What it was was foolish. And why on earth did you have to compound your foolishness by talking about a school for the blind? Why would you care about that?" Warren stretched his legs in front of him, crossing them at the ankles. "There are schools in other places. The parents can send them there."

Barrett tried not to wince at the memory that he'd once advocated exactly that. But that was before he understood the price both Charlotte and David would have paid.

"What if the parents don't want to send their children away?"

Warren shrugged. "That's their problem, not yours."

And that was where he was wrong. "It is my problem. Charlotte's son is blind."

His eyes narrowing, Warren stared at Barrett for a long moment before he spoke. "You're considering marrying her, aren't you?"

"What if I were?" Barrett wouldn't answer directly, not when Warren was in this mood.

"Then I'd say you were as blind as her boy. The voters want to see a perfect family, not one with a damaged child."

When Barrett started to protest the term, Warren held up a hand, silencing him. "I don't care how pretty she is; don't throw away your chance at power for a pretty face."

Charlotte was more than a pretty face. She was a warm, caring woman, a woman of deep loyalty and unshakable integrity. The fact that she was also beautiful was only a small part of her appeal. But Barrett would not tell Warren that, for he doubted the older man would understand. When he'd first entertained the thought of running for office, it had been for selfish reasons. Though he had not admitted it to either Warren or Richard, Barrett had been more concerned about impressing his brothers than serving the citizens of Wyoming. That had changed. As the months had passed, he'd realized how wrong he'd been, and it was all because of Charlotte.

"It isn't power I want," he said firmly. "It's to be in a position where I can make a difference." That was the challenge Charlotte had given him, and now more than ever before, Barrett was determined to answer that challenge.

Warren snorted. "You're only fooling yourself if you believe that. Every man wants power."

"Then why don't you run for office?" Though it was a question Barrett had asked himself a dozen times, this was the first time he'd voiced it.

"I would if I were twenty years younger."

17

She refused — she absolutely refused — to dwell on the fact that Barrett had finally declared his love to Miriam and that their engagement would likely be announced any day now. When memories of Miriam's radiant smile resurfaced, Charlotte forced herself to smile and then to remind herself that she had more important things to worry about, starting with the school.

Though Barrett had done his best, it appeared that the decision makers of Wyoming Territory did not share Charlotte's belief that a school for the blind and deaf was essential. She couldn't let them stop her. There had to be something she could do to help David and Nancy. In the meantime, she would do what she could for the unfortunate women who took their meals at Mrs. Kendall's boardinghouse.

Charlotte shivered as she hurried toward 15th Street. January was supposed to be the coldest month, but this year February seemed to be trying for that dubious honor. With the mercury dipping below zero and a stiff wind turning snowflakes into icy pellets, it was not a night for a stroll. Perhaps she should have waited another day, but when she'd finished the brown calico dress, she had been filled with a sense of urgency, and so she'd donned her heaviest coat, thankful that the veil she always wore to Mrs. Kendall's provided at least a measure of protection for her face.

"C'mon in, honey." As she had expected, even though it wasn't quite five o'clock, Mrs. Kendall was bustling around the kitchen. "I got some coffee ready, and if you can wait a few minutes, there'll be cinnamon buns fresh outta the oven."

Though the aroma was enticing, Charlotte shook her head. "I can't stay that long."

"Nonsense." Mrs. Kendall pulled out a chair and glared at it, as if willing Charlotte to remove her coat and sit there. "You need to warm up. I cain't have you turnin' into an icicle."

Flexing her fingers, Charlotte realized that the tips were tingling from the cold. It would be foolish to return home until they'd warmed a bit. She unbuttoned her coat and hung it on the hook near the door, smiling when Mrs. Kendall grabbed the coat and draped it over the chair nearest the stove so that it would warm more quickly.

"You need some coffee too," she announced. "I reckon you could drink it without takin' off your veil if you was careful."

Charlotte heard the slightly miffed tone in the older woman's voice and realized that she had insulted her by not revealing her identity. Though initially she had been worried about her customers, that concern had paled when Charlotte had learned that the baron was a frequent patron of Sylvia's. She could not take the risk of lifting her veil, for the baron must never discover that she and David lived in Cheyenne. "Thank you," Charlotte said. "Your coffee smells delicious. But first I want to show you what I brought. There are two more dresses," she explained as she opened the package she'd wrapped in an old sheet. "The brown is my favorite."

Mrs. Kendall fingered the calico. "It's perfect. They're both perfect." She poured coffee into a tin mug and pushed it across the table toward Charlotte. "I wish you could see the difference havin' proper clothes makes. The gals don't just look different, they act different too. More modest-like." She sipped her coffee. "Now, drink yours."

Charlotte complied, though it was difficult to maneuver the cup to her mouth without removing her veil. At last, frustrated by the layers of tulle, she raised it enough to clear her mouth, holding it back with her left hand while she lifted the cup with her right.

"I heerd from Sally and Laura," Mrs. Kendall continued. "They're the two of Sylvia's gals what went to Laramie last month. Sally done got herself a job as a washerwoman, and Laura's working as a cook. It wouldn't a' happened without your dresses."

It was a nice thought, but Charlotte couldn't accept the credit for the young women's transformation. "It takes more than a new dress to change a person's life. You have to want to change."

"Mebbe so, but decent clothing helps." Mrs. Kendall rose, opening the oven door and withdrawing a pan of fragrant rolls. "I shore wish I could sew like you."

"It's not difficult," Charlotte said when she'd tasted the delicious pastry. "Anyone can learn if they have the right teacher."

The right teacher. Charlotte started to laugh when she heard her own words. That could be the answer.

"What's so funny?"

"Nothing, really. I've been trying to solve a problem, and I realized that the answer's been here all along. Thank you, Mrs. Kendall. You unlocked the door."

Though the other woman looked dubious, Charlotte was not, and her words echoed through her mind as she walked home. If the legislators wouldn't approve a school, someone else had to do something. Who better than Charlotte? It was true that she had been frustrated by the book Barrett had given her. Although it was a beginning, it wasn't enough. She now knew that what she needed was the right teacher. It wasn't as if Charlotte was inexperienced. She had taught children long enough to know that she would be able to teach blind children, if she had the right schooling. What she needed was to be trained by someone who had actually taught blind children.

Charlotte grimaced as she crossed 16th Street and the wind buffeted her. It wouldn't be easy. She knew that. She would have to find someone who had been trained at the Perkins School. Barrett's book had been written by a woman who had studied there, and she had indicated that it was one of the finest schools devoted to the education of blind children. That was what Charlotte wanted and what David and Nancy deserved: the best.

Perhaps someone who had trained there could spend a few months in Cheyenne with Charlotte. If not, she would go to Watertown, Massachusetts, and study at the school. It would be expensive, for she would have to close the store while she and David traveled east. With no money coming in and substantial expenses, her savings would be depleted in a few months. Unless . . . Charlotte smiled as she thought of Mrs. Cox. The woman had said she would do anything to give Nancy the life she deserved, and she had made it clear that she was far from destitute. She would probably help defray the costs while Charlotte studied, since the training would benefit Nancy.

Her heart suddenly lighter, Charlotte climbed the steps to her apartment. There were many things to consider, but she believed she was headed in the right direction, and that felt good. Very good.

Miriam glanced around the room. If anyone had forgotten that they were celebrating Valentine's Day, one look at the parlor and the dining room would have reminded them. Her friend Betty's mother had outdone herself tonight, decorating the entire first floor of their home in shades of red and pink in honor of the occasion. Swags of red crepe were draped on the curving staircase, while a pink tablecloth and red linen napkins transformed the dining room into a Valentine. Even the candles in the parlor chandelier had been replaced with pink ones.

As Miriam flexed her fingers inside the satin gloves Charlotte had made for her, the string quartet rose and bowed, signaling the beginning of a brief intermission.

"Would you like a cup of punch?"

Miriam fanned her face. It was silly to be so flustered. After all, she had known that Richard would be one of the guests. But now that he was at her side, speaking to her for the first time this evening, she could not stop the blood from rushing to her face.

"No, thank you," she said, laying her hand on his arm, "but I would like to find a quiet corner."

Richard gave her a crooked smile. "That may be an impossible quest," he said as he glanced around the room. He took a step toward the archway that separated the parlor from the entry hall. After peering around the corner, he grinned. "Success. Not only is there no one in the hallway right now, but there's a place to sit."

When they reached the padded oak bench and Miriam had arranged her skirts, Richard's smile faded. "I'm surprised you're not with Barrett. I saw you dancing together." Though his voice remained even, Richard clenched his fists. "Everyone says you're the perfect couple."

Surely he didn't believe that. Surely he realized that she loved him as much as he did her. But perhaps he did not. Perhaps he believed that she viewed him as nothing more than a friend. After all, she hadn't told him that she loved him. The day he'd admitted his love, Richard had refused to discuss it further, his face turning so stony that Miriam had known the time was not right for her own declaration. Tonight might not be the right time, either, but she could not let Richard continue to believe she cared for Barrett, and so, though her mother would be appalled by her forwardness, she spoke.

"Barrett and I could only be the perfect couple if we loved each other. We don't. I don't love Barrett, and I doubt that he's ever loved me. You know the truth, Richard. It was a business arrangement. Barrett wanted my father's endorsement, and my parents thought he'd be a good husband for me. Now that the party seems to have disowned Barrett, my mother's having doubts about him. She wants me to marry a man with prospects."

Miriam kept her eyes fixed on Richard. Though she had thought he might respond, he remained silent, his hands so tightly fisted that his knuckles whitened.

"I love my parents," she continued. "I'd do almost anything to make them happy, but I won't marry a man I don't love." This was his chance to tell her that he loved her, to ask if she returned his love, but Richard said nothing. Miriam was ready to scream in frustration. When they discussed books or music, Richard was eloquent, never at a loss for words. Tonight, when the subject was far more important, he was silent.

She took a deep breath. It went against all the rules, but she couldn't continue in this state of limbo, believing Richard loved her but not knowing whether they had a future together. "I love you, Richard," she said, slowly and distinctly. "You said you loved me. If that's true, won't you marry me?" There. She'd done it. She had actually proposed to a man. Now it was up to Richard to agree.

But he did not. Though his eyes had brightened when she'd declared her love, they were once again somber. "You know your parents would never approve. I'm too old, and I'll never be a senator."

Miriam shook her head. "I don't care that you're older." She would not say "too old," for he was not. "I don't care about anything but being your wife."

"It's not that simple." There was a note of resignation in his voice. Miriam hated it and the fact that his eyes no longer sparkled.

"It is simple. We don't need my parents' permission. I'm old enough to make my own decisions. We can elope."

It wasn't only that the sparkle had disappeared from Richard's eyes. Now they were filled with sadness. "You'd regret it."

"I would not. Besides, before you know it, Mama and Papa will relent."

"What if they didn't? Could you go through the rest of your life being estranged from them?"

Though it was a prospect she had not considered, Miriam nodded. "You're more important to me than they are." She tried to infuse enthusiasm into her voice, but she knew that Richard heard her hesitation.

"I'm sorry, my love, but I can't take that risk."

"I'm glad we're finally getting our chance to have tea at Rue de Rivoli," Barrett said as he opened the front door to the impressive sandstone edifice. Though Charlotte had tried to refuse Barrett's invitation, believing it unwise to be seen in public with him when he was close to announcing his engagement to Miriam, he had insisted that this would be a business meeting. She might still have refused, but the disappointment on Barrett's face had convinced her to accept. And so here they were.

Unlike the entrances to many buildings situated on a street corner, Rue de Rivoli's door was angled so that it faced the corner rather than favor either street. Apparently the architect who'd designed the massive building hadn't been able to decide whether Ferguson or 16th Street would be the more prominent and had hedged his bets. In Charlotte's opinion, the angled entry gave the building a special appeal. Barrett smiled as if he shared her opinion and escorted her inside.

"I hope you enjoy the afternoon," he said as the waiter showed them to a table near the front window.

"When I heard that Cheyenne's most prominent women come here for tea, I thought you might get some new customers if people saw you here."

Charlotte waited to respond until Barrett had ordered tea and afternoon sandwiches.

"I may not want any more customers," she told him. "If everything goes the way I hope, I won't have time to sew many gowns."

She had spent hours scribbling on a slate, erasing one set of numbers after another, making notes about everything that could go wrong. Now that she was comfortable with her plans, Charlotte was eager to discuss them with Barrett. This would be a business meeting, simply not the one he had envisioned. Although she thought her plans were complete, she knew that Barrett would tell her if she'd missed something important or if her assumptions were too optimistic.

When he raised an eyebrow, encouraging her to continue, she said, "I realized there's a way to turn my dream of a school into reality."

"And that is . . ."

Before she could answer, Mr. and Mrs. Slater entered the dining room. The flash of recognition followed by surprise that crossed Mr. Slater's face told Charlotte he knew Barrett but had not expected to see him here. Or perhaps he had not expected Charlotte to be with Barrett.

"Madame Charlotte. It's so good to see you." Mrs. Slater's greeting was genuine. She turned to her husband, loudly declaring that Charlotte was the woman who'd made her new gowns. If Barrett had wanted advertising for Charlotte, he'd gotten it.

When the older couple left for their table at the opposite side of the rapidly filling room, Barrett reminded Charlotte that they'd been discussing the school. "What did you discover?"

"I realized that I could be the teacher." Barrett said nothing, merely nodding as Charlotte explained her plan to gain the specialized training she needed. "The school won't have everything I once envisioned. I won't be able to hire other teachers, at least not initially, so I thought I'd start with only blind children."

"That seems to make sense." Barrett leaned forward, his expression intent. "Have you picked a location?"

Charlotte nodded. "If I could afford it, I'd buy Mr. Yates's store and use it, but since I can't do that, I thought I could divide my store in half, putting the school on one side and the shop on the other."

For the first time, Barrett seemed surprised. "You're going to keep Élan open?"

"I don't have any choice. I'll need more money than I can charge for tuition, so I thought I'd have the store open on Saturdays when there's no school. My customers can come for fittings then, but I'll do the actual sewing at night."

"It'll be a lot of work."

When the waiter had set a pot of tea in front of them, Charlotte poured herself and Barrett a cup. "You're right," she said as she stirred sugar into her tea. "At first, it felt daunting, but I think I can do it. I've never been afraid of hard work. I don't know about your family, but my parents raised the three of us to believe that working was a way of worshiping the Lord. They told us that's why he gave us talents."

As Barrett smiled, his eyes deepened to the color of an August sky. "My parents would have liked yours. They felt the same way." He took a sip of tea. "It sounds as if you're not planning for the school to be a boarding school."

"Not at first," she agreed. "I don't have enough room. Even if I closed the shop and used the whole ground floor, I don't think it would be large enough. I suspect I'll have only two pupils at the beginning: David and Nancy Cox." Charlotte would post notices of the school in the newspaper, just in case there were other blind children in Cheyenne, but she couldn't advertise outside the city when there was no place to house students.

"Will they learn as quickly as they would

at a boarding school?"

Trust Barrett to go to the heart of the matter. That question had bothered Charlotte too. "I don't know. I thought I'd ask the Perkins School when I inquire about becoming trained. I picked them because I've heard they're the best."

Barrett nodded. "Then you ought to start there. That's a lesson I learned from my parents. They told me to never settle for second best."

His demeanor had changed, the faint furrows between his eyes disappearing, replaced by a calm acceptance. Charlotte sensed that he had no further questions, and so she asked one of her own. "Do you think the school is a good idea?"

Instead of responding with a nod or a shake of the head, Barrett leaned forward slightly. "That depends," he said softly.

"On what?"

"Are you certain this is what you want to do with your life? Once you begin, it wouldn't be fair to your pupils or their parents to stop."

"I agree." Charlotte waited until the waiter had placed a platter on the table before she spoke again. "It's hard to explain," she said as she selected an egg salad sandwich. "The more I think about it, the more excited I become. I can't ever remember feeling this way, but I feel as if this is what I'm meant to do."

When Barrett said nothing, she took a bite of the sandwich, chewing carefully as she phrased her next sentence. After she washed the sandwich down with a swallow of tea, she said, "At first, I didn't understand. I asked God why my baby wasn't perfect and why he'd given me this cross to bear. Then my prayers changed, and I asked him what David had done to deserve being blind. There were no answers, but today I feel as if the school is the reason. There's a need for a school for the blind here. If David hadn't been born blind, I would never have realized that, and I certainly would not have considered starting one, but if it works out the way I hope it will, I'll be able to help other children, not just mine."

"And make the world a better place." Though there was no special inflection to his voice, the corners of Barrett's lips curved.

"You remember that?"

He arched an eyebrow. "I remember most things you've told me. I don't know what it is about you, Charlotte, but you're a hard woman to forget."

Feeling a blush steal its way to her cheeks,

Charlotte lowered her head and stirred another lump of sugar into her tea. She didn't need the additional sweetness, but stirring gave her a chance to settle her thoughts.

"I'll take that as a compliment."

When she looked up, Barrett was grinning. "It was meant as one. As for the school, if that's the way you feel, you definitely should open it."

Charlotte felt the warmth of his gaze as she offered to refill his teacup. She doubted he had any idea how his smile made her heart leap and the blood rush through her veins, and yet there was something special in his eyes, a tenderness that she hadn't seen before. It made no sense, for he had told Miriam he loved her, and yet Charlotte could not deny that Barrett's expression was almost lover-like.

"Thank you, Barrett. You're a good friend and a businessman." She emphasized the word *friend.* "That's why your opinion means so much to me."

To Charlotte's surprise, faint color stained his cheeks. It was almost as if he were as affected by her nearness as she was by his. Barrett cleared his throat. "I plan to go to the ranch for a few days. We'll talk again when I return. Who knows? I may have some new ideas for you. But never doubt it, Charlotte. The school is a good idea."

She took a deep breath, exhaling slowly as relief washed over her. There was only one hurdle left. She needed to tell Abigail and Elizabeth about David and her change of direction. She'd do that tonight, and then while she waited for their response, she would begin planning for her school.

Her fingers, her toes, every inch of her tingling with pleasure, she smiled at Barrett. He approved. He wanted to help her. He found her unforgettable. Somehow, silly as it was, it was the last thought that brought her the greatest happiness.

The buzzards were circling. Barrett tried to tamp down the dread that continued to well up inside him. He hadn't wanted to say anything to Charlotte — she'd been so excited about the prospect of opening a school for the blind — but for days now he'd been unable to dismiss his worries about the livestock. Several of the other cattle barons had scoffed when he'd mentioned his concerns. Cattle were sturdy animals, they'd told him. But Barrett knew that even the sturdiest of animals had its limits. There was only one way to allay his fears, and that was to see for himself.

So far, February had been a strange month. It hadn't been his imagination, Barrett knew, that prominent members of the party were displeased with him. Though they had offered greetings when they'd seen him at Betty Dawson's Valentine's Day dance, those had been at best perfunctory, at worst cold. And then there was Miriam. She had refused his offer to escort her to the party, saying she had received her own invitation and would go unaccompanied. Once there, she had seemed happy when he'd asked her to dance, although she had disappeared soon after that. That wasn't like Miriam, nor were the tears he'd seen glistening in her eyes when she'd returned to the dance floor. But when he'd expressed his concern, she had denied that anything was wrong.

Women. Barrett doubted he'd ever understand them. Fortunately, he'd had no trouble understanding Charlotte's desire for a school. While other women might have bewailed their fate, cursing God for afflicting them with a blind child, Charlotte had transformed her pain into a plan to help others in the same position. Barrett frowned as he thought of the challenges she faced. There had to be a way he could help her, but first he had to reach the ranch and discover what was happening to his cattle.

The buzzards were not a good sign. Though they'd been common enough in Pennsylvania, this was the first time he'd seen them in Wyoming. And even back East, when he'd seen a buzzard, it had been one or two, not the huge flocks that now circled overhead, marring the cloudless sky with their appearance.

As he rode north, Barrett's spirits continued to plummet. The reason for the buzzards' arrival wasn't hard to find. Dozens of dead cattle littered the ground. Though the cold had helped preserve their bodies, the inevitable decay had begun, attracting the birds of prey. The cattle had died of starvation. The buzzards would not.

"Is it as bad as I think?" Barrett asked Dustin as he removed his hat and drew closer to the stove. Though he'd thought the foreman might be riding the range, Barrett had found him sitting inside the main house, his slumped shoulders and gloomy expression mute evidence that he was as depressed as Barrett.

Dustin ran his fingers through his curly blond hair, frowning as he stared at the floor. Other than the brief look he'd given Barrett when he'd entered the building, Dustin had kept his eyes glued to the floor.

"Probably worse," he muttered. " 'Pears to me we done lost half the herd, and it ain't even March."

"What happened?" Though Barrett thought he knew, Dustin was the expert. He wanted his foreman to confirm his fears.

"They couldn't break through the ice to get to the grass. I cleared out as much as I could, but it weren't enough." The anguish he heard in Dustin's voice told Barrett the man was suffering as deeply as he was. "The ponds stayed frozen, so they couldn't drink, neither. When I chopped at 'em, all I got was ice. They was frozen clear to the bottom. Poor critters."

Starvation and dehydration. Barrett shuddered. "It's not a pretty way to die."

Dustin looked up, his eyes filled with pain. "I ain't never seen nothin' like it. There's no easy way to say this . . ."

He broke off, leaving Barrett to complete the sentence. "I'm ruined, and so are all the other stock growers."

" 'Fraid so." Dustin opened the stove and poked at the wood. "I'll pack my bags and head back to Missouri. Ain't no reason to stay here. I just waited so's I could tell you where I was headin' and why."

It was what he had feared. Barrett knew that pain and anger would come, but for the moment he was numb. The only pain that registered was Dustin's. His foreman had had more time to see the devastation and to recognize the consequences. Unlike Barrett, Dustin had no emergency fund. Barrett hadn't lost everything. Not quite, and with what remained, he could ease Dustin's worries. "There are still some cattle alive. We'll need to round them up this spring. I want you to do that."

His eyes widening with surprise, Dustin stared at Barrett. "You sure, Boss?"

"Sure enough to pay you in advance." Barrett reached into his pocket, withdrawing his wallet. "Here you go." Four months' pay wasn't a lot of money for Barrett, but it would make a difference for his foreman.

Dustin looked at the bills. "You trust me with that?" It was customary to pay cowboys for the work they'd completed, not to give them an advance on wages.

Barrett nodded. "I trusted you with my cattle, and you never let me down. Money's nothing compared to those animals." He closed his eyes, trying to blot out the image of the carcasses. "Yes, Dustin, I trust you won't leave until you've earned that pay. I only wish it hadn't ended this way."

Because, no matter what anyone might say, Barrett's life as a cattle rancher was over. He couldn't go through this again, watching animals suffer and die from starvation. Even Dustin, normally the most optimistic of men, didn't try to contradict him when Barrett said the best thing was to sell all the cattle that survived the winter.

The two men sat around the stove, sharing a can of beans, occasionally muttering a desultory word or two, but mostly lost in their thoughts. When he prepared to leave the next morning, Barrett clapped Dustin on the shoulder. "Thanks," he said. "You did everything you could. A man couldn't ask more."

But as he rode home, Barrett couldn't stop the questions from whirling through his mind. *What do you want from me, Lord?* he asked as he caught sight of yet another buzzard settling onto a dead steer. *My plans to run for office are gone. The cattle are gone.* Though Barrett had told Harrison he had enough money to restock, he knew he wouldn't do it, for there was no promise that the new herd would survive. Barrett had seen the signs of overgrazing. Even though the grass was resilient, it needed time to recover. He didn't know whether all this snow and water would help or hinder the prairie. What he did know was that if the next summer was another dry one, there might not be enough grass to keep a herd alive. He wouldn't take a chance of more innocent creatures dying slowly and painfully.

What should I do? Barrett raised his eyes to the sky, looking for a sign, hoping for an answer. There was none. All he saw were dead cattle and buzzards, and that made him want to weep. *Is this what Egypt looked like after one of the plagues? How could Pharaoh harden his heart when he saw such a loss of life?* Barrett tightened his grip on the reins. Never again. He couldn't bear the thought of facing such loss again.

"This is not what I'm meant to do." To Barrett's surprise, he spoke the words aloud, his voice so emphatic that Midnight turned, as if startled. Barrett wasn't meant to be a cattle baron. Hadn't Harrison told him that? Now he was hearing the same message from God. The question was, what was he meant to do?

Charlotte had no doubts. She knew the school was what the Lord intended for her future. She even believed that was the reason her son had been born blind. Charlotte had found her way. Barrett was still stumbling.

Perhaps the death of the cattle was a sign. Perhaps the party's disavowal of his candidacy was another sign. The problem was, all the signs were negative. He'd heard the messages. He wasn't meant to run for office. He wasn't meant to raise cattle. What was he meant to do?

As he closed his eyes, images filled his brain. Charlotte, that first day he'd seen her in her shop. Charlotte at the opera house. Charlotte sipping hot chocolate in his dining room. Charlotte blushing as she poured him a cup of tea at Rue de Rivoli. Charlotte. Charlotte. Charlotte. Was she his future?

Barrett's eyes sprang open, and he stared at the horizon as if he expected to see her suddenly appear. He hadn't been flattering her when he'd told her that she was unforgettable. Never before had a woman caught his imagination the way Charlotte did. Never before had a woman haunted his dreams the way she did. Never before had he cared so desperately for a woman.

He loved her.

Barrett laughed out loud as the words reverberated through his brain. He loved Charlotte. He wanted to marry her. It was no wonder he had never asked Miriam to be his bride, for he'd never felt this way about her. No matter how often Warren and Richard had advised him to marry Miriam,

Barrett had never been able to imagine a life with her. Now when he thought of the future, Charlotte was the one concrete thing he could envision. Everything else was still shrouded in mist, but Charlotte's face was as clear as the Laramie range on a summer day.

He closed his eyes for a second, picturing himself and Charlotte walking arm in arm through his house, taking David for drives in the park, laughing about everything and nothing at all. That was what he wanted: a future with Charlotte.

Barrett's laughter faded as his eyes focused on another dead steer. He might want a future with Charlotte, but how could he ask her to marry him when he had so little to offer her?

18

"It's over."

Warren stared at the man who stood in the door of his office. He'd seen Barrett happy, he'd seen him angry, he'd seen him disappointed, but never before had he seen him looking like this. Warren's most important client appeared defeated. His shoulders slumped, his eyes were clouded, his skin looked almost gray. It seemed as if he were turning into a shadow.

Warren felt the blood drain from his own face as Barrett took one of the chairs in front of his desk, not bothering to remove his hat or coat. On an ordinary day, Barrett would be joking, pretending that the decision of whether to sit in the dark green leather chair rather than the one covered in deep red suede was a momentous one. Today he was not joking.

Though it was clear that something was terribly wrong, Warren had no idea what it could be. Barrett was like that mythical King Midas. Everything he touched turned to gold. That was why Warren had allied himself with him. It wasn't simply that the work associated with Barrett's cattle raising was lucrative or that other cattle barons had sought Warren's counsel because of his connection to Barrett. That was good, but what was even better were the possibilities if Barrett gained public office. When he'd realized that political patronage could be a gold mine for the candidate's advisers, Warren had chuckled. Working for Senator Landry would be far more profitable and decidedly less strenuous than actually mining gold. All Warren had to do was wait for the man to send work his way. But now it appeared that his dreams of wealth were in jeopardy.

"What do you mean?" Warren demanded, his voice harsher than he'd intended. "If you play your cards right, the party will come around."

For the first time since he'd entered Warren's office, Barrett's eyes showed a spark of light. "If you believe that," he said, his lips curving into a rueful smile, "you're probably the only person in the territory who does. Even Richard tells me I have no chance. He advises me to wait at least a year until everyone has forgotten that I mentioned regulating stock growers."

"That wasn't your finest moment."

"It could have been."

Barrett shook his head when Warren offered him a cigar. The man didn't appreciate good tobacco, but that wasn't going to stop Warren from enjoying a smoke.

Warren lit the cigar and took a deep puff. "I still think you have a chance."

Turning his head when the smoke rings drifted in his direction, Barrett tapped his fingers on the chair arms. "Did you hear about Betty Dawson's Valentine's party?"

Warren felt his muscles tighten. Was Barrett asking a simple question, or was he reminding him that, no matter how much he tried, Warren wasn't yet accepted by the cream of Cheyenne society? It rankled him to know that he was considered good enough to manage their legal affairs, but he wasn't invited to dinners and other social occasions.

"No," he said abruptly.

"Half the party leadership was there, or so it seemed. I can tell you that, despite the occasion, their hearts were not filled with love, at least not toward me. They barely acknowledged my existence."

"They'll get over it. Their memories are

notoriously short."

Though he had expected Barrett to smile, the man shook his head. "I doubt that. I'm beginning to believe you're right, that I don't have the starch that's needed." Before Warren could protest, Barrett continued. "Besides, I have bigger problems than running a political campaign now. My days as a cattle rancher are over."

"That can't be true." Warren didn't want to consider the possibility of ruin. The money Barrett paid him to handle the cattle business's affairs was too important to lose, especially if there would be no political patronage. "You have one of the finest herds in the territory."

"Had, Warren. Past tense. At least half the herd is dead, and I have no idea how many more I'll lose before spring." Barrett looked directly at Warren, his eyes once more bleak. "It's over."

Five hours later, Warren stared out the window, his hands fisted, his rage still simmering. This wasn't the way it was supposed to play out. It was bad enough that Barrett appeared obstinate about not running for office. Though Warren had counted on that extra money, he might have been able to survive the loss of it, were it not for Barrett's other news. That had turned his stomach sour. He had bet money — far too much money — on this year's cattle profits. It was supposed to be a sure thing. Prices were cyclical, and this was the year they should have risen. Warren had counted on '87 being as good a year as '83. Now it appeared that it would be a disaster. If Barrett's livestock were dying, they all were.

Spring, which was supposed to have brought him wealth, privilege, and a wife, was starting to look bleak. It was true that he had the Franklin ranch, small as it was, but that wasn't enough to convince the Cheyenne Club to admit him, and it certainly wasn't enough to show Gwen how much he valued her. He couldn't let her slip through his fingers. No, sirree. Gwen Amos was a fine woman, part of his ticket to acceptance, and he intended to dress her in jewels and furs and make her Mrs. Warren Duncan before spring ended. To do that, he needed money.

Warren pounded the windowsill in frustration. Money. He'd been so close, and now . . . Now there was only one answer. He had to find the money Jeffrey Crowley had taken. Once he had that, there would be no more problems. He'd be richer than Barrett Landry or F. E. Warren or Joseph Carey ever dreamt. He'd find that money.

He would. But in the meantime . . .

Warren reached into his bottom desk drawer and pulled out his mask. It was time to pay Sylvia a visit.

Someone was pounding on the door. Though his bedchamber was at the back of the house, the noise was loud enough to rouse Barrett from a sound sleep. Thrusting his feet into slippers and donning his dressing robe, he hurried downstairs. By the time he reached the door, Mr. Bradley, similarly clad in nightclothes, was opening it.

"Where is she?" Cyrus Taggert's face was contorted with rage, the bulging veins so prominent that Barrett feared they would burst. "Don't try lying. I know she's here."

There was no question who he meant. "Miriam's not here. I haven't seen her in several days." Barrett kept his voice low and calm as he ushered Miriam's father into the parlor. "Why did you think she was here?" He forbore pointing out that Miriam's presence in a man's house at 5:30 would be highly scandalous.

"This is why." Cyrus held out a crumpled sheet of paper. "Mrs. Taggert thought she heard a strange noise. When I went downstairs to investigate, I found this on the breakfast table."

Barrett smoothed the paper and read. *Dearest Mama and Papa, please forgive me, but I cannot live without him. I love him more than I ever thought possible. I love you too, but my future is with him. Miriam.*

"Where is she?" Miriam's father repeated. "She's got to be here. You're . . ."

It might be rude to interrupt, but Barrett couldn't let Cyrus Taggert continue. "I'm sorry, Mr. Taggert, but Miriam is not here. I'm not the man she loves."

The older man's face sagged. "Then who?"

Though Barrett had a strong suspicion, he would not voice it until he was certain. "Why don't you go home? I'm sure your wife needs you to comfort her. I'll search for Miriam."

"Will you bring her home?"

Barrett wouldn't lie. "I won't force her, but I'll tell her how worried you and her mother are."

Cyrus Taggert nodded as he made his way to the door, his gait that of a much older man. "Thank you, Barrett. You're a better man than I thought."

Someone was following her. At first Charlotte had thought it was her imagination. After all, she had never before seen anyone

372

out at this time of the early morning once she turned onto Ferguson. While it was true that she'd passed an occasional vagrant on 15th Street, the homeless men had paid her no attention. This was different. Whoever it was hadn't wanted her to be aware of his presence, not at the beginning. The first few times she had heard what she believed were footsteps, she had turned to look but had seen no one. Now there was no doubt. The man was becoming careless. Either that or he wanted her to know he was there. The last two times he had barely concealed himself in a doorway, his sleeve protruding.

Charlotte increased her pace. In another block, she'd be home. She'd be safe then. The footsteps were closer now, and for the first time she heard the man. It was nothing more than a chuckle, and yet the sound sent shivers down her spine. Whoever it was was evil. When the chuckle was repeated, she turned, and as she did, Charlotte felt her heart stop. Her pursuer did not bother to hide. He stood there, as if taunting her, a figure clothed in black, his face hidden by a mask. The baron.

Charlotte began to run.

By the time Barrett was dressed, Mr. Bradley had the carriage ready. It would have been easier to simply saddle Midnight, but Barrett wanted the carriage in case he was able to persuade Miriam to return to her parents' home. He doubted he'd succeed. If she was with Richard as he believed, she was unlikely to leave.

She loved Richard, and unless Barrett was sorely mistaken, Richard loved her. Barrett smiled as he climbed into the carriage and seized the reins. He was surprised by the notion, and yet he knew he shouldn't be. The signs had been there, but he had been too blind to see them.

When he'd taken Barrett to task for neglecting Miriam, Richard had practically confessed tender feelings for her. As for Miriam, she'd made it clear that she sought a man who shared her love of music and literature. Richard did. If the Taggerts didn't interfere and insist that Miriam marry a man with a future in politics, she and Richard would be an ideal couple.

As Barrett had expected, Ferguson was deserted at this time of night. It was still hours before the shops would open, and so the majority of houses were dark, the few lighted windows possibly the sign of a fussy child. Was David awake? Barrett pushed the thought aside. This was no time to be thinking about Charlotte and her son. He needed to find Miriam and then do whatever he could to smooth matters between her and her parents.

Barrett was about to turn onto 18th Street when he saw her. Though the street was dark and she was clad all in black, there was no mistaking the fact that a woman was running.

"Help me!" she cried, and as she did, Barrett's blood ran cold. He knew that voice.

"Charlotte!" Barrett flicked the reins, drawing them in when he reached her. "Get in." In the dim light from the stars, he saw that the woman with Charlotte's voice had her face covered with a heavy veil. "Charlotte?" This time he made it a question.

"Yes. Thank God you're here. He's after me." As she climbed into the carriage, her voice trembled so much that Barrett could barely understand her.

"Who?"

She shuddered, and Barrett reached out, wrapping his arm around her to draw her closer to him.

"The . . ." She stopped, her teeth chattering from cold or fear or perhaps both. "A man. He was right behind me." She pointed south on Ferguson.

"I don't see anyone."

"At first he hid in doorways." Her voice was stronger now. "Then he came out, as if he wanted me to know he was there. Oh, Barrett, I've never been so scared."

Barrett tightened his grip on Charlotte. "We'll find him," he assured her. But though he drove slowly, pausing to look at each doorway and every narrow passageway between the buildings, he saw no one.

"He's gone." If he really existed. Charlotte wasn't a woman given to flights of fancy, but there was no evidence of anyone lurking in the darkness. Perhaps she had heard a stray dog and her imagination had run wild. Anything was possible at this hour when the streets were empty and the shadows long.

"Why were you out?" Though he tried to keep his voice even, now that the danger was past, he found himself recoiling with horror over what might have happened if she was being pursued. Charlotte was a resourceful woman, but she was no match for a man bent on harming her.

"I was delivering dresses to a boarding-house on 15th Street."

Barrett blinked in astonishment. "At five in the morning?" He hadn't thought Charlotte foolish, but that was the height of foolhardiness. Fifteenth Street was not a place for gently bred ladies, particularly at this hour.

"It was the safest time," she insisted. "No one's out then."

"That wasn't true today. You could have been hurt or worse." Though he hadn't intended it, anger crept into his voice. "If you'd asked me, I would have taken you there at a reasonable time."

Charlotte stiffened and pulled away from him. "I will not be coddled." Her voice was once again ragged, but this time Barrett recognized anger as well as fear. "I told you what my childhood was like, so surely you understand that I've spent too much of my life being protected. This was something I had to do by myself. I don't want to be treated like a hothouse flower."

"It's not coddling to want you to be safe, Charlotte. It's called caring. I care about you." What he felt was far deeper than mere caring, but this was neither the time nor the place to tell her that. "Let's get you home."

She nodded. To Barrett's relief, her trembling stopped and her breathing returned to normal. When they reached her house, he alighted from the carriage and helped her out.

"I want to see you safely inside," he told

her as he took her arm and led her to the stairs.

She nodded again. It was only when she had lit the kitchen lamp that she turned to Barrett. "Thank you for being there." A look of mild confusion flitted across her face. "I know God sent you. It had to be his hand that led you there at exactly the right time, but I don't understand why you were outside at this hour."

"I was looking for Miriam."

A quarter hour later, Barrett was still looking for her. When he'd reached Richard's house, all the first floor lights were blazing, but when Barrett knocked on the door, no one answered. He'd waited a minute, rapping constantly, but Richard did not appear. Finally, Barrett had opened the door and gone from room to room. All empty. He did not doubt that Miriam had been here, for her perfume lingered in the parlor, nor did he doubt that she and Richard had left together. What he did not know was where they'd gone. It could be anywhere. Though he hated the message he would have to deliver, there was no choice. He had to tell Cyrus Taggert that he had failed to find his daughter.

Barrett was not surprised when he saw

the lights on at the Taggert mansion. Undoubtedly Cyrus and Amelia were waiting for him. He was not surprised when their butler greeted him as if there were nothing unusual about callers arriving before dawn. However, Barrett was surprised when he entered the parlor and saw Miriam and Richard seated on the long couch, his arm wrapped around her waist.

"We're going to be married," Miriam announced. Though her cheeks were stained with tears, her smile was brilliant. "Mama and Papa have agreed that we'll have a small wedding this afternoon. Will you come?"

"Of course."

19

"Did you hear the news?" Gwen was breathless as she stood in the doorway of Charlotte's workroom. "I was buying groceries, and it was all anyone could talk about."

Charlotte shook her head as she looked up at Gwen. She'd been thankful that she had no customers this morning, for it had given her time to think. And, oh, how she'd needed that. Her thoughts were as turbulent as the mountain stream she'd seen in Vermont, with water swirling and tumbling as it fought for supremacy with the boulders that tried to block its passage.

The baron had found her. Charlotte shuddered each time she remembered the sight of the masked figure. She hadn't imagined him. It might not have been the baron, but it was difficult to believe there were two men in Cheyenne who wore hoods over their faces, two men who frequented 15th Street. Though she tried to convince herself that he might not have recognized her, for she had been careful to keep her identity concealed, Charlotte could not dismiss the belief that the man had known exactly who she was and that he was following her. "He's a dangerous man," the prisoner at Fort Laramie had said. Charlotte did not doubt that for a second. The baron was dangerous, and he was evil.

While she trembled at the memory of those stealthy footsteps, Charlotte could not forget the comfort she had felt when Barrett had wrapped his arm around her. His strength, his warmth, his caring had helped to banish the terror. For the moments that she had been so close to him, she had felt safe and cherished. But then Barrett had admitted that he was searching for Miriam. He might care for Charlotte, but Miriam was the woman he loved. Though Charlotte did not know why he'd been looking for her at that hour, it did not matter. He loved Miriam, and if Charlotte had any sense at all, she would not forget that.

"What happened?" It was difficult to muster enthusiasm for the latest gossip when her heart felt as if it had been shredded.

"It's Miriam Taggert." Gwen put her hand on her chest as she attempted to catch her breath. "She's getting married this afternoon."

"That's nice." Somehow, Charlotte managed to keep her voice even. "I hope she and Barrett are happy together."

Shaking her head vigorously, Gwen grinned. "That's why everyone's so excited. It's not Barrett. She's marrying Richard Eberhardt."

Though Barrett doubted it was the kind of wedding Amelia Taggert had envisioned for her daughter, the simple ceremony in the Taggerts' parlor was one he would long remember, if only because of the bride and groom's palpable happiness. Richard looked as if he'd been given the most precious gift imaginable, while Miriam's smile was so wide her cheeks must have hurt. And though Amelia Taggert's smile appeared forced, Cyrus seemed genuinely pleased by his daughter's happiness.

"I trust you'll keep last night's events quiet," Cyrus said when the service ended and the few guests had made their way into the dining room for a cold collation, cake, and punch.

Barrett nodded. He had no plan to tell anyone that Miriam had gone to Richard's town house, intent on compromising her reputation so that Richard would have no alternative but to marry her. "All that matters is that they're wed."

Cyrus Taggert gave Barrett a long look. "I've been doing a lot of thinking, and I think the party is wrong. You'd make a fine senator. If you decide to run, you'll have my endorsement."

It was more than Barrett had expected. A week ago, he might have been elated. Today he was not. "Thank you, sir. I appreciate it, but a man's got to find his place. Mine isn't in Washington."

The question remained: where was it? Barrett wanted to believe that his place was with Charlotte. The fear that he'd known when he'd heard her scream had deepened his conviction that she was the only woman he would ever love. In that moment, he had wanted nothing more than to keep her safe, to protect her and David, to create a life for the three of them. But what kind of life would that be?

Mere months ago, he'd been confident of what the future would bring. Now . . . now his world looked completely different. Barrett knew that if he was patient and listened, he would learn what the Lord had in store for him. But until that happened, until he was confident that he could create a secure future for Charlotte and David, he would say nothing. It would be wrong to promise something he might not be able to deliver. Charlotte deserved the best, and if he could not give her that, he would simply walk away.

In the meantime, there was one thing he could do for her. He had realized that when he'd entered the Taggert mansion to witness two of his friends being joined in holy matrimony. As he'd looked at the spacious foyer of a building that was far too large for two people, Barrett had known he had at least one answer. He'd tell her tomorrow.

Charlotte had heard people say that their jaws dropped, but she had thought it was simply a figure of speech. She had been wrong. Her jaw had most definitely dropped. She stared at Barrett. "I don't understand," she said when she had managed to regain a modicum of composure.

Those dark blue eyes that she envisioned even when she closed her own sparkled. "It's simple," he said as he leaned forward ever so slightly. "I want to give you my house."

"That's what I thought you said. I just didn't believe my ears." She hadn't been surprised when Barrett entered the store.

She had expected him to come, if only to assure himself that she had suffered no ill effects from her fright. When he'd arrived, she had wondered whether she should broach the subject of Miriam or simply pretend that she was unaware of the wedding. Barrett had perched on the edge of the chair rather than settling back and relaxing, his expression so serious that she feared Miriam's marriage had devastated him. As Charlotte struggled to find words to comfort him, he'd shocked her by offering his home for the school.

"Are you certain?" To Charlotte's dismay, her voice cracked more than it had when Barrett had rescued her from the baron. She'd been frightened then, but now . . . now she wasn't sure what she felt other than overwhelmed.

Barrett took a quick look out the window, as if assuring himself there were no customers on the doorstep. "If you think this was an impulsive gesture, I can assure you that it isn't. I've given it considerable thought. The simple fact is, I no longer need a house of that size. I'm not going to run for office, so there's no need to entertain on a grand scale. Quite simply, it's too large for one person."

Charlotte nodded slowly. Though Barrett

claimed it wasn't a hasty decision, she suspected it was precipitated by Miriam's marriage. Without a bride and the possibility of children, Barrett did not need a mansion.

"I'm sorry about Miriam," she said softly. "The news must have hurt."

Barrett's eyes widened for a second. "Is that what the rumor mill is claiming, that I'm in the depths of despair because Miriam married Richard?" When Charlotte nodded, he laughed. "It couldn't be further from the truth. I'm happy for both of them. I would have danced at their wedding, only there was no dancing, so I had to be content with toasting their happiness."

Charlotte tried to make sense of his words. "Then you don't . . ." She stopped, not daring to ask such a personal question.

"If you're asking whether I was in love with Miriam, the answer is no. It's true that I considered marrying her, but for all the wrong reasons. The truth is, she loves Richard. I suspect she always has."

Of course. Charlotte smiled as the pieces fell into place. No wonder Miriam had been so concerned about Gwen's possibly marrying an older man. She had been thinking about herself and Richard. And when she'd expressed her admiration for the man who shared her love of music and literature, it hadn't been Barrett. Richard was the man Miriam loved. Richard was the one whose declaration of love had excited her. Of course.

"Then I'm glad for all of you." Charlotte was more than glad. She was thrilled, for Barrett's explanation reignited the flame of hope she'd tried so desperately to extinguish.

Barrett opened his mouth as if to speak, then shook his head. Clearing his throat, he gestured toward the flocked walls. "It would be a shame to divide this building. You'd wind up with a store and a school, but they'd both be too small. If you moved to my house, you'd be able to have more pupils and to make it a boarding school." He paused for a second before adding, "I imagine you could persuade Mrs. Melnor to stay, even if you couldn't pay her full salary. You wouldn't need much other staff initially."

Charlotte took a deep breath, trying to control her emotions. There was no doubt that Barrett's mansion would be a far better site for a school than her shop. There was no doubt that his offer was incredibly generous. There was also no doubt that she could not agree to it.

"Oh, Barrett," Charlotte said, searching for the words to make him understand. She didn't want to hurt or insult him by refusing a gift of this magnitude. "I appreciate your offer. Truly, I do. I never dreamt that anyone would offer me so much. But I can't accept."

He blinked, as if surprised by her response. "Why not? I don't believe it would be too difficult to convert it to a school."

"It wouldn't." Charlotte shook her head, remembering her first impression of his home. "I never told you, but your house reminded me a bit of the academy where Abigail and I used to teach. It has the same spacious rooms and the feeling that a child would be welcome, even if he slid down the banister or dropped food on the carpet."

"Then what's the problem?" Barrett appeared perplexed and, though she sensed he was trying to hide it, a bit angry.

"I can't take it. It wouldn't be right."

Shaking his head, Barrett fixed his gaze on her. "Now I'm the one who doesn't understand."

How could she explain without making it sound as if she sought something more from him? It would have been difficult enough if he and Miriam were engaged — of course, if that were the case, Barrett would not be offering Charlotte his home — but now it might seem as if she was angling for marriage. "It wouldn't be proper," she said, hoping he'd understand how rigid some rules were.

Comprehension glimmered in his eyes. "Because I'm a man and you're a woman?"

"Exactly. Widows have a good deal more freedom than unmarried women, but a gift of a house would be frowned upon. There would be speculation about our . . ." Though she had intended to say "relationship," Charlotte bit off the word. "It would be seen as at least slightly scandalous, and if there's one thing a school does not need, it's any hint of scandal."

Though Barrett frowned, he did not appear discouraged. "If the gift is a problem, we'll make it a sale. I'll sell the building to you for a dollar. Warren can do all the paperwork, and no one needs to know what you paid. I imagine by now everyone's aware my fortunes are on the skids, so they won't be surprised when I sell the house."

As reports of the enormous loss of cattle had reached Cheyenne, conjecture had begun over which of the cattle barons would be the first to declare bankruptcy and leave Wyoming. Though Charlotte had tried not to dwell on the possibility, she hated the thought that Barrett might return to Pennsylvania.

"That's another reason why I cannot accept your offer. You shouldn't be giving away your greatest asset. I don't mean to pry into your personal affairs, but how would you live?" While he might not be able to recoup the full cost of the house, Barrett would certainly be able to sell it for far more than a dollar.

He leaned forward and took her hand in his. "You needn't worry about me. Unlike some of my fellow stock growers, I'm not in debt. I even have some savings."

His hand tightened, and the warmth from his palm spread up Charlotte's arm. It was silly, but she felt almost lightheaded. It must be the shock of Barrett's offer. Surely it wasn't the fact that this man who was so dear to her, the man who'd admitted that he cared for her, held her hand. She was reading too much into it, feeling cherished simply because he held her hand in his.

If Barrett was affected by their entwined fingers, he gave no sign of it. His expression was calm, his voice even. "When I was a boy, my father used to tell us we should have emergency funds. I can't speak for Harrison or Camden, but I took that advice to heart. My mother said it was rude to talk about money, so I won't tell you how much I have saved, but I will say that I can live for at least a year on it. Admittedly, I won't be living in a mansion, but I'll have a roof over my head, and I won't starve."

Though he'd been staring into the distance, Barrett returned his gaze to her face, his eyes meeting hers. "Tell me you'll take the house. Please, Charlotte. I want to give it to you and David. I want to help make your dream come true."

It was a wonderful offer, an almost irresistible one, from a wonderful, almost irresistible man. Barrett was kind, caring, unbelievably generous. He believed in Charlotte's dreams, and he wanted to help her achieve them. He was everything she had dreamt of. That was the problem.

"I can't, Barrett. I can't let you make that kind of sacrifice."

He shook his head, as if he didn't understand. "Why not?"

Charlotte took a deep breath. She should have told him months ago. She knew that, just as she knew she had been making excuses each time she'd postponed the discussion. Landry never lies, but Charlotte had. She could argue that she had good reasons for the deceptions, but the simple fact was, she had lied. Now it was time for the truth.

She took another deep breath, exhaling slowly, keeping her eyes fixed on Barrett as she said, "I'm not the woman you think I am."

20

As Barrett's eyes widened, Charlotte saw shock and disbelief reflected in them. Next would come revulsion, once he understood what she'd done. She had known that was inevitable, that the man who prized honesty would want nothing to do with a woman who'd built her life on lies. That was one of the reasons she'd waited so long to tell him the truth.

"What do you mean?"

To Charlotte's surprise, she heard no condemnation in his voice, only a simple question. She rose and drew the curtains over the front windows, then turned the door sign to "closed."

Willing her hands not to tremble, she settled back into the chair across from Barrett. Though she longed for the comfort his touch had given her, Charlotte knew she did not deserve it. "I'd better start at the beginning. My name isn't Charlotte Harding." She shook her head, contradicting herself. "That's not really true. That was my name until I married Jeffrey. Then I became Charlotte Crowley."

Barrett looked at her steadily. Someone else might have missed the momentary tightening of his lips at the realization that she had lied, but Charlotte did not. It was what she had expected. Barrett would not easily excuse what she had done. When he spoke, his voice was almost harsh. "Why didn't you keep his name? Was he a cruel man?" The way Barrett clenched and unclenched his fists told Charlotte that thought disturbed him, and a glimmer of hope rekindled itself. Perhaps that was the reason he looked so somber, and it wasn't solely because she'd been less than honest.

"No," she hastened to assure him. "He was foolish, perhaps, but not cruel. Jeffrey loved me, but sometimes it seemed that he loved money more. He gambled and did some very foolish things, because he thought we needed more than his lieutenant's pay."

Though Barrett seemed to relax a bit with her reassurance, his eyes widened in surprise at her final words. "Your husband was a soldier? I thought he was a farmer."

Another lie. "Jeffrey hated farming. His parents had a farm and could barely make ends meet. I think that's one of the reasons money was so important to him — he had lived with so little. As soon as he could, he escaped from the farm and went to West Point."

"A very different life."

"Yes, it was. He chafed at the restrictions and complained about the pay, but he admitted it was better than being a farmer." Charlotte managed a small smile, remembering the times when Jeffrey had seemed happy. "He was stationed at Fort Laramie. That's how I came to Wyoming."

"So you weren't lying when you said that your husband brought you here." Once again, there was no censure, merely a simple statement of fact. Charlotte felt some of the tension that had stiffened her spine begin to ebb. This was more than she had dared hope, for Barrett's reaction wasn't what she had feared.

"I tried not to lie any more than necessary, but I couldn't let anyone know I was Jeffrey Crowley's widow."

"Why not? Were you ashamed of his gambling?"

If only Jeffrey had limited himself to gambling, she wouldn't have had to lie, but he had wanted more money than gambling provided. Though she had never asked for it, Jeffrey had believed that Charlotte craved a life of luxury, and so he'd done whatever he could to pay for fancy china and silver, a Steinway piano, a cook and housekeeper. He had never asked whether Charlotte would have been happy without those things, and she'd been equally at fault, for she had never questioned the source of the money. It was only when it was too late to change anything that Charlotte had realized that if they'd talked more, Jeffrey might still be alive.

"It wasn't only gambling," she told Barrett. "Jeffrey was a thief too. He got involved in stagecoach robberies."

Barrett nodded, his expression so calm that Charlotte wondered if anything she could say would shock him. Once he'd learned that Jeffrey had not been abusive, he'd relaxed. "In its heyday, there was a lot of gold on the Black Hills line."

The coaches that used to run from the Black Hills gold mines in Deadwood to Cheyenne were famous for the cargoes they carried, and until the company added specially armored coaches, they had been prey to robberies. After that, although passengers had been robbed of their belongings, there had been no spectacular holdups. And then, with the extension of the railroad, an era had ended. Since there was no further need for stagecoaches, the last one had left Cheyenne less than two weeks ago.

"Jeffrey never got any gold, but one of his . . ." Charlotte searched for the correct word. "Partners," she said at last. "One of his partners believes he found Big Nose Parrott's stash, and he wants it. The man has already killed at least one woman trying to find the money." Charlotte looked at Barrett, willing him to understand. "That's why I've been lying. It's not shame; it's fear. I'm afraid he'll find me and that he'll hurt David to make me give him the money." She clasped her hands together to still their trembling. "I thought we were safe in Cheyenne, but then I learned he was here. I think he was the man who followed me the other night."

"No wonder you were so frightened." Barrett's voice was warm and comforting. "Don't worry, Charlotte. We'll find him. Then you'll be safe."

She wanted to believe him. Oh, how she did. Charlotte swallowed deeply, trying to tamp down the fears that thoughts of the baron raised. "I hope that's true. I've hated living with lies, but I had to do whatever I could to keep my son safe."

Barrett was silent for a moment, and

Charlotte sensed that he was trying to absorb everything she had told him. When he spoke, his voice was gentle. "I understand." He paused, then added, "As well as anyone who's not a parent can."

"Then you don't hate me for lying?" The question slipped out, unbidden. She had heard no condemnation in his voice and had seen no revulsion on his face, and yet she had to be certain.

"I could never hate you. Surely you realize that. I care for you and David. I want you both to be safe and happy."

This was the second time Barrett had said he cared for her, and this time he had included David in that declaration. Warmth flooded Charlotte's cheeks, and her hands ceased their trembling.

"If you're going to be safe," Barrett continued, "we have to find out who this man is. If he's a murderer, he deserves to be behind bars until a jury can decide his fate. What does he look like?"

"I don't know. I never saw him. The woman at Fort Laramie who warned me about him only told me his name. She called him the baron." Charlotte frowned, remembering that day. She had been so frightened by the woman's words that she hadn't been thinking clearly. By the time she regained her common sense, it had been too late. "I wanted to ask her more, but she was killed that night. I think the baron was responsible. She said he was ruthless and that nothing would stop him from getting the money." Charlotte gripped the chair arms. "I don't have it, but he doesn't know that."

Barrett laid his hand on hers, and once again she drew strength from his warmth. "You'll be all right, Charlotte. We'll find the baron." Though he'd said it before, Barrett seemed to know that Charlotte needed the reassurance.

"Are you sure he's actually a baron?" Barrett appeared skeptical. "We have a number of cattle barons here, but no one uses that as a title. We've even got some blue bloods from Europe. There's a viscount and a couple earls, but no barons."

"It probably isn't a real title," Charlotte admitted, "but he still uses it." She shuddered, remembering the stories she had heard. "I can't believe that there are two such cruel men living in Wyoming and calling themselves the baron. It has to be the same one." Quickly, she explained about how she knew that Sylvia's girls feared him. "The worst part is, no one knows what he looks like because he wears a mask."

Barrett seemed disturbed. "If this Sylvia knows he's cruel, why does she let him into her establishment? Surely the money can't be worth it."

Charlotte had asked the same question. "It's not just the money. Mrs. Kendall said he threatened to burn down the brothel with everyone inside. Sylvia believed he'd do that, and so do I. He seems to be a truly evil man."

Barrett rose and began to pace the floor. "Someone must know who he is. I'll make some discreet inquiries."

It was necessary. Charlotte knew that, and yet she couldn't help shuddering. What would happen if the baron learned that she was Jeffrey's widow before Barrett found him?

Barrett seemed to understand, for he stood next to her chair and looked down at her, his expression warm and comforting. "I won't do anything to endanger you. I'll only speak to my friends."

"Thank you." Charlotte nodded as relief settled over her like a soft blanket.

She was a remarkable woman. A truly remarkable woman. Barrett leaned forward, urging Midnight to gallop. He needed a chance to clear his head, and riding with the wind blowing across his face was the best way Barrett knew to do that. He could only hope that Midnight was enjoying the gallop as much as he was.

The ride was giving him a chance to think. Though he ought to be focusing on finding the baron, Barrett couldn't stop thinking about Charlotte and all that he'd learned about her. He'd been right in believing she had secrets, but never had he imagined either the depths of those secrets or the extent of her courage. She'd been frightened — *terrified* was probably a better word — by what had happened at Fort Laramie and the danger she and David faced. And yet she'd overcome that fear, replacing it with determination to make a new life.

She could have returned to Vermont. She could have lived with one of her sisters. She could have remarried. Any of those alternatives would have been easy, but Charlotte hadn't taken the easy way. Instead, she had chosen to remain independent and create a life for herself and David. Amazing. Charlotte Harding Crowley was an amazing woman.

Barrett frowned as he looked at the sky. Buzzards continued to circle, reminding him of the devastation he'd seen the last time he'd headed north. It was worse today.

Though it had been less than a week since he'd traveled this route, the number of carcasses was higher, some of the bodies so stiff with rigor mortis that he knew their death had been recent. Barrett didn't want to look. He didn't want to see the destruction of so many men's dreams, and yet he could not ignore it. Cattle continued to die. Though the loss of life saddened him, what was worse was the knowledge that he could do nothing to change it. If, as Charlotte claimed, he was put on Earth to make it a better place, being a cattle rancher was certainly not the way to accomplish that. Helping Charlotte just might be.

Midnight whinnied, and Barrett wondered whether he was disturbed by the dead cattle or whether he sensed Barrett's own distress. In either case, there was nothing Barrett could do for his horse. Charlotte's situation was different. He wouldn't accept defeat where she was concerned. He wouldn't give up until he'd found the baron, for until he did, Charlotte would continue to live in fear. There was only one solution. The baron must be brought to justice. That was why Barrett was on his way to Fort Laramie. He hadn't spoken to Richard and Warren, for he doubted they could help him. The answers, he was certain, were at the fort. And so he'd saddled his horse at daybreak and was headed toward the Army post.

By the time he reached the fort that stood at the confluence of the Laramie and Platte Rivers the next day, Barrett was tired. So, too, was Midnight. They both needed rest and food.

"State your business," the sentry barked as Barrett approached the post.

Barrett looked around, surprised that the fort resembled a small town more than a military establishment. With no surrounding walls, a mixture of architectural styles, and ladies strolling along boardwalks, it did not meet his mental image of a fort.

"I want to see Captain Westland." Charlotte had given him the name of the company commander, adding that she wasn't certain the man would still be there. The Army, it seemed, transferred its men regularly.

"That way, sir." The sentry pointed toward a large L-shaped building at the southeast corner of the parade ground. "That's the administration building. You'll find him there."

One hurdle passed. The captain was still here. Now all Barrett needed was for him to know the baron's identity. Glad to stretch his legs after the hours on horseback,

Barrett lengthened his stride as he passed what appeared to be barracks on the way to the limestone building the sentry had indicated. Less than a minute later, he was introduced to the fort's commanding officer.

"What can I do for you?" Captain Westland proved to be a stocky, bespectacled man whose graying hair made him appear to be about the same age as Warren. He was also as matter-of-fact as Barrett's attorney, eschewing any small talk once the introductions had been made.

Taking the seat the captain indicated, Barrett looked around the room. While it couldn't compare to Cheyenne's mansions, the room was less stark than he had expected. The crossed flags — United States and Army — on top of the mantel were no surprise, but the beautifully carved cherry-wood desk and bookcases were, as was the potted plant that had grown spindly, trying to reach the windowsill.

"I want to learn what I can about Jeffrey Crowley's death and a man called the baron," Barrett said, fixing his eyes on the captain.

The commander frowned slightly. "You know that I can't discuss an officer's military record with you."

"I wouldn't expect you to. I realize that's confidential information."

Barrett's response appeared to surprise the captain. "Then why are you here?"

"I trust that what I'm going to tell you will remain as confidential as Lieutenant Crowley's record." Barrett looked back at the door, ensuring that it was fully closed.

"Certainly."

"I've met his widow."

The captain's surprise deepened. "How? Where? You said you were from Cheyenne, but I heard she had gone back to Vermont."

Barrett debated how much to tell the commanding officer, finally deciding on the basics. "Mrs. Crowley" — it felt strange to refer to her by that name — "moved to Cheyenne. She's worried that the baron might be searching for her."

Captain Westland removed his spectacles, polishing them carefully as he said, "That could be. The man's a bit of a legend. No one seems to know where he came from, where he lives, or even how he got his name. An eyewitness said he was the one who killed Lieutenant Crowley, but he stayed in the shadows so no one could identify him. Whoever he is, the baron is a wily man."

After hearing the captain's explanation, Barrett agreed with Charlotte that the man who frightened Sylvia's girls was likely the same one who'd led Jeffrey deeper into crime. He might have traded the shadows for a mask, but he hadn't changed his nature. Charlotte had said he was evil. Barrett agreed, especially now that he knew the baron had killed at least two people.

"I heard the baron might have been involved in stagecoach robberies," Barrett said.

"I heard that too." The captain replaced his spectacles and peered over them at Barrett. "There's no proof, though. The robberies stopped when Crowley died."

"And now the stagecoach has ceased running."

"Precisely." Captain Westland frowned. "I'm afraid I haven't been much help."

While it was true that the captain hadn't been able to identify the baron, Barrett had learned at least one new facet of the man's past. Whether he'd tell Charlotte that the baron was responsible for her husband's death remained to be seen.

"Thank you, anyway. I appreciate your time." Barrett rose and took a step toward the door, turning abruptly. "One more thing. Could you tell me where Lieutenant and Mrs. Crowley lived?" It wouldn't help him find the baron, but it might help him understand Charlotte.

"Certainly." The captain led Barrett outside and pointed to the west. "See that white house there?" he asked, indicating a good-sized building at the curve of the road. "It's divided into two residences. The left side was theirs."

Barrett walked the short distance and stared at the place where Charlotte had once lived. It was a pleasant enough building, two stories high with three dormers on the front and two on the back of the second story. Judging from the placement of the windows and chimneys, Barrett guessed the first floor contained a parlor and dining room and that the one-story addition to the back housed the kitchen. Though not huge by any standards, it was considerably larger than the apartment Charlotte now shared with three others. Did she feel cramped in Cheyenne? Did she miss the wide wraparound porch? Barrett could picture her sitting there, rocking slowly on a warm summer night.

He peered around the side of the building, noting that in addition to the normal outbuildings, the yard contained what appeared to be a small garden. Perhaps Charlotte had been the one who'd hoed the ground in that backyard garden. Perhaps she had done her sewing sitting by that front window, watching soldiers march on the parade ground. Or perhaps her days had been whiled away visiting with other officers' wives. There was so much Barrett wanted to know, so much he needed to understand about her past. If they were going to have a future together — and he was determined that they would — they both needed to know what had made them the people they were today. But first he had to find the baron.

"Tomorrow is March 1, and we haven't had any snow for ten days." Gwen looked up from the lace she was attaching to a collar, her face wreathed in a smile. "Spring can't be far away."

"I hope so. It seems like all of us are waiting for spring." Charlotte didn't add that she was also waiting for Barrett to return from Fort Laramie. She hoped he'd discover something there but wasn't optimistic. Instead, she worried that the only thing he would discover was more dead cattle along the way. At least the action of pulling a thread and needle through fabric helped settle her nerves. That was one of the reasons she was sewing tonight, that and the fact that she wanted to get another dress to Mrs. Kendall by the end of the week. This time, though, she would not make her delivery on foot. Barrett had insisted that he would take her in his carriage, and remembering the fear she had felt when she'd known she was being followed, Charlotte had not argued with him. It would be safer, not to mention more enjoyable, to go with Barrett, and, since she was no longer trying to expand her dressmaking business, she wouldn't worry about her customers learning what she was doing.

Gwen knotted her thread. "This awful winter has to end. It's making everyone miserable. Even Warren's been in a disagreeable mood." She frowned, then looked up at Charlotte, a question in her eyes. "I hope it's nothing to do with me."

"I'm sure it isn't." Charlotte had managed to overcome her initial reaction to Warren, telling herself that while he wasn't a man she would want to marry, he was kind to Gwen and Rose and had brought a sparkle to Charlotte's friend's eyes. "As you said, everyone's discouraged. According to today's paper, the loss of cattle is staggering. That will affect everyone, not just the cattle growers. Warren will have fewer clients if they go out of business."

Gwen wasn't convinced. "As awful as it

sounds, I hope you're right and that's the only reason Warren's been out of sorts," she said, a tremor in her voice. "I don't know what I'll do if Warren doesn't love me. He's everything I ever dreamt of." Tears welled in Gwen's eyes. "I thought he loved me, but if he does, he should have declared himself by now." She dashed the tears from her cheeks. "Why hasn't he? I want to know that we have a future together. Rose and I need him."

Charlotte tried not to frown at Gwen's use of the word *need.* Her parents had taught their daughters that marriage should be based on love and respect, not need, but Gwen didn't want to hear that. And perhaps there was no reason for Charlotte to say anything, for it appeared that Gwen did love Warren, not simply the idea that he would take care of her and her daughter.

"Lent has started," Charlotte said, grasping at straws. "He may be waiting until it ends. You know that almost no one marries between Ash Wednesday and Easter." It was such a solemn time of the year that few engagements were announced then, and there were even fewer weddings.

Gwen's tears vanished, replaced by a smile. "You must be right. Warren wouldn't do anything that wasn't proper." Laying her sewing aside, she rose and hugged Charlotte. "Thank you. You've made me feel much better." When she returned to her seat, she raised an eyebrow. "Wouldn't it be perfect if Warren and Barrett proposed at the same time? We could have a double wedding."

Charlotte couldn't let Gwen continue to weave fantasies that would not come true, fantasies that Charlotte only admitted in her dreams. "I don't expect to remarry," she said firmly. "The school will be my life."

"I thought you'd given up that idea." Gwen stuck her needle into the fabric and looked up, frowning. "Honestly, Charlotte, I think you're mistaken. Why would you want to spend your life teaching other people's children when you could have a life with Barrett? He'd take care of you and David. You could even have other children. Don't you see? It would be perfect."

Perfect appeared to be Gwen's favorite word today. The problem was, her idea of perfect was different from Charlotte's. "The school is important."

"It is," Gwen agreed, "but you don't have to be the teacher. If you married Barrett, you could use some of his money to hire someone. You don't have to do everything yourself."

It wasn't the first time Charlotte had heard that advice. "That's what Abigail and Elizabeth said." Her sisters had not been enthusiastic about her plan for a school. Part of the reason, Charlotte suspected, was that they had been hurt that she hadn't confided the truth of David's blindness sooner, and that feeling of hurt colored everything else.

"You should listen to us," Gwen said, a smug smile on her face. "We can't all be wrong."

But they were. Establishing the school was what God wanted her to do. Charlotte was certain of that.

Charlotte was helping a customer the next day when Barrett entered the shop. Though he said nothing beyond a brief greeting, the slump of his shoulders told Charlotte his trip had been discouraging.

As soon as the customer left, she turned to Barrett. "Welcome back," she said, infusing her voice with as much enthusiasm as she could. "I'm glad you're here."

"You won't be when you hear what I have to say." Barrett refused the chair she offered, and so Charlotte remained standing rather than have to crane her neck to look at him.

"What I learned at the fort is that the

baron is even more dangerous than you feared," he said, his voice tinged with regret. "I know the school is important to you, but I'd advise waiting until we've found him."

Barrett swallowed, and Charlotte realized there was much he wasn't telling her. Though anger mingled with regret that he felt the need to shelter her from unpleasant news, Charlotte said nothing. After all, Barrett was only trying to help her. He would probably argue that it was caring, not coddling. Perhaps he was right and she was being overly sensitive.

"I don't want to wait," she said quietly.

"I know that, but if the baron learns that you're Jeffrey's widow, there's no telling what he might do. As you said, he's an evil man. I'm afraid you might be putting not just David but Nancy and the other children at risk."

Barrett had raised the one argument that would make Charlotte stop. Slowly, she nodded. Her dream would have to be postponed.

21

She was falling behind. Though her ragged breathing told him she was running as quickly as she could, there was no way she could win the race. Even if she were not burdened by the child she carried, even if she did not catch her foot in one of the holes that pocked the prairie, even if the blazing summer sun did not sap her energy, her legs were no match for the man's. The man who pursued her had everything on his side: size, strength, and, most of all, the knife. Its silver blade gleamed in the sunshine, a wicked glint that matched the evil twist of his lips. While the woman was clad in only a thin nightdress, the man was dressed for the elements, leather chaps protecting his legs from the spiky leaves of the yucca and the thorns of the tumbleweeds. He was prepared. She was not.

The woman glanced behind her, and the fear he saw on her face stabbed at Barrett. She was right to fear her pursuer, for his intent was all too obvious. The man would kill her and leave her body and that of her child for the buzzards. He would laugh as he laughed now, untroubled by the death of two innocent souls. Charlotte's pursuer was evil incarnate, afraid to show his face in the sunlight. This was the masked man she feared. This was the baron. And somehow he had found her.

Barrett stared at the man, wondering who hid behind the ugly mask. More like a hood than an ordinary mask, it covered his head and face, leaving only his lips and eyes visible. Black as night, the disguise was the most ominous thing Barrett had ever seen, for he knew what was behind it: a man without a conscience, a man who planned to kill the woman Barrett loved.

"Stop!" Barrett shouted as he lunged toward the man. He had no knife, no weapon other than his hands, but somehow he would stop him. If it was the last thing he did, he would keep the baron from killing Charlotte and David. But though he ran faster than ever before, he could not reach the man. For each step he took, the baron took two.

"Stop!"

The man turned, his lips twisting into a sneer as he laughed. A second later, he grabbed Charlotte's arm, wrenching it backward. She stumbled and started to fall, and as she did, the man raised the knife, plunging it down-ward.

"No!"

Barrett wakened, his heart pounding, his body drenched with sweat. Springing out of bed, he stopped when the cold from the floor penetrated the soles of his feet. It had been a dream. Nothing but a dream. It was winter in Cheyenne, not summer on the prairie. Charlotte and David were safe. Or were they? Perhaps the dream was a premonition, a warning like the ones the Bible recounted. Ma had told him that the Lord used dreams to prepare people. Barrett shuddered, wondering if anyone could be prepared for the evil he'd seen shining from the baron's eyes. Only God could defeat that evil.

Keep them safe, Barrett prayed as he slid his feet into slippers and wrapped a robe around him. *Keep Charlotte and David safe.* Sleep was gone. Though the nightmare had destroyed any hopes of peaceful rest, it had strengthened Barrett's resolve. If the dream was a warning, he would not ignore it, any more than he had ignored Charlotte's fears the night he'd discovered her fleeing from a masked man. Somehow, some way, he would keep her and David safe, for nothing was more important than that. Charlotte's dream of a school might not come true; he might not be able to give her the financially secure future she deserved, but he could offer her protection . . . and love.

Barrett smiled as the word echoed through his mind, and he found himself wondering whether this was how Camden had felt when he asked Susan to marry him. It couldn't be. No one else could have experienced this wonderful warm feeling, the sense that he had found the one woman in the world who was meant for him. Others might have similar experiences, but they weren't the same. Just as Charlotte was one of a kind, what Barrett felt for her was unique.

Even when he'd tried to convince himself that Miriam was the wife he needed, he'd never experienced anything close to the feelings that surged through him now. It was as if every fiber of his body had become sensitized, heightening every thought of Charlotte. Picturing her smile, remembering the softness of her skin, recalling the delicate trill of her laughter filled Barrett with an almost inexpressible joy. At the same time, the prospect of anyone harming her sent anger and a fierce determination to keep her safe surging through him.

There was no doubt about it. He loved

Charlotte. He loved her, and he wanted to protect her and David.

Barrett wanted — oh, how he wanted — to ask Charlotte to marry him today. But that wouldn't be fair to her. He could not forget the day Ma had lined her three boys in a row in front of her and had given them lessons on marriage. Ladies, she had informed them, deserved to be wooed. A man shouldn't assume that the woman he favored loved him and that just because he could buy her a house and a carriage meant that she would agree to marry him. A man shouldn't simply ask a woman to be his wife. She needed to be courted first.

Barrett grinned as he switched on the lights. Charlotte would have her courtship. Oh, it might not be quite what Ma had envisioned — after all, Ma's advice hadn't included the etiquette for wooing a widow with a child — but by the time he was done, Charlotte would know that he loved her. And if he was very, very lucky, she would agree to become his wife. But first he had to start.

As he drew back the drapes and looked outside, Barrett's grin widened. Fresh snow. Perfect.

"I'm glad to see you have no customers this

morning," he said as he entered Élan a few hours later. Wyoming snow was fickle. Even on a frigid day, the sun could be bright enough to melt it. That was why he'd come to the shop earlier than normal.

Charlotte wrinkled her nose. Had he ever noticed how attractive she was when she did that? He must have, but this morning she seemed more beautiful than ever.

"You may be happy, but I'm not," she said with a quick gesture at the rack of partially sewn dresses. "I don't know how I'll finish these. Molly's sick and Gwen has a blister on her finger. That leaves just me." She wrinkled her nose again. "I need to get back to work."

"You also need to play. Both you and David."

"We do play," she countered, her fingers plying the needle and thread with the expertise that came from years of practice. "Just because David won't bowl without you doesn't mean we don't play."

"But you don't play the way I intend. Now, won't you close the store and dress yourself and David in warm clothes? We're going for a ride."

Though he saw the curiosity in her eyes, she shook her head. "I can't, Barrett."

"Yes, you can. C'mon, Charlotte. This

could be the last snow of the season. You wouldn't want to deprive David of a new experience, would you?"

As he'd known she would, she took the bait. While Charlotte would never play hooky for herself, she would do almost anything for her son.

"Hurry. I'll be waiting for you."

Sooner than he'd expected, she descended the steps, David in her arms. Both were so warmly dressed that they appeared to have gained a substantial amount of weight. It was almost as if she knew what he had planned, for the extra clothing would provide padding as well as warmth.

"Hello, David," Barrett said, taking him from Charlotte so she could climb into the wagon that he'd parked in front of her shop.

"Bowl!" A grin wreathed the child's face.

"Not today. We're going to do something that's even more fun."

As Charlotte settled David on the bench between herself and Barrett, she raised an eyebrow. "That's an ambitious claim. I'm not sure there's anything David enjoys more than bowling."

"Wait and see." Though she was normally curious, it appeared that Charlotte had not noticed the blanket-covered object in the back of the wagon. That was good. Excellent, in fact, for it meant that their destination could remain a surprise.

As they headed north on Ferguson, Charlotte laid a hand on Barrett's sleeve. "Where are we going?"

Though he would do nothing to discourage her touch, he couldn't help smiling at the eagerness he heard in her voice. "Who's the child, you or David?" he asked softly. David was bouncing up and down on the seat, crooning to himself. "It seems to me you're as excited as he is."

"I am," Charlotte admitted. "It's rare for me to go outside the city."

When they reached the city limits, Ferguson turned from a street lined with houses and shops into an open road with few buildings in sight. A few minutes later, Barrett turned east, heading toward the snow-covered hill that was their destination. As he had hoped, though the sun was bright, it had yet to melt the snow. Instead, its brilliance made the tiny crystals sparkle more than the diamonds he'd seen in Mr. Mullen's store.

"It almost hurts my eyes," Charlotte said, shielding hers with a hand.

"I know, but it's beautiful, isn't it?"

She nodded. "Cheyenne's snow is special. We had more snow in Vermont, and it was different. Softer."

"Plus, it probably fell straight down, not sideways."

Charlotte laughed. "That's true. My sisters didn't believe me when I told them about sideways snow."

"You miss them, don't you?"

She nodded, and though her smile did not fade, Barrett caught a glimpse of wistfulness in her eyes. "Sometimes I miss being a child. Things seemed simpler then. On a day like this, the three of us would have gone sledding."

Barrett fought the grin that threatened to split his face. Keeping his voice as neutral as he could, he asked, "Have you ever taken David sledding?"

"No." Something in his voice must have alerted her, for Charlotte turned to look at the wagon bed where he'd stowed the sled. "Is that what we're going to do?"

There was no reason to lie. "Yes. What do you think of the idea?"

The wistfulness was gone. Now Charlotte's eyes sparkled with happiness. "I think it's marvelous." She laid her hand on David's head and turned his face toward her. "David, we're going to have so much fun today."

And they did. Barrett positioned himself

at the rear of the sled, placing Charlotte in front of him, David in her arms. With his legs stretched out on either side, he was able to steer the sled with his feet while he kept his arms around Charlotte. There was only one problem: he couldn't see her face or David's as they sped down the hill. But he could hear David's shrieks of delight and Charlotte's soft laughter.

"I thought he might have been frightened," Barrett said when they reached the bottom. It would be a long climb back up the hill, but that was the price for the seconds of excitement.

Charlotte's grin told him she'd enjoyed the ride as much as her son. "There's no reason for him to be scared when we're with him. He knows we'll keep him safe."

Barrett felt as if his buttons would burst. She had said "we." Twice. It was a simple pronoun, a mere two letters, and yet it warmed his heart more than the brilliant sunshine. Perhaps it was only wishful thinking, but it seemed as if Charlotte had begun to think of them as a couple. Perhaps she did not need a long courtship. That would be wonderful.

"I had an ulterior motive for asking you both to come."

Warren raised an eyebrow when Barrett made the announcement. He had waited until the serving dishes had been placed on the table and the butler had left, as if to ensure there would be no interruptions. Warren had been surprised by the timing of the invitation, since Richard was Barrett's other guest. While the newlyweds were waiting until summer to take a wedding trip, they had remained practically sequestered in Richard's town house, and when they'd emerged, it had always been together. Until today.

Warren looked at Barrett. As was normally the case when they dined at the Landry mansion, their host was seated at the head of the table, with Richard on one side of him, Warren on the other. It was a matter of amusement for Warren that one time he would be seated on the right, the next on the left. Barrett Landry was a man of scruples, even to the point of avoiding a hint of favoritism among his friends. What would he think if he knew of Warren's scruples, or — more precisely — the lack thereof? Fortunately, that subject would never be addressed.

Richard feigned shock as he helped himself to a serving of roast beef. "I thought you invited us so we could enjoy another of

Mrs. Melnor's fine meals. You'd better be careful, Barrett," he said playfully. "Miriam wants me to hire her away from you. She says no one does a roast as well as your cook."

Barrett nodded. "Miriam's correct. Mrs. Melnor is a gem, but that's not what I want to discuss."

When it was evident that Richard was more interested in the beef and potatoes or perhaps thoughts of his bride than Barrett's motives, Warren spoke. "So, why did you summon us?"

The way Barrett's face clouded told Warren this was no trivial matter. He only hoped Barrett wasn't going to announce that he was leaving Cheyenne. He'd been counting on Barrett's support when his application for membership in the Cheyenne Club was reviewed.

Barrett's lips tightened as he said, "I heard a rumor that there's someone in Cheyenne who calls himself the baron. I wondered if either of you knew anything about him."

Thank goodness he was eating. Warren took another bite of meat to give himself the excuse of a full mouth, then busied himself with buttering a slice of bread. He dared not look at Barrett for fear that his expression might reveal his shock. No one important was supposed to know about the baron. Oh, it was true that the girls at Sylvia's knew him by that name, but that was by design. Surely Barrett hadn't gone to Sylvia's. Not straitlaced Barrett. So how had he heard the name?

Richard looked up from his plate, his face showing only a modicum of interest. "The baron? I haven't heard of anyone with that name. He could be a newcomer."

Barrett shook his head. "Not from the stories I heard. This man's been here for a few years." He turned toward Warren, pointing his fork at him. "What about you, Warren? You know more people than I do. Has anyone mentioned him to you?"

Warren almost laughed. The way the question was phrased, he didn't have to lie. Perjury didn't bother him under special circumstances, and this was certainly one of those, but he tried to avoid lies — and self-incrimination — whenever he could. "I'm afraid not." He forced a light tone to his voice. "While I'd like to claim that my clientele is the most exclusive in the city, it doesn't include any barons."

Barrett's frown deepened. "Despite the moniker, it doesn't sound as if this baron is someone we'd meet at the club. He frequents one of the seedier brothels on 15th

Street, and he has a reputation for being rough on the women."

Whoever they were, Barrett's sources were good. There had to be a way to deflect his interest. "Don't be so prudish, Barrett. I suspect a number of the Cheyenne Club's members employ the services of prostitutes."

"Perhaps." Barrett helped himself to a serving of green beans. "Whether he visits whorehouses is not what concerns me. I want to meet this man."

On the opposite side of the table, Richard sputtered. "Why on earth?"

Yes, why did Barrett care about the baron? Warren fixed his gaze on Barrett, trying to fathom his motives.

"He has a key to something I want."

"A key? What kind of key?" The questions spilled out before Warren knew what was happening.

"It doesn't matter now." Though he'd intrigued Warren, Barrett dismissed the subject. "I doubted either of you would have heard of him, but I needed to ask. Now, let's talk about something more pleasant."

An hour later as he walked home, Warren clenched his fists. It had taken all the composure he could muster to avoid grabbing Barrett by the throat and demanding to know why he wanted to learn about the baron and — just as importantly — who had told him about Warren's alter ego. But, though he'd seethed inside, he had forced himself to sit there as quietly as if they were discussing nothing more important than the weather.

What had happened? The question reverberated through his brain. There should have been no way that Barrett would ever hear of the baron. The baron didn't travel in the same circles, and despite what Warren had said to Barrett, the members of the Cheyenne Club did not frequent establishments like Sylvia's. There were other houses that catered to men with money and influence. But somehow the baron had come to Barrett's notice.

It might not be a problem. Barrett might forget all about the baron in a day or two. Warren pounded a fist into his hand. He was deluding himself if he believed that. Barrett Landry was nothing if not tenacious. If he was able to ferret out the truth, everything Warren had worked so hard to establish would be lost. He had taken every precaution to avoid having his name linked with the baron's. The mask, the clandestine visits, disguising his voice. And yet, there was always the chance that he had missed something. All it took was one little slip.

He couldn't let that happen. He couldn't let Barrett connect the baron and Warren Duncan. And he wouldn't. First he had to discover why Barrett had suddenly become so interested in the baron. Warren thought back, remembering the night — early morning, really — when he'd followed a woman north on Ferguson. At first it had been nothing more than a lark, an opportunity to demonstrate his power by frightening her. But when the gracefulness of her walk told him she was younger than he'd thought, the game had changed. His night at Sylvia's had left him dissatisfied. Perhaps a kiss or two — maybe something more — would sate his desires. He'd almost reached her when he saw the carriage headed toward him. Nothing, not even the sweetest of kisses, was worth being discovered, and so he'd faded into the shadows and made his way home.

Had that been Barrett's carriage? Of course not. Barrett had no reason to be out at that hour. Barrett's interest had been piqued by something different.

The sudden interest in the baron must have something to do with Barrett's trip to Fort Laramie. When he'd mentioned that he had gone there, Barrett had refused to explain his reasons, claiming they were personal. To Warren's knowledge, Barrett had never kept secrets, but he'd been different since he'd returned.

Warren shuddered. He had sworn he would never again set foot on that fort. The dangers were too high. But the dangers in not going seemed equally threatening. As distasteful as the prospect of entering the Army post was, he had to learn why Barrett had gone there and what he had found. Warren would go to Fort Laramie tomorrow. And then, one way or another, he would ensure that Barrett Landry did not discover the baron's identity.

22

"He's courting you."

Gwen leaned against the door frame while Charlotte pulled on woolen socks in preparation for her next outing with Barrett. When he had invited her and David, he had refused to say where they were going or what they would do. All he'd told Charlotte was that it was something new and to dress warmly.

"I told you he cared about you," Gwen continued. "Now, if only Warren would speak, we could have a double wedding." Weddings were Gwen's favorite topic of conversation, and for her sake, Charlotte hoped that Warren did propose. Barrett was another story.

"He's simply being kind." Admittedly, the smiles he had given her were warmer than mere courtesy demanded, and he touched her hand more frequently than absolutely necessary. And then there had been the time his hand had brushed her cheek. Though it might have been an accident, the way it had lingered seemed to say otherwise. But courting? Charlotte doubted that.

Gwen's lips twisted as she shook her head. "A man who's simply being kind doesn't find an excuse to spend time with a woman every day. Mark my words, Charlotte. He's smitten, and you'd be a fool if you didn't take advantage of that. You won't find a better husband than Barrett."

"You're right." Charlotte had told herself that she would not remarry unless she found a man who would love both her and David. She hadn't expected that to happen, and yet she could not deny that Barrett seemed to care for David. She wouldn't claim that he treated David like any other boy, for he did not. Instead, he recognized David's blindness but sought ways to give him experiences that would make his life as close to normal as possible. That was caring. If Charlotte let herself dream, she would say that it was more than caring, that it was love.

Barrett was the kindest, most wonderful man she had ever met. When they were together, her heart beat faster, and every one of her senses seemed more acute. She was aware of the lightest of scents, the faintest of sounds, and even a gentle touch set her blood to pounding. When they were apart, she felt bereft, as if the world had suddenly faded to pale gray.

Gwen took a step into the room, a satisfied smile on her face. "Then you admit it. You love him."

Charlotte pulled out her heaviest flannel petticoat. Though it spoiled the lines of her gown, it would keep her warm if they were outside for an extended period, and with her long cloak covering it, no one would realize that Madame Charlotte was not dressed in the latest fashion.

"I do, but . . ."

"No buts. Oh, Charlotte, can't you see how perfect this is? This is what God intended for you, not teaching school. He brought Barrett into your life so you could marry him."

Charlotte wished she were as certain as her friend. Though she had believed that God wanted her to open the school, Barrett's inability to discover the baron's identity made her wonder if she'd been mistaken. Perhaps it had been nothing more than a passing dream, not one that she was supposed to turn into reality. Each morning, every night, and many times in between, Charlotte prayed for guidance, but she had heard no answer. If the Lord was going to speak, it seemed he was giving her a lesson in patience first.

"We'll have to see what the future brings." Charlotte fastened the last button. "Right now, it's time for me to get David ready."

Ten minutes later, she heard Barrett's knock on the door.

"Hello, my boy," he said as David raced across the floor to fling his arms around Barrett's legs. "Are you ready?"

While her son nodded vigorously, a smile lighting his face, Charlotte felt a lump rise to her throat. Though he probably meant nothing by it, the sound of Barrett calling David "my boy" brought tears to her eyes. Gwen was right. This was what she wanted, a man who would be a father for David and a husband for her. "Sled?" David chortled with glee when Barrett picked him up and swung him around. The brief swing had become a tradition, and judging from the grin on David's face, it was one he enjoyed.

"He's learned a new word," Charlotte told Barrett as they descended the steps. Today he'd brought his carriage rather than the wagon, confirming his statement that they would not be sledding. Though it would have been possible to put the sled at the back of the carriage where luggage was often carried, it was easier to load it into a wagon bed.

"I'm afraid there'll be no sledding today." Barrett placed David in the center of the seat, then helped Charlotte in beside him. "But both of you might like this even more. You can learn a new word too."

"And what word would that be?" Charlotte asked as she settled into her spot.

He chuckled. "In your case, *patience.*"

As Barrett flicked the reins and the horse began to trot, Charlotte laughed. "You've discovered one of my weaknesses. I'm not very patient."

"Which is why you have to wait until we reach our destination before I tell you what we're going to do."

When they approached 17th Street, Barrett turned east, continuing past Central. Charlotte's smile broadened. Without a horse, she rarely came this far from home, but it was pleasant riding with Barrett, seeing the elaborate homes in this part of the city, enjoying the sparkle of the sun on the snow. Though last week's snow had melted, as Barrett had predicted, another inch had fallen yesterday, making the yards once more pristine and white.

Barrett slowed the horse when they reached what could only be a park. While

435

few trees were visible, the road led to a series of lagoons and a small lake, all of which appeared to be frozen. In the distance, several children ran across the ice, sliding on the slippery surface, while their mothers kept watch from the gently sloping banks.

"Oh, it's beautiful!" Charlotte wrapped her arms around David, drawing him closer. "There's ice here, David." She looked up at Barrett. "Does the park have a name?"

"Of course. Minnehaha. It's the city's newest park." As he slowed the carriage even further, Barrett explained that a few years earlier, the town fathers had decided the city needed a park on its eastern boundary. "They dug ditches to bring water from Sloan's Lake so there could be a lake here."

Charlotte nodded. "I've heard of the park, of course. Miriam told me it was her favorite and that she especially enjoyed boating on the lagoons."

"That would be a little difficult right now," Barrett said with a chuckle. "I checked the ice this morning, and it's safe. Would you like to skate? And don't tell me you have no skates. Mr. Yates was happy to sell me three pairs."

Charlotte flushed. She should have realized that Barrett would provide everything they needed. After all, he'd bought a sled so that David could enjoy the thrill of sliding down a hill. Sledding had been marvelous, but skating presented new challenges.

"Three pairs? David can hardly walk."

Barrett busied himself hitching the horse to one of the posts, then returned to the carriage to help Charlotte dismount. "I don't want David to miss the opportunity. If we both take an arm, he should be able to skate. Or," he said, his lips twisting into a crooked grin, "what passes for skating for a one-year-old. If he shuffles his feet, we can call it skating."

This was what she wanted, what she'd dreamt of, the opportunity for David to live a close to normal life, and thanks to Barrett, her dream was coming true. Blinking back tears of happiness, Charlotte turned to her son. "Oh, David, you're going to have so much fun."

"I hope you will too," Barrett said as he pulled the bag of skates from the back of the carriage and led her to a bench that had been placed at the side of the lagoon, perhaps as a place for skaters to rest.

"I know I'll have fun if my ankles support me. It's been a long time since I've skated."

When Barrett handed her two pairs of skates, Charlotte shook her head. "First I need to introduce David to ice." She gathered him into her arms and carried him to the edge of the lagoon, then removed one of his mittens. "Ice, David," she said as she placed his hand on the frozen surface. "It's cold, and it's hard. We're going to skate on it." Returning to the bench, she handed him one of the small skates and let him discover the shape and texture. "These go on your feet," she explained. A puzzled expression crossed David's face. "It's more fun than walking," she promised.

After fastening the runners to David's boots, Charlotte put on her own, then tried to rise. As she had feared, her ankles wobbled, but within a few minutes, the three of them were gliding slowly across the ice. David refused to move his legs, clinging tightly to her hand and Barrett's, but as they propelled him along, he began to smile.

"It's fun, isn't it, David?" Charlotte asked, delighted with his progress. He might be too young to recall his first sledding and skating trips, but she knew the memories were engraved on her brain. A year ago, she had despaired of her son ever living a normal life, and now — thanks in great part to the man who stood so close to her — David was doing better than she had dreamt possible.

Charlotte looked at Barrett. "Thank you for making this possible."

The tiny crinkles at the corners of his eyes disappeared as his smile faded, and his voice was sober as he said, "I'm always happy to help. All you have to do is ask. I'd do anything for you and David."

Charlotte felt a flush color her cheeks. If Gwen were here, she would declare that Barrett's words were proof he was courting her. Though Charlotte had worried that Barrett might consider her and David a burden, especially when he realized that life with a blind child would never be completely normal, it seemed that he didn't mind the extra work David required. Like David himself, Barrett seemed to be having fun.

"You're enjoying this, aren't you?" she asked.

Barrett nodded. "Very much. I can't think of anything I'd rather be doing than spending the day with you and David."

"Even though neither of us can skate very well?"

"Maybe *because* you aren't the best skaters on the lagoon. It makes me feel useful."

Barrett's words echoed through Charlotte's mind that night. As she gave her hair its ritual hundred strokes, she replayed the time they'd shared at the lagoon. *"It makes me feel useful,"* he had said, his expression asking whether she understood. She did. Oh, how she understood.

Charlotte drew the brush through her hair again, smiling as the long tresses crackled with electricity. Helping others made her feel useful. She had lived her life believing that her purpose for being on this earth was to help others. That was one reason establishing a school appealed to her so greatly. It was a reason she enjoyed sewing clothing for others. Even though her customers paid her, she was rewarded with more than money. Knowing that they felt better about themselves when they were dressed in flattering colors and styles was a reward too. And then there were the garments she made for Mrs. Kendall. Though she received no money for them, the knowledge that those dresses helped Mrs. Kendall's residents and Sylvia's girls build new lives was worth more than a dozen gold coins.

Being needed, helping others, and feeling useful were basic human needs. Charlotte laid the brush on the dresser and began to braid her hair. Why hadn't she realized that? She wasn't the only one who wanted to feel useful, and David wasn't the only one who was blind. Though her fingers moved methodically, Charlotte's brain skittered as the thoughts tumbled through it. How wrong she had been! She had believed she needed to do everything herself. Asking for help was a sign of weakness, or so she had thought. It would mean that others were coddling her, proving that she was incapable of helping herself.

She had been wrong. So very wrong. She had been so blind that she hadn't realized that by struggling to do everything herself, she was depriving others of the opportunity to be needed. It had been a matter of pride, of deluding herself into thinking she could — and should — be self-sufficient. That was why she hadn't told her sisters about David's blindness, even though they would have given her much-needed comfort. That was why she hadn't let Gwen help her deliver dresses to Mrs. Kendall, although Gwen might have enjoyed the opportunity to bring a bit of beauty to the women's lives. That was why she hadn't wanted to accept Barrett's help, even his wonderfully generous offer of his home. She had forgotten that the simple act of giving brought so much pleasure, and so she had deprived Barrett of that.

Thanks to Charlotte's foolish pride, her life had been more difficult and decidedly less pleasant than it could have been. It was time to change.

23

As the clock on the church steeple chimed the hour, Barrett shook his head at the realization that once again he had arrived early for a rendezvous with Charlotte.

Ever since he'd returned from Fort Laramie, he had found a reason to spend time with her each day. Some days he included David; others he and Charlotte simply spent a half hour or so together. It didn't matter what they did or what they discussed. What was important was that they were together. Ma had been right. Courtship was a good thing. According to her, the purpose of courting was to let the woman know that the man cared about her, that he was interested in more than friendship. What Ma hadn't told her boys was that courtship benefited the man too. At least it did Barrett. The time he spent with Charlotte deepened his love for her and strengthened his conviction that she was the one woman he would love for the rest of his life.

Courtship was good. Though he had yet to mention words like *love* and *marriage,* Barrett did not believe he was mistaken in thinking that Charlotte harbored tender feelings for him. Those lovely brown eyes warmed when she greeted him, and the smiles she gave him were unlike those she bestowed on others. It was true that she was disappointed that he'd been unable to discover the baron's identity, but she seemed less anxious than she had a few weeks ago. "We'll find him," she said confidently.

Barrett wished he shared that confidence. He'd continued his inquiries, even going to Sylvia's to talk to some of the girls. He'd learned little from them other than that his dream had been eerily accurate. The girls could not describe anything more than his eyes. Light blue, they had said, and he smelled of cigars. Unfortunately, there were dozens of men in Cheyenne with light blue eyes who smoked cigars.

Barrett shook his head again as the chimes faded. He wouldn't think about the baron. Not when he had the opal ring that he'd bought for Charlotte nestled in his pocket. It had taken less time than he'd expected to exchange Miriam's diamond for the ring that had caught his fancy the first time he'd entered Mr. Mullen's store. That was why he was so early. A full half hour early.

Barrett couldn't interrupt Charlotte, not when she had customers, but he didn't want to return home, either. He smiled, knowing there was another place where he'd be welcome. Seconds later, he pushed open the door of Yates's Dry Goods.

"No, I'm sorry, but that's not quite right." The woman's querulous voice carried to the doorway. Judging from the pile of garments on the counter, the short, heavyset woman with the navy blue hat had said that a number of times before.

Though he looked up when the bell signaled Barrett's arrival, Mr. Yates did nothing more than nod at him. The fussy customer must have rattled the elderly man more than usual, for normally he had a warm smile for anyone who entered his store.

Barrett scanned the interior of the shop. No wonder Mr. Yates looked so harried. He had two other customers waiting, the tapping of one woman's toe signaling her impatience. Both were well-dressed, the tall, toe-tapping one in a maroon cloak and hat, the shorter one in a shade of brown that reminded Barrett of Charlotte's eyes. Years of experience in his family's store told

Barrett they were serious shoppers, not women like the fussy one who'd spend an hour looking at dozens of articles but would leave without purchasing a single one.

Barrett turned and started to leave, but as he did, he overheard the taller of the women addressing her companion.

"Come, Mildred. It is obvious Mr. Yates does not need our business. We shall see if Mr. Myers can wait on us."

Though she started to turn, the woman called Mildred put a restraining hand on the tall shopper's arm. "But, Gertrude, my Horace likes Mr. Yates's shirts."

Barrett's gaze moved to Mr. Yates. The flicker of pain in the shopkeeper's eyes confirmed his fear of losing this sale. One morning when Barrett had been visiting, the older man had confided that sales had declined over the winter and that he was concerned that any further losses would discourage a prospective buyer. At the time, though Barrett had been sympathetic, he had had no idea how to help Mr. Yates. Today was different. Surely Mr. Yates wouldn't object to what he hoped to do.

Stepping forward, Barrett bowed to the two women. "Good afternoon, ladies. Perhaps I can assist you." He glanced to the side and saw Mr. Yates's shoulders straighten ever so slightly. He didn't disapprove.

The women turned toward Barrett, and the shorter one's eyes widened. "I know you. You're Barrett Landry. You don't work here."

"You are correct, madam, but I grew up in a mercantile, and I know what fine merchandise Mr. Yates carries." He kept his gaze fixed on her as he added, "It's true that there are other dry goods establishments in Cheyenne, but I wouldn't want you to settle for lesser quality."

The woman named Gertrude frowned. "I don't know, Mildred. It doesn't seem quite right to have Mr. Landry helping us."

Mildred was wavering. Barrett could see that. If he didn't do something quickly, the two women would leave the shop, possibly never to return. The anticipation of salvaging a sale coursed through his veins, startling him with its intensity. It had been years since he'd worked in a mercantile, and it seemed he'd forgotten how heady the challenge of convincing customers could be.

Barrett gave both women a warm smile but focused his attention on Gertrude, who appeared to be the dominant one. "Would you deprive me of the pleasure of serving two lovely ladies?" Gertrude raised an eyebrow. It would take more than a little flattery to convince her. "We rarely had such discerning customers in my family's store."

Mildred eyed a stack of shirts as she said, "We're here, Gertrude. Let's stay."

"Oh, all right." Though the words were less than gracious, Barrett didn't mind. What mattered was that the women had not left. That and the surprising feeling that he was exactly where he was supposed to be. It hadn't been coincidence that he'd arrived at Élan early and that he'd been drawn into Mr. Yates's store.

"I appreciate your confidence in me, ladies. Now, what can I show you?"

"I need some shirts," Mildred said as she pointed toward the ones she had been eyeing. "My Horace always wears those."

Barrett nodded. He retrieved one from the shelf along with a shirt from a different stack. When he placed both on the end of the counter, he addressed Mildred. "This is a very fine shirt," he said, gesturing toward the one she said her husband preferred, "but you might want to consider this." He laid a hand on the other shirt he'd selected. "If you feel the cotton, you'll see that it's a smoother weave. Some gentlemen prefer these, believing they're worth the extra cost."

Mildred hesitated. "I don't know . . ."

"Let me see." Gertrude jostled her companion so she could touch the shirt Barrett had recommended. "You're right, Mr. Landry. These are better. They're just what my Benjamin needs. I'll take half a dozen."

That was all the encouragement Mildred needed. "So will I."

Barrett gave Mr. Yates a glance. Though he was still attempting to please the fussy customer, the wrinkle lines between his eyes seemed to have lessened. "You've made a fine choice, ladies. I knew women of your refinement would appreciate the superior quality," Barrett said as he smiled at his customers. "Have you seen the new cravats? The silk ones are particularly attractive." He broadened his smile, directing it at Gertrude. "I know, because I bought one last week."

She took the bait. "Show me which one you chose."

By the time the women were finished, Barrett had sold them not just shirts and cravats for their husbands but stockings and corset covers for themselves. It was true they'd looked askance when he'd mentioned the corset covers, until he assured them that his mother had taught him what ladies sought in their undergarments. "She wouldn't sell something unless it was pretty," he explained. "She told my brothers and me that a lady should be elegant from head to toe, but there's no need for me to tell you that. Your clothing shows you understand fashion far better than my mother ever did."

When the women had declared their shopping complete, Gertrude looked at the pile of garments she had acquired and frowned. "Oh, my. How will I ever carry all this home? Perhaps I should take only one or two shirts."

As Mildred nodded, Barrett gave them another smile. "Surely you weren't planning to carry anything at all. The James Sisters have some new spring hats," he said, referring to the millinery shop that was less than a block away. "You wouldn't want to miss them, and I'm certain you don't want to worry about carrying packages when you're trying on a hat." Both women nodded. "If you'll give me your addresses, I'll have your purchases delivered to your homes later today."

Pursing her lips, Gertrude gave Barrett a long look. "Mr. Yates has never done that."

"Perhaps he didn't mention that's a new service he's considering."

The fussy customer must have overheard

Barrett, for she fixed her gaze on Mr. Yates. "Is that true?" When he nodded reluctantly, she pointed to two pairs of shoes that she had discarded. "In that case, I'll take these too."

Minutes later, when the three women had left the shop, Mr. Yates slumped onto a chair. Though he appeared weary, his voice was firm. "Delivery service?" he demanded. "When did I consider that? And, more to the point, how will I pay for it?"

"I'm sorry, sir." Barrett was sorry that he'd worried Mr. Yates, though he could not regret the decision. "It seems old habits are hard to break. My parents taught all of us not to let a sale get away, but I'm afraid my tongue ran away with itself." He reached for the sheet of paper with the women's addresses. "Mr. Bradley will deliver their purchases."

Mr. Yates was not mollified. "That's fine for today, but what am I to do going forward? You know those three women will tell everyone about my free delivery service."

Biting back a smile, Barrett said, "I want to talk to you about that. I have a plan."

The place had not improved. It had been dark the last time, and though daylight made many things more attractive, that was not the case with Fort Laramie. A collection of mismatched buildings; soldiers marching on the parade ground for no good reason; a passel of stray dogs running around the perimeter. Unlike Cheyenne's Fort D.A. Russell, this was not Warren's idea of an ideal military installation.

"I need to see your commanding officer," he announced to the guard who asked his business. The flunkies might know something, but Warren was betting that the man in charge would be a better source of information.

The soldier nodded. "Captain Westland's office is in the Administration Building." He pointed to an L-shaped building at the opposite corner of the parade ground.

"Thank you, soldier. I can find my way."

As he crossed the boardwalks that lined this side of the parade ground, Warren looked at the square stone building on the opposite side. For some reason, it was situated at an odd angle, rather than lining up with the barracks alongside it. That was the Army for you. Couldn't do anything right, including making a proper guardhouse. Warren's lips twisted. He'd never thought he'd kill a woman. In fact, he had once declared that that was the one thing he would never do. And yet he had. Right there in that crooked guardhouse, he'd slit a woman's throat. It had been easier than he'd thought, and once the deed was done, he'd realized that he would do it again. If it was the only way to get the money Jeffrey Crowley had stolen, he'd kill women, he'd kill children, he'd kill anyone who stood in his way.

"How can I help you?"

As he entered the CO's office, Warren gave the man a quick assessment. Though he estimated Captain Westland's age to be about the same as his, it was clear that Army living had taken its toll on him. Westland wore spectacles, and the paunch around his middle told Warren he hadn't spent much time marching with his men.

"I'm trying to reach an old friend of mine," Warren said as he took the chair the captain indicated. "The last time I heard from him, he was stationed here. I'm hoping he still is." Warren concluded the story he had fabricated with a piece of truth. "His name wa— is Jeffrey Crowley. Lieutenant Crowley." He'd almost given himself away there, using the past tense. Fortunately, the captain didn't seem to have noticed.

The man shook his head. "I'm sorry to be the one to tell you this, but Lieutenant Crowley was killed over a year ago."

"Killed?" Warren hoped his shock sounded sincere. "How did it happen?"

"I'm not at liberty to say, other than that the circumstances were unfortunate. Most unfortunate."

Indeed they were, for even though Jeffrey and the woman who'd wound up in the guardhouse were dead, Warren did not have Big Nose's stash.

"And his wife? Is she still here?" Surely it was reasonable for a man who claimed to be an old friend to inquire about the grieving widow.

To Warren's surprise, Captain Westland stared at him for a moment, his expression veiled. "No, sir," he said at last. "She's not here."

"Do you know where she went? I'd like to send her my condolences. They may be belated, but . . ."

The captain's expression altered, and this time there was no doubt about it. He was cautious. If Warren hadn't known better, he would have said that the man was wary of him. That couldn't be. Westland knew nothing about the baron and even less about Warren Duncan.

"I believe she went back East," Westland said. "New Hampshire, Vermont, somewhere like that."

He was lying. Oh, Warren would grant that he was a good liar, but a poker player like Warren knew when he was being bluffed. He also knew that he'd learned everything he could from this man.

"Thank you, Captain. I appreciate your help."

He wouldn't admit defeat. There had to be someone on this miserable Army fort who knew where Mrs. Crowley had gone. As he strolled around the parade ground, more slowly this time, Warren looked at the men who were marching. They had the look of new recruits. No point in asking them. He'd try the post store. Chances were that the men working there had been here a while.

"You just passing through?" the clerk inquired when Warren asked what kind of tobacco he stocked.

"You could say that. I thought I'd be here longer, but I learned that the friend I'd come to visit died. It doesn't seem right that Jeffrey's not here." He looked at the clerk, as if a thought had just occurred to him. "I don't suppose you knew him. Lieutenant Crowley?"

The man nodded. "Sure did. Fine man. Had a pretty wife too."

Exultation raced through Warren's veins.

He'd been right in believing that the answers were here. Now all he had to do was extract them. It didn't appear that would be too difficult, for the clerk seemed to be the talkative sort. "I don't suppose you know where she went, do you? I'd like to see her and tell her how much I valued her husband." He had. Until that last day, Jeffrey Crowley had been valuable.

The clerk scrunched his nose, possibly trying to encourage his memory. "I don't know where she went," he said. "It seemed mighty odd that she left before her sister got hitched."

"Her sister?" Warren had forgotten that Jeffrey's sister-in-law had come to the fort.

"Yeah." The clerk grinned. "Miss Harding was even prettier than Mrs. Crowley."

Harding. Warren tried not to frown. He knew he'd heard that name before, but he could not remember when. He paid for the tobacco he didn't want and left the store. It was only when he'd mounted his horse that the memory resurfaced. Though she was always addressed as Madame Charlotte, Barrett had mentioned that her name was Charlotte Harding. Of course! It was no coincidence. Jeffrey's wife had been named Charlotte. If her sister was Miss Harding, that meant that Jeffrey's wife had once been

Charlotte Harding.

The fool! She could have gone to London or Paris, but Jeffrey's widow thought she was smart by hiding in plain sight. She'd soon learn that Warren was smarter. Smarter and more determined. He clenched the reins as his anger began to simmer. There was a long, tedious ride ahead, but at least he'd accomplished his goal. He knew where to find Widow Crowley.

Charlotte's fingers trembled as she fastened the last of the fourteen jet black buttons on the front of her bodice. It was silly, really. She shouldn't be so nervous. It wouldn't be the first time she had shared a meal with Barrett, but it would be the first time she had been the only guest for dinner at his home. Gwen was convinced that Barrett planned to propose and that was why he'd asked Gwen if she would be able to care for David. Charlotte didn't know what to think. It was true that Barrett had seemed different the last few days, and he had appeared almost nervous when he'd invited her to have dinner with him. "I have something I'd like to discuss with you," he'd said, his face uncharacteristically pale. They'd spent so much time together over the past month that Charlotte had learned to read Barrett's moods. This one said that she should not ask, that he wasn't ready to tell her his reasons.

Smoothing the skirts of the blue silk dress she'd made especially for tonight, Charlotte tried but failed to still the trembling of her fingers. With its square neckline edged with pleated trim and the black Venice lace she'd ordered from New York, the dress was beautiful. She knew that. She looked her best. She knew that too. But still she couldn't help being nervous. It was true that she loved Barrett, that he had aroused feelings that exceeded anything she had shared with Jeffrey, but if he did ask her to marry him, she wasn't certain she should accept. She had to be certain that he loved her the way she did him and that his proposal — if indeed there was one — was not motivated by pity.

Taking a deep breath, Charlotte reached for the Bible that she kept on her night-stand. The Psalms never failed to soothe her. But as she started to open the Bible, she shook her head. She needed the comfort of her old Bible, the one that had been a part of her life for so long. Charlotte opened the drawer and pulled it out, finding her fingers steadier as she stroked the familiar leather.

"He's here!" Gwen called a few minutes later.

Charlotte glanced at the clock, grateful that her earlier nervousness had fled, chased away by the promises she'd found in God's Word. Barrett was ten minutes early. Mama had always said that a lady should let the gentleman wait, but Charlotte couldn't do that. Setting the Bible aside, she grabbed her cloak and hurried into the kitchen.

"You look more beautiful than ever." Barrett held out his arms for the cloak and settled it over her shoulders, smiling all the while.

"Thank you." Charlotte wished the blood hadn't rushed to her cheeks. She wasn't a schoolgirl. A man's admiration shouldn't cause her to blush. As she kissed her son good night, she stole another glance at Barrett. He was breathtakingly handsome with his suit carefully brushed, his hair freshly cut, his face devoid of even the slightest hint of a beard. But though the sight of him made Charlotte's pulse race, she doubted he wanted to be told he was handsome. Instead, she focused on his clothing. "Is that a new cravat? It almost matches some fabric I received last week."

Barrett nodded as he escorted her down the steps and into his carriage. "It is new. I bought it from Mr. Yates yesterday." Though the words were ordinary, Barrett's eyes sparkled, and his lips curved in an almost secretive smile.

She settled in the carriage for the short ride to Barrett's house. Though the March days were growing longer, the sun had already set, and there were far fewer people out than during the day. Memories of the last time she had ridden with Barrett after dark flitted through Charlotte's brain. The circumstances could not have been more different. Then she'd been frightened. Today she was filled with anticipation. Then she'd been disguised in her widow's weeds. Today she wore iridescent dupioni silk and sat next to a man who found the occasion worthy of a haircut and a new cravat. Most importantly, then she'd believed Barrett loved Miriam. Today she knew otherwise.

Her nervousness returning at the thought of love, Charlotte tried to keep her voice even as she said, "I'm sure Mr. Yates appreciated the sale. He's been worried that dwindling business will make it more difficult for him to find a buyer for the store."

"I know." Barrett sounded almost as if he were laughing, but that wasn't possible. Barrett was not a man who would take pleasure in another's distress. "He's a nice man."

"That he is. Even David seems to agree."

Charlotte turned slightly so she could watch Barrett's expression. "I hope you won't feel slighted, but David bowls with Mr. Yates."

As she had expected, Barrett's eyebrows rose in surprise. "Really?"

"I couldn't believe it myself. Gwen and I invite Mr. Yates to join us for supper occasionally. One time he saw the blocks arranged and asked what they were for. When we explained, he said the word *bowl.* That was all David needed. He ran for his ball and rolled it toward Mr. Yates, even though the blocks were on the other side of the room. I don't know who was more surprised, Mr. Yates or me."

Barrett shrugged. "Perhaps he thinks bowling is something only men do."

"I don't know, but we tried it again. When Gwen called to him, he refused to play, but when Mr. Yates did, it was just as if you were there."

"I'm not sure whether or not I should be flattered by being compared to a man who's close to seventy." A chuckle accompanied Barrett's words, telling Charlotte he found the prospect amusing.

"Well," she said, affecting a slow drawl, "I can see where David might be confused. After all, you both wear trousers and have deep voices."

"And the similarity ends there." When he'd handed the reins to one of his servants, Barrett helped Charlotte out of the carriage, then opened the front door to his home. "Shall we see what Mrs. Melnor has in store for us?"

It was a delicious meal. A delicate fish soup was followed by succulent roast beef and all the trimmings, and though Charlotte didn't think she could eat another bite, when Mr. Bradley set a piece of chess pie in front of her, she couldn't resist. It would have been the most wonderful meal of her life, had it not been for her nervousness and the fact that Barrett seemed equally apprehensive. His hands didn't tremble the way hers did, and his voice never quavered, but she sensed a hesitancy in him. Perhaps that was why, although he had said he wanted to discuss something, he kept the conversation light while they ate. He spoke of spring, of Miriam and Richard's wedding, of David's progress. But not once did he venture into any serious subjects.

When they had finished their dessert, Barrett smiled at Charlotte. "Shall we go into the parlor?" He pulled out her chair, placing his hand on the small of her back as they walked across the hallway to the front parlor. As the warmth of his hand penetrated her clothing, Charlotte's smile broadened. No matter what he wanted to discuss, she would always remember how good it had felt to be walking like this.

Gesturing toward one of the tapestry-covered wingback chairs that flanked the stove, Barrett waited until she was seated before he settled into the other. Though his expression remained calm, Charlotte saw a telltale vein throbbing on his neck. It was what she had thought. Barrett was as nervous as she.

"The first time I met you, I asked for your honest opinion," he said. "I'm asking for that again."

Her opinion. Gwen had been wrong. Barrett wasn't planning to ask her to marry him. He wanted to discuss something far more mundane. Charlotte tried to bite back her disappointment and forced herself to smile as she said, "Of course."

"Thank you. I knew I could rely on you." Barrett cleared his throat and looked away for a moment before turning his gaze back to Charlotte. "I've reached a crossroads in my life," he said, his voice solemn. "My plans to run for office are gone. My life as a cattle baron is ending. I needed to find a new direction, and I believe that I have."

Charlotte took a deep breath, trying to

keep the smile fixed on her face. Oh, how she hoped he was not going to tell her he was returning to Pennsylvania. Even if Barrett didn't love her and didn't want to marry her, she didn't want to lose his friendship.

"I would say it was a coincidence," Barrett continued, "but you and I both know there are no coincidences. This was part of the plan."

As Barrett recounted his experience helping Mr. Yates's customers, Charlotte watched his face. The hesitancy she had seen before was gone, replaced by more enthusiasm than she'd ever seen. His eyes sparkled, his lips curved in easy smiles, his voice rang with sincerity. When he'd finished, Charlotte laughed, imagining Mr. Yates's reaction to the announcement. "You told them delivery was a new policy Mr. Yates was considering? What did he say?"

Barrett's smile broadened. "He was concerned until I told him I wanted to buy his business."

"Buy his business?" Though Charlotte hadn't thought Barrett could surprise her, he had. Whenever he'd spoken of his parents' mercantile, she'd had the impression that he disliked working there, and when she'd mentioned Mr. Yates's dilemma,

Barrett had claimed he had no interest in running another store. Something had obviously changed, for there was no denying his enthusiasm. "You want to stay in Cheyenne and take over Mr. Yates's business?"

Barrett nodded. "I realized that I enjoyed serving those two ladies more than almost anything I've done in years." He leaned forward, placing his hands on his knees. "When Harrison was here, he told me he thought I belonged with people, not cattle. At first I didn't agree. I thought he was just being Harrison, my bossy oldest brother. But the more I thought about it, the more I realized that he was right, and that no matter how much money I made raising and selling cattle, it wasn't particularly fulfilling. Politics seemed like the answer. It involved people, so I told myself that's what I should do. It wasn't."

Barrett raised his gaze, meeting Charlotte's. "Being a shopkeeper might not be as glamorous as being a senator, but I feel it's what I was meant to do." He paused, his expression once again serious as he asked, "What do you think?"

This was the opinion he wanted. This was the reason he'd arranged that wonderful dinner. Gwen had been wrong. Charlotte managed a small smile, though her heart ached at the knowledge that she'd been as mistaken as Gwen.

"Your face tells me everything," she said firmly. "When you talked about the customers, you looked happy and excited. Even when you spoke about water rights, there wasn't the same enthusiasm. I know you felt deeply about that, but this is different. This seems as if it's part of you." Charlotte took a deep breath as she thought about Barrett in the shop next to Élan. He'd be so close that she could see him every day, perhaps more than once. It wasn't the future she'd dreamt of, but it was still good.

As she started to nod, a thought assailed Charlotte. "You said the shop couldn't be profitable unless it was larger."

"That's true." Though he'd been leaning forward, Barrett settled back in the chair. "That's the real reason I wanted to talk to you tonight."

Of course. This was why Barrett had seemed so apprehensive. He hadn't been certain she would agree to sell him her store. After all, until they found the baron, they had both agreed it would not be safe for Charlotte to open her school. In the meantime, she needed the income from Élan to pay her expenses. The prudent course would be to tell Barrett he would have to wait until she had the school established, but Charlotte wasn't feeling prudent. She didn't want to do anything to destroy Barrett's happiness. If she had to, she could run her business the way she'd heard some dressmakers did, by conducting all the meetings and fittings in her clients' homes. It wouldn't be as convenient as having a showroom, and she'd probably lose some sales, but it was a small price to pay for Barrett's happiness.

"You want my shop." She made it a statement, not a question as she tried to tamp down her disappointment. It wasn't Barrett's fault that she had hoped for a different outcome from tonight.

"Yes, but —"

She wouldn't let him apologize. She wouldn't let him rationalize. Friends didn't do that to friends. Before he could continue, Charlotte said, "You may have it."

Though she had expected to see relief reflected on his face, Barrett appeared almost annoyed. That was undoubtedly her imagination. She had just given him what he wanted. Of course he was not annoyed.

"You haven't heard everything," he said.

"I've heard enough. It's a fine idea, Barrett. An excellent one." When he looked as if he were going to say something, Char

25

His dreams were coming true. He could feel it in his bones. Slowing the horse as he reached the outskirts of Cheyenne, Warren grinned. He'd ridden harder than normal, but there'd been no choice, not unless he was willing to waste another day, and that was something he wouldn't do. Though he didn't like to abuse good horseflesh, he didn't want to wait until morning. That was why he was still riding, though it was well past sunset. He might be tired, the horse might be winded, but he was here.

He had it all planned. The red-hot fury he'd felt when he'd realized that Widow Crowley had tried to outsmart him had faded, but in its wake, he'd found a new resolve. She would pay for the time he'd waited for the money. She would pay, and so would that brat of hers.

Two days ago, all he'd wanted was the money. Now he wanted more. He deserved

lotte continued to outline the reasons Barrett's plan was ideal. "Mr. Yates will be able to move to Arizona, you'll have the future you deserve, and the citizens of Cheyenne will have a newly expanded place to buy their dry goods." If only she didn't feel so horribly empty inside, everything would be perfect.

Barrett said nothing, and the silence stretched between them, an awkward silence as Charlotte wondered why he wasn't responding. Hadn't she said what he wanted to hear? What more did he want from her?

At last he cleared his throat. "Now may I tell you why I invited you to dinner?"

Blinking in confusion, Charlotte stared at him. "You already have."

He shook his head. "That was the prelude. Yes, it's true that I would like to buy Mr. Yates's store. It's also true that I would like to expand it by incorporating what is now Élan, but none of that matters unless I have what I want most in life."

Pausing for a moment, Barrett stretched his hands out, capturing hers in his. "I'm supposed to be the man with the golden tongue," he said, his lips twisting with irony. "Folks say I can convince anyone of anything. Now, when it matters more than ever before, I feel like a tongue-tied schoolboy."

He cleared his throat again. "You know what a difficult winter this has been. I've been like everyone else in Cheyenne, waiting for spring. I told myself that everything would be better then, and it will be, if you . . ." He stopped abruptly. "There I go, getting ahead of myself." Though he shook his head in apparent self-disgust, his eyes sparkled.

Charlotte stared at Barrett, her breath catching at what she saw in his eyes. When he'd spoken of buying the dry goods store, she had seen enthusiasm. When he'd recounted the story of helping the customers, she had seen satisfaction. But now his eyes reflected something softer and yet stronger than either enthusiasm or satisfaction. Love.

Barrett raised her hands to his lips and pressed a kiss on them. "I love you, Charlotte. I love you with all my heart, with every breath in my body."

She started to smile. This was what she had hoped for. This was what she had dreamt of. She tugged Barrett's hands and turned them over, slowly raising them to her lips so that she could return the kiss he had given her, but he shook his head. "Please let me finish."

As she nodded, Barrett's lips curved into a smile. "The store is important, but if I

were there alone, it would be mean need more. I want more. I want to you and spend the rest of my life wi and David. That's what is important t Will you do it, Charlotte? Will you mak life complete? Will you be my wife?"

Her heart pounding so furiously t Charlotte feared it would break through h chest, she nodded. "Yes, Barrett, I will."

Dreams did come true.

more. It was no longer enough to send her a demand for the money or to wear his mask when he confronted her. Now he wanted to see her face when she realized who he was and what he intended to do. That was why he'd decided that he needed to visit Charlotte tonight.

Her shop would be closed, so he wouldn't run the risk of encountering any of her customers. He didn't want anyone — especially Gwen — overhearing their conversation. That was why he'd tell Charlotte they had business to discuss and that it would be best if they went to the store. She'd agree. Just as she'd agree to tell no one of his demands. Of course she would, for Warren was a most persuasive man. He'd make sure she knew that her son's life was at stake. Silly Charlotte wouldn't realize that he had every intention of killing both her and the boy. That was the only way he could ensure her silence. Besides, if Charlotte were dead, the victim of an unfortunate accident, Gwen would have no one to turn to but him.

Warren's grin widened. By tomorrow, he would have the money — his money. And the next day he would ask Gwen to marry him. His grin turned into a chuckle. In less than forty-eight hours, his future would be secured.

Once he'd hitched the horse, he climbed the steps leading to the second floor apartment and knocked on Charlotte's door. The time of reckoning had arrived.

"Warren?" Gwen's eyes widened in surprise as she opened the door. "I didn't expect you," she said as she ushered him into an immaculately clean kitchen. "Did Barrett send you? Has something happened to Charlotte?"

Warren stifled a curse. This wasn't going the way he had planned, for Jeffrey's widow was not here.

"Where is Charlotte?" His words came out harsher than he'd planned, causing Gwen to flinch. *Careful, Warren,* he admonished himself. *You don't want to lose control now. Gwen must never know what you've done and what you intend to do.* Sweet, innocent Gwen would not marry a murderer and a thief.

"She's having dinner with Barrett." Gwen tilted her head to one side in the gesture he found so endearing. "At his house. I don't know what came over me. Of course there's nothing wrong. It was foolish of me to think otherwise. I was just so surprised to see you."

Warren's mind began to whirl. Though there would be an unfortunate delay, perhaps he could turn it to his advantage. He might be able to learn something from Gwen, and even if he didn't, he'd have the pleasure of her company.

"May I stay for a few minutes?"

Gwen started to nod, then shook her head, her indecision apparent. "I'm not sure it would be proper, since we have no chaperone."

"Didn't you say Charlotte was with Barrett at his house?"

"Yes," she admitted, "but there are servants there. No one's here but Rose and David, and they'd hardly qualify as chaperones, even if they were awake."

Her protests only heightened his determination. Everything she did and said underscored what a perfect wife she would be. Once they were wed, no one, not even the most persnickety member of the committee, would question Warren's suitability for the Cheyenne Club.

"Please, Gwen. I missed you while I was gone. No one will know I'm here." Warren's thoughts flew to the horse that was hitched in front of the store. It was a gray, and grays were not common in Cheyenne. That had been part of the gelding's appeal. It was also the reason he never rode to Sylvia's. That was one place where he could not afford to be recognized. This was another. He hadn't expected to be here long enough for anyone to notice his horse, and so he hadn't taken his normal precautions, but now . . . Warren tossed caution aside. "I'd like to spend some time with you," he told Gwen.

She hesitated again, then nodded. "All right. Come in."

As she led him into what appeared to be the parlor area of the apartment, Warren saw that she was wearing house slippers. Perhaps that was another reason she was so reluctant to invite him in. A lady like Gwen would feel uncomfortable entertaining a man in her slippers. But soon, if everything went the way Warren planned, he would see her house slippers every day. He grinned at the prospect of sharing a house and a life with this woman.

While Warren waited until Gwen seated herself, he looked around the room. Since he'd been inside Mr. Yates's store, he was familiar with the basic dimensions of the apartment. He'd known it would not be large, but to Warren's surprise, there was no sign of wealth. To the contrary, the furniture was well-worn, and though a table had been placed over it, he spotted a hole in the carpet. Apparently Charlotte had not lavished any of Big Nose's gold here. It made no sense. If he had all that money, he

476

wouldn't be living in a small apartment with used furnishings, but he didn't pretend to understand the workings of a woman's mind. Perhaps Charlotte had a conscience and knew the money wasn't hers.

As he settled himself on the chair Gwen indicated, Warren nodded. That must be the case. Hadn't Jeffrey mentioned that his wife's father was a minister? It figured that a parson's daughter would have scruples. Warren almost laughed out loud. Charlotte's scruples meant more money for him.

Tiny furrows appeared between Gwen's eyes. "Are you certain nothing is wrong?"

"Why would you think anything is amiss?" Plenty was wrong, but Warren didn't want to worry Gwen.

"Your expression when you were looking at the room. I never saw you look quite like that."

Warren shrugged as he feigned nonchalance. He hadn't realized Gwen was so perceptive. He'd have to be careful after they were married, especially on the days when he planned to visit Sylvia's. Whatever else he did, he couldn't let Gwen learn about that side of his life.

"If I'm looking strange, it must be because I'm so tired." Determined to change the subject, he made a show of looking around the room, this time keeping his expression neutral. "This is the first time I've seen where you live. It's not what I expected."

Gwen seemed surprised, but at least she was no longer studying his face. "Why not?"

"I thought it would be bigger." He wouldn't say that he had thought it would be nicer, because the furnishings weren't Gwen's fault. He knew she had little money. That was why she lived here, working as a glorified servant for Charlotte Crowley, a woman who could afford a mansion. It was Charlotte who was to blame for these modest surroundings. Tamping down his anger, Warren searched for proof that Charlotte Harding, proprietor of Élan, was actually Jeffrey Crowley's widow. The parlor was barren of personal touches other than some children's toys and a sewing basket.

"I'm surprised you have no photographs of your family here." He gestured toward the mantel and the wall. "Most homes I've visited do."

Gwen looked at the bare walls as if seeing them for the first time. "There's a portrait of Mike in my bedchamber." A faint blush stained her cheeks, and he wondered if she'd broken some rule of etiquette by mentioning her sleeping quarters. "I keep it out because I don't want Rose to forget her father."

This was the opening Warren needed. As casually as he could, he asked, "And Charlotte? Does she have a picture of her husband? What was his name?" He paused for a second, as if racking his brain. "Jeffrey?"

Though he hadn't intended it, confusion clouded Gwen's eyes. He must have sounded like he was cross-examining a hostile witness. He'd have to be more careful. Gwen shook her head slowly. "There are no photographs of him, but it doesn't matter. I'm sure Charlotte's like me, and she'll never forget her husband's face. As for David, the poor child wouldn't know if there were a dozen portraits of his father."

That might be true, but the absence of photos struck Warren as suspicious. Only a woman with something to hide would have changed her name and hidden all evidence of her past. Warren stared into the distance, acting as casual as he could. "She must have loved Jeffrey very much if she can't bear to see reminders of her marriage."

It was the wrong thing to say, for Gwen started to bristle. Perhaps she thought he was questioning her love for Mike, since she kept his portrait on display. "Why do you keep saying 'Jeffrey'?" she demanded. "I don't believe that was his name."

But it had to be. There couldn't be two Charlotte Hardings in Wyoming Territory. "Then what was his name?"

Gwen pursed her lips. "I don't know. Charlotte doesn't talk about him very often, and when she does, she refers to him as 'my husband.' "

"Then she never mentioned Jeffrey Crowley?"

"No."

"And she never told you she lived at Fort Laramie?"

"No." Gwen's face began to flush. "Warren, I don't know where you got those ideas. You must be mistaken." She looked at him, her eyes dark with anger. "I know Charlotte. She's my dearest friend. If what you're saying were true, she would have told me."

"Unless she's a liar."

Charlotte sighed as she wrapped her arms around Barrett's neck. Never had she dreamt that his kisses would be so enticing. At first they'd been feather light, teasing her with a gentle brushing across her lips. And then he'd deepened them, pressing his lips to hers, kissing her with an intensity that left her breathless and longing for more.

"Oh, Barrett, I love you," she whispered

when they broke apart.

"I will never, ever tire of hearing you say that." His words were little more than a murmur before his lips captured hers again. When at length he ended the kiss, he kept his arms around her waist and smiled at her. "I have so many questions for you, but when you're this close, it's hard to remember them."

With obvious reluctance, he dropped his arms and stepped back a pace, leaving Charlotte feeling oddly bereft. Her eyes lighted on the ormolu clock. Was it possible that it had been less than half an hour since they'd entered the parlor? So much had changed in so little time. Half an hour ago she hadn't known what was in Barrett's heart. Now she wore his ring — the most beautiful ring she had ever seen — and they were making plans to marry.

Barrett's lips curved into a crooked smile as he gestured toward the chairs they'd used before. "I'd better keep my distance. Otherwise all I can think about is kissing you again." He waited until she was seated before taking the other chair. "There, that's better. Now I can ask my questions. Let's start with the most important one. When would you like to be married?" He reached out and clasped her right hand between his, leaving the left one with the exquisite opal resting on the chair arm. "If it were up to me, I'd say tomorrow, but I know that brides need more time to prepare."

His impatience was endearing, warming Charlotte as much as his kisses had. "Tomorrow sounds wonderful, but it wouldn't be right." She hoped Barrett would understand her reasons. "We need to wait until after Easter. I know not everyone adheres to convention, but my father felt strongly that Lent was a time for solemn reflection. That's why he would not marry a couple during Lent. Even though he's no longer here, I want to abide by his wishes."

"Certainly." Barrett tightened the grip on her hand. Though his words were matter-of-fact, his expression was anything but. His eyes sparkled, and his lips curved into the sweetest of smiles, leaving her no doubt that this man who'd haunted so many of her dreams and even more of her waking moments loved her. "Will that give your sisters enough time to come here? I imagine you want them with you."

"I do," she admitted, "but not if it means delaying our wedding." As dearly as she loved her sisters, she loved Barrett more. Perhaps she was being greedy, but she wanted their life together to begin as soon as possible. Charlotte raised her left hand, smiling at the ring that changed colors as she moved it, revealing new depths and beauty. Still smiling, she met Barrett's gaze. "Let's not wait for my sisters. Elizabeth couldn't come until school ends, and that's months from now. I don't know whether Abigail is able to travel at all. She might be in a delicate condition." Barrett's nod told Charlotte he understood her reference. "What about your brothers?" she asked, mindful that her family was not the only one to consider. "Will they come?"

"Not both of them. They can't leave the store for that long, and by now Camden's bride may also be in a delicate condition. Let's pick a date and see how many of our family can make it. If none of them can, we'll visit them on our wedding trip." Barrett uncrossed his ankles and leaned forward. "Easter's April 10. Would April 11 be too soon?"

Charlotte chuckled, amused and yet pleased that he was as eager for their marriage as she. "It's less than four weeks, but I can be ready. If Abigail can't come, I'll ask Gwen to be my attendant." A thought assailed her. It wasn't only her life that was about to change. "I've been selfish. I haven't considered how this will affect her and

Rose." While it was possible that Warren would marry her, Charlotte could not assume that.

"I'd hardly call you selfish." Waiting until the clock finished chiming the hour, Barrett added, "Gwen can stay in the apartment, if that's what's bothering you. I won't need the space for the store, and I assume you and I will live here." His eyes brightened. "Would you like to see the upstairs? I'm not sure what you'll want to change for the school."

How could she have forgotten the school? The prospect of becoming Barrett's wife must have turned her brain to cornmeal mush.

"What about the baron?"

Barrett had a ready answer. "I'm going to hire a Pinkerton to look for him. The baron may be clever, but he's no match for a Pinkerton. So, Charlotte Harding Crowley soon to become Charlotte Landry, let's talk about your school."

"Are you certain you don't mind the idea of having a school here? You've seen how noisy David can be. It'll be much worse if we have a dozen or so pupils." When Barrett didn't respond immediately, Charlotte added, "Perhaps I should reconsider. It might be better if it wasn't a boarding school."

"Better for whom?" Barrett rose and settled her hand on his arm. "If you're worried about me, don't be. This house has been quiet for too long." He opened the door and escorted her toward the lovely carved staircase.

"It won't be quiet if we have children living with us."

"And that's good. It'll be alive." Barrett waited until they reached the second floor before he spoke again. "So, we're agreed. We'll be married on April 11, and then we'll begin planning for your school and my new store."

He led her along the hallway, opening the doors to each of the six bedrooms. Though less ornately furnished than the first floor rooms, it was obvious to Charlotte that a great deal of planning had been involved in decorating chambers that would rarely have been used. The first two rooms on each side had connecting doors, and though the wallpaper in each was a different color, the patterns were similar enough to be pleasing. One side, which Charlotte immediately appropriated for the girls, was predominantly pink and lavender, while the other was decorated in shades of blue and green. The two rooms that formed a suite at the back of the house were clearly Barrett's personal domain, and Charlotte felt a twinge of uneasiness entering them. Boasting maroon drapes with gold tassels and a matching bedspread, the main room was masculine, and yet not overly so. Charlotte could imagine living here. And the smaller room, which reversed the color scheme, appeared almost feminine.

"What do you think?" Barrett asked when they returned to the hallway. "There are another ten rooms on the third floor. They're smaller, of course, because they're intended for servants."

"Or teachers." Charlotte looked around the second floor. "This is perfect." It could easily accommodate the dozen pupils she thought she might have eventually, and if the need arose, she could expand the school to twenty. "We'll have the girls here," she said, gesturing toward the pink and lavender rooms. "The older girls in the front room, the younger ones next to them. And the boys will be in the blue and green rooms."

Barrett's lips twisted as if he were trying to squelch a smile. "And the last two rooms?"

Charlotte felt herself blushing. How silly. She had been married before, and yet she was acting like a schoolgirl. "They're for us," she said as calmly as she could. "We can turn the gold room into a sitting area. It'll give us a quiet place to escape."

"A sanctuary." Barrett's lips twisted into one of the crooked grins she loved as he added, "Or a nursery."

"How can you even suggest that?" As Warren watched, the blood drained from Gwen's face. "Charlotte wouldn't lie to me."

Though he wished there were a way to spare her, there wasn't. Eventually Gwen would know the truth about her so-called friend. "She did. I'm certain of it. The woman you know as Charlotte Harding is really Charlotte Crowley, Lieutenant Jeffrey Crowley's widow. He was stationed at Fort Laramie until his death." Gwen needed to know that, but she most definitely did not need to know that it was Warren who had killed the hapless lieutenant.

Gwen's light blue eyes flashed with anger. She didn't like the truth, learning that dear, sweet Charlotte, her best friend, was a liar. "I won't believe it. I . . ." Before she could complete her sentence, a child started to scream. Gwen jumped to her feet. "It's David. He probably realizes that Charlotte isn't here." She gave Warren a stern look. "Goodbye, Warren. I need to comfort David, and you need to go. I don't want to hear any more of your lies about Charlotte."

Though she gestured toward the back door, Warren did not move. He wouldn't leave. Not like this, with anger between them. With a small harrumph, Gwen entered the room off the kitchen, switching on the light. "It's all right, David," he heard her say, her voice gentle now that she wasn't speaking to him. "Everything will be all right."

Just as everything would be all right between him and Gwen. He would wait until the child was asleep, and then he'd make her understand.

Settling back in the chair, Warren listened as Gwen crooned to Charlotte's son. "There, there. Mama will be home soon. It's time to sleep." Her voice rose and fell as if she were singing. It was a soothing sound, and yet the child continued to wail. "All right," she said when it appeared that David was not responding to her comforting words. "I'll read you a story. Mama always has a book on her nightstand. We'll find a good story." The word *story* seemed to have penetrated the boy's brain, for his wails subsided into little whimpers.

Warren heard Gwen's firm footsteps and

suspected she was picking out a book. He closed his eyes, wondering how long she would have to read before Charlotte's brat fell asleep. But there were no sounds other than a brief gasp. Warren opened his eyes, curious about whatever had surprised Gwen.

Seconds later, she appeared in the doorway, her expression distraught. "You were right, Warren," she said, holding out a Bible. "Charlotte lied. The proof is here."

26

"Something's wrong." Charlotte felt her heart begin to race as they approached the house, and she turned toward Barrett, placing her hand on his arm. She wanted — no, she needed — the reassurance that he was next to her. Perhaps it was her imagination, but ever since they'd left his house, her nerves had been on edge. There was no logical reason. The night was cold and clear, and for once the wind was not howling. Ferguson Street looked as peaceful as ever; no masked strangers lurked in the shadows. And yet Charlotte could not dismiss her feeling that something was terribly wrong. The closer they came to her home, the stronger the fear had grown. Now as Barrett halted the carriage, Charlotte knew she had not been mistaken.

"What do you mean? What's wrong?"

Trying to keep her hand from trembling, Charlotte pointed toward the stairway, which was now shrouded in darkness. "There's no light on the steps. Gwen always turns it on when one of us is out after sunset."

Barrett laid his hand over hers, the warmth sending waves of comfort through her veins. "She must have forgotten."

His voice was as comforting as his touch, but still the fear remained. Something was wrong. Not only was the stairway light extinguished, but there were no lights on in the apartment. Surely Gwen would have wanted to hear about Charlotte's evening with Barrett. She had been so certain that it was going to be a special one. And it had been.

"I might have forgotten the light, but Gwen would not." Gwen was almost ritualistic in the way she followed a routine. "Something's wrong," Charlotte repeated when Barrett helped her out of the carriage and they began to climb the darkened steps. When they reached the landing, her fear deepened. "Look, Barrett. The door's ajar. Gwen would never have left it like that." Even during the summer, when they would have benefited from a cool breeze, Gwen had insisted that critters, as she called them, might enter the apartment unless the door was completely shut. And now when winter still gripped Cheyenne, despite the calendar's claim that spring was only a few days away, she was too frugal to have allowed cold air into the apartment.

Barrett wrapped his arm around Charlotte's shoulders and gave them a quick squeeze. "Let me go first." He pushed the door open, then fumbled for a light. "Where's the switch?" Seconds later, the room was bright. "Everything looks normal," he reported.

Charlotte shivered as she entered her house. Barrett was correct. There were no signs of an intruder. That wasn't the problem. "It doesn't feel right," she said as she looked at the modest room that had been her home for almost a year and a half. "It feels empty. Look, Barrett," she said, pointing at the door to the room she and David shared. It was ajar. "We always keep that door closed at night," she told Barrett as she raced across the kitchen. "David's so sensitive to sounds that even footsteps can waken him."

Though they were both whispering, the fear that had lodged in her stomach shrieked that there was no need for whispers. *Please, Lord,* she prayed as she flicked on the light in her bedroom. *Let David be safe.* But he was not. The crib was empty, the blankets tossed aside, the pillow discarded on the floor. Even the wooden ball that David insisted on having by his side each night was missing.

As darkness threatened to engulf her and her legs turned to rubber, Charlotte gripped the crib rail. "Barrett!" she cried. "David's gone!"

He was there in a second, drawing her close to him. "Maybe he's in Gwen's room."

If only that were true. But Charlotte knew it was not. Gwen wasn't here. Opening the door to her friend's bedchamber merely confirmed Charlotte's premonition that something was terribly wrong. The apartment was empty. David was gone, and so were Gwen and Rose.

"Perhaps there's an innocent explanation." Barrett's embrace was comforting, but it wasn't enough. There would be no comfort until Charlotte had David back in her arms.

"There's nothing innocent about this. Gwen would never take the children out this late." Switching off the light in the front bedroom, Charlotte returned to the center of the apartment. Barrett stayed close to her, but he had let his arms drop, as if he knew that she needed to move without impediment. Where had Gwen gone, and why? The questions reverberated through Charlotte's brain, and with each iteration, her dread increased. The only answer made no sense. The baron. But if he had discovered her identity, there was no reason to have involved Gwen.

Charlotte looked around the apartment, her eyes searching for a clue. Nothing appeared out of place. And yet . . . She took another step into the parlor area, drawn by the sight of a folded sheet of paper on the table next to the settee. It wasn't normal to have paper there, but somehow she had missed it when she'd rushed into Gwen's room.

"What is it?" Barrett's voice was rough with emotion. Though David was her son, Charlotte knew he loved the boy almost as dearly as she did.

Her hands trembling, she opened the paper, shuddering as she read the scribbled words. "He's found me. The baron has found me." Though there was no signature, only one person on Earth could have written the note.

Gently, Barrett touched Charlotte's shoulders and led her toward the settee. "You'd better sit down. I don't want you to collapse." When they were both seated, he drew her close to him. "What did he say?"

Charlotte began to read. " 'Mrs. Crowley.' It has to be the baron, and now he knows my real name. 'If you want to see your son again, bring me the money your husband stole.' He still thinks Jeffrey took Big Nose's stash, but he didn't."

Barrett stroked her hair, trying to comfort her. It was the same gesture Charlotte had used countless times to soothe David, particularly when he'd had a nightmare. Only this was no nightmare. It was real.

"What else did he say?"

"He told me what he wants. 'If I don't have . . .' " Charlotte sobbed as she read the amount. " 'One hundred thousand dollars by noon tomorrow, your son will die.' "

"Anything else?"

Charlotte handed the page to Barrett. "There are directions to the place where he's taken David." Gripping Barrett's arm, Charlotte whispered the final words. "He says if I bring anyone with me, he'll kill David." Her sweet, innocent little boy was in the grip of a madman. "I can't lose David. I can't."

Barrett shook his head, and Charlotte knew he was trying to encourage her. "The baron won't kill David. He has no reason to. You'll give him the money, and he'll release your son."

"I don't have the money. You know that, Barrett. Even with the gambling and the thefts, Jeffrey never had that much money." Charlotte bit her lip, trying to keep from crying. "I feel so powerless, trying to imagine what it must be like for David, being in a strange place with a strange man."

Barrett continued the rhythmic stroking of Charlotte's hair. "David's not alone. Gwen and Rose are with him. It's the only thing that makes any sense. Gwen will keep David safe until you deliver the money."

"What money? I don't have a hundred thousand dollars, and the banks aren't likely to lend me that much."

"Don't worry about the money. We don't even have to wait for the banks to open. That's why we're going to my house." Barrett rose and drew Charlotte to her feet. "I can ransom David."

He had told her that he had money saved, but Charlotte had not considered that it might be a fortune.

"Your savings? Your emergency money?"

"Exactly." Barrett headed for the door. "My parents didn't trust banks after the panic of '57, so I have a safe at home. I have a little more than a hundred thousand dollars in it. Come on, Charlotte," he said, tugging at her hand. "David is waiting."

Charlotte's legs refused to cooperate. She doubted they would support her, for they felt weaker than they had the summer she was expecting David, when she'd been so ill for so long.

"You'd give me all your money?" she asked, still not believing what she'd heard. Perhaps she shouldn't have been surprised, for Barrett had offered her his house, which was worth many times the ransom. Still, this was an incredibly generous offer, since the money represented his last measure of security.

As her legs buckled at the evidence of Barrett's love, he put his arm around her waist. "I love you, Charlotte. Both you and David. I'd do anything in my power to keep you safe."

Charlotte swallowed deeply, trying to corral her emotions. Fears for David mingled with relief that one hurdle had been surmounted. Thanks to this wonderful, wonderful man, she would soon be able to ransom her son.

"I don't know what to say, Barrett. 'Thank you' seems inadequate."

The tension on his face subsided, and he smiled. "I'll collect payment when David is safe."

"Payment? How will I . . . ?"

His smile turned into a grin. "Trust me. You can afford what I have in mind. But first things first. There's no time to waste. Your son is waiting."

When they reached Barrett's house, if Mr. Bradley was surprised to see Charlotte again, he was too well trained to give any indication. He merely nodded when Barrett asked him to have two horses saddled. "I'm afraid we have no side saddles," Barrett said when Mr. Bradley marched toward the back door, his spine as stiff as if there were nothing out of the ordinary.

"I can ride astride." It wouldn't be comfortable, particularly in a silk gown, but that was unimportant. What was important was reaching David. Charlotte shivered inside her warm cloak. "Why did you ask for two horses?"

Barrett raised an eyebrow. "You don't think I'd let you go alone, do you? It's nighttime. You don't know the way, and I don't know who else is out there."

"But the baron said . . ."

"I know what he said, but he won't see me. I promise you that. Now, let me get the money."

Taking the stairs two at a time, Barrett raced to the second floor. When he returned, he was carrying a leather satchel. As he waited for Mr. Bradley to bring the horses out of the stable, Barrett unfolded the paper and stared at the baron's written demands, his expression pensive. "The handwriting looks familiar," he told Charlotte, "but it's so scribbled that I can't identify it. I know the place, though. It's the Franklin ranch. I heard the family gave up ranching last summer and moved back East. Richard mentioned that someone bought it, but he didn't know who. My guess is that the new owners haven't moved in, and somehow the baron learned that the place was deserted."

When the horses were ready, Barrett helped Charlotte mount hers, then sprang onto his. Turning to Mr. Bradley, he said, "If we're not back in three hours, tell the sheriff we went to the Franklin ranch."

Charlotte shuddered. "We can't tell anyone. The baron said . . ."

"I know what he said. That's why Mr. Bradley will wait before he calls the sheriff, but I want to be sure that we have backup. Just in case."

Riding was more difficult than Charlotte had anticipated. It was true that she had ridden astride, but that had been as a child, one day when the boys next door had challenged her and Abigail to ride like them. Tonight was far different. Unlike the sturdy wool riding habit she'd had at Fort Laramie, her silk gown with its waterfall skirt and short train was not designed for the constant abrasion of a saddle. Unfortunately, not even the habit would have made riding astride easy. Her skirts hiked to a scandalous height, Charlotte clung to the reins, hoping she would manage to remain seated. What had seemed like an adventure when she was a child was now an ordeal, and yet Charlotte would not complain, for she knew that whatever David was enduring was worse. Much worse.

They were headed directly west of the city, Barrett told her as they rode toward the Franklin ranch. Though the sky was spangled with stars, the moon was almost new, the tiny sliver casting little light. The conditions were far from ideal for traveling, but the darkness would help conceal Barrett once they arrived. Though he'd promised he'd remain hidden, Charlotte suspected he had something in mind. What it was, she did not know. She had no plans beyond rescuing David. Getting her son out of the baron's clutches and into her arms was all she cared about.

Keep him safe, Lord, she prayed. *Help Gwen keep David from worrying.* When she glanced at Barrett, Charlotte saw his lips moving ever so slightly, and she wondered if he was praying, too.

"How much farther do you think it is?" she asked after what seemed like an hour had passed.

"Not much more than another mile. We'll be there soon." Barrett patted the satchel that he'd tied behind his saddle. "I'll give you this when we split up." As they'd ridden, he had told Charlotte that he remembered the layout of the ranch. Though he was puzzled about why the baron had set the meeting for a work shed rather than the house itself, he had explained that he'd circle around and approach the shed from the back so that he would not be seen.

"In less than an hour, we'll all be on our way back." Though he had been tempted to bring a third horse so that Gwen would have a mount for herself and Rose, Barrett had worried about the additional noise and had told Charlotte that once David was free they'd figure out the best way for the five of them to return to Cheyenne. But first, she had to find the baron and give him the ransom money.

And before that, they had to reach the ranch. They'd turned off the main road onto a narrow lane that was little more than a path. Pitted with squirrel and fox holes, it was the most dangerous road yet. Though Charlotte wanted to stare into the distance, that was foolhardy. Not only was there nothing to see, but she felt compelled to watch the ground. Although she wasn't certain she could see any better than the horse, she wanted to guide it around obstacles. When they reached what appeared to be a smooth stretch, she glanced up. For a second, Charlotte doubted her eyes, but when she blinked, it was still there. Her heart began to pound.

"Look, Barrett." She pointed toward the figure she'd seen. "There's someone on the road."

"I don't see anyone."

"There's someone there. I know it." There was no time to explain that she'd always been able to see well in the dark. Charlotte squinted, trying to identify the figure. "It's a woman, and she's carrying a child." Dread and hope twisted themselves around her heart, leaving her breathless. This close to their destination, it could only be one woman. "It's Gwen. I know it is." Somehow she had gotten free from the baron. That was good. What wasn't good was that Charlotte could see only one child. Surely Gwen wouldn't leave either David or Rose behind. Perhaps it was David she was carrying, and

Rose was walking behind her, hidden by her skirts.

Without waiting for Barrett's response, Charlotte flicked the reins and raced toward the woman. It was Gwen, she confirmed even before she reached her friend. She recognized her walk. Charlotte squinted, hope battling with fear as she tried to identify the child Gwen was carrying. Rose. There was no doubt, just as there was no sign of David. Biting back the despair that threatened to overwhelm her, Charlotte leaned over the horse's neck, wanting to be closer to Gwen. Judging from her slow pace and the slump of her shoulders, her friend was exhausted and overwrought.

"What happened? Where's David?" Charlotte cried, her words little more than a sob.

"Yes, where is David?" Barrett had reached Charlotte's side. His normally pleasant voice was harsh, perhaps because he was as distraught as Charlotte.

In the dim light, she saw Gwen recoil. "He's still got him." Gwen set Rose on her feet, admonishing her not to stray. "He brought us here on a horse. Oh, Charlotte, it was awful. He had this crazy look in his eyes, and he was laughing all the while, telling me he was going to be a wealthy man. I told him I didn't care about money, but he just laughed harder. He said everyone cares about money."

Charlotte's thoughts began to whirl. It sounded as if Gwen knew the baron. Surely that wasn't possible, and yet . . .

"Why are you walking?" Though his voice was still firm, Barrett did not bark at Gwen.

"He took Rose and me into the house and made me promise that we wouldn't leave. He said it was going to be ours soon, so we should make ourselves comfortable while he waited for the money." She looked up at Charlotte, her face contorted with anguish, and in that moment Charlotte knew who the baron was. Gwen was suffering, not only because of what had happened but also because of who was responsible.

"I didn't want to leave David with him, but I couldn't fight him." When Gwen covered her face with her hands and began to weep, Rose clutched her skirts and hid her face in them. "The only thing I could do was try to get help."

"The baron plans to kill David." Charlotte wouldn't pronounce his real name, for that would give him a touch of humanity that he did not deserve, not now when her worst fear had been confirmed.

Barrett reached over and laid a hand on her shoulder. "Not necessarily. He won't do anything until he has the money. He knows you won't give it to him unless you see that David is safe."

It made sense, and yet Charlotte could not dismiss her worries. Her son, her precious little boy, was being held hostage by a madman.

Gwen wiped her eyes and looked up at Charlotte. "I'm so sorry. It's all my fault. He told me you were lying when you called yourself Charlotte Harding. He said you were really some Army lieutenant's wife. I didn't believe him, but then I saw the Bible."

There was only one Bible that would have changed Gwen's mind, but it was kept hidden. Or was it? Charlotte closed her eyes, trying to visualize her room, trying to recall whether she had put the Bible back in the drawer before she left for her evening with Barrett. She couldn't remember opening the drawer again. She had left it out, and that meant that David's capture was her fault, not Gwen's.

Charlotte shook her head slowly. Gwen must have misunderstood, for her face crumpled, and she looked as if she were going to cry again. "I'm sorry, Charlotte. I shouldn't have done it, but I read the family pages. When I saw that he was right, I told him." Her shoulders shook, and tears began to roll down her cheeks. "I never knew he was evil."

"Who?" The question came from Barrett.

"Warren."

"Warren?" Charlotte heard the shock in Barrett's voice and felt his hand tighten on her shoulder as Gwen confirmed what she had surmised. Warren was the baron. She should have recognized it before. After all, her instincts had warned her that something was amiss from the first time she'd met him. If only she'd heeded them, perhaps tonight would not have happened. As it was, both Barrett and Gwen had been betrayed, and Charlotte's son was in mortal danger.

Keep him safe, she prayed again. *Soften Warren's heart.*

"I thought he loved me." Gwen's wail wrenched Charlotte's heart.

"He does." She reached down, extending her hand toward her friend. "He loves you in his own way." Just as Jeffrey had loved her as best he could. It wasn't the way Charlotte had wanted to be loved. It wasn't the way Barrett loved her. But it was all that Jeffrey had been able to offer.

Barrett dismounted and strode toward Gwen. Though Charlotte imagined that he was still reeling from the revelation of Warren's perfidy, his voice was devoid of emotion. "Can you ride astride?" When Gwen nodded, he gestured toward Charlotte. "Take Charlotte's horse and go home. There's nothing more you can do here, and you and Rose need to be out of the cold."

It was sound advice. As Charlotte prepared to dismount, Barrett reached up and lifted her off the horse, drawing her close to him for the briefest of moments. "I love you," he whispered. "Remember that." She would. No matter what happened, she would never forget that this wonderful man loved her . . . and her son.

"Can you forgive me?" Gwen asked as Charlotte approached her. "I didn't mean to hurt David."

"I know. It wasn't your fault." Charlotte gave her a quick hug. "Keep Rose safe."

Barrett helped Gwen mount, then handed Rose up to her. When they were headed toward the city, he put his arm around Charlotte's shoulder, squeezing gently as he said, "We'll ride together until we get close to the ranch. I'll get off then." He lifted Charlotte onto his horse, climbing on behind her and wrapping his arms around her so that he could control the reins. "I visited the ranch a couple times. There's a bend in the road right before we reach it. If we turn left, we can come up behind the shed where Warren's holding David. The only opening is a door in the front. He won't see you until you're right there."

Charlotte wasn't certain that her arrival needed to be a surprise, but she knew that Warren must have no idea that Barrett was close by. There was no telling what he might do if he realized she hadn't followed his instructions.

They were a hundred or so yards from the shed when Barrett dismounted. "Stall if you can," he said when he'd placed the reins in her hand. "That'll give me time to get there. My instincts tell me that we need to be ready to leave the moment you give him the money."

Though Barrett said nothing more, Charlotte knew he did not trust his friend. His former friend. Nor did she. Madmen were unpredictable, and that made them dangerous.

Charlotte nodded, though her heart was pounding so fiercely that she could hardly hear over its frantic beat. "I don't know what I'm going to do when I see him. I'm angry and scared at the same time. I'm so afraid he'll hurt David."

Barrett laid his hand on hers. "You're not alone. You know that. You're never alone."

When she reached the front of the shed,

she saw that Barrett was correct. There were no windows, only a single door with light seeping out around its frame. Oddly, there were no sounds. She had expected to hear David wailing and Warren shouting at him. Instead, there was an eerie silence. There was only one explanation Charlotte could imagine: David was asleep. She murmured a silent prayer of thanksgiving as she dismounted and headed toward the door. She rapped on the door, then opened it and gasped. David wasn't asleep. He was lying in a crate, tied hand and foot. Even worse, he had been gagged. That monster of a baron had treated her son as if he were a sack of potatoes. Charlotte saw the trace of tears on David's face and watched as he started to squirm when he heard the sound of her footsteps.

"David!" She lunged, desperate to reach him and end his ordeal, but the baron stepped in her path, pointing a gun at her heart.

"Give me the money, or I'll kill both you and your brat."

27

Charlotte glared at the man who'd once hidden his evil behind a mask, the man with eyes as cold as January ice. Though she'd suspected the baron was the man who'd shot Jeffrey, seeing him now confirmed her fears. This man was a killer. He'd murdered before, and he'd do it again. In all likelihood, he planned to kill her and David as soon as she gave him the money. Murmuring a silent prayer that she could somehow outwit him, Charlotte refused to flinch as she met his gaze.

"You won't get anything from me until I'm sure my son is unharmed." Somehow she would get David out of here, even if she had to die to do it. Though she hated the thought of leaving her son, Charlotte knew David would not be alone if she were killed, for Barrett would raise him as if he were his own. But first she had to free him.

As if he sensed her determination, Warren

lowered his gun, allowing Charlotte to pass. In her haste to reach David, she stumbled, her eyes widening in surprise when she recognized the object that had tripped her: David's ball. He must have refused to relinquish it and had carried it all the way here. Or perhaps Gwen, knowing his attachment to the toy, had hidden it in her cloak. Whatever the reason, David's ball was here.

Charlotte scooped her son into her arms, needing to hold him close, to assure herself that he was alive, before she untied him. Reluctantly, she laid him back in the crate. "It'll be all right," she crooned as she removed the gag and ropes. Like a spring that had been released, David began to flail his arms and legs. "You're safe, David. You're safe." Reaching down to stroke his forehead, Charlotte prayed that was true.

As David's whimpers turned into full-fledged screams, Warren scowled. "Shut him up! All he does is howl. It's enough to drive a man crazy."

Charlotte lifted the still struggling child into her arms and turned him so his cries were muffled by her body. "He's a child, Warren," she said, fixing her eyes on the man who was responsible for her son's distress. "A child who cannot see. You took him from his home and put him in a strange place. How did you expect him to react? He's tired, he's probably hungry, and he's scared. Of course he's going to cry."

As Warren's scowl deepened, he began to wave his gun at her. "I don't need a lecture from you, Mrs. Crowley." The name was delivered with a sneer. "You thought you were smart enough to hide from me, but you were wrong." He took a step toward her, his posture menacing. "Now, where's the money?"

"I don't have it." She wouldn't give this evil man Barrett's savings if she could help it, for if what she feared was true, it would not save David's life. She had to get her son out of here, but first she needed to be certain that Barrett was waiting.

Warren's face reddened, making his nose look more like a raptor's beak than ever. "What do you mean? Of course you have it. Jeffrey gave it to you."

As David's wails turned to whimpers, Charlotte shook her head. "Jeffrey had no money. He wouldn't have gotten involved in the stagecoach robberies if he had."

Though she hadn't thought it possible, Warren's face turned an even deeper shade of red. "You're lying. Jeffrey found Big Nose's stash."

"No, he did not. So you see, Warren, you

accomplished nothing by kidnapping David. I have no money to give you."

Warren took a deep breath, exhaling slowly. "You're not a very good liar, Mrs. Crowley. I think you do have money. It may not be Big Nose's, but you have money. We'll wait for Barrett."

"Barrett?"

"You needn't feign innocence, Mrs. Crowley." Warren sneered again, as if pronouncing the name gave him pleasure. "I know you had dinner with him, and I'm sure that being the gentleman he is" — another sneer accompanied Warren's words — "he accompanied you home. That means he knows about my demands." Warren's eyes narrowed as he kept his gaze focused on Charlotte. "If I had it, I'd be willing to bet Big Nose's stash that Barrett did not let you come here alone. I expect him to burst through that door any minute now, so let's get ready." He gestured toward the shed's sole seating, a spindle-back chair with one spindle and most of its paint missing. "Sit down."

"And if I don't?"

"I'll shoot your brat." He cocked the gun.

Charlotte sat.

"Put the boy on the floor."

Charlotte complied.

"Now put your hands behind the chair." He grabbed two ropes from the table.

"Why?" It was a rhetorical question. Charlotte was stalling, hoping that Barrett would arrive before the baron could restrain her.

Warren's lip curled. "Surely you're not that stupid. You must realize I'm going to tie you to the chair. Without the money, you're of no value to me other than as a bargaining piece. If Barrett cares about you, he'll give me what I want."

Charlotte took a deep breath. There was no sense in arguing with a man with a gun. Even without the weapon, Warren was bigger and stronger. Her only hope was to use her wits. With a silent prayer for wisdom, she settled onto the chair. At least Warren wasn't threatening to gag and tie David again. Her son would be free to escape when Barrett arrived.

After stroking David's head once more and admonishing him to sit quietly, Charlotte allowed Warren to tie her wrists, hoping he wouldn't notice how far she had kept her hands from the spindle. If the rope was loose enough, she might be able to slip her hands out when he returned to his post by the door. But he tugged the rope so hard that she knew that plan had failed. If he secured her legs as tightly, she would be as powerless as David had been. Charlotte couldn't let that happen. When Warren moved in front of her to tie her legs, she took a deep breath. It was time. Mustering every ounce of strength she possessed, she kicked. Her feet missed their target, and even though she had kicked as hard as she could, Warren remained standing.

His face contorted with rage, he glared at her for a second. Then slowly and deliberately, so she would know what was about to happen, he clenched his fist, drew back his arm, and swung it forward. When his knuckles collided with her face, the impact left Charlotte speechless. She felt her head jerk backward, and then she saw nothing but stars. By the time she had regained her vision, her ankles were bound. At her side, David whimpered softly, but though she longed to comfort him with a touch, she could not. For the first time in David's short life, though his mother was nearby, she could not wrap him in her arms.

"I'm sorry, David," she whispered.

"You'll be more than sorry if you try anything like that again." Warren's voice held a menacing note. "I won't pull the next punch." He pressed his knuckles to her cheek, grinning when Charlotte winced from the pain. "It would be a shame to bloody your face, wouldn't it?"

He looked down at David and aimed a kick in his direction, stopping short of actually hitting him.

"No!" Charlotte cried. "Don't hurt my son. He's no threat to you." The pain in her face was nothing compared to the fear that Warren would harm her child.

"You're right," Warren agreed. "Your brat is no threat, and neither is Barrett. When he sees you, he'll do exactly what I want. Now all I have to do is wait." He strode across the room, positioning himself next to the door, his gun cocked and ready to fire.

Please, Lord, no. Don't let him kill Barrett and David. Charlotte looked around, searching for a way to distract Warren. Though Barrett was armed, he was walking into an ambush. If he could get into the shed without being shot, he might be able to disarm Warren, and without a gun, Warren would be far less dangerous. Charlotte suspected he was a man who liked to intimidate those he considered weaker. Barrett was no weakling, but he was also no match for a madman with a gun. There had to be a way to even the odds.

Charlotte looked down at her son, who was sitting by her side as if afraid to move. As she did, she spied an object. That might be the answer.

"David, let's find your ball," she said softly. "It's not far away."

"What are you doing?"

Charlotte forced herself to meet Warren's eyes, hoping her expression did not betray the glimmer of hope that had lodged deep inside her. "Keeping my son from crying," she replied. "You said you didn't like that."

"And I don't." Apparently mollified, Warren leaned against the wall, his gun clutched at his side.

"A little farther," Charlotte coached her son. "You're a smart boy. That's the right direction." When he discovered his beloved toy, David began to chortle with happiness. "That's good. Now come back to Mama."

Warren's curled lip left no doubt that he considered David a nuisance, a necessary evil in his plan to obtain the fortune he believed he deserved. The only good thing Charlotte could say about Warren's obvious disdain for her son was that he was no longer staring at the door. Though she had turned her head so that the direction of her gaze was not obvious, Charlotte was watching the door carefully. There were no sounds, nothing to betray Barrett's approach. Only the increasing darkness along the door frame told Charlotte he was here.

She turned toward David. The time had come.

"Bowl, David," she said, raising her voice slightly. It was a signal to Barrett as well as David. As she had expected, her son gave her a quizzical look but refused to move.

"What are you talking about?" Warren demanded. "Bowl?"

That was all David needed. The sound of a man's voice pronouncing the magic word triggered his reaction. He sent the ball rolling across the floor toward Warren. Perhaps he pitched it faster than normal. Perhaps it was only because the floor was slightly tilted. All Charlotte knew was that when it collided with Warren's foot, their captor gave out a loud "ouch." It was the distraction Barrett needed. A moment later, he had entered the shed, his pistol drawn.

"Put your gun down," Barrett ordered, his voice steely as he stared at the man who had once been his friend and adviser.

A sneer greeted his command. "I knew you'd come." Warren swung around, pointing his weapon at Charlotte. "But you won't do anything. You didn't have enough starch to be a politician, and you're too lily-livered to shoot me. You won't take the chance that I can shoot Charlotte first." His eyes narrowed, and though he kept his eyes and weapon focused on Charlotte, his words were directed to Barrett. "You know I'm a crack shot, and — unlike you — I'm not burdened with cowardly scruples. I killed a woman before. It wouldn't bother me to do it again."

"What do you want?" As Barrett moved farther into the shed, his gaze met Charlotte's, and she saw his concern. Perhaps he was wondering why she hadn't given Warren the satchel of money. Surely he must realize that it would not satisfy Warren, that he wouldn't want anyone to live to tell what he'd done.

"You know what I want. Money."

"What are you going to do with it?" Charlotte asked. It might not work, but maybe if she kept Warren talking, he'd lower his gun and Barrett would be able to disarm him.

"Why do you care?"

"If I'm going to die, I might as well know why."

Charlotte heard Barrett's intake of breath and saw his fingers tighten on the trigger.

"It's for Gwen," Warren said, his voice deepening with emotion. "She deserves to be treated like a lady. I'm going to build her a fancy house so she can live like a queen. And when I do, no one at the Cheyenne Club will dare refuse me membership."

He cared for Gwen. Charlotte could hear that in his voice and see it in the fire flashing in his eyes. As for Gwen, Charlotte knew she loved the man she thought he was. But now that Warren had shown his true colors, everything had changed.

"Do you think she'll still marry you?" Though Charlotte kept her gaze fixed on Warren, from the corner of her eye she saw Barrett moving closer.

"Why wouldn't she?" Warren demanded, apparently oblivious to the fact that Barrett was now within striking range. He was staring at Charlotte, wide-eyed. Whether it was rage or shock that kept his gaze fixed on her didn't matter. What mattered was keeping Warren from noticing Barrett.

"Gwen won't marry you, because she's seen the real you," Charlotte announced as calmly as if she were discussing the weather. "She wouldn't marry a man who killed her friends."

Warren's face contorted with anger as Charlotte's words hit their mark. "You know nothing! You're nothing but a liar, and you know what liars deserve?" He raised his gun and pointed it at Charlotte. "They deserve to die." He narrowed his eyes and pulled the trigger. The report was deafening, almost obliterating Warren's cry of rage when the gun flew from his hand, propelled by the force of Barrett's arm, and the bullet lodged in the ceiling. "You!" Warren snarled as he tackled Barrett. "You deserve to die too."

A second later, the two men were on the floor, grunting with pain as their punches landed, rolling across the floor as each tried to gain supremacy. Charlotte winced each time Barrett groaned, but there was nothing she could do except pray that he would not be seriously hurt. Though Barrett had the advantage of age, Warren's fury lent him unexpected strength. Neither man spoke except with fists and the animal-like grunts and groans that those fists provoked.

The fight was more brutal than anything Charlotte had ever witnessed, and yet she knew it could have been worse. If Warren still had his weapon, blood would have been shed. He would have tried to kill Barrett, and Barrett would have had no choice but to retaliate. As it was, both men had a chance of survival.

Charlotte closed her eyes for a second, trying to block out the horrible sights, but that was worse. Deprived of sight, her imagination conjured a scene that was worse than reality. Poor David. He had no way of knowing what was happening. It was no wonder that he'd scrambled to his feet and stood at her side, clinging to her. But, though he was clearly terrified, Charlotte was powerless to do anything but croon to him, trying to reassure him that the strange sounds he heard, sounds which must be even more frightening for him than they were for her, would stop.

And they did. Though it seemed as if hours had passed, Charlotte knew it was only minutes later when Warren began to tire. Barrett flipped him over, using his body to pin Warren to the floor, then pulled back his arm and punched the older man on the jaw. Even a trained boxer would have been proud of the knockout punch.

Somehow, though his muscles must have protested, Barrett found the energy to get to his feet. Once standing, he sprinted the few yards to Charlotte's side. "Are you all right?" His eyes narrowed as he touched her bruised cheek. "Did he do that?" When Charlotte nodded, Barrett frowned. "I should have hit him harder."

"I'll live." Two simple words, and yet they were the answer to prayer. Despite everything Warren had tried to do, all four of them were still alive.

Within seconds, Barrett had untied her. Charlotte rubbed her wrists and flexed her toes, trying to restore the circulation. As soon as she thought her arms were strong enough, she lifted David into her arms. "You're safe, David. Mama's here, and so is Mr. Landry. He kept you safe."

With the resiliency of the very young, David seemed to have forgotten his ordeal. "Bowl?" he asked, turning toward Barrett.

Charlotte shook her head. "Not now, young man. We're going home, and you're going to bed." Patting David's back, Charlotte started to rise, then froze. It couldn't be, and yet it was. Warren had regained consciousness and was crawling toward his gun.

"Barrett! Look out!"

It was too late. Warren had the weapon clutched in his hand.

"You can't stop me!" A wild laugh accompanied his words. Though Barrett lunged toward him, there was nothing he could do. In less than a second, Warren had pressed the revolver to his forehead and pulled the trigger.

28

"I was such a fool." Gwen's red-rimmed eyes bore witness to her sleepless night and the tears she had shed. Exhausted by their ordeal, both David and Rose were still in bed, leaving Gwen and Charlotte alone at the breakfast table. Neither woman had much of an appetite, although both had drunk extra cups of coffee. "How could I have even imagined that a man like Warren would love a dumpy woman like me? I should have realized that something was wrong."

Charlotte's heart ached for her friend, but she gave thanks that Gwen hadn't been in the shed to see Warren's final moments. After last night's horror faded, Gwen might still be left with some happy memories.

"Nothing is wrong with you. Everything was wrong with Warren," Charlotte said firmly. Instinctively, she touched her bruised cheek, regretting the movement when she saw a flash of pain in Gwen's eyes. It was still difficult to believe that the baron was gone and that Charlotte no longer needed to fear that he would harm David. Though she had prayed that the baron would be found and put behind bars, she had never sought his death. Warren had been a troubled man, but so long as he lived, there was the possibility that he would change. Now that chance was gone, and Gwen was suffering.

"He didn't hurt me until last night," Gwen said, "and then it was with words, not his fists." She stirred a spoonful of sugar into her coffee and tasted it before adding another. "What am I going to do now? I can't hold my head up."

"Oh, Gwen, that's not true. You may feel like that right now, but what Warren did was his fault. It doesn't reflect on you."

Gwen shook her head. "I know you want to help me, but you don't know how I feel."

"Yes, I do." Charlotte took a sip of coffee as she prepared to reveal parts of her past that she had tried desperately to hide. Though she hated dredging up painful memories, she couldn't let her friend blame herself for Warren's sins. "I know how you feel, because my husband did some terrible things." Slowly she outlined what had happened at Fort Laramie and why she had called herself Charlotte Harding. "At first I was ashamed of what Jeffrey had done. It took me a long time to realize that I wasn't responsible. I tried to change him, but the truth is, none of us can change another person. We can give them advice and we can point them in the right direction, but the decision has to be theirs. Jeffrey wasn't willing to change. Warren was like that too. There was nothing you could do. You're not responsible."

Gwen sipped her coffee, her expression thoughtful as she settled the cup back on the saucer. "I wish I could believe that."

Morning sun spilled into the parlor, sending a shaft of light over the carpet. Though Charlotte felt as if she'd aged years, it had been less than twelve hours since Warren had been here, writing his note and forcing Gwen and the children to go with him. But the night of terror had ended, and so Gwen's anguish would, too, in time.

"Believe it," Charlotte said. "And believe that God has good things in store for you, perhaps even another husband."

"I doubt that." As Gwen spoke, tears welled in her eyes. "No one will want me once they learn about what Warren did and how gullible I was to believe him. They'll say I'm a fool, and I was. I was so anxious for Rose to have a father that I didn't think clearly." A single tear rolled down Gwen's cheek. "I lost my chance. Now I need to resign myself to the fact that I'll be a widow for the rest of my life."

"I felt that way too," Charlotte confided. "I was certain I'd never remarry. At first I worried that people would think I was like Jeffrey and would shun me for that reason. Then when I discovered that David was blind, I believed any man who might have considered marrying me would find David too much of a burden. I was wrong." Charlotte looked at the ring that adorned her left hand. "God sent me a man who loves my son as much as I do."

"You were blessed." Gwen brushed her tears away, giving Charlotte a forced smile. "You don't need to worry about me. I'll be all right. Rose and I have survived on our own before."

Barely. Charlotte remembered the day she had met Gwen and how desperate the woman had appeared. "Are you worried about where you'll live after Barrett and I marry?" Perhaps that had added to Gwen's distress this morning.

When Gwen nodded, Charlotte reached across the table and laid her hand on her friend's. "Barrett and I've talked about that. If you like, you can stay right here. With David and me gone, you'll have more space. Rose can even have her own room." Gwen nodded slowly. Though Charlotte hadn't discussed the next idea with Barrett, she ventured it anyway. "If you want to be part of the school, there's a place for you. I'll need someone to watch over the children when they're not in classes, and I can't think of anyone better suited for that than you. It would mean you'd have to move to Barrett's house, but the quarters on the third floor are as nice as our rooms here."

Gwen's eyes widened, and she clutched Charlotte's hand. "You'd do that?" she asked, her voice filled with surprise and wonder. "You'd trust me to care for your pupils after what I did?"

So that was what was bothering Gwen. She feared that Charlotte would condemn her for showing Warren the Bible.

"Of course. We all make mistakes." Charlotte had made more than her share, including not hiding the Bible.

Gwen smiled as she dashed new tears from her cheeks. "Thank you, Charlotte. You're the best friend I've ever had."

"Are you ready?" Barrett asked as he entered the apartment.

It was early afternoon, and though he'd sent her several messages, this was the first time Charlotte had seen Barrett since he'd brought her and David home last night. The first message had told her that the authorities had been advised of what had happened at the Franklin ranch. The second detailed the simple burial he had arranged for Warren. The third had said there was an urgent matter regarding their wedding and that he would call for her this afternoon. Though she'd been puzzled, there had been no time to ask for an explanation, and now it no longer mattered, for Barrett was here, looking as handsome as ever, despite the evidence of his fight with Warren.

"The minister apologized," he told Charlotte, "but he needs to meet with us today." Barrett chuckled. "Actually, his wife needs to meet with us. She's the organist. It seems she's leaving tomorrow for a trip to Omaha and wants us to choose our hymns before she leaves."

So that was the reason. "I'm ready." Tying her bonnet ribbons, Charlotte looked down at her son, who clung to her skirts. "I'll be back soon, David," she said. "You can play with Rose while I'm gone."

At the sound of her name, the little girl

scampered across the room and took David's hand. "I play with you. I and you have fun."

"Is David all right?" Barrett asked as he and Charlotte descended the steps.

She nodded. "He will be. He's been more clingy than normal today, but I'm not surprised. Last night must have been frightening for him." There was nothing she could do other than lavish love on him and hope that the memories would fade quickly.

Charlotte looked up at Barrett when they reached the street. Though he'd smiled when he'd arrived, his eyes were clouded, and she knew his memories would not be so quick to fade. "Are you all right? You look troubled."

He bent his arm and placed her hand on it. While it was less than a block to the parsonage, a distance she had walked without assistance many times, Barrett was a stickler for courtesy. Charlotte didn't mind. In fact, she welcomed the opportunity to be close to him, especially this afternoon when she sensed that he needed comfort. Not simply the salves she had applied to his face and hands to soothe his cuts and bruises, but loving touches to heal the wounds that last night had inflicted. Those wounds would linger long after the bruises faded.

"I'm angry with myself for not seeing behind the mask." Barrett spoke so softly that Charlotte had to strain to hear him. It was, she knew, a measure of his distress and perhaps his shame that he did not want to be overheard. "I thought Warren was my friend. Now I know he was only using me."

"You shouldn't blame yourself." Charlotte tightened her grip on Barrett's arm as she found herself using the same words she had with Gwen just a few hours earlier. Unlike Gwen, who had been able to release some of her sorrow through tears, Charlotte was certain that Barrett had not allowed himself to cry.

"Warren did wear a mask," she said firmly. "He wore a real one when he visited Sylvia's girls, but I think the one he donned when he was with you was even thicker. He didn't plan for anyone to see through it, and we didn't. He fooled us all." Even she, who should have known better, had dismissed her concerns, telling herself that she was mistaken.

They had reached the front of Mr. Yates's store. When a woman came out of the shop, Barrett raised his hat and greeted her. In another month, she would be one of his customers. In another month, he and Charlotte would be wed. But first he had to heal.

"I should have realized what was happening. I should have stopped it."

Charlotte heard the anguish in Barrett's voice and knew he was berating himself for the loss of a man he had once considered a friend. She slowed her steps, then stopped, forcing Barrett to stop too. What she wanted to say was best said when she had his full attention. She looked up at him, hoping he'd understand.

"We can't change the past. It took me a long time to accept that and realize that all I can do is make the present the best it can be."

Barrett nodded slowly, and the corners of his mouth started to twitch. Though she hadn't thought she had said anything funny, Charlotte would not quibble if her words amused him. Anything she could do to lighten Barrett's mood was good.

"You told me something like that the first time we met." There was no doubt about it. He was smiling now, the lines of pain receding, his eyes brightening. "At the time, I thought you were an impractical idealist."

On another day she might have feigned indignation over the description, but not today. "And now? Have you changed your mind?"

"Now I know you're the woman I love,

the one who's seen me at my worst moments and who still wants to marry me." His expression sobered. "I suppose I should ask you the same question you asked me. Have you changed your mind? Now that you've seen what a poor judge of people I am, are you sure you want to marry me?"

Tightening her grip on his arm again, Charlotte smiled at the man she loved. "More than ever." Barrett's face might be battered; his hands might be bruised; but to Charlotte he had never looked more handsome. The wounds he bore were wounds of honor, sustained defending her and David. They were visible proof of Barrett's love, and though she might wish he had not had to incur them, she could not help but be moved by them.

The momentary doubt in his eyes vanished, replaced by the sparkle of happiness. "I love you, Charlotte."

"And I love you."

As his lips started to curve into another smile, he flattened them, and for an instant Charlotte thought he would scowl. She couldn't imagine what had changed his mood so suddenly.

"Is something wrong?" she asked.

Barrett appeared startled. "No. Yes. Maybe." He refused to meet her gaze.

Instead, he stared into the distance as he said, "I suppose I ought to thank you for not giving Warren the ransom money, but you've created a problem."

"A problem?" He was making no sense. Charlotte had heard that people who sustained injuries to their heads could be confused for several days. Perhaps Warren had hurt Barrett more seriously than she had realized. Perhaps they should be on their way to see a physician, not a minister. "How can there be a problem?"

Barrett's lips quivered again, and once again Charlotte had the impression that he was trying to fight his smile. "Now I can't collect the payment," he announced.

"I don't understand."

Barrett's eyebrows rose in what appeared to be astonishment. "How could you forget? Don't you remember that when you insisted I should not sacrifice my savings, I told you I'd ask for payment when David was safe?" Charlotte nodded as the memory resurfaced. "That's the payment I want to collect. The problem is, your son is safe, but it doesn't seem quite fair to ask for anything when I still have all the money."

Though Barrett's voice was solemn, his eyes sparkled with ill-concealed mirth, and Charlotte realized that he was neither serious nor injured. He was in his right mind, trying to bring a little levity to a day that had had more than its share of tragedy.

"What kind of payment did you have in mind?" Charlotte tried to match Barrett's solemnity, though the twinkle in his eyes told her that the payment he wanted couldn't be onerous.

"A huge one."

"How huge?"

"Enormous."

She pursed her lips, pretending to be annoyed. "But you said I'd be able to afford it."

Barrett nodded. "You can. The question is whether you will want to pay it."

This was a side of Barrett Charlotte had not seen today, playful and joking, and — oh! — how she liked it. Living with a man like this would never be boring.

"Unless you tell me what you have in mind, I'll have no choice but to refuse. My mother taught me never to buy a pig in a poke."

"A what?"

"A pig in a poke." When Barrett did not seem to recognize the term, Charlotte explained. "Poke is an old-fashioned word for a sack. Not buying a pig in a poke means you shouldn't take something without looking at it. If it's still in the sack, you don't know whether it's a healthy pig or whether it's a pig at all."

"I assure you, the payment I have in mind is no pig." Oddly, the muffled noise that accompanied Barrett's words sounded like a pig's snort.

"Then what is it?"

"It's simple and yet complex."

"Sounds like a pig in a poke." Charlotte shook her head in feigned indignation. "Just tell me, Barrett."

"All right." As the sun dipped behind a cloud, Barrett's lips curved into the sweetest smile Charlotte had ever seen. "The payment I want is a kiss."

Her smile matched his as she thought of the kisses they had shared last night. The prospect of a lifetime of those kisses broadened her smile. How glorious it would be to be married to this man!

"That's all?" she asked, pretending disbelief. "You were prepared to give up your entire fortune, and all you want is a kiss?"

"Not just any kiss. I wanted a kiss from you."

"One kiss?" He'd given her many more than that last night.

He nodded. "That's all."

"Then you shall have it." Though it was

clear that Barrett expected his payment later, Charlotte had other ideas. Barrett was the man of her dreams, the one she'd been waiting for her whole life. He was the man who'd filled her heart with love and happiness. He was her hero. And so, in full view of anyone passing by, Charlotte wrapped her arms around his neck and pressed her lips to his.

"I love you, Barrett Landry," she murmured.

Summer of Promise, even though he's not human.

As always, I look forward to hearing from you. For more information, including my email address, I invite you to visit my website (www.amandacabot.com). You can also find me on Facebook, and you might be interested in my blog where my "Wednesday in Wyoming" posts give you an insider's look at the state.

Blessings,
Amanda Cabot

ACKNOWLEDGMENTS

I am privileged to have a team of talented, dedicated professionals working to turn my stories from rough manuscripts into finished books. The staff at Revell is, without exception, a true delight. To list everyone who's been part of this book would take several pages, but I would like to single out four women whose efforts have made a huge difference.

Vicki Crumpton's title may be Executive Editor, but I call her Editor Extraordinaire. She has an innate sense of what readers want — and don't want — in a book. That, combined with her wonderful sense of humor, makes revisions fun. Well . . . almost fun. Vicki's the perfect editor: part cheerleader, part coach, completely fabulous.

My project editor, Kristin Kornoelje, describes her comments as picky. I find them brilliantly insightful. Kristin's the one who catches inconsistencies, overuse of individual words, and unclear motivation. I thank her, and so should you, because my stories are better as a result of her pickiness.

Michele Misiak continues to amaze me with her innovative methods of promoting my books and her boundless energy. Although her title is Marketing Manager, she coordinates so many aspects of the publishing process that she's become my go-to person whenever I have a question. And, even though her inbox is overflowing and her schedule packed, she's unfailingly quick to respond. Thanks, Michele!

Art Director Cheryl Van Andel is an author's dream come true. She's never content with a merely good cover but keeps working with the artists to make each one great. Since she's given me consistently beautiful covers, I had high expectations for this one. What I didn't expect was that Cheryl would leave me speechless. Those of you who've met me know that doesn't happen very often, but when I received an email from Cheryl saying that the artist couldn't find a suitable gown for the cover model and that she was going to have one made specifically for my book, I was flabbergasted, flattered, and — yes — speechless. As if that weren't enough, Cheryl let me select the gown's design and color. What can I say other than that I was thrilled to be part of the process and even more thrilled with the final product?

I am deeply grateful to Vicki, Kristin, Michele, Cheryl, and the rest of the Revell staff for everything they do to make my books the best possible.

ABOUT THE AUTHOR

Dreams have always been an important part of **Amanda Cabot**'s life. For almost as long as she can remember, she dreamt of being an author. Fortunately for the world, her grade-school attempts as a playwright were not successful, and she turned her attention to writing novels. Her dream of selling a book before her thirtieth birthday came true, and she's been spinning tales ever since. She now has more than twenty-five novels to her credit under a variety of pseudonyms.

Amanda is a member of ACFW, a charter member of Romance Writers of America, and an avid traveler. She married her high school sweetheart, who shares her love of travel and who's driven thousands of miles to help her research her books. A few years ago they fulfilled a longtime dream and are now living in the American West.